THE CTHULHU STORIES OF ROBERT E. HOWARD

ROBERT E. HOWARD

WFP
WORDFIRE PRESS

CONTENTS

THE CTHULHU STORIES OF ROBERT E. HOWARD
copyright © 2020, WordFire Press
Additional copyright information at the end of book

EBook ISBN: 978-1-68057-097-7
Trade Paperback ISBN: 978-1-68057-096-0
Hardcover ISBN: 978-1-68057-098-4

Edited by M. Scott Lee
Cover design by Janet McDonald
Cover artwork "Spawn of the Stars" by Sofyan Syarief
Kevin J. Anderson, Art Director
Published by
WordFire Press, LLC
PO Box 1840
Monument CO 80132
Kevin J. Anderson & Rebecca Moesta, Publishers
WordFire Press eBook Edition 2019
WordFire Press Trade Paperback Edition 2019
WordFire Press Hardcover Edition 2019
Printed in the USA
Join our WordFire Press Readers Group for
sneak previews, updates, new projects, and giveaways.
Sign up at wordfirepress.com

❀ Created with Vellum

FOREWORD

Tentacles, Terrible Tomes, and Broadswords

by Paul Di Filippo

The Cthulhu Mythos is an early example of open-source software.

Think about it: an intangible product, originating perhaps from the initial vision of a lone individual, whose refinement and expansion depends on the efforts of myriad selfless contributors, ungoverned by rigid hierarchies of command. Wikipedia, Linux, Firefox ... H.P. Lovecraft and company constituted the Silicon Valley of Horror of their era!

Seriously, we shouldn't stretch this comparison too far. Coding and scribbling are two distinct pastimes. Nonetheless, Lovecraft's willingness to have other writers play in his painstakingly conceived and reified cosmic sandbox is rare and exemplary and farsighted, an early instance of the "information wants to be free" credo of the computer age.

Of course, this kind of enterprise, where several creators world-build together, existed before Lovecraft. In the *Science Fiction Encyclopedia*, John Clute nominates perhaps the earliest instance: "It could be argued that the first shared-world anthology to make a significant impact on the Western World was the Christian *New Testament* ..." Indeed the *New Testament* experience of a multiplicity of authors all working to chronicle a shared experience or vision strikes to the heart of what HPL and his buddies were doing, a more secular and literary enterprise which today goes by several names, such as "shared-world fiction" or "franchise fiction" or even, clunkily, "multi-author braided meganovels." The pejorative term "share-cropping" has also been tossed about.

When fans think of major contributors to the Mythos, they instantly summon up the names of Clark Ashton Smith, Robert Bloch, August Derleth, Fritz Leiber, Ramsey Campbell and others. But not quite so much attention gets paid to Lovecraft's good friend, Robert E. Howard, he of Conanesque literary fame. But Howard did indeed contribute to the Mythos, and this volume you now peruse—ably compiled by Scott Lee—gives us the major instances of Howard's dabbling in the eldritch shared swamp of the Old Ones.

Although the official "launch" of the Mythos is now dated to HPL's 1919 story "Dagon," the heyday of the "franchise" did not begin until 1928, with the publication of "The Call of Cthulhu." We know that Howard was reading Lovecraft via their shared issues of *Weird Tales*, and their lifelong correspondence (lasting till REH's suicide in 1936) began in 1930, when Howard sent a letter praising HPL's "The Rats in the Walls" to editor Farnsworth Wright, who forwarded it to Lovecraft's home in Providence. "A rich and vibrant correspondence immediately ensued," says the dustjacket copy to the assembled correspondence of the two vastly different creators, *A Means to Freedom: The Letters of H.P. Lovecraft and Robert E. Howard*.

Howard was no slavish imitator, and his Mythos tales reflect his own themes and style and interests in a unique manner. Some approach HPL's efforts more closely than others. Let's take a quick look at them, in order of publication, before trying to summarize their effects.

"The Shadow Kingdom" (1929) forms part of Howard's series on the Atlantean barbarian-cum-king named Kull, and hence slots soundly right into Howard's Thurian-Hyborian cycle, being for the most part straight-up sword and sorcery. It was in all likelihood written before the influence of "The Call of Cthulhu." Yet we see Howard's early fascination with the same unknowable cosmic vistas that tantalized HPL. Brule the Pict tells Kull:

"[We] are but barbarians—infants compared to the Seven Empires. Not even they themselves know how old they are. Neither the memory of man nor the annals of the historians reach back far enough to tell us when the first men came up from the sea and built cities on the shore. But Kull, men were not always ruled by men!"

Next up is "Skull-Face" (1929), and this heady, hypnotic, feverish pulp adventure, while basically a Sax Rohmer-ish tale of an evil mastermind and the noble forces arrayed against his plans for world domination, also contains some tantalizing references to horrid precursors to mankind. Here the villain Kathulos expatiates:

"Know you who I am? Kathulos of Egypt! Bah! They knew me in the old days! I reigned in the dim misty sea lands ages and ages before the sea rose and engulfed the land. I died, not as men die; the magic draft of life everlasting was ours! I drank deep and slept. Long I slept in my lacquered case! My flesh withered and grew hard; my blood dried in my veins. I became as one dead. But still within me burned the spirit of life, sleeping but anticipating the awakening. The great cities crumbled to dust. The sea drank the land. The tall shrines and the lofty spires sank beneath the green waves. All this I knew as I slept, as a man knows in dreams. Kathulos of Egypt? Faugh! Kathulos of Atlantis!"

I uttered a sudden involuntary cry. This was too grisly for sanity.
"Aye, the magician, the sorcerer.

"And down the long years of savagery, through which the barbaric
races struggled to rise without their masters, the legend came of the day of
empire, when one of the Old Race would rise up from the sea. Aye, and
lead to victory the black people who were our slaves in the old days."

That evildoer's name, by the way, proved to be a mere coinci-
dence, not the first nod to HPL, as Howard himself explained:
"A writer in the Eyrie, a Mr. O'Neail, I believe, wondered if I did
not use some myth regarding this Cthulhu in 'Skull Face'. The
name Kathulos might suggest that, but in reality, I merely manu-
factured the name at random, not being aware at the time of any
legendary character named Cthulhu—if indeed there is."

"The Gods of Bal-Sagoth" (1931) continues in the vein of our
first two tales, being the initial adventure of one Turlogh
O'Brien, an exiled Gaelic swordsman wandering the world in
historical Viking times. This particular exploit brings him to a
mysterious island where he encounters a figure reminiscent of
Lovecraft's Charles Dexter Ward.

He was very old; he alone of all the throng was bearded, and his
beard was as white as the long hair which fell about his shoulders. He
was very tall and very lean, and his great dark eyes blazed as from a
hidden fire. Turlogh knew without being told that this man was Gothan,
priest of the Black God. The ancient exuded a very aura of age and
mystery. His great eyes were like windows of some forgotten temple,
behind which passed like ghosts his dark and terrible thoughts. Turlogh
sensed that Gothan had delved too deep in forbidden secrets to remain
altogether human. He had passed through doors that had cut him off from
the dreams, desires and emotions of ordinary mortals. Looking into those
unwinking orbs Turlogh felt his skin crawl, as if he had looked into the
eyes of a great serpent.

At last, with "The Black Stone" (1931), we enter the arena of
explicit Cthulhuiana. Our protagonist—suddenly a literary gent,
and not a big-thewed barbarian—is studying Von Junzt's *Nameless*

Cults, a primo HPL talisman. His unwise investigations bring him to an unsavory monolith in Hungary.

"The Children of the Night" (1931) returns to Von Junzt, and also gives a shoutout to "The Call of Cthulhu" itself! Something of a "club story," the piece follows our hero as he mentally time-slips back to a prehuman era.

Good old essential Von Junzt and his damnable book return in "The Thing on the Roof " (1932), which involves a visit to the Latin American Temple of the Toad.

Another of Howard's barbarian heroes, Bran Mak Morn, who lived during Classical Roman times, is front and center in "Worms of the Earth" (1932). With explicit allusions to HPL's drowned city of R'lyeh, the tale conjures up a different species of ancient monsters, half-human, half-other.

Allied to "The Children of the Night," "People of the Dark" (1932) features another modern-day man again psychically voyaging to an earlier era to encounter:

The Little People—I wondered if those anthropologists were correct in their theory of a squat Mongoloid aboriginal race, so low in the scale of evolution as to be scarcely human, yet possessing a distinct, though repulsive, culture of their own. They had vanished before the invading races, theory said, forming the base of all Aryan legends of trolls, elves, dwarfs and witches. Living in caves from the start, these aborigines had retreated farther and farther into the caverns of the hills, before the conquerors, vanishing at last entirely, though folklore fancy pictures their descendants still dwelling in the lost chasms far beneath the hills, loathsome survivors of an outworn age.

A surprisingly poignant story of a man whose wife becomes possessed and deadly, "The Haunter of the Ring" (1934) offers a great instance of the incursion into the mortal plane of forces from the Outer Dark:

And then at last Vrolok wheeled, with an awful shriek, throwing his arms above his head in a gesture of wild despair. And for one brain-shattering instant he was blotted out by a great black shadow—Kirowan grasped my arm and we fled from that accursed chamber, blind with horror.

A famous round-robin exercise involving Lovecraft, Howard, A. Merritt, C.L. Moore and Frank Belknap Long, "The Challenge from Beyond" (1935) is *echt* Cthulhu due to Lovecraft's usurpation of the plot to dovetail with his "The Shadow Out of Time." In the penultimate chapter, Howard takes Lovecraft's hapless human in an alien's body and turns him into, basically, King Kull, a conqueror of the galaxy!

"The Fire of Asshurbanipal" (1936) could be an episode in the career of Indiana Jones, as our white man hero and his Moslem sidekick discover a lost desert city where the Elder Gods have wreaked a certain curse.

"As Xuthltan died," continued the old Bedouin, "he cursed the stone whose magic had not saved him, and he shrieked aloud the fearful words which undid the spell he had put upon the demon in the cavern, and set the monster free. And crying out on the forgotten gods, Cthulhu and Koth and Yog-Sothoth, and all the pre-Adamite Dwellers in the black cities under the sea and the caverns of the earth, he called upon them—to take back that which was theirs, and with his dying breath pronounced doom on the false king, and that doom was that the king should sit on his throne holding in his hand the Fire of Asshurbanipal until the thunder of Judgment Day.

Lastly, "Dig Me No Grave" (1937) features some of the recurring characters of the intermittent "club tales" herein, and shows us the posthumous fate of a nigh-immortal fellow who delved too deeply into the occult: "Before manne was, ye Elder ones were, & even yet their lord dwelleth amonge ye shadows to which if a manne sette his foote he maye not turn upon his track."

Emerging from these swift-flowing, enthralling, riotous, shivery tales, the reader who is familiar with the corpus of Lovecraft's work and its effects can judge exactly how integral Howard's contributions were to the Mythos, and whether they achieved any of the same frissons. For my part, I find that

Howard deliberately eschewed many of the touchstones of Lovecraft's writings. The sense of hopelessness and helplessness and
madness is generally underplayed. Howard was just too vigorous
a proponent of Conanesque *elan vital* to embrace the neuras-
thenic sensitives that HPL favored. Howard's protagonists
generally emerge alive from their encounters with the Great
Ones and their minions, and don't plunge into permanent insanity. Likewise absent is a distaste for foreignness. Howard's actors
revel in travel and encountering other cultures. And despite
Howard's deft employment of several bookish talismans—Von
Junzt, etc—his heroes are doers and men of action, not acade-
mics or scientists or recluses.

What Howard did heartily embrace and convey from Lovecraft's literary repository was the sense of vast depths of
unrecorded time, and the smallness of man's place in the
universe. This haunting riff Howard had pioneered on his own, a
case of independent literary invention, and so he must have
perked up to find in Lovecraft a fellow enthusiast along these
lines.

Ultimately, Howard's forays into the Cthulhu Mythos showed
a comradely joy in sharing some of the superficial tokens of a
friend's imagination. But one feels that the hot-blooded Texan
never fully inhabited the cool meticulous mindset or deracinated
worldview of his gloomy Yankee pal, as did, say, Smith or Bloch
or Leiber. Howard could write only Howardian tales, sagas of
mortals contending, foolishly or valiantly, with non-human forces
older and larger than mankind, while refusing ever to admit
defeat. I am sure that if, say, Bran Mak Morn or Kull ever had to
face a shoggoth, their response would not be a gibbering descent
into incoherence, but a sharp blade sunk into a gelatinous hulk!

THE SHADOW KINGDOM

A KING COMES RIDING

The blare of the trumpets grew louder, like a deep golden tide surge, like the soft booming of the evening tides against the silver beaches of Valusia. The throng shouted; women flung roses from the roofs as the rhythmic chiming of silver hosts came clearer and the first of the mighty array swung into view in the broad white street that curved round the golden-spired Tower of Splendor.

First came the trumpeters, slim youths, clad in scarlet, riding with a flourish of long, slender golden trumpets; next the bowmen, tall men from the mountains; and behind these the heavily armed footmen, their broad shields clashing in unison, their long spears swaying in perfect rhythm to their stride. Behind them came the mightiest soldiery in all the world, the Red Slayers, horsemen, splendidly mounted, armed in red from helmet to spur. Proudly they sat their steeds, looking neither to right nor to left, but aware of the shouting for all that. Like bronze statues they were, and there was never a waver in the forest of spears that reared above them.

Behind those proud and terrible ranks came the motley files of the mercenaries, fierce, wild-looking warriors, men of Mu and of Kaa-u and of the hills of the east and the isles of the west.

They bore spears and heavy swords, and a compact group that marched somewhat apart were the bowmen of Lemuria. Then came the light foot of the nation, and more trumpeters brought up the rear.

A brave sight, and a sight which aroused a fierce thrill in the soul of Kull, king of Valusia. Not on the Topaz Throne at the front of the regal Tower of Splendor sat Kull, but in the saddle, mounted on a great stallion, a true warrior king. His mighty arm swung up in reply to the salutes as the hosts passed. His fierce eyes passed the gorgeous trumpeters with a casual glance, rested longer on the following soldiery; they blazed with a ferocious light as the Red Slayers halted in front of him with a clang of arms and a rearing of steeds, and tendered him the crown salute. They narrowed slightly as the mercenaries strode by. They saluted no one, the mercenaries. They walked with shoulders flung back, eyeing Kull boldly and straightly, albeit with a certain appreciation; fierce eyes, unblinking; savage eyes, staring from beneath shaggy manes and heavy brows.

And Kull gave back a like stare. He granted much to brave men, and there were no braver in all the world, not even among the wild tribesmen who now disowned him. But Kull was too much the savage to have any great love for these. There were too many feuds. Many were age-old enemies of Kull's nation, and though the name of Kull was now a word accursed among the mountains and valleys of his people, and though Kull had put them from his mind, yet the old hates, the ancient passions still lingered. For Kull was no Valusian but an Atlantean.

The armies swung out of sight around the gem-blazing shoulders of the Tower of Splendor, and Kull reined his stallion about and started toward the palace at an easy gait, discussing the review with the commanders that rode with him, using not many words, but saying much.

"The army is like a sword," said Kull, "and must not be allowed to rust." So down the street they rode, and Kull gave no heed to any of the whispers that reached his hearing from the throngs that still swarmed the streets.

"That is Kull, see! Valka! But what a king! And what a man! Look at his arms! His shoulders!"

And an undertone of more sinister whispering: "Kull! Ha, accursed usurper from the pagan isles."

"Aye, shame to Valusia that a barbarian sits on the Throne of Kings."

Little did Kull heed. Heavy-handed had he seized the decaying throne of ancient Valusia and with a heavier hand did he hold it, a man against a nation.

After the council chamber, the social palace where Kull replied to the formal and laudatory phrases of the lords and ladies, with carefully hidden grim amusement at such frivolities; then the lords and ladies took their formal departure, and Kull leaned back upon the ermine throne and contemplated matters of state until an attendant requested permission from the great king to speak, and announced an emissary from the Pictish embassy.

Kull brought his mind back from the dim mazes of Valusian statecraft where it had been wandering and gazed upon the Pict with little favor. The man gave back the gaze of the king without flinching. He was a lean-hipped, massive-chested warrior of middle height, dark, like all his race, and strongly built. From strong, immobile features gazed dauntless and inscrutable eyes.

"The chief of the Councilors, Ka-nu of the tribe, right hand of the king of Pictdom, sends greetings and says: 'There is a throne at the feast of the rising moon for Kull, king of kings, lord of lords, emperor of Valusia.'"

"Good," answered Kull. "Say to Ka-nu the Ancient, ambassador of the western isles, that the king of Valusia will quaff wine with him when the moon floats over the hills of Zalgara."

Still the Pict lingered. "I have a word for the king, not—" with a contemptuous flirt of his hand "—for these slaves."

Kull dismissed the attendants with a word, watching the Pict warily.

The man stepped nearer and lowered his voice: "Come alone to feast tonight, lord king. Such was the word of my chief."

The king's eyes narrowed, gleaming like gray sword steel, coldly.

"Alone?"

"Aye."

They eyed each other silently, their mutual tribal enmity seething beneath their cloak of formality. Their mouths spoke the cultured speech, the conventional court phrases of a highly polished race, a race not their own, but from their eyes gleamed the primal traditions of the elemental savage. Kull might be the king of Valusia and the Pict might be an emissary to her courts, but there in the throne hall of kings, two tribesmen glowered at each other, fierce and wary, while ghosts of wild wars and world-ancient feuds whispered to each.

To the king was the advantage and he enjoyed it to its fullest extent. Jaw resting on hand, he eyed the Pict, who stood like an image of bronze, head flung back, eyes unflinching.

Across Kull's lips stole a smile that was more a sneer.

"And so I am to come—alone?" Civilization had taught him to speak by innuendo and the Pict's dark eyes glittered, though he made no reply. "How am I to know that you come from Ka-nu?"

"I have spoken," was the sullen response.

"And when did a Pict speak truth?" sneered Kull, fully aware that the Picts never lied, but using this means to enrage the man.

"I see your plan, king," the Pict answered imperturbably. "You wish to anger me. By Valka, you need go no further! I am angry enough. And I challenge you to meet me in single battle, spear, sword, or dagger, mounted or afoot. Are you king or man?"

Kull's eyes glinted with the grudging admiration a warrior must needs give a bold foeman, but he did not fail to use the chance of further annoying his antagonist.

"A king does not accept the challenge of a nameless savage," he sneered, "nor does the emperor of Valusia break the Truce of Ambassadors. You have leave to go. Say to Ka-nu I will come alone."

The Pict's eyes flashed murderously. He fairly shook in the grasp of the primitive bloodlust; then, turning his back squarely upon the king of Valusia, he strode across the Hall of Society and vanished through the great door.

Again, Kull leaned back upon the ermine throne and meditated.

So, the chief of the Council of Picts wished him to come alone? But for what reason? Treachery? Grimly Kull touched the hilt of his great sword. But scarcely. The Picts valued too greatly the alliance with Valusia to break it for any feudal reason. Kull might be a warrior of Atlantis and hereditary enemy of all Picts, but too, he was king of Valusia, the most potent ally of the Men of the West.

Kull reflected long upon the strange state of affairs that made him ally of ancient foes and foe of ancient friends. He rose and paced restlessly across the hall, with the quick, noiseless tread of a lion. Chains of friendship, tribe and tradition had he broken to satisfy his ambition. And, by Valka, god of the sea and the land, he had realized that ambition! He was king of Valusia—a fading, degenerate Valusia, a Valusia living mostly in dreams of bygone glory, but still a mighty land and the greatest of the Seven Empires. Valusia—Land of Dreams, the tribesmen named it, and sometimes it seemed to Kull that he moved in a dream. Strange to him were the intrigues of court and palace, army and people. All was like a masquerade, where men and women hid their real thoughts with a smooth mask. Yet the seizing of the throne had been easy—a bold snatching of opportunity, the swift whirl of swords, the slaying of a tyrant of whom men had wearied unto death, short, crafty plotting with ambitious statesmen out of favor at court—and Kull, wandering adventurer, Atlantean exile, had swept up to the dizzy heights of his dreams: he was lord of

Valusia, king of kings. Yet now it seemed that the seizing was far easier than the keeping. The sight of the Pict had brought back youthful associations to his mind, the free, wild savagery of his boyhood. And now a strange feeling of dim unrest, of unreality, stole over him as of late it had been doing. Who was he, a straightforward man of the seas and the mountain, to rule a race strangely and terribly wise with the mysticisms of antiquity? An ancient race—

"I am Kull!" said he, flinging back his head as a lion flings back his mane. "I am Kull!"

His falcon gaze swept the ancient hall. His self-confidence flowed back ... And in a dim nook of the hall a tapestry moved —slightly.

THUS SPAKE THE SILENT HALLS OF VALUSIA

The moon had not risen, and the garden was lighted with torches aglow in silver cressets when Kull sat down on the throne before the table of Ka-nu, ambassador of the western isles. At his right hand sat the ancient Pict, as much unlike an emissary of that fierce race as a man could be. Ancient was Ka-nu and wise in statecraft, grown old in the game. There was no elemental hatred in the eyes that looked at Kull appraisingly; no Tribal traditions hindered his judgments. Long associations with the statesmen of the civilized nations had swept away such cobwebs. Not: who and what is this man? was the question ever foremost in Ka-nu's mind, but: can I use this man, and how? Tribal prejudices he used only to further his own schemes.

And Kull watched Ka-nu, answering his conversation briefly, wondering if civilization would make of him a thing like the Pict. For Ka-nu was soft and paunchy. Many years had stridden across the sky-rim since Ka-nu had wielded a sword. True, he was old, but Kull had seen men older than he in the forefront of battle. The Picts were a long-lived race. A beautiful girl stood at Ka-nu's elbow, refilling his goblet, and she was kept busy. Meanwhile Ka-nu kept up a running fire of jests and comments, and Kull, secretly contemptuous of his garrulity, nevertheless missed none of his shrewd humor.

At the banquet were Pictish chiefs and statesmen, the latter jovial and easy in their manner, the warriors formally courteous, but plainly hampered by their tribal affinities. Yet Kull, with a tinge of envy, was cognizant of the freedom and ease of the affair as contrasted with like affairs of the Valusian court. Such freedom prevailed in the rude camps of Atlantis—Kull shrugged his shoulders.

After all, doubtless Ka-nu, who had seemed to have forgotten he was a Pict as far as time-hoary custom and prejudice went, was right and he, Kull, would better become a Valusian in mind as in name.

At last, when the moon had reached her zenith, Ka-nu, having eaten and drunk as much as any three men there, leaned back upon his divan with a comfortable sigh and said, "Now, get you gone, friends, for the king and I would converse on such matters as concern not children. Yes, you too, my pretty; yet first let me kiss those ruby lips—so; now, dance away, my rose bloom."

Ka-nu's eyes twinkled above his white beard as he surveyed Kull, who sat erect, grim and uncompromising.

"You are thinking, Kull," said the old statesman, suddenly, "that Ka-nu is a useless old reprobate, fit for nothing except to guzzle wine and kiss wenches!"

In fact, this remark was so much in line with his actual thoughts, and so plainly put, that Kull was rather startled, though he gave no sign.

Ka-nu gurgled, and his paunch shook with his mirth. "Wine is red and women are soft," he remarked tolerantly. "But—ha! ha!—think not old Ka-nu allows either to interfere with business."

Again, he laughed, and Kull moved restlessly. This seemed much like being made sport of, and the king's scintillating eyes began to glow with a feline light.

Ka-nu reached for the wine-pitcher, filled his beaker and glanced questioningly at Kull, who shook his head irritably.

"Aye," said Ka-nu equably, "it takes an old head to stand strong drink. I am growing old, Kull, so why should you young men begrudge me such pleasures as we oldsters must find? Ah me, I grow ancient and withered, friendless and cheerless."

But his looks and expressions failed far of bearing out his words. His rubicund countenance fairly glowed, and his eyes sparkled, so that his white beard seemed incongruous. Indeed, he looked remarkably elfin, reflected Kull, who felt vaguely resentful. The old scoundrel had lost all of the primitive virtues of his race and of Kull's race, yet he seemed more pleased in his aged days than otherwise.

"Hark ye, Kull," said Ka-nu, raising an admonitory finger, "'tis a chancy thing to laud a young man, yet I must speak my true thoughts to gain your confidence."

"If you think to gain it by flattery—"

"Tush. Who spake of flattery? I flatter only to disguard."

There was a keen sparkle in Ka-nu's eyes, a cold glimmer that did not match his lazy smile. He knew men, and he knew that to gain his end he must smite straight with this tigerish barbarian, who, like a wolf scenting a snare, would scent out unerringly any falseness in the skein of his wordweb.

"You have power, Kull," said he, choosing his words with more care than he did in the council rooms of the nation, "to make yourself mightiest of all kings, and restore some of the lost glories of Valusia. So. I care little for Valusia—though the women and wine be excellent—save for the fact that the stronger Valusia is, the stronger is the Pict nation. More, with an Atlantean on the throne, eventually Atlantis will become united—"

Kull laughed in harsh mockery. Ka-nu had touched an old wound.

"Atlantis made my name accursed when I went to seek fame and fortune among the cities of the world. We—they—are age-old foes of the Seven Empires, greater foes of the allies of the Empires, as you should know."

Ka-nu tugged his beard and smiled enigmatically.

"Nay, nay. Let it pass. But I know whereof I speak. And then warfare will cease, wherein there is no gain; I see a world of peace and prosperity—man loving his fellow man—the good supreme. All this can you accomplish—if you live!"

"Ha!" Kull's lean hand closed on his hilt and he half rose, with a sudden movement of such dynamic speed that Ka-nu, who fancied men as some men fancy blooded horses, felt his old blood leap with a sudden thrill. Valka, what a warrior! Nerves and sinews of steel and fire, bound together with the perfect coordination, the fighting instinct, that makes the terrible warrior.

But none of Ka-nu's enthusiasm showed in his mildly sarcastic tone.

"Tush. Be seated. Look about you. The gardens are deserted, the seats empty, save for our selves. You fear not me?"

Kull sank back, gazing about him warily.

"There speaks the savage," mused Ka-nu. "Think you if I planned treachery I would enact it here where suspicion would be sure to fall upon me? Tut. You young tribesmen have much to learn. There were my chiefs who were not at ease because you were born among the hills of Atlantis, and you despise me in your secret mind because I am a Pict. Tush. I see you as Kull, king of Valusia, not as Kull, the reckless Atlantean, leader of the raiders who harried the western isles. So you should see in me, not a Pict but an international man, a figure of the world. Now to that figure, hark! If you were slain tomorrow who would be king?"

"Kaanuub, baron of Blaal."

"Even so. I object to Kaanuub for many reasons, yet most of all for the fact that he is but a figure-head."

"How so? He was my greatest opponent, but I did not know that he championed any cause but his own."

"The night can hear," answered Ka-nu obliquely. "There are worlds within worlds. But you may trust me and you may trust Brule, the Spear-slayer. Look!" He drew from his robes a bracelet of gold representing a winged dragon coiled thrice, with three horns of ruby on the head.

"Examine it closely. Brule will wear it on his arm when he comes to you tomorrow night so that you may know him. Trust Brule as you trust yourself and do what he tells you to. And in proof of trust, look ye!"

And with the speed of a striking hawk, the ancient snatched something from his robes, something that flung a weird green light over them, and which he replaced in an instant.

"The stolen gem!" exclaimed Kull recoiling. "The green jewel from the Temple of the Serpent! Valka! You! And why do you show it to me?"

"To save your life. To prove my trust. If I betray your trust, deal with me likewise. You hold my life in your hand. Now I could not be false to you if I would, for a word from you would be my doom."

Yet for all his words the old scoundrel beamed merrily and seemed vastly pleased with himself.

"But why do you give me this hold over you?" asked Kull, becoming more bewildered each second.

"As I told you. Now, you see that I do not intend to deal you false, and tomorrow night when Brule comes to you, you will follow his advice without fear of treachery. Enough. An escort waits outside to ride to the palace with you, lord."

Kull rose. "But you have told me nothing."

"Tush. How impatient are youths!" Ka-nu looked more like a mischievous elf than ever. "Go you and dream of thrones and power and kingdoms, while I dream of wine and soft women and roses. And fortune ride with you, King Kull."

As he left the garden, Kull glanced back to see Ka-nu still reclining lazily in his seat, a merry ancient, beaming on all the world with jovial fellowship.

A mounted warrior waited for the king just without the garden, and Kull was slightly surprised to see that it was the same that had brought Ka-nu's invitation. No word was spoken as Kull swung into the saddle, nor as they clattered along the empty streets.

The color and the gayety of the day had given way to the eerie stillness of night. The city's antiquity was more than ever apparent beneath the bent, silver moon. The huge pillars of the mansions and palaces towered up into the stars. The broad stair-ways, silent and deserted, seemed to climb endlessly until they vanished in the shadowy darkness of the upper realms. Stairs to the stars, thought Kull, his imaginative mind inspired by the weird grandeur of the scene.

Clang! clang! clang! sounded the silver hoofs on the broad, moon-flooded streets, but otherwise there was no sound. The age of the city, its incredible antiquity, was almost oppressive to the king; it was as if the great silent buildings laughed at him, noiselessly, with unguessable mockery. And what secrets did they hold?

"You are young," said the palaces and the temples, and the shrines, "but we are old. The world was wild with youth when we were reared. You and your tribe shall pass, but we are invincible, indestructible. We towered above a strange world, ere Atlantis and Lemuria rose from the sea; we still shall reign when the green waters sigh for many a restless fathom above the spires of Lemuria and the hills of Atlantis, and when the isles of the Western Men are the mountains of a strange land.

"How many kings have we watched ride down these streets before Kull of Atlantis was even a dream in the mind of Ka, bird of Creation? Ride on, Kull of Atlantis; greater shall follow you; greater came before you. They are dust; they are forgotten; we stand; we know; we are. Ride, ride on, Kull of Atlantis; Kull the king, Kull the fool!"

And it seemed to Kull that the clashing hoofs took up the silent refrain to beat it into the night with hollow re-echoing mockery; "Kull-the-king! Kull-the-fool!"

Glow, moon; you light a king's way! Gleam, stars; you are torches in the train of an emperor! And clang, silver-shod hoofs; you herald that Kull rides through Valusia.

Ho! Awake, Valusia! It is Kull that rides, Kull the king!

"We have known many kings," said the silent halls of Valusia.

And so in a brooding mood Kull came to the palace, where his bodyguard, men of the Red Slayers, came to take the rein of the great stallion and escort Kull to his rest. There the Pict, still sullenly speechless, wheeled his steed with a savage wrench of the rein and fled away in the dark like a phantom; Kull's heightened imagination pictured him speeding through the silent streets like a goblin out of the Elder World.

There was no sleep for Kull that night, for it was nearly dawn and he spent the rest of the night hours pacing the throne-room, and pondering over what had passed. Ka-nu had told him nothing, yet he had put himself in Kull's complete power. At what had he hinted when he had said the baron of Blaal was naught but a figurehead? And who was this Brule who was to come to him by night, wearing the mystic armlet of the dragon? And why? Above all, why had Ka-nu shown him the green gem of terror, stolen long ago from the temple of the Serpent, for which the world would rock in wars were it known to the weird and terrible keepers of that temple, and from whose vengeance not even Ka-nu's ferocious tribesmen might be able to save him? But Ka-nu knew he was safe, reflected Kull, for the statesman was too shrewd to expose himself to risk without profit. But was it to throw the king off his guard and pave the way to treachery? Would Ka-nu dare let him live now? Kull shrugged his shoulders.

THEY THAT WALK THE NIGHT

The moon had not risen when Kull, hand to hilt, stepped to a window. The windows opened upon the great inner gardens of the royal palace, and the breezes of the night, bearing the scents of spice trees, blew the filmy curtains about. The king looked out. The walks and groves were deserted; carefully trimmed trees were bulky shadows; fountains nearby flung their slender sheen of silver in the starlight and distant fountains rippled steadily. No guards walked those gardens, for so closely were the outer walls guarded that it seemed impossible for any invader to gain access to them.

Vines curled up the walls of the palace, and even as Kull mused upon the ease with which they might be climbed, a segment of shadow detached itself from the darkness below the window and a bare, brown arm curved up over the sill. Kull's great sword hissed halfway from the sheath; then the King halted. Upon the muscular forearm gleamed the dragon armlet shown him by Ka-nu the night before.

The possessor of the arm pulled himself up over the sill and into the room with the swift, easy motion of a climbing leopard.

"You are Brule?" asked Kull, and then stopped in surprise not unmingled with annoyance and suspicion; for the man was he whom Kull had taunted in the Hall of Society; the same who had escorted him from the Pictish embassy.

"I am Brule, the Spear-slayer," answered the Pict in a guarded voice; then swiftly, gazing closely in Kull's face, he said, barely above a whisper:

"*Ka nama kaa lajerama!*"

Kull started. "Ha! What mean you?"

"Know you not?"

"Nay, the words are unfamiliar; they are of no language I ever heard—and yet, by Valka!—somewhere—I have heard—"

"Aye," was the Pict's only comment. His eyes swept the room, the study room of the palace. Except for a few tables, a divan or two, and great shelves of books of parchment, the room was barren compared to the grandeur of the rest of the palace.

"Tell me, king, who guards the door?"

"Eighteen of the Red Slayers. But how come you, stealing through the gardens by night and scaling the walls of the palace?"

Brule sneered. "The guards of Valusia are blind buffaloes. I could steal their girls from under their noses. I stole amid them and they saw me not nor heard me. And the walls—I could scale them without the aid of vines. I have hunted tigers on the foggy beaches when the sharp east breezes blew the mist in from seaward, and I have climbed the steppes of the western sea mountain. But come—nay, touch this armlet."

He held out his arm and, as Kull complied wonderingly, gave an apparent sigh of relief.

"So. Now throw off those kingly robes; for there are ahead of you this night such deeds as no Atlantean ever dreamed of."

Brule himself was clad only in a scanty loincloth through which was thrust a short, curved sword.

"And who are you to give me orders?" asked Kull, slightly resentful.

"Did not Ka-nu bid you follow me in all things?" asked the Pict irritably, his eyes flashing momentarily. "I have no love for you, lord, but for the moment I have put the thought of feuds from my mind. Do you likewise. But come."

Walking noiselessly, he led the way across the room to the door. A slide in the door allowed a view of the outer corridor, unseen from without, and the Pict bade Kull look.

"What see you?"

"Naught but the eighteen guardsmen."

The Pict nodded, motioned Kull to follow him across the room. At a panel in the opposite wall Brule stopped and fumbled there a moment. Then with a light movement he stepped back, drawing his sword as he did so. Kull gave an exclamation as the panel swung silently open, revealing a dimly lighted passageway.

"A secret passage!" swore Kull softly. "And I knew nothing of it! By Valka, someone shall dance for this!"

"Silence!" hissed the Pict.

Brule was standing like a bronze statue as if straining every nerve for the slightest sound; something about his attitude made Kull's hair prickle slightly, not from fear but from some eery anticipation. Then, beckoning, Brule stepped through the secret doorway which stood open behind them. The passage was bare, but not dustcovered as should have been the case with an unused secret corridor. A vague, gray light filtered through somewhere, but the source of it was not apparent. Every few feet Kull saw doors, invisible, as he knew, from the outside, but easily apparent from within.

"The palace is a very honeycomb," he muttered. "Aye. Night and day, you are watched, king, by many eyes."

The king was impressed by Brule's manner. The Pict went forward slowly, warily, half crouching, blade held low and thrust forward. When he spoke, it was in a whisper and he continually flung glances from side to side.

The corridor turned sharply, and Brule warily gazed past the turn.

"Look!" he whispered. "But remember! No word! No sound— on your life!"

Kull cautiously gazed past him. The corridor changed just at the bend to a flight of steps. And then Kull recoiled. At the foot of those stairs lay the eighteen Red Slayers who were that night stationed to watch the king's study room. Brule's grip upon his mighty arm and Brule's fierce whisper at his shoulder alone kept Kull from leaping down those stairs.

"Silent, Kull! Silent, in Valka's name!" hissed the Pict. "These corridors are empty now, but I risked much in showing you, that you might then believe what I had to say. Back now to the room of study." And he retraced his steps, Kull following; his mind in a turmoil of bewilderment.

"This is treachery," muttered the king, his steel-gray eyes a-smolder, "foul and swift! Mere minutes have passed since those men stood at guard."

Again, in the room of study, Brule carefully closed the secret panel and motioned Kull to look again through the slit of the outer door. Kull gasped audibly. For without stood the eighteen guardsmen!

"This is sorcery!" he whispered, half-drawing his sword. "Do dead men guard the king?"

"Aye!" came Brule's scarcely audible reply; there was a strange expression in the Pict's scintillant eyes. They looked squarely into each other's eyes for an instant, Kull's brow wrinkled in a puzzled scowl as he strove to read the Pict's inscrutable face. Then Brule's lips, barely moving, formed the words:

"The—snake—that—speaks!"

"Silent!" whispered Kull, laying his hand over Brule's mouth. "That is death to speak! That is a name accursed!"

The Pict's fearless eyes regarded him steadily.

"Look, again, King Kull. Perchance the guard was changed."

"Nay, those are the same men. In Valka's name, this is sorcery —this is insanity! I saw with my own eyes the bodies of those men, not eight minutes agone. Yet there they stand."

Brule stepped back, away from the door, Kull mechanically following.

"Kull, what know ye of the traditions of this race ye rule?"

"Much—and yet, little. Valusia is so old—"

"Aye," Brule's eyes lighted strangely, "we are but barbarians—infants compared to the Seven Empires. Not even they themselves know how old they are. Neither the memory of man nor the annals of the historians reach back far enough to tell us when the first men came up from the sea and built cities on the shore. But Kull, men were not always ruled by men!"

The king started. Their eyes met.

"Aye, there is a legend of my people—"

"And mine!" broke in Brule. "That was before we of the isles were allied with Valusia. Aye, in the reign of Lion-fang, seventh war chief of the Picts, so many years ago no man remembers how many. Across the sea we came, from the isles of the sunset, skirting the shores of Atlantis, and falling upon the beaches of Valusia with fire and sword. Aye, the long white beaches resounded with the clash of spears, and the night was like day from the flame of the burning castles. And the king, the king of Valusia, who died on the red sea sands that dim day—" His voice trailed off; the two stared at each other, neither speaking; then each nodded.

"Ancient is Valusia!" whispered Kull. "The hills of Atlantis and Mu were isles of the sea when Valusia was young."

The night breeze whispered through the open window. Not the free, crisp sea air such as Brule and Kull knew and reveled in, in their land, but a breath like a whisper from the past, laden with musk, scents of forgotten things, breathing secrets that were hoary when the world was young.

The tapestries rustled, and suddenly Kull felt like a naked child before the inscrutable wisdom of the mystic past. Again, the sense of unreality swept upon him. At the back of his soul stole dim, gigantic phantoms, whispering monstrous things. He sensed that Brule experienced similar thoughts. The Pict's eyes were fixed upon his face with a fierce intensity. Their glances met. Kull felt warmly a sense of comradeship with this member of an enemy tribe. Like rival leopards turning at bay against hunters, these two savages made common cause against the inhuman powers of antiquity.

Brule again led the way back to the secret door. Silently they entered, and silently they proceeded down the dim corridor, taking the opposite direction from that in which they previously traversed it. After a while the Pict stopped and pressed close to one of the secret doors, bidding Kull look with him through the hidden slot.

"This opens upon a little-used stair which leads to a corridor running past the study-room door."

They gazed, and presently, mounting the stair silently, came a silent shape.

"Tu! Chief councilor!" exclaimed Kull. "By night and with bared dagger! How, what means this, Brule?"

"Murder! And foulest treachery!" hissed Brule. "Nay—" as Kull would have flung the door aside and leaped forth "—we are lost if you meet him here, for more lurk at the foot of those stairs. Come!"

Half running, they darted back along the passage. Back through the secret door Brule led, shutting it carefully behind them, then across the chamber to an opening into a room seldom used. There he swept aside some tapestries in a dim corner nook and, drawing Kull with him, stepped behind them. Minutes dragged. Kull could hear the breeze in the other room blowing the window curtains about, and it seemed to him like the murmur of ghosts. Then through the door, stealthily, came Tu, chief councilor of the king. Evidently, he had come through the study room and, finding it empty, sought his victim where he was most likely to be.

He came with upraised dagger, walking silently. A moment he halted, gazing about the apparently empty room, which was lighted dimly by a single candle. Then he advanced cautiously, apparently at a loss to understand the absence of the king. He stood before the hiding place—and—

"Slay!" hissed the Pict.

Kull with a single mighty leap hurled himself into the room. Tu spun, but the blinding, tigerish speed of the attack gave him no chance for defense or counterattack. Sword steel flashed in the dim light and grated on bone as Tu toppled backward, Kull's sword standing out between his shoulders.

Kull leaned above him, teeth bared in the killer's snarl, heavy brows ascowl above eyes that were like the gray ice of the cold sea. Then he released the hilt and recoiled, shaken, dizzy, the hand of death at his spine.

For as he watched, Tu's face became strangely dim and unreal; the features mingled and merged in a seemingly impossible manner. Then, like a fading mask of fog, the face suddenly vanished and, in its stead gaped and leered a monstrous serpent's head!

"Valka!" gasped Kull, sweat beading his forehead, and again; "Valka!"

Brule leaned forward, face immobile. Yet his glittering eyes mirrored something of Kull's horror.

"Regain your sword, lord king," said he. "There are yet deeds to be done."

Hesitantly Kull set his hand to the hilt. His flesh crawled as he set his foot upon the terror which lay at their feet, and as some jerk of muscular reaction caused the frightful mouth to gape suddenly, he recoiled, weak with nausea. Then, wrathful at himself, he plucked forth his sword and gazed more closely at the nameless thing that had been known as Tu, chief councilor. Save for the reptilian head, the thing was the exact counterpart of a man.

"A man with the head of a snake!" Kull murmured. "This, then, is a priest of the serpent god?"

"Aye. Tu sleeps unknowing. These fiends can take any form

they will. That is, they can, by a magic charm or the like, fling a web of sorcery about their faces, as an actor dons a mask, so that they resemble anyone they wish to."

"Then the old legends were true," mused the king; "the grim old tales few dare even whisper, lest they die as blasphemers, are no fantasies. By Valka, I had thought—I had guessed—but it seems beyond the bounds of reality. Ha! The guardsmen outside the door—"

"They too are snake-men. Hold! What would you do?"

"Slay them!" said Kull between his teeth.

"Strike at the skull if at all," said Brule. "Eighteen wait without the door and perhaps a score more in the corridors. Hark ye, king. Ka-nu learned of this plot. His spies have pierced the inmost fastnesses of the snake priests and they brought hints of a plot. Long ago he discovered the secret passageways of the palace, and at his command I studied the map thereof and came here by night to aid you, lest you die as other kings of Valusia have died. I came alone for the reason that to send more would have roused suspicion. Many could not steal into the palace as I did. Some of the foul conspiracy you have seen. Snake-men guard your door, and that one, as Tu, could pass anywhere else in the palace; in the morning, if the priests failed, the real guards would be holding their places again, nothing knowing, nothing remembering; there to take the blame if the priests succeeded. But stay you here while I dispose of this carrion."

So saying, the Pict shouldered the frightful thing stolidly and vanished with it through another secret panel. Kull stood alone, his mind awhirl. Neophytes of the mighty serpent, how many lurked among his cities? How might he tell the false from the true? Aye, how many of his trusted councilors, his generals, were men? He could be certain—of whom?

The secret panel swung inward and Brule entered.

"You were swift."

"Aye!" The warrior stepped forward, eyeing the floor. "There is gore upon the rug. See?"

Kull bent forward; from the corner of his eye he saw a blur of movement, a glint of steel. Like a loosened bow he whipped erect, thrusting upward. The warrior sagged upon the sword, his own clattering to the floor. Even at that instant Kull reflected grimly that it was appropriate that the traitor should meet his death upon the sliding, upward thrust used so much by his race. Then, as Brule slid from the sword to sprawl motionless on the floor, the face began to merge and fade, and as Kull caught his breath, his hair aprickle, the human features vanished and there the jaws of a great snake gaped hideously, the terrible beady eyes venomous even in death.

"He was a snake priest all the time!" gasped the king. "Valka! What an elaborate plan to throw me off my guard! Ka-nu there, is he a man? Was it Ka-nu to whom I talked in the gardens? Almighty Valka!" as his flesh crawled with a horrid thought; "are the people of Valusia men or are they all serpents?"

Undecided he stood, idly seeing that the thing named Brule no longer wore the dragon armlet. A sound made him wheel.

Brule was coming through the secret door.

"Hold!" Upon the arm upthrown to halt the king's hovering sword gleamed the dragon armlet. "Valka!" The Pict stopped short. Then a grim smile curled his lips.

"By the gods of the seas! These demons are crafty past reckoning. For it must be that one lurked in the corridors and seeing me go carrying the carcass of that other, took my appearance. So I have another to do away with."

"Hold!" There was the menace of death in Kull's voice; "I have seen two men turn to serpents before my eyes. How may I know if you are a true man?"

Brule laughed. "For two reasons, King Kull. No snake-man wears this—" he indicated the dragon armlet "—nor can any say these words," and again Kull heard the strange phrase; "Ka nama kaa lajerama."

"Ka nama kaa lajerama" Kull repeated mechanically. "Now,

where, in Valka's name, have I heard that? I have not! And yet—
and yet—"

"Aye, you remember, Kull," said Brule. "Through the dim
corridors of memory those words lurk; though you never heard
them in this life, yet in the bygone ages they were so terribly
impressed upon the soul mind that never dies, that they will
always strike dim chords in your memory, though you be reincar-
nated for a million years to come. For that phrase has come
secretly down the grim and bloody eons, since when, uncounted
centuries ago, those words were watchwords for the race of men
who battled with the grisly beings of the Elder Universe. For
none but a real man of men may speak them, whose jaws and
mouth are shaped different from any other creature. Their
meaning has been forgotten but not the words themselves."

"True," said Kull. "I remember the legends—Valka!" He
stopped short, staring, for suddenly, like the silent swinging wide
of a mystic door, misty, unfathomed reaches opened in the
recesses of his consciousness and for an instant he seemed to
gaze back through the vastness that spanned life and life; seeing
through the vague and ghostly fogs dim shapes reliving dead
centuries—men in combat with hideous monsters, vanquishing a
planet of frightful terrors. Against a gray, ever-shifting background moved strange nightmare forms, fantasies of lunacy and
fear; and man, the jest of the gods, the blind, wisdomless striver
from dust to dust, following the long bloody trail of his destiny,
knowing not why, bestial, blundering, like a great murderous
child, yet feeling somewhere a spark of divine fire ... Kull drew a
hand across his brow, shaken; these sudden glimpses into the
abysses of memory always startled him.

"They are gone," said Brule, as if scanning his secret mind;
"the bird-women, the harpies, the bat-men, the flying fiends, the
wolf-people, the demons, the goblins—all save such as this being
that lies at our feet, and a few of the wolf-men. Long and terrible
was the war, lasting through the bloody centuries, since first the

first men, risen from the mire of apedom, turned upon those who then ruled the world."

"And at last mankind conquered, so long ago that naught but dim legends come to us through the ages. The snake-people were the last to go, yet at last men conquered even them and drove them forth into the waste lands of the world, there to mate with true snakes until some day, say the sages, the horrid breed shall vanish utterly. Yet the Things returned in crafty guise as men grew soft and degenerate, forgetting ancient wars. Ah, that was a grim and secret war! Among the men of the Younger Earth stole the frightful monsters of the Elder Planet, safeguarded by their horrid wisdom and mysticisms, taking all forms and shapes, doing deeds of horror secretly. No man knew who was true man and who false. No man could trust any man. Yet by means of their own craft they formed ways by which the false might be known from the true. Men took for a sign and a standard the figure of the flying dragon, the winged dinosaur, a monster of past ages, which was the greatest foe of the serpent. And men used those words which I spoke to you as a sign and symbol, for as I said, none but a true man can repeat them. So mankind triumphed. Yet again the fiends came after the years of forgetfulness had gone by—for man is still an ape in that he forgets what is not ever before his eyes. As priests they came; and for that men in their luxury and might had by then lost faith in the old religions and worships, the snake-men, in the guise of teachers of a new and truer cult, built a monstrous religion about the worship of the serpent god. Such is their power that it is now death to repeat the old legends of the snake-people, and people bow again to the serpent god in new form; and blind fools that they are, the great hosts of men see no connection between this power and the power men overthrew eons ago. As priests the snake-men are content to rule—and yet—" He stopped.

"Go on." Kull felt an unaccountable stirring of the short hair at the base of his scalp.

"Kings have reigned as true men in Valusia," the Pict whis-

pered, "and yet, slain in battle, have died serpents—as died he
who fell beneath the spear of Lion-fang on the red beaches when
we of the isles harried the Seven Empires. And how can this be.
Lord Kull? These kings were born of women and lived as men!
Thus—the true kings died in secret—as you would have died
tonight—and priests of the Serpent reigned in their stead, no
man knowing."

Kull cursed between his teeth. "Aye, it must be. No one has
ever seen a priest of the Serpent and lived, that is known. They
live in utmost secrecy."

"The statecraft of the Seven Empires is a mazy, monstrous
thing," said Brule. "There the true men know that among them
glide the spies of the Serpent, and the men who are the Serpent's
allies—such as Kaanuub, baron of Blaal—yet no man dares seek
to unmask a suspect lest vengeance befall him. No man trusts his
fellow, and the true statesmen dare not speak to each other what
is in the minds of all. Could they be sure, could a snake-man or
plot be unmasked before them all, then would the power of the
Serpent be more than half broken; for all would then ally and
make common cause, sifting out the traitors. Ka-nu alone is of
sufficient shrewdness and courage to cope with them, and even
Ka-nu learned only enough of their plot to tell me what would
happen—what has happened up to this time. Thus far I was
prepared; from now on we must trust to our luck and our craft.
Here and now I think we are safe; those snake-men without the
door dare not leave their post lest true men come here unexpectedly. But tomorrow they will try something else, you may be
sure. Just what they will do, none can say, not even Ka-nu; but we
must stay at each other's sides, King Kull, until we conquer or
both be dead. Now come with me while I take this carcass to the
hiding-place where I took the other being."

Kull followed the Pict with his grisly burden through the
secret panel and down the dim corridor. Their feet, trained to
the silence of the wilderness, made no noise. Like phantoms they
glided through the ghostly light, Kull wondering that the corri-

dors should be deserted; at every turn he expected to run full upon some frightful apparition. Suspicion surged back upon him; was this Pict leading him into ambush? He fell back a pace or two behind Brule, his ready sword hovering at the Pict's unheeding back. Brule should die first if he meant treachery. But if the Pict was aware of the king's suspicion, he showed no sign. Stolidly he tramped along, until they came to a room, dusty and long unused, where moldy tapestries hung heavy. Brule drew aside some of these and concealed the corpse behind them.

Then they turned to retrace their steps, when suddenly Brule halted with such abruptness that he was closer to death than he knew; for Kull's nerves were on edge.

"Something moving in the corridor," hissed the Pict. "Ka-nu said these ways would be empty, yet—"

He drew his sword and stole into the corridor, Kull following warily.

A short way down the corridor a strange, vague glow appeared that came toward them. Nerves a-leap, they waited, backs to the corridor wall; for what they knew not, but Kull heard Brule's breath hiss through his teeth and was reassured as to Brule's loyalty.

The glow merged into a shadowy form. A shape vaguely like a man it was, but misty and illusive, like a wisp of fog, that grew more tangible as it approached, but never fully material. A face looked at them, a pair of luminous great eyes, that seemed to hold all the tortures of a million centuries. There was no menace in that face, with its dim, worn features, but only a great pity— and that face—that face—

"Almighty gods!" breathed Kull, an icy hand at his soul; "Eal-lal, king of Valusia, who died a thousand years ago!"

Brule shrank back as far as he could, his narrow eyes widened in a blaze of pure horror, the sword shaking in his grip, unnerved for the first time that weird night. Erect and defiant stood Kull, instinctively holdng his useless sword at the ready; flesh acrawl, hair a-prickle, yet still a king of kings, as ready to challenge the powers of the unknown dead as the powers of the living.

The phantom came straight on, giving them no heed; Kull shrank back as it passed them, feeling an icy breath like a breeze from the arctic snow. Straight on went the shape with slow, silent footsteps, as if the chains of all the ages were upon those vague feet; vanishing about a bend of the corridor.

"Valka!" muttered the Pict, wiping the cold beads from his brow; "that was no man! That was a ghost!"

"Aye!" Kull shook his head wonderingly. "Did you not recognize the face? That was Eallal, who reigned in Valusia a thousand years ago and who was found hideously murdered in his throne room—the room now known as the Accursed Room. Have you not seen his statue in the Fame Room of Kings?"

"Yes, I remember the tale now. Gods, Kull! that is another sign of the frightful and foul power of the snake priests—that king was slain by snake-people and thus his soul became their slave, to do their bidding throughout eternity! For the sages have ever maintained that if a man is slain by a snake-man his ghost becomes their slave."

A shudder shook Kull's gigantic frame. "Valka! But what a fate! Hark ye—" his fingers closed upon Brule's sinewy arm like steel "—hark ye! If I am wounded unto death by these foul monsters, swear that ye will smite your sword through my breast lest my soul be enslaved."

"I swear," answered Brule, his fierce eyes lighting. "And do ye the same by me, Kull."

Their strong right hands met in a silent sealing of their bloody bargain.

MASKS

K ull sat upon his throne and gazed broodily out upon the sea of faces turned toward him. A courtier was speaking in evenly modulated tones, but the king scarcely heard him. Close by, Tu, chief councilor, stood ready at Kull's command, and each time the king looked at him, Kull shuddered inwardly. The surface of court life was as the unrippled surface of the sea between tide and tide. To the musing king the affairs of the night before seemed as a dream, until his eyes dropped to the arm of his throne. A brown, sinewy hand rested there, upon the wrist of which gleamed a dragon armlet; Brule stood beside his throne and ever the Pict's fierce secret whisper brought him back from the realm of unreality in which he moved.

No, that was no dream, that monstrous interlude. As he sat upon his throne in the Hall of Society and gazed upon the courtiers, the ladies, the lords, the statesmen, he seemed to see their faces as things of illusion, things unreal, existent only as shadows and mockeries of substance. Always he had seen their faces as masks, but before he had looked on them with contemptuous tolerance, thinking to see beneath the masks shallow, puny souls, avaricious, lustful, deceitful; now there was a grim undertone, a sinister meaning, a vague horror that lurked beneath the smooth masks. While he exchanged courtesies with some nobleman or counsellor he seemed to see the smiling face fade like smoke and the frightful jaws of a serpent gaping there. How many of those he looked upon were horrid, inhuman monsters, plotting his death, beneath the smooth mesmeric illusion of a human face?

Valusia—land of dreams and nightmares—a kingdom of the shadows, ruled by phantoms who glided back and forth behind the painted curtains, mocking the futile king who sat upon the throne—himself a shadow.

And like a comrade shadow Brule stood by his side, dark eyes glittering from immobile face. A real man, Brule! And Kull felt his friendship for the savage become a thing of reality and sensed that Brule felt a friendship for him beyond the mere necessity of statecraft.

And what, mused Kull, were the realities of life? Ambition, power, pride? The friendship of man, the love of women—which Kull had never known—battle, plunder, what? Was it the real Kull who sat upon the throne or was it the real Kull who had scaled the hills of Atlantis, harried the far isles of the sunset, and laughed upon the green roaring tides of the Atlantean sea? How could a man be so many different men in a lifetime? For Kull knew that there were many Kulls, and he wondered which was the real Kull. After all, the priests of the Serpent went a step further in their magic, for all men wore masks, and many a different mask with each different man or woman; and Kull wondered if a serpent did not lurk under every mask.

So he sat and brooded in strange, mazy thought-ways, and the courtiers came and went and the minor affairs of the day were completed, until at last the king and Brule sat alone in the Hall of Society save for the drowsy attendants.

Kull felt a weariness. Neither he nor Brule had slept the night before, nor had Kull slept the night before that, when in the gardens of Ka-nu he had had his first hint of the weird things to be. Last night nothing further had occurred after they had returned to the study room from the secret corridors, but they had neither dared nor cared to sleep. Kull, with the incredible vitality of a wolf, had aforetime gone for days upon days without sleep in his wild savage days, but now his mind was edged from constant thinking and from the nerve-breaking eeriness of the past night. He needed sleep, but sleep was furthest from his mind.

And he would not have dared sleep if he had thought of it. Another thing that had shaken him was the fact that though he and Brule had kept a close watch to see if, or when, the study-room guard was changed, yet it was changed without their knowledge; for the next morning those who stood on guard were able to repeat the magic words of Brule, but they remembered nothing out of the ordinary. They thought that they had stood at guard all night, as usual, and Kull said nothing to the contrary. He believed them true men, but Brule had advised absolute secrecy, and Kull also thought it best.

Now Brule leaned over the throne, lowering his voice so not even a lazy attendant could hear: "They will strike soon, I think, Kull. A while ago Ka-nu gave me a secret sign. The priests know that we know of their plot, of course, but they know not, how much we know. We must be ready for any sort of action. Ka-nu and the Pictish chiefs will remain within hailing distance now until this is settled one way or another. Ha, Kull, if it comes to a pitched battle, the streets and the castles of Valusia will run red!"

Kull smiled grimly. He would greet any sort of action with a ferocious joy. This wandering in a labyrinth of illusion and magic was extremely irksome to his nature. He longed for the leap and clang of swords, for the joyous freedom of battle.

Then into the Hall of Society came Tu again, and the rest of the councilors.

"Lord king, the hour of the council is at hand, and we stand ready to escort you to the council room."

Kull rose, and the councilors bent the knee as he passed through the way opened by them for his passage, rising behind

him, and following. Eyebrows were raised as the Pict strode defi-
antly behind the king, but no one dissented. Brule's challenging
gaze swept the smooth faces of the councilors with the defiance
of an intruding savage. The group passed through the halls and came at last to the
council chamber. The door was closed, as usual, and the councilors arranged themselves in the order of their rank before the
dais upon which stood the king. Like a bronze statue Brule took
up his stand behind Kull.

Kull swept the room with a swift stare. Surely no chance of
treachery here. Seventeen councilors there were, all known to
him; all of them had espoused his cause when he ascended the
throne.

"Men of Valusia—" he began in the conventional manner,
then halted, perplexed. The councilors had risen as a man and
were moving toward him. There was no hostility in their looks,
but their actions were strange for a council room. The foremost
was close to him when Brule sprang forward, crouched like a
leopard.

"Ka nama kaa lajerama!" His voice crackled through the
sinister silence of the room and the foremost councilor recoiled,
hand flashing to his robes; and like a spring released, Brule
moved, and the man pitched headlong and lay still while his face
faded and became the head of a mighty snake.

"Slay, Kull!" rasped the Pict's voice. "They be all serpent
men!"

The rest was a scarlet maze. Kull saw the familiar faces dim
like fading fog and in their places gaped horrid reptilian visages
as the whole band rushed forward. His mind was dazed but his
giant body faltered not.

The singing of his sword filled the room, and the onrushing
flood broke in a red wave. But they surged forward again, seemingly willing to fling their lives away in order to drag down the
king. Hideous jaws gaped at him; terrible eyes blazed into his
unblinkingly; a frightful fetid scent pervaded the atmosphere—

the serpent scent that Kull had known in southern jungles. Swords and daggers leaped at him, and he was dimly aware that they wounded him. But Kull was in his element; never before had he faced such grim foes but it mattered little; they lived, their veins held blood that could be spilt, and they died when his great sword cleft their skulls or drove through their bodies. Slash, thrust, thrust and swing. Yet Kull had died there but for the man who crouched at his side, parrying and thrusting. For the king was clear berserk, fighting in the terrible Atlantean way, that seeks death to deal death; he made no effort to avoid thrusts and slashes, standing straight up and ever plunging forward, no thought in his frenzied mind but to slay. Not often did Kull forget his fighting craft in his primitive fury, but now some chain had broken in his soul, flooding his mind with a red wave of slaughter-lust. He slew a foe at each blow, but they surged about him, and time and again Brule turned a thrust that would have slain, as he crouched beside Kull, parrying and warding with cold skill, slaying not as Kull slew with long slashes and plunges, but with short overhand blows and upward thrusts.

Kull laughed, a laugh of insanity. The frightful faces swirled about him in a scarlet blaze. He felt steel sink into his arm and dropped his sword in a flashing arc that cleft his foe to the breastbone. Then the mists faded, and the king saw that he and Brule stood alone above a sprawl of hideous crimson figures who lay still upon the floor.

"Valka! What a killing!" said Brule, shaking the blood from his eyes. "Kull, had these been warriors who knew how to use the steel, we had died here. These serpent priests know naught of swordcraft and die easier than any men I ever slew. Yet had there been a few more, I think the matter had ended otherwise."

Kull nodded. The wild berserker blaze had passed, leaving a mazed feeling of great weariness. Blood seeped from wounds on breast, shoulder, arm, and leg. Brule, himself bleeding from a score of flesh wounds, glanced at him in some concern.

"Lord Kull, let us hasten to have your wounds dressed by the women."

Kull thrust him aside with a drunken sweep of his mighty arm.

"Nay, we'll see this through ere we cease. Go you, though, and have your wounds seen to—I command it."

The Pict laughed grimly. "Your wounds are more than mine, lord king—" he began, then stopped as a sudden thought struck him. "By Valka, Kull, this is not the council room!"

Kull looked about and suddenly other fogs seemed to fade. "Nay, this is the room where Eallal died a thousand years ago—since unused and named 'Accursed.'"

"Then by the gods, they tricked us after all!" exclaimed Brule in a fury, kicking the corpses at their feet. "They caused us to walk like fools into their ambush! By their magic they changed the appearance of all—"

"Then there is further deviltry afoot," said Kull, "for if there be true men in the councils of Valusia, they should be in the real council room now. Come swiftly."

And, leaving the room with its ghastly keepers, they hastened throught halls that seemed deserted until they came to the real council room. Then Kull halted with a ghastly shudder. From the council room sounded a voice speaking, and—the voice was his!

With a hand that shook he parted the tapestries and gazed into the room. There sat the councilors, counterparts of the men he and Brule had just slain, and upon the dais stood Kull, king of Valusia.

He stepped back, his mind reeling.

"This is insanity!" he whispered. "Am I Kull? Do I stand here or is that Kull yonder in very truth, and am I but a shadow, a figment of thought?"

Brule's hand clutching his shoulder, shaking him fiercely, brought him to his senses.

"Valka's name, be not a fool! Can you yet be astounded after all we have seen? See you not that those are true men bewitched by a snake-man who has taken your form, as those others took their forms? By now you should have been slain, and yon monster reigning in your stead, unknown by those who bowed to you. Leap and slay swiftly or else we are undone. The Red Slayers, true men, stand close on each hand and none but you can reach and slay him. Be swift!"

Kull shook off the onrushing dizziness, flung back his head in the old, defiant gesture. He took a long, deep breath as does a strong swimmer before diving into the sea; then, sweeping back the tapestries, made the dais in a single lion-like bound. Brule had spoken truly. There stood men of the Red Slayers, guardsmen trained to move quick as the striking leopard; any but Kull had died ere he could reach the usurper. But the sight of Kull, identical with the man upon the dais, held them in their tracks, their minds stunned for an instant, and that was long enough. He upon the dais snatched for his sword. but even as his fingers closed upon the hilt, Kull's sword stood out behind his shoulders, and the thing that men had thought the king pitched forward from the dais to lie silent upon the floor.

"Hold!" Kull's lifted hand and kingly voice stopped the rush that had started, and while they stood astounded he pointed to the thing which lay before them—whose face was fading into that of a snake. They recoiled, and from one door came Brule and from another came Ka-nu.

These grasped the king's bloody hand and Ka-nu spoke: "Men of Valusia, you have seen with your own eyes. This is the true Kull, the mightiest king to whom Valusia has ever bowed. The power of the Serpent is broken and ye be all true men. King Kull, have you commands?"

"Lift that carrion," said Kull, and men of the guard took up the thing.

"Now follow me," said the king, and he made his way to the Accursed Room. Brule, with a look of concern, offered the support of his arm but Kull shook him off.

The distance seemed endless to the bleeding king, but at last he stood at the door and laughed fiercely and grimly when he heard the horrified ejaculations of the councilors.

At his orders the guardsmen flung the corpse they carried beside the others, and motioning all from the room Kull stepped out last and closed the door.

A wave of dizziness left him shaken. The faces turned to him, pallid and wondering, swirled and mingled in a ghostly fog. He felt the blood from his wound trickling down his limbs and he knew that what he was to do, he must do quickly or not at all.

His sword rasped from its sheath.

"Brule, are you there?"

"Aye!" Brule's face looked at him through the mist, close to his shoulder, but Brule's voice sounded leagues and eons away.

"Remember our vow, Brule. And now, bid them stand back."

His left arm cleared a space as he flung up his sword. Then with all his waning power he drove it through the door into the jamb, driving the great sword to the hilt and sealing the room forever.

Legs braced wide, he swayed drunkenly, facing the horrified councilors. "Let this room be doubly accursed. And let those rotting skeletons lie there forever as a sign of the dying might of the Serpent. Here I swear that I shall hunt the serpent-men from land to land, from sea to sea, giving no rest until all be slain, that good triumph, and the power of Hell be broken. This thing I swear—I—Kull—king—of—Valusia."

His knees buckled as the faces swayed and swirled. The councilors leaped forward, but ere they could reach him, Kull slumped to the floor, and lay still, face upward.

The councilors surged about the fallen king, chattering and shrieking. Ka-nu beat them back with his clenched fists, cursing savagely.

"Back, you fools! Would you stifle the little life that is yet in him? How, Brule, is he dead or will he live?"—to the warrior who bent above the prostrate Kull.

"Dead?" sneered Brule irritably. "Such a man as this is not so

easily killed. Lack of sleep and loss of blood have weakened him
—by Valka, he has a score of deep wounds, but none of them
mortal. Yet have those gibbering fools bring the court women
here at once."

Brule's eyes lighted with a fierce, proud light.

"Valka, Ka-nu, but here is such a man as I knew not existed
in these degenerate days. He will be in the saddle in a few scant
days and then may the serpentmen of the world beware of Kull
of Valusia. Valka, but that will be a rare hunt! Ah, I see long years
of prosperity for the world with such a king."

SKULL-FACE

THE FACE IN THE MIST

"We are no other than a moving row
Of Magic Shadow-shapes that come and go."

—Omar Khayyam

The horror first took concrete form amid that most unconcrete of all things—a hashish dream. I was off on a timeless, spaceless journey through the strange lands that belong to this state of being, a million miles away from earth and all things earthly; yet I became cognizant that something was reaching across the unknown voids—something that tore ruthlessly at the separating curtains of my illusions and intruded itself into my visions.

I did not exactly return to ordinary waking life, yet I was conscious of a seeing and a recognizing that was unpleasant and seemed out of keeping with the dream I was at that time enjoying. To one who has never known the delights of hashish, my explanation must seem chaotic and impossible. Still, I was aware of a rending of mists and then the Face intruded itself into my sight. I though at first it was merely a skull; then I saw that it was a hideous yellow instead of white, and was endowed with some horrid form of life. Eyes glimmered deep in the sockets and the jaws moved as if in speech. The body, except for the high, thin shoulders, was vague and indistinct, but the hands, which floated in the mists before and below the skull, were horribly vivid and filled me with crawling fears. They were like the hands of a mummy, long, lean, and yellow, with knobby joints and cruel, curving talons.

Then, to complete the vague horror which was swiftly taking possession of me, a voice spoke—imagine a man so long dead that his vocal organ had grown rusty and unaccustomed to speech. This was the thought which struck me and made my flesh crawl as I listened.

"A strong brute and one who might be useful somehow. See that he is given all the hashish he requires."

Then the face began to recede, even as I sensed that I was the subject of conversation, and the mists billowed and began to close again. Yet for a single instant a scene stood out with startling clarity. I gasped—or sought to. For over the high, strange shoulder of the apparition another face stood out clearly for an instant, as if the owner peered at me. Red lips, half-parted, long dark eyelashes, shading vivid eyes, a shimmery cloud of hair. Over the shoulder of horror, breathtaking beauty for an instant looked at me.

THE HASHISH SLAVE

"Up from Earth's center through the Seventh Gate
I rose, and on the Throne of Saturn sate."

—Omar Khayyam

M y dream of the skull-face was borne over that usually
uncrossable gap that lies between hashish enchantment
and humdrum reality. I sat cross-legged on a mat in Yun Shatu's
Temple of Dreams and gathered the fading forces of my
decaying brain to the task of remembering events and faces.

This last dream was so entirely different from any I had ever
had before, that my waning interest was roused to the point of
inquiring as to its origin. When I first began to experiment with
hashish, I sought to find a physical or psychic basis for the wild
flights of illusion pertaining thereto, but of late I had been
content to enjoy without seeking cause and effect.

Whence this unaccountable sensation of familiarity in regard
to that vision? I took my throbbing head between my hands and
laboriously sought a clue. A living dead man and a girl of rare
beauty who had looked over his shoulder. Then I remembered.

Back in the fog of days and nights which veils a hashish

addict's memory, my money had given out. It seemed years or possibly centuries, but my stagnant reason told me that it had probably been only a few days. At any rate, I had presented myself at Yun Shatu's sordid dive as usual and had been thrown out by the great Negro Hassim when it was learned I had no more money.

My universe crashing to pieces about me, and my nerves humming like taut piano wires for the vital need that was mine, I crouched in the gutter and gibbered bestially, till Hassim swaggered out and stilled my yammerings with a blow that felled me, half-stunned.

Then as I presently rose, staggeringly and with no thought save of the river which flowed with cool murmur so near me—as I rose, a light hand was laid like the touch of a rose on my arm. I turned with a frightened start, and stood spellbound before the vision of loveliness which met my gaze. Dark eyes limpid with pity surveyed me and the little hand on my ragged sleeve drew me toward the door of the Dream Temple. I shrank back, but a low voice, soft and musical, urged me, and filled with a trust that was strange, I shambled along with my beautiful guide.

At the door Hassim met us, cruel hands lifted and a dark scowl on his ape-like brow, but as I cowered there, expecting a blow, he halted before the girl's upraised hand and her word of command which had taken on an imperious note.

I did not understand what she said, but I saw dimly, as in a fog, that she gave the black man money, and she led me to a couch where she had me recline and arranged the cushions as if I were king of Egypt instead of a ragged, dirty renegade who lived only for hashish. Her slim hand was cool on my brow for a moment, and then she was gone and Yussef Ali came bearing the stuff for which my very soul shrieked—and soon I was wandering again through those strange and exotic countries that only a hashish slave knows.

Now as I sat on the mat and pondered the dream of the skull-face, I wondered more. Since the unknown girl had led me

back into the dive, I had come and gone as before, when I had
plenty of money to pay Yun Shatu. Someone certainly was paying
him for me, and while my subconscious mind had told me it was
the girl, my rusty brain had failed to grasp the fact entirely, or to
wonder why. What need of wondering? So someone paid and the
vivid-hued dreams continued, what cared I? But now I
wondered. For the girl who had protected me from Hassim and
had brought the hashish for me was the same girl I had seen in
the skull-face dream.

Through the soddenness of my degradation the lure of her
struck like a knife piercing my heart and strangely revived the
memories of the days when I was a man like other men—not yet
a sullen, cringing slave of dreams. Far and dim they were, shimmery islands in the mist of years—and what a dark sea lay
between!

I looked at my ragged sleeve and the dirty, claw-like hand
protruding from it; I gazed through the hanging smoke which
fogged the sordid room, at the low bunks along the wall whereon
lay the blankly staring dreamers—slaves, like me, of hashish or of
opium. I gazed at the slippered Chinamen gliding softly to and
fro bearing pipes or roasting balls of concentrated purgatory
over tiny, flickering fires. I gazed at Hassim standing, arms
folded, beside the door like a great statue of black basalt.

And I shuddered and hid my face in my hands because with
the faint dawning of returning manhood, I knew that this last
and most cruel dream was futile—I had crossed an ocean over
which I could never return, had cut myself off from the world of
normal men or women. Naught remained now but to drown this
dream as I had drowned all my others—swiftly and with hope
that I should soon attain that Ultimate Ocean which lies beyond
all dreams.

So these fleeting moments of lucidity, of longing, that tear
aside the veils of all dope slaves—unexplainable, without hope of
attainment.

So I went back to my empty dreams, to my phantasmagoria

of illusions; but sometimes, like a sword cleaving a mist, through the high lands and the low lands and seas of my visions floated, like half-forgotten music, the sheen of dark eyes and shimmery hair.

You ask how I, Stephen Costigan, American and a man of some attainments and culture, came to lie in a filthy dive of London's Limehouse? The answer is simple—no jaded debauchee I, seeking new sensations in the mysteries of the Orient. I answer—Argonne! Heavens, what deeps and heights of horror lurk in that one word alone! Shell-shocked—shell-torn. Endless days and nights without end and roaring red hell over No Man's Land where I lay shot and bayoneted to shreds of gory flesh. My body recovered, how I know not; my mind never did.

And the leaping fires and shifting shadows in my tortured brain drove me down and down, along the stairs of degradation, uncaring until at last I found surcease in Yun Shatu's Temple of Dreams, where I slew my red dreams in other dreams—the dreams of hashish whereby a man may descend to the lower pits of the reddest hells or soar into those unnamable heights where the stars are diamond pinpoints beneath his feet.

Not the visions of the sot, the beast, were mine. I attained the unattainable, stood face to face with the unknown and in cosmic calmness knew the unguessable. And was content after a fashion, until the sight of burnished hair and scarlet lips swept away my dream-built universe and left me shuddering among its ruins.

THE MASTER OF DOOM

"And He that toss'd you down into the Field,
He knows about it all—He knows! He knows!"

—Omar Khayyam

A hand shook me roughly as I emerged languidly from my
latest debauch.

"The Master wishes you! Up, swine!"

Hassim it was who shook me and who spoke.

"To Hell with the Master!" I answered, for I hated Hassim—
and feared him.

"Up with you or you get no more hashish," was the brutal
response, and I rose in trembling haste.

I followed the huge black man and he led the way to the rear
of the building, stepping in and out among the wretched
dreamers on the floor.

"Muster all hands on deck!" droned a sailor in a bunk. "All
hands!"

Hassim flung open the door at the rear and motioned me to
enter. I had never before passed through that door and had
supposed it led into Yun Shatu's private quarters. But it was

furnished only with a cot, a bronze idol of some sort before which incense burned, and a heavy table.

Hassim gave me a sinister glance and seized the table as if to spin it about. It turned as if it stood on a revolving platform and a section of the floor turned with it, revealing a hidden doorway in the floor. Steps led downward in the darkness.

Hassim lighted a candle and with a brusque gesture invited me to descend. I did so, with the sluggish obedience of the dope addict, and he followed, closing the door above us by means of an iron lever fastened to the underside of the floor. In the semi-darkness we went down the rickety steps, some nine or ten I should say, and then came upon a narrow corridor.

Here Hassim again took the lead, holding the candle high in front of him. I could scarcely see the sides of this cave-like passageway but knew that it was not wide. The flickering light showed it to be bare of any sort of furnishings save for a number of strange-looking chests which lined the walls—receptacles containing opium and other dope, I thought.

A continuous scurrying and the occasional glint of small red eyes haunted the shadows, betraying the presence of vast numbers of the great rats which infest the Thames waterfront of that section.

Then more steps loomed out of the dark in front of us as the corridor came to an abrupt end. Hassim led the way up and at the top knocked four times against what seemed the underside of a floor. A hidden door opened, and a flood of soft, illusive light streamed through.

Hassim hustled me up roughly, and I stood blinking in such a setting as I had never seen in my wildest flights of vision. I stood in a jungle of palm trees through which wriggled a million vivid-hued dragons! Then, as my startled eyes became accustomed to the light, I saw that I had not been suddenly transferred to some other planet, as I had at first thought. The palm trees were there, and the dragons, but the trees were artificial and stood in great pots and the dragons writhed across heavy tapestries which hid the walls.

The room itself was a monstrous affair—inhumanly large, it seemed to me. A thick smoke, yellowish and tropical in suggestion, seemed to hang over all, veiling the ceiling and baffling upward glances. This smoke, I saw, emanated from an altar in front of the wall to my left. I started. Through the saffron-billowing fog two eyes, hideously large and vivid, glittered at me. The vague outlines of some bestial idol took indistinct shape. I flung an uneasy glance about, marking the Oriental divans and couches and the bizarre furnishings, and then my eyes halted and rested on a lacquer screen just in front of me.

I could not pierce it and no sound came from beyond it, yet I felt eyes searing into my consciousness through it, eyes that burned through my very soul. A strange aura of evil flowed from that strange screen with its weird carvings and unholy decorations.

Hassim salaamed profoundly before it and then, without speaking, stepped back and folded his arms, statue-like.

A voice suddenly broke the heavy and oppressive silence.

"You who are a swine, would you like to be a man again?"

I started. The tone was inhuman, cold—more, there was a suggestion of long disuse of the vocal organs—the voice I had heard in my dream!

"Yes," I replied, trance-like, "I would like to be a man again."

Silence ensued for a space; then the voice came again with a sinister whispering undertone at the back of its sound like bats flying through a cavern.

"I shall make you a man again because I am a friend to all broken men. Not for a price shall I do it, nor for gratitude. And I give you a sign to seal my promise and my vow. Thrust your hand through the screen."

At these strange and almost unintelligible words I stood perplexed, and then, as the unseen voice repeated the last command, I stepped forward and thrust my hand through a slit

which opened silently in the screen. I felt my wrist seized in an
iron grip and something seven times colder than ice touched the
inside of my hand. Then my wrist was released, and drawing
forth my hand I saw a strange symbol traced in blue close to the
base of my thumb—a thing like a scorpion.

The voice spoke again in a sibilant language I did not understand, and Hassim stepped forward deferentially. He reached
about the screen and then turned to me, holding a goblet of
some amber-colored liquid which he proffered me with an iron-
ical bow. I took it hesitatingly.

"Drink and fear not," said the unseen voice. "It is only an
Egyptian wine with life-giving qualities."

So I raised the goblet and emptied it; the taste was not
unpleasant, and even as I handed the beaker to Hassim again, I
seemed to feel new life and vigor whip along my jaded veins.

"Remain at Yun Shatu's house," said the voice. "You will be
given food and a bed until you are strong enough to work for
yourself. You will use no hashish nor will you require any. Go!"

As in a daze, I followed Hassim back through the hidden
door, down the steps, along the dark corridor and up through the
other door that let us into the Temple of Dreams.

As we stepped from the rear chamber into the main room of
the dreamers, I turned to the Negro wonderingly.

"Master? Master of what? Of Life?"

Hassim laughed, fiercely and sardonically.

"Master of Doom!"

THE SPIDER AND THE FLY

"There was the Door to which I found no Key;
There was the Veil through which I might not see."

—Omar Khayyam

I sat on Yun Shatu's cushions and pondered with a clearness of
mind new and strange to me. As for that, all my sensations
were new and strange. I felt as if I had wakened from a
monstrously long sleep, and though my thoughts were sluggish, I
felt as though the cobwebs which had dogged them for so long
had been partly brushed away.

I drew my hand across my brow, noting how it trembled. I
was weak and shaky and felt the stirrings of hunger—not for
dope but for food. What had been in the draft I had quenched
in the chamber of mystery? And why had the "Master" chosen
me, out of all the other wretches of Yun Shatu's, for
regeneration?

And who was this Master? Somehow the word sounded
vaguely familiar—I sought laboriously to remember. Yes—I had
heard it, lying half-waking in the bunks or on the floor—whispered sibilantly by Yun Shatu or by Hassim or by Yussef Ali, the

Moor, muttered in their low-voiced conversations and mingled always with words I could not understand. Was not Yun Shatu, then, master of the Temple of Dreams? I had thought and the other addicts thought that the withered Chinaman held undisputed sway over this drab kingdom and that Hassim and Yussef Ali were his servants. And the four China boys who roasted opium with Yun Shatu and Yar Khan the Afghan and Santiago the Haitian and Ganra Singh, the renegade Sikh—all in the pay of Yun Shatu, we supposed—bound to the opium lord by bonds of gold or fear.

For Yun Shatu was a power in London's Chinatown and I had heard that his tentacles reached across the seas into high places of mighty and mysterious *tongs*. Was that Yun Shatu behind the lacquer screen? No; I knew the Chinaman's voice and besides I had seen him puttering about in the front of the temple just as I went through the back door.

Another thought came to me. Often, lying half-torpid, in the late hours of night or in the early grayness of dawn, I had seen men and women steal into the temple, whose dress and bearing were strangely out of place and incongruous. Tall, erect men, often in evening dress, with their hats drawn low about their brows, and fine ladies, veiled, in silks and furs. Never two of them came together, but always they came separately and, hiding their features, hurried to the rear door, where they entered and presently came forth again, hours later sometimes. Knowing that the lust for dope finds resting place in high positions sometimes, I had never wondered overmuch, supposing that these were wealthy men and women of society who had fallen victims to the craving, and that somewhere in the back of the building there was a private chamber for such. Yet now I wondered—sometimes these persons had remained only a few moments—was it always opium for which they came, or did they, too, traverse that strange corridor and converse with the One behind the screen?

My mind dallied with the idea of a great specialist to whom came all classes of people to find surcease from the dope habit.

Yet it was strange that such a one should select a dope-joint from which to work—strange, too, that the owner of that house should apparently look on him with so much reverence.

I gave it up as my head began to hurt with the unwonted effort of thinking, and shouted for food. Yussef Ali brought it to me on a tray, with a promptness which was surprizing. More, he salaamed as he departed, leaving me to ruminate on the strange shift of my status in the Temple of Dreams.

I ate, wondering what the One of the screen wanted with me. Not for an instant did I suppose that his actions had been prompted by the reasons he pretended; the life of the underworld had taught me that none of its denizens leaned toward philanthropy. And underworld the chamber of mystery had been, in spite of its elaborate and bizarre nature. And where could it be located? How far had I walked along the corridor? I shrugged my shoulders, wondering if it were not all a hashish-induced dream; then my eye fell upon my hand—and the scorpion traced thereon.

"Muster all hands!" droned the sailor in the bunk. "All hands!"

To tell in detail of the next few days would be boresome to any who have not tasted the dire slavery of dope. I waited for the craving to strike me again—waited with sure sardonic hopelessness. All day, all night—another day—then the miracle was forced upon my doubting brain. Contrary to all theories and supposed facts of science and common sense, the craving had left me as suddenly and completely as a bad dream! At first I could not credit my senses but believed myself to be still in the grip of a dope nightmare. But it was true. From the time I quaffed the goblet in the room of mystery, I felt not the slightest desire for the stuff which had been life itself to me. This, I felt vaguely, was somehow unholy and certainly opposed to all rules of nature. If the dread being behind the screen had discovered the secret of breaking hashish's terrible power, what other monstrous secrets had he discovered and what unthinkable dominance was his? The suggestion of evil crawled serpentlike through my mind.

I remained at Yun Shatu's house, lounging in a bunk or on cushions spread upon the floor, eating and drinking at will, but now that I was becoming a normal man again, the atmosphere became most revolting to me, and the sight of the wretches writhing in their dreams reminded me unpleasantly of what I myself had been, and it repelled, nauseated me.

So one day, when no one was watching me, I rose and went out on the street and walked along the waterfront. The air, burdened though it was with smoke and foul scents, filled my lungs with strange freshness and aroused new vigor in what had once been a powerful frame. I took new interest in the sounds of men living and working, and the sight of a vessel being unloaded at one of the wharfs actually thrilled me. The force of long-shoremen was short, and presently I found myself heaving and lifting and carrying, and though the sweat coursed down my brow and my limbs trembled at the effort, I exulted in the thought that at last I was able to labor for myself again, no matter how low or drab the work might be.

As I returned to the door of Yun Shatu's that evening— hideously weary but with the renewed feeling of manhood that comes of honest toil—Hassim met me at the door.

"You been where?" he demanded roughly.

"I've been working on the docks," I answered shortly.

"You don't need to work on docks," he snarled. "The Master got work for you."

He led the way, and again I traversed the dark stairs and the corridor under the earth. This time my faculties were alert, and I decided that the passageway could not be over thirty or forty feet in length. Again I stood before the lacquer screen, and again I heard the inhuman voice of living death.

"I can give you work," said the voice. "Are you willing to work for me?"

I quickly assented. After all, in spite of the fear which the voice inspired, I was deeply indebted to the owner.

"Good. Take these."

As I started toward the screen a sharp command halted me, and Hassim stepped forward and, reaching behind, took what was offered. This was a bundle of pictures and papers, apparently.

"Study these," said the One behind the screen, "and learn all you can about the man portrayed thereby. Yun Shatu will give you money; buy yourself such clothes as seamen wear and take a room at the front of the temple. At the end of two days, Hassim will bring you to me again. Go!"

The last impression I had, as the hidden door closed above me, was that the eyes of the idol, blinking through the everlasting smoke, leered mockingly at me.

The front of the Temple of Dreams consisted of rooms for rent, masking the true purpose of the building under the guise of a waterfront boarding house. The police had made several visits to Yun Shatu but had never got any incriminating evidence against him.

So in one of these rooms I took up my abode and set to work studying the material given me.

The pictures were all of one man, a large man, not unlike me in build and general facial outline, except that he wore a heavy beard and was inclined to blondness whereas I am dark. The name, as written on the accompanying papers, was Major Fairlan Morley, special commissioner to Natal and the Transvaal. This office and title were new to me, and I wondered at the connection between an African commissioner and an opium house on the Thames waterfront.

The papers consisted of extensive data evidently copied from authentic sources and all dealing with Major Morley, and a number of private documents considerably illuminating on the major's private life.

An exhaustive description was given of the man's personal appearance and habits, some of which seemed very trivial to me. I wondered what the purpose could be, and how the One behind the screen had come in possession of papers of such intimate nature.

I could find no clue in answer to this question but bent all my energies to the task set out for me. I owed a deep debt of gratitude to the unknown man who required this of me, and I was determined to repay him to the best of my ability. Nothing, at this time, suggested a snare to me.

THE MAN ON THE COUCH

*"What dam of lances sent thee forth to jest at dawn
with Death?"*

—Rudyard Kipling

At the expiration of two days, Hassim beckoned me as I
stood in the opium room. I advanced with a springy,
resilient tread, secure in the confidence that I had culled the
Morley papers of all their worth. I was a new man; my mental
swiftness and physical readiness surprized me—sometimes it
seemed unnatural.

Hassim eyed me through narrowed lids and motioned me to
follow, as usual. As we crossed the room, my gaze fell upon a man
who lay on a couch close to the wall, smoking opium. There was
nothing at all suspicious about his ragged, unkempt clothes, his
dirty, bearded face or the blank stare, but my eyes, sharpened to
an abnormal point, seemed to sense a certain incongruity in the
clean-cut limbs which not even the slouchy garments could
efface.

Hassim spoke impatiently and I turned away. We entered the
rear room, and as he shut the door and turned to the table, it

moved of itself and a figure bulked up through the hidden doorway. The Sikh, Ganra Singh, a lean sinister-eyed giant, emerged
and proceeded to the door opening into the opium room, where
he halted until we should have descended and closed the secret
doorway.

Again I stood amid the billowing yellow smoke and listened
to the hidden voice.

"Do you think you know enough about Major Morley to
impersonate him successfully?"

Startled, I answered, "No doubt I could, unless I met
someone who was intimate with him."

"I will take care of that. Follow me closely. Tomorrow you
sail on the first boat for Calais. There you will meet an agent of
mine who will accost you the instant you step upon the wharfs,
and give you further instructions. You will sail second class and
avoid all conversation with strangers or anyone. Take the papers
with you. The agent will aid you in making up and your
masquerade will start in Calais. That is all. Go!"

I departed, my wonder growing. All this rigmarole evidently
had a meaning, but one which I could not fathom. Back in the
opium room Hassim bade me be seated on some cushions to
await his return. To my question he snarled that he was going
forth as he had been ordered, to buy me a ticket on the Channel
boat. He departed and I sat down, leaning my back against the
wall. As I ruminated, it seemed suddenly that eyes were fixed on
me so intensely as to disturb my sub-mind. I glanced up quickly,
but no one seemed to be looking at me. The smoke drifted
through the hot atmosphere as usual; Yussef Ali and the Chinese
glided back and forth tending to the wants of the sleepers.

Suddenly the door to the rear room opened, and a strange
and hideous figure came haltingly out. Not all of those who
found entrance to Yun Shatu's back room were aristocrats and
society members. This was one of the exceptions, and one whom
I remembered as having often entered and emerged therefrom.
A tall, gaunt figure, shapeless and ragged wrappings, and nonde-

script garments, face entirely hidden. Better that the face be hidden, I thought, for without doubt the wrapping concealed a grisly sight. The man was a leper, who had somehow managed to escape the attention of the public guardians and who was occasionally seen haunting the lower and more mysterious regions of East End—a mystery even to the lowest denizens of Limehouse.

Suddenly my supersensitive mind was aware of a swift tension in the air. The leper hobbled out the door, closed it behind him. My eyes instinctively sought the couch whereon lay the man who had aroused my suspicions earlier in the day. I could have sworn that cold steely eyes glared menacingly before they flickered shut. I crossed to the couch in one stride and bent over the prostrate man. Something about his face seemed unnatural—a healthy bronze seemed to underlie the pallor of complexion.

"Yun Shatu!" I shouted. "A spy is in the house!"

Things happened then with bewildering speed. The man on the couch with one tigerish movement leaped erect and a revolver gleamed in his hand. One sinewy arm flung me aside as I sought to grapple with him and a sharp decisive voice sounded over the babble which broke forth.

"You there! Halt! Halt!"

The pistol in the stranger's hand was leveled at the leper, who was making for the door in long strides!

All about was confusion; Yun Shatu was shrieking volubly in Chinese, and the four China boys and Yussef Ali were rushing in from all sides, knives glittering in their hands.

All this I saw with unnatural clearness even as I marked the stranger's face. As the fleeing leper gave no evidence of halting, I saw the eyes harden to steely points of determination, sighting along the pistol barrel—the features set with the grim purpose of the slayer. The leper was almost to the outer door, but death would strike him down ere he could reach it.

And then, just as the finger of the stranger tightened on the trigger, I hurled myself forward and my right fist crashed against his chin. He went down as though struck by a trip-hammer, the revolver exploding harmlessly in the air.

In that instant, with the blinding flare of light that sometimes comes to one, I knew that the leper was none other than the Man Behind the Screen!

I bent over the fallen man, who though not entirely senseless had been rendered temporarily helpless by that terrific blow. He was struggling dazedly to rise, but I shoved him roughly down again and, seizing the false beard he wore, tore it away. A lean bronzed face was revealed, the strong lines of which not even the artificial dirt and greasepaint could alter.

Yussef Ali leaned above him now, dagger in hand, eyes slits of murder. The brown sinewy hand went up—I caught the wrist.

"Not so fast, you black devil! What are you about to do?"

"This is John Gordon," he hissed, "the Master's greatest foe! He must die, curse you!"

John Gordon! The name was familiar somehow, and yet I did not seem to connect it with the London police nor account for the man's presence in Yun Shatu's dope-joint. However, on one point I was determined.

"You don't kill him, at any rate. Up with you!" This last to Gordon, who with my aid staggered up, still very dizzy.

"That punch would have dropped a bull," I said in wonderment; "I didn't know I had it in me."

The false leper had vanished. Yun Shatu stood gazing at me as immobile as an idol, hands in his wide sleeves, and Yussef Ali stood back, muttering murderously and thumbing his dagger edge, as I led Gordon out of the opium room and through the innocent-appearing bar which lay between that room and the street.

Out in the street I said to him: "I have no idea as to who you are or what you are doing here, but you see what an unhealthful place it is for you. Hereafter be advised by me and stay away."

His only answer was a searching glance, and then be turned and walked swiftly though somewhat unsteadily up the street.

THE DREAM GIRL

"I have reached these lands but newly
From an ultimate dim Thule."

—Edgar Allan Poe

Outside my room sounded a light footstep. The doorknob turned cautiously and slowly; the door opened. I sprang erect with a gasp. Red lips, half-parted, dark eyes like limpid seas of wonder, a mass of shimmering hair—framed in my drab doorway stood the girl of my dreams!

She entered, and half-turning with a sinuous motion, closed the door. I sprang forward, my hands outstretched, then halted as she put a finger to her lips.

"You must not talk loudly," she almost whispered. "*He* did not say I could not come; yet—"

Her voice was soft and musical, with just a touch of foreign accent which I found delightful. As for the girl herself, every intonation, every movement proclaimed the Orient. She was a fragrant breath from the east. From her night-black hair, piled high above her alabaster forehead, to her little feet, encased in high-heeled pointed slippers, she portrayed the highest ideal of Asiatic loveliness—an effect which was heightened rather than lessened by the English blouse and skirt which she wore.

"You are beautiful!" I said dazedly. "Who are you?"

"I am Zuleika," she answered with a shy smile. "I—I am glad you like me. I am glad you no longer dream hashish dreams."

Strange that so small a thing should set my heart to leaping wildly!

"I owe it all to you, Zuleika," I said huskily. "Had not I dreamed of you every hour since you first lifted me from the gutter, I had lacked the power of even hoping to be freed from my curse."

She blushed prettily and intertwined her white fingers as if in nervousness.

"You leave England tomorrow?" she said suddenly.

"Yes. Hassim has not returned with my ticket—" I hesitated suddenly, remembering the command of silence.

"Yes, I know, I know!" she whispered swiftly, her eyes widening. "And John Gordon has been here! He saw you!"

"Yes!"

She came close to me with a quick lithe movement.

"You are to impersonate some man! Listen, while you are doing this, you must not ever let Gordon see you! He would know you, no matter what your disguise! He is a terrible man!"

"I don't understand," I said, completely bewildered. "How did the Master break me of my hashish craving? Who is this Gordon and why did he come here? Why does the Master go disguised as a leper—and who is he? Above all, why am I to impersonate a man I never saw or heard of?"

"I cannot—I dare not tell you!" she whispered, her face paling. "I—"

Somewhere in the house sounded the faint tones of a Chinese gong. The girl started like a frightened gazelle.

"I must go! *He* summons me!"

She opened the door, darted through, halted a moment to electrify me with her passionate exclamation: "Oh, be careful, be very careful, sahib!"

Then she was gone.

THE MAN OF THE SKULL

"What the hammer? What the chain?
In what furnace was thy brain?
What the anvil? What dread grasp
Dare its deadly terrors clasp?"

—William Blake

A while after my beautiful and mysterious visitor had left, I sat in meditation. I believed that I had at last stumbled onto an explanation of a part of the enigma, at any rate. This was the conclusion I had reached: Yun Shatu, the opium lord, was simply the agent or servant of some organization or individual whose work was on a far larger scale than merely supplying dope addicts in the Temple of Dreams. This man or these men needed co-workers among all classes of people; in other words, I was being let in with a group of opium smugglers on a gigantic scale. Gordon no doubt had been investigating the case, and his presence alone showed that it was no ordinary one, for I knew that he held a high position with the English government, though just what, I did not know.

Opium or not, I determined to carry out my obligation to

the Master. My moral sense had been blunted by the dark ways I had traveled, and the thought of despicable crime did not enter my head. I was indeed hardened. More, the mere debt of gratitude was increased a thousandfold by the thought of the girl. To the Master I owed it that I was able to stand up on my feet and look into her clear eyes as a man should. So if he wished my services as a smuggler of dope, he should have them. No doubt I was to impersonate some man so high in governmental esteem that the usual actions of the customs officers would be deemed unnecessary; was I to bring some rare dream-producer into England?

These thoughts were in my mind as I went downstairs, but ever back of them hovered other and more alluring suppositions—what was the reason for the girl, here in this vile dive—a rose in a garbage-heap—and who was she?

As I entered the outer bar, Hassim came in, his brows set in a dark scowl of anger, and, I believed, fear. He carried a newspaper in his hand, folded.

"I told you to wait in opium room," he snarled.

"You were gone so long that I went up to my room. Have you the ticket?"

He merely grunted and pushed on past me into the opium room, and, standing at the door, I saw him cross the floor and disappear into the rear room. I stood there, my bewilderment increasing. For as Hassim had brushed past me, I had noted an item on the face of the paper, against which his black thumb was tightly pressed as if to mark that special column of news.

And with the unnatural celerity of action and judgment which seemed to be mine those days, I had in that fleeting instant read:

"AFRICAN SPECIAL COMMISSIONER FOUND MURDERED!

The body of Major Fairlan Morley was yesterday discovered in a rotting ship's hold at Bordeaux ..."

No more I saw of the details, but that alone was enough to

make me think! The affair seemed to be taking on an ugly aspect. Yet—

Another day passed. To my inquiries, Hassim snarled that the plans had been changed and I was not to go to France. Then, late in the evening, he came to bid me once more to the room of mystery.

I stood before the lacquer screen, the yellow smoke acrid in my nostrils, the woven dragons writhing along the tapestries, the palm trees rearing thick and oppressive.

"A change has come in our plans," said the hidden voice. "You will not sail as was decided before. But I have other work that you may do. Mayhap this will be more to your type of usefulness, for I admit you have somewhat disappointed me in regard to subtlety. You interfered the other day in such manner as will no doubt cause me great inconvenience in the future."

I said nothing, but a feeling of resentment began to stir in me.

"Even after the assurance of one of my most trusted servants," the toneless voice continued, with no mark of any emotion save a slightly rising note, "you insisted on releasing my most deadly enemy. Be more circumspect in the future."

"I saved your life!" I said angrily.

"And for that reason alone I overlook your mistake—this time!"

A slow fury suddenly surged up in me.

"This time! Make the best of it this time, for I assure you there will be no next time. I owe you a greater debt than I can ever hope to pay, but that does not make me your slave. I have saved your life—the debt is as near paid as a man can pay it. Go your way and I go mine!"

A low, hideous laugh answered me, like a reptilian hiss.

"You fool! You will pay with your whole life's toil! You say you are not my slave? I say you are—just as black Hassim there beside you is my slave—just as the girl Zuleika is my slave, who has bewitched you with her beauty."

These words sent a wave of hot blood to my brain and I was conscious of a flood of fury which completely engulfed my reason for a second. Just as all my moods and senses seemed sharpened and exaggerated those days, so now this burst of rage transcended every moment of anger I had ever had before.

"Hell's fiends!" I shrieked. "You devil—who are you and what is your hold on me? I'll see you or die!"

Hassim sprang at me, but I hurled him backward and with one stride reached the screen and flung it aside with an incredible effort of strength. Then I shrank back, hands outflung, shrieking. A tall, gaunt figure stood before me, a figure arrayed grotesquely in a silk brocaded gown which fell to the floor.

From the sleeves of this gown protruded hands which filled me with crawling horror—long, predatory hands, with thin bony fingers and curved talons—withered skin of a parchment brownish-yellow, like the hands of a man long dead.

The hands—but, oh God, the face! A skull to which no vestige of flesh seemed to remain but on which taut brownish-yellow skin grew fast, etching out every detail of that terrible death's-head. The forehead was high and in a way magnificent, but the head was curiously narrow through the temples, and from under penthouse brows great eyes glimmered like pools of yellow fire. The nose was high-bridged and very thin; the mouth was a mere colorless gash between thin, cruel lips. A long, bony neck supported this frightful vision and completed the effect of a reptilian demon from some medieval hell.

I was face to face with the skull-faced man of my dreams!

BLACK WISDOM

"By thought a crawling ruin,
By life a leaping mire.
By a broken heart in the breast of the world
And the end of the world's desire."

—G. K. Chesterton

The terrible spectacle drove for the instant all thought of rebellion from my mind. My very blood froze in my veins and I stood motionless. I heard Hassim laugh grimly behind me. The eyes in the cadaverous face blazed fiendishly at me and I blanched from the concentrated satanic fury in them.

Then the horror laughed sibilantly.

"I do you a great honor, Mr. Costigan; among a very few, even of my own servants, you may say that you saw my face and lived. I think you will be more useful to me living than dead."

I was silent, completely unnerved. It was difficult to believe that this man lived, for his appearance certainly belied the thought. He seemed horribly like a mummy. Yet his lips moved when he spoke and his eyes flamed with hideous life.

"You will do as I say," he said abruptly, and his voice had

taken on a note of command. "You doubtless know, or know of, Sir Haldred Frenton?"

"Yes."

Every man of culture in Europe and America was familiar with the travel books of Sir Haldred Frenton, author and soldier of fortune.

"You will go to Sir Haldred's estate tonight—"

"Yes?"

"And kill him!"

I staggered, literally. This order was incredible—unspeakable! I had sunk low, low enough to smuggle opium, but to deliberately murder a man I had never seen, a man noted for his kindly deeds! That was too monstrous even to contemplate.

"You do not refuse?"

The tone was as loathly and as mocking as the hiss of a serpent.

"Refuse?" I screamed, finding my voice at last. "Refuse? You incarnate devil! Of course I refuse! You—"

Something in the cold assurance of his manner halted me—froze me into apprehensive silence.

"You fool!" he said calmly. "I broke the hashish chains—do you know how? Four minutes from now you will know and curse the day you were born! Have you not thought it strange, the swiftness of brain, the resilience of body—the brain that should be rusty and slow, the body that should be weak and sluggish from years of abuse? That blow that felled John Gordon—have you not wondered at its might? The ease with which you mastered Major Morley's records—have you not wondered at that? You fool, you are bound to me by chains of steel and blood and fire! I have kept you alive and sane—I alone. Each day the lifesaving elixir has been given you in your wine. You could not live and keep your reason without it. And I and only I know its secret!"

He glanced at a queer timepiece which stood on a table at his elbow.

"This time I had Yun Shatu leave the elixir out—I anticipated rebellion. The time is near—ha, it strikes!"

Something else he said, but I did not hear. I did not see, nor
did I feel in the human sense of the word. I was writhing at his
feet, screaming and gibbering in the flames of such hells as men
have never dreamed of.

Aye, I knew now! He had simply given me a dope so much
stronger that it drowned the hashish. My unnatural ability was
explainable now—I had simply been acting under the stimulus of
something which combined all the hells in its makeup, which
stimulated, something like heroin, but whose effect was unno-
ticed by the victim. What it was, I had no idea, nor did I believe
anyone knew save that hellish being who stood watching me
with grim amusement. But it had held my brain together,
instilling into my system a need for it, and now my frightful
craving tore my soul asunder.

Never, in my moments of worst shell shock or my moments
of hashish craving, have I ever experienced anything like that. I
burned with the heat of a thousand hells and froze with an
iciness that was colder than any ice, a hundred times. I swept
down to the deepest pits of torture and up to the highest crags
of torment—a million yelling devils hemmed me in, shrieking
and stabbing. Bone by bone, vein by vein, cell by cell, I felt my
body disintegrate and fly in bloody atoms all over the universe—
and each separate cell was an entire system of quivering,
screaming nerves. And they gathered from far voids and reunited
with a greater torment.

Through the fiery bloody mists I heard my own voice
screaming, a monotonous yammering. Then with distended eyes
I saw a golden goblet, held by a claw-like hand, swim into view—
a goblet filled with an amber liquid.

With a bestial screech, I seized it with both hands, being
dimly aware that the metal stem gave beneath my fingers, and
brought the brim to my lips. I drank in frenzied haste, the liquid
slopping down onto my breast.

KATHULOS OF EGYPT

"Night shall be thrice night over you,
And Heaven an iron cope."

—G. K. Chesterton

The Skull-faced One stood watching me critically as I sat panting on a couch, completely exhausted. He held in his hand the goblet and surveyed the golden stem, which was crushed out of all shape. This my maniac fingers had done in the instant of drinking.

"Superhuman strength, even for a man in your condition," he said with a sort of creaky pedantry. "I doubt if even Hassim here could equal it. Are you ready for your instructions now?"

I nodded, wordless. Already the hellish strength of the elixir was flowing through my veins, renewing my burnt-out force. I wondered how long a man could live as I lived being constantly burned out and artificially rebuilt.

"You will be given a disguise and will go alone to the Frenton estate. No one suspects any design against Sir Haldred and your entrance into the estate and the house itself should be a matter of comparative ease. You will not don the disguise—which will be of unique nature—until you are ready to enter the estate. You will then proceed to Sir Haldred's room and kill him, breaking his neck with your bare hands—this is essential—"

The voice droned on, giving the ghastly orders in a frightfully casual and matter-of-fact way. The cold sweat beaded my brow.

"You will then leave the estate, taking care to leave the imprint of your hand somewhere plainly visible, and the automobile, which will be waiting for you at some safe place nearby, will bring you back here, you having first removed the disguise. I have, in case of complications, any amount of men who will swear that you spent the entire night in the Temple of Dreams and never left it. But there must be no detection! Go warily and perform your task surely, for you know the alternative."

I did not return to the opium house but was taken through winding corridors, hung with heavy tapestries, to a small room containing only an Oriental couch. Hassim gave me to understand that I was to remain here until after nightfall and then left me. The door was closed, but I made no effort to discover if it was locked. The Skull-faced Master held me with stronger shackles than locks and bolts.

Seated upon the couch in the bizarre setting of a chamber which might have been a room in an Indian zenana, I faced fact squarely and fought out my battle. There was still in me some trace of manhood left—more than the fiend had reckoned, and added to this were black despair and desperation. I chose and determined on my only course.

Suddenly the door opened softly. Some intuition told me whom to expect, nor was I disappointed. Zuleika stood, a glorious vision before me—a vision which mocked me, made blacker my despair and yet thrilled me with wild yearning and reasonless joy.

She bore a tray of food which she set beside me, and then she seated herself on the couch, her large eyes fixed upon my face. A flower in a serpent den she was, and the beauty of her took hold of my heart.

"Steephen!" she whispered, and I thrilled as she spoke my name for the first time.

Her luminous eyes suddenly shone with tears and she laid her little hand on my arm. I seized it in both my rough hands.

"They have set you a task which you fear and hate!" she faltered.

"Aye," I almost laughed, "but I'll fool them yet! Zuleika, tell me—what is the meaning of all this?"

She glanced fearfully around her.

"I do not know all—" she hesitated "—your plight is all my fault but I—I hoped—Steephen, I have watched you every time you came to Yun Shatu's for months. You did not see me but I saw you, and I saw in you, not the broken sot your rags proclaimed, but a wounded soul, a soul bruised terribly on the ramparts of life. And from my heart I pitied you. Then when Hassim abused you that day—" again tears started to her eyes "—I could not bear it and I knew how you suffered for want of hashish. So I paid Yun Shatu, and going to the Master I—I—oh, you will hate me for this!" she sobbed.

"No—no—never—"

"I told him that you were a man who might be of use to him and begged him to have Yun Shatu supply you with what you needed. He had already noticed you, for his is the eye of the slaver and all the world is his slave market! So he bade Yun Shatu do as I asked; and now—better if you had remained as you were, my friend."

"No! No!" I exclaimed. "I have known a few days of regeneration, even if it was false! I have stood before you as a man, and that is worth all else!"

And all that I felt for her must have looked forth from my eyes, for she dropped hers and flushed. Ask me not how love comes to a man; but I knew that I loved Zuleika—had loved this mysterious Oiental girl since first I saw her—and somehow I felt that she, in a measure, returned my affection. This realization made blacker and more barren the road I had chosen; yet—for pure love must ever strengthen a man—it nerved me to what I must do.

"Zuleika," I said, speaking hurriedly, "time flies and there are things I must learn; tell me—who are you and why do you remain in this den of Hades?"

"I am Zuleika—that is all I know. I am Circassian by blood and birth; when I was very little I was captured in a Turkish raid and raised in a Stamboul harem; while I was yet too young to marry, my master gave me as a present to—to *Him*."

"And who is he—this skull-faced man?"

"He is Kathulos of Egypt—that is all I know. My master."

"An Egyptian? Then what is he doing in London—why all this mystery?"

She intertwined her fingers nervously.

"Steephen, please speak lower; always there is someone listening everywhere. I do not know who the Master is or why he is here or why he does these things. I swear by Allah! If I knew I would tell you. Sometimes distinguished-looking men come here to the room where the Master receives them—not the room where you saw him—and he makes me dance before them and afterward flirt with them a little. And always I must repeat exactly what they say to me. That is what I must always do—in Turkey, in the Barbary States, in Egypt, in France and in England. The Master taught me French and English and educated me in many ways himself. He is the greatest sorcerer in all the world and knows all ancient magic and everything."

"Zuleika," I said, "my race is soon run, but let me get you out of this—come with me and I swear I'll get you away from this fiend!"

She shuddered and hid her face.

"No, no, I cannot!"

"Zuleika," I asked gently, "what hold has he over you, child—dope also?"

"No, no!" she whimpered. "I do not know—I do not know— but I cannot—I never can escape him!"

I sat, baffled for a few moments; then I asked, "Zuleika, where are we right now?"

"This building is a deserted storehouse back of the Temple of Silence."

"I thought so. What is in the chests in the tunnel?"

"I do not know."

Then suddenly she began weeping softly. "You too, a slave, like me—you who are so strong and kind—oh Steephen, I cannot bear it!"

I smiled. "Lean closer, Zuleika, and I will tell you how I am going to fool this Kathulos."

She glanced apprehensively at the door.

"You must speak low. I will lie in your arms and while you pretend to caress me, whisper your words to me."

She glided into my embrace, and there on the dragon-worked couch in that house of horror I first knew the glory of Zuleika's slender form nestling in my arms—of Zuleika's soft cheek pressing my breast. The fragrance of her was in my nostrils, her hair in my eyes, and my senses reeled; then with my lips hidden by her silky hair I whispered, swiftly:

"I am going first to warn Sir Haldred Frenton—then to find John Gordon and tell him of this den. I will lead the police here and you must watch closely and be ready to hide from *Him*—until we can break through and kill or capture him. Then you will be free."

"But you!" she gasped, paling. "You must have the elixir, and only he—"

"I have a way of outdoing him, child," I answered.

She went pitifully white and her woman's intuition sprang at the right conclusion.

"You are going to kill yourself!"

And much as it hurt me to see her emotion, I yet felt a torturing thrill that she should feel so on my account. Her arms tightened about my neck.

"Don't, Steephen!" she begged. "It is better to live, even—"

"No, not at that price. Better to go out clean while I have the manhood left."

She stared at me wildly for an instant; then, pressing her red lips suddenly to mine, she sprang up and fled from the room. Strange, strange are the ways of love. Two stranded ships on the shores of life, we had drifted inevitably together, and though no word of love had passed between us, we knew each other's heart —through grime and rags, and through accouterments of the slave, we knew each other's heart and from the first loved as naturally and as purely as it was intended from the beginning of time.

The beginning of life now and the end for me, for as soon as I had completed my task, ere I felt again the torments of my curse, love and life and beauty and torture should be blotted out together in the stark finality of a pistol ball scattering my rotting brain. Better a clean death than—

The door opened again and Yussef Ali entered.

"The hour arrives for departure," he said briefly. "Rise and follow."

I had no idea, of course, as to the time. No window opened from the room I occupied—I had seen no outer window whatever. The rooms were lighted by tapers in censers swinging from the ceiling. As I rose the slim young Moor slanted a sinister glance in my direction.

"This lies between you and me," he said sibilantly. "Servants of the same Master we—but this concerns ourselves alone. Keep your distance from Zuleika—the Master has promised her to me in the days of the empire."

My eyes narrowed to slits as I looked into the frowning, handsome face of the Oriental, and such hate surged up in me as I have seldom known. My fingers involuntarily opened and closed, and the Moor, marking the action, stepped back, hand in his girdle.

"Not now—there is work for us both—later perhaps." Then in a sudden cold gust of hatred, "Swine! Ape-man! When the

Master is finished with you I shall quench my dagger in your heart!"

I laughed grimly.

"Make it soon, desert-snake, or I'll crush your spine between my hands."

THE DARK HOUSE

"Against all man-made shackles and a man-made hell—
Alone—at last—unaided—I rebel!"

—Talbot Mundy

I followed Yussef Ali along the winding hallways, down the steps—Kathulos was not in the idol room—and along the tunnel, then through the rooms of the Temple of Dreams and out into the street, where the streetlamps gleamed drearily through the fogs and a slight drizzle. Across the street stood an automobile, curtains closely drawn.

"That is yours," said Hassim, who had joined us. "Saunter across natural-like. Don't act suspicious. The place may be watched. The driver knows what to do."

Then he and Yussef Ali drifted back into the bar and I took a single step toward the curb.

"Steephen!"

A voice that made my heart leap spoke my name! A white hand beckoned from the shadows of a doorway. I stepped quickly there.

"Zuleika!"

"Shhh!"

She clutched my arm, slipped something into my hand; I made out vaguely a small flask of gold.

"Hide this, quick!" came her urgent whisper. "Don't come back but go away and hide. This is full of elixir—I will try to get you some more before that is all gone. You must find a way of communicating with me."

"Yes, but how did you get this?" I asked amazedly.

"I stole it from the Master! Now please, I must go before he misses me."

And she sprang back into the doorway and vanished. I stood undecided. I was sure that she had risked nothing less than her life in doing this, and I was torn by the fear of what Kathulos might do to her, were the theft discovered. But to return to the house of mystery would certainly invite suspicion, and I might carry out my plan and strike back before the Skull-faced One learned of his slave's duplicity.

So I crossed the street to the waiting automobile. The driver was a Negro whom I had never seen before, a lanky man of medium height. I stared hard at him, wondering how much he had seen. He gave no evidence of having seen anything, and I decided that even if he had noticed me step back into the shadows he could not have seen what passed there nor have been able to recognize the girl.

He merely nodded as I climbed in the back seat, and a moment later we were speeding away down the deserted and fog-haunted streets. A bundle beside me I concluded to be the disguise mentioned by the Egyptian.

To recapture the sensations I experienced as I rode through the rainy, misty night would be impossible. I felt as if I were already dead, and the bare and dreary streets about me were the roads of death over which my ghost had been doomed to roam forever. A torturing joy was in my heart, and bleak despair—the despair of a doomed man. Not that death itself was so repellent —a dope victim dies too many deaths to shrink from the last—

but it was hard to go out just as love had entered my barren life. And I was still young.

A sardonic smile crossed my lips—they were young, too, the men who died beside me in No Man's Land. I drew back my sleeve and clenched my fists, tensing my muscles. There was no surplus weight on my frame, and much of the firm flesh had wasted away, but the cords of the great biceps still stood out like knots of iron, seeming to indicate massive strength. But I knew my might was false, that in reality I was a broken hulk of a man, animated only by the artificial fire of the elixir, without which a frail girl might topple me over.

The automobile came to a halt among some trees. We were on the outskirts of an exclusive suburb and the hour was past midnight. Through the trees I saw a large house looming darkly against the distant flares of nighttime London.

"This is where I wait," said the Negro. "No one can see the automobile from the road or from the house."

Holding a match so that its light could not be detected outside the car, I examined the "disguise" and was hard put to restrain an insane laugh. The disguise was the complete hide of a gorilla! Gathering the bundle under my arm I trudged toward the wall which surrounded the Frenton estate. A few steps and the trees where the Negro hid with the car merged into one dark mass. I did not believe he could see me, but for safety's sake I made, not for the high iron gate at the front, but for the wall at the side where there was no gate.

No light showed in the house. Sir Haldred was a bachelor, and I was sure that the servants were all in bed long ago. I negotiated the wall with ease and stole across the dark lawn to a side door, still carrying the grisly "disguise" under my arm. The door was locked, as I had anticipated, and I did not wish to arouse anyone until I was safely in the house, where the sound of voices would not carry to one who might have followed me. I took hold of the knob with both hands, and, exerting slowly the inhuman strength that was mine, began to twist. The shaft turned in my hands and the lock within shattered suddenly, with a noise that was like the crash of a cannon in the stillness. An instant more and I was inside and had closed the door behind me.

I took a single stride in the darkness in the direction I believed the stair to be, then halted as a beam of light flashed into my face. At the side of the beam I caught the glimmer of a pistol muzzle. Beyond a lean shadowy face floated.

"Stand where you are and put up your hands!"

I lifted my hands, allowing the bundle to slip to the floor. I had heard that voice only once but I recognized it—knew instantly that the man who held that light was John Gordon.

"How many are with you?"

His voice was sharp, commanding.

"I am alone," I answered. "Take me into a room where a light cannot be seen from the outside and I'll tell you some things you want to know."

He was silent; then, bidding me take up the bundle I had dropped, he stepped to one side and motioned me to precede him into the next room. There he directed me to a stairway and at the top landing opened a door and switched on lights.

I found myself in a room whose curtains were closely drawn. During this journey Gordon's alertness had not relaxed, and now he stood, still covering me with his revolver. Clad in conventional garments, he stood revealed a tall, leanly but powerfully built man, taller than I but not so heavy—with steel-gray eyes and clean-cut features. Something about the man attracted me, even as I noted a bruise on his jawbone where my fist had struck in our last meeting.

"I cannot believe," he said crisply, "that this apparent clumsiness and lack of subtlety is real. Doubtless you have your own reasons for wishing me to be in a secluded room at this time, but Sir Haldred is efficiently protected even now. Stand still."

Muzzle pressed against my chest, he ran his hand over my garments for concealed weapons, seeming slightly surprized when he found none.

"Still," he murmured as if to himself, "a man who can burst an iron lock with his bare hands has scant need of weapons."

"You are wasting valuable time," I said impatiently. "I was sent here tonight to kill Sir Haldred Frenton—"

"By whom?" the question was shot at me.

"By the man who sometimes goes disguised as a leper."

He nodded, a gleam in his scintillant eyes.

"My suspicions were correct, then."

"Doubtless. Listen to me closely—do you desire the death or arrest of that man?"

Gordon laughed grimly.

"To one who wears the mark of the scorpion on his hand, my answer would be superfluous."

"Then follow my directions and your wish shall be granted."

His eyes narrowed suspiciously.

"So that was the meaning of this open entry and non-resistance," he said slowly. "Does the dope which dilates your eyeballs so warp your mind that you think to lead me into ambush?"

I pressed my hands against my temples. Time was racing and every moment was precious—how could I convince this man of my honesty?

"Listen; my name is Stephen Costigan of America. I was a frequenter of Yun Shatu's dive and a hashish addict—as you have guessed, but just now a slave of stronger dope. By virtue of this slavery, the man you know as a false leper, whom Yun Shatu and his friends call 'Master,' gained dominance over me and sent me here to murder Sir Haldred—why, God only knows. But I have gained a space of respite by coming into possession of some of this dope which I must have in order to live, and I fear and hate this Master. Listen to me and I swear, by all things holy and unholy, that before the sun rises the false leper shall be in your power!"

I could tell that Gordon was impressed in spite of himself.

"Speak fast!" he rapped.

Still I could sense his disbelief and a wave of futility swept over me.

"If you will not act with me," I said, "let me go and somehow I'll find a way to get to the Master and kill him. My time is short —my hours are numbered and my vengeance is yet to be realized."

"Let me hear your plan, and talk fast," Gordon answered.

"It is simple enough. I will return to the Master's lair and tell him I have accomplished that which he sent me to do. You must follow closely with your men and while I engage the Master in conversation, surround the house. Then, at the signal, break in and kill or seize him."

Gordon frowned. "Where is this house?"

"The warehouse back of Yun Shatu's has been converted into a veritable Oriental palace."

"The warehouse!" he exclaimed. "How can that be? I had thought of that first, but I have carefully examined it from without. The windows are closely barred and spiders have built webs across them. The doors are nailed fast on the outside, and the seals that mark the warehouse as deserted have never been broken or disturbed in any way."

"They tunneled up from beneath," I answered. "The Temple of Dreams is directly connected with the warehouse."

"I have traversed the alley between the two buildings," said Gordon, "and the doors of the warehouse opening into that alley are, as I have said, nailed shut from without just as the owners left them. There is apparently no rear exit of any kind from the Temple of Dreams."

"A tunnel connects the buildings, with one door in the rear room of Yun Shatu's and the other in the idol room of the warehouse."

"I have been in Yun Shatu's back room and found no such door."

"The table rests upon it. You noted the heavy table in the center of the room? Had you turned it around, the secret door

would have opened in the floor. Now this is my plan: I will go in
through the Temple of Dreams and meet the Master in the idol
room. You will have men secretly stationed in front of the warehouse and others upon the other street, in front of the Temple
of Dreams. Yun Shatu's building, as you know, faces the waterfront, while the warehouse, fronting the opposite direction,
faces a narrow street running parallel with the river. At the signal
let the men in this street break open the front of the warehouse
and rush in, while simultaneously those in front of Yun Shatu's
make an invasion through the Temple of Dreams. Let these
make for the rear room, shooting without mercy any who may
seek to deter them, and there open the secret door as I have
said. There being, to the best of my knowledge, no other exit
from the Master's lair, he and his servants will necessarily seek to
make their escape through the tunnel. Thus we will have them
on both sides."

Gordon ruminated while I studied his face with breathless
interest.

"This may be a snare," he muttered, "or an attempt to draw
me away from Sir Haldred, but—"

I held my breath.

"I am a gambler by nature," he said slowly. "I am going to
follow what you Americans call a hunch—but God help you if
you are lying to me!"

I sprang erect.

"Thank God! Now aid me with this suit, for I must be
wearing it when I return to the automobile waiting for me."

His eyes narrowed as I shook out the horrible masquerade
and prepared to don it.

"This shows, as always, the touch of the master hand. You
were doubtless instructed to leave marks of your hands, encased
in those hideous gauntlets?"

"Yes, though I have no idea why."

"I think I have—the Master is famed for leaving no real clues
to mark his crimes—a great ape escaped from a neighboring zoo

earlier in the evening and it seems too obvious for mere chance, in the light of this disguise. The ape would have gotten the blame of Sir Haldred's death."

The thing was easily gotten into and the illusion of reality it created was so perfect as to draw a shudder from me as I viewed myself in a mirror.

"It is now two o'clock," said Gordon."Allowing for the time it will take you to get back to Limehouse and the time it will take me to get my men stationed, I promise you that at half-past four the house will be closely surrounded. Give me a start—wait here until I have left this house, so I will arrive at least as soon as you."

"Good!" I impulsively grasped his hand. "There will doubtless be a girl there who is in no way implicated with the Master's evil doings, but only a victim of circumstances such as I have been. Deal gently with her."

"It shall be done. What signal shall I look for?"

"I have no way of signaling for you and I doubt if any sound in the house could be heard on the street. Let your men make their raid on the stroke of five."

I turned to go.

"A man is waiting for you with a car, I take it? Is he likely to suspect anything?"

"I have a way of finding out, and if he does," I replied grimly, "I will return alone to the Temple of Dreams."

FOUR THIRTY-FOUR

"Doubting, dreaming dreams no mortal ever dared to dream before."

—Edgar Allan Poe

The door closed softly behind me, the great dark house looming up more starkly than ever. Stooping, I crossed the wet lawn at a run, a grotesque and unholy figure, I doubt not, since any man had at a glance sworn me to be not a man but a giant ape. So craftily had the Master devised!

I clambered the wall, dropped to the earth beyond and made my way through the darkness and the drizzle to the group of trees which masked the automobile.

The Negro driver leaned out of the front seat. I was breathing hard and sought in various ways to simulate the actions of a man who has just murdered in cold blood and fled the scene of his crime.

"You heard nothing, no sound, no scream?" I hissed, gripping his arm.

"No noise except a slight crash when you first went in," he answered. "You did a good job—nobody passing along the road could have suspected anything."

"Have you remained in the car all the time?" I asked. And when he replied that he had, I seized his ankle and ran my hand over the soles of his shoe; it was perfectly dry, as was the cuff of his trouser leg. Satisfied, I climbed into the back seat. Had he taken a step on the earth, shoe and garment would have showed it by the telltale dampness.

I ordered him to refrain from starting the engine until I had removed the apeskin, and then we sped through the night, and I fell victim to doubts and uncertainties. Why should Gordon put any trust in the word of a stranger and a former ally of the Master's? Would he not put my tale down as the ravings of a dope-crazed addict, or a lie to ensnare or befool him? Still, if he had not believed me, why had he let me go?

I could but trust. At any rate, what Gordon did or did not do would scarcely affect my fortunes ultimately, even though Zuleika had furnished me with that which would merely extend the number of my days. My thought centered on her, and more than my hope of vengeance on Kathulos was the hope that Gordon might be able to save her from the clutches of the fiend. At any rate, I thought grimly, if Gordon failed me, I still had my hands and if I might lay them upon the bony frame of the Skull-faced One—

Abruptly I found myself thinking of Yussef Ali and his strange words, the import of which just occurred to me, *"The Master has promised her to me in the days of the empire!"*

The days of the empire—what could that mean?

The automobile at last drew up in front of the building which hid the Temple of Silence—now dark and still. The ride had seemed interminable, and as I dismounted, I glanced at the timepiece on the dashboard of the car. My heart leaped—it was four thirty-four, and unless my eyes tricked me I saw a movement in the shadows across the street, out of the flare of the streetlamp. At this time of night it could mean only one of two things—some menial of the Master watching for my return, or else Gordon had kept his word. The Negro drove away and I opened the door, crossed the deserted bar, and entered the opium room. The bunks and the floor were littered with the dreamers, for such places as these know nothing of day or night as normal people know, but all lay deep in sottish slumber.

The lamps glimmered through the smoke and a silence hung mist-like overall.

THE STROKE OF FIVE

"He saw gigantic tracks of death,
And many a shape of doom."

—G.K. Chesterton

Two of the China boys squatted among the smudge fires, staring at me unwinkingly as I threaded my way among the recumbent bodies and made my way to the rear door. For the first time I traversed the corridor alone and found time to wonder again as to the contents of the strange chests which lined the walls.

Four raps on the underside of the floor, and a moment later I stood in the idol room. I gasped in amazement—the fact that across a table from me sat Kathulos in all his horror was not the cause of my exclamation. Except for the table, the chair on which the Skull-faced One sat and the altar—now bare of incense—the room was perfectly bare! Drab, unlovely walls of the unused warehouse met my gaze instead of the costly tapestries I had become accustomed to. The palms, the idol, the lacquered screen—all were gone.

"Ah, Mr. Costigan, you wonder, no doubt."

The dead voice of the Master broke in on my thoughts. His serpent eyes glittered balefully. The long yellow fingers twined sinuously upon the table.

"You thought me to be a trusting fool, no doubt!" he rapped suddenly. "Did you think I would not have you followed? You fool, Yussef Ali was at your heels every moment!"

An instant I stood speechless, frozen by the crash of these words against my brain; then as their import sank home, I launched myself forward with a roar. At the same instant, before my clutching fingers could close on the mocking horror on the other side of the table, men rushed from every side. I whirled, and with the clarity of hate, from the swirl of savage faces I singled out Yussef Ali, and crashed my right fist against his temple with every ounce of my strength. Even as he dropped, Hassim struck me to my knees and a Chinaman flung a man-net over my shoulders. I heaved erect, bursting the stout cords as if they were strings, and then a blackjack in the hands of Ganra Singh stretched me stunned and bleeding on the floor.

Lean sinewy hands seized and bound me with cords that cut cruelly into my flesh. Emerging from the mists of semi-unconsciousness, I found myself lying on the altar with the masked Kathulos towering over me like a gaunt ivory tower. About in a semicircle stood Ganra Singh, Yar Khan, Yun Shatu, and several others whom I knew as frequenters of the Temple of Dreams. Beyond them—and the sight cut me to the heart—I saw Zuleika crouching in a doorway, her face white and her hands pressed against her cheeks, in an attitude of abject terror.

"I did not fully trust you," said Kathulos sibilantly, "so I sent Yussef Ali to follow you. He reached the group of trees before you, and, following you into the estate, heard your very interesting conversation with John Gordon—for he scaled the house-wall like a cat and clung to the window ledge! Your driver delayed purposely so as to give Yussef Ali plenty of time to get back—I have decided to change my abode anyway. My furnishings are already on their way to another house, and as soon as we have disposed of the traitor—you!—we shall depart also, leaving a little surprise for your friend Gordon when he arrives at five-thirty."

My heart gave a sudden leap of hope. Yussef Ali had misunderstood, and Kathulos lingered here in false security while the London detective force had already silently surrounded the house. Over my shoulder I saw Zuleika vanish from the door.

I eyed Kathulos, absolutely unaware of what he was saying. It was not long until five—if he dallied longer—then I froze as the Egyptian spoke a word, and Li Kung, a gaunt, cadaverous Chinaman, stepped from the silent semicircle and drew from his sleeve a long thin dagger. My eyes sought the timepiece that still rested on the table and my heart sank. It was still ten minutes until five. My death did not matter so much, since it simply hastened the inevitable, but in my mind's eye I could see Kathulos and his murderers escaping while the police awaited the stroke of five.

The Skull-face halted in some harangue, and stood in a listening attitude. I believe his uncanny intuition warned him of danger. He spoke a quick staccato command to Li Kung and the Chinaman sprang forward, dagger lifted above my breast.

The air was suddenly supercharged with dynamic tension. The keen dagger-point hovered high above me—loud and clear sounded the skirl of a police whistle and on the heels of the sound there came a terrific crash from the front of the warehouse!

Kathulos leaped into frenzied activity. Hissing orders like a cat spitting, he sprang for the hidden door and the rest followed him. Things happened with the speed of a nightmare. Li Kung had followed the rest, but Kathulos flung a command over his shoulder, and the Chinaman turned back and came rushing toward the altar where I lay, dagger high, desperation in his countenance.

A scream broke through the clamor, and, as I twisted desperately about to avoid the descending dagger, I caught a glimpse of Kathulos dragging Zuleika away. Then with a frenzied wrench I toppled from the altar just as Li Kung's dagger, grazing my breast, sank inches deep into the dark-stained surface and quivered there.

I had fallen on the side next to the wall and what was taking place in the room I could not see, but it seemed as if far away I could hear men screaming faintly and hideously. Then Li Kung wrenched his blade free and sprang, tigerishly, around the end of the altar. Simultaneously a revolver cracked from the doorway—the Chinaman spun clear around, the dagger flying from his hand—he slumped to the floor.

Gordon came running from the doorway where a few moments earlier Zuleika had stood, his pistol still smoking in his hand. At his heels were three rangy, clean-cut men in plain clothes. He cut my bonds and dragged me upright.

"Quick! Where have they gone?"

The room was empty of life save for myself, Gordon and his men, though two dead men lay on the floor.

I found the secret door and after a few seconds' search located the lever which opened it. Revolvers drawn, the men grouped about me and peered nervously into the dark stairway. Not a sound came up from the total darkness.

"This is uncanny!" muttered Gordon. "I suppose the Master and his servants went this way when they left the building—as they are certainly not here now!—and Leary and his men should have stopped them either in the tunnel itself or in the rear room of Yun Shatu's. At any rate, in either event they should have communicated with us by this time."

"Look out, sir!" one of the men exclaimed suddenly, and Gordon, with an ejaculation, struck out with his pistol barrel and crushed the life from a huge snake which had crawled silently up the steps from the blackness beneath.

"Let us see into this matter," said he, straightening.

But before he could step onto the first stair, I halted him; for, flesh crawling, I began dimly to understand something of what had happened—I began to understand the silence in the tunnel, the absence of the detectives, the screams I had heard some minutes previously while I lay on the altar. Examining the lever which opened the door, I found another smaller lever—I began to believe I knew what those mysterious chests in the tunnel contained.

"Gordon," I said hoarsely, "have you an electric torch?"

One of the men produced a large one.

"Direct the light into the tunnel, but as you value your life, do not put a foot upon the steps."

The beam of light struck through the shadows, lighting the tunnel, etching out boldly a scene that will haunt my brain all the rest of my life. On the floor of the tunnel, between the chests which now gaped open, lay two men who were members of London's finest secret service. Limbs twisted and faces horribly distorted they lay, and above and about them writhed, in long glittering scaly shimmerings, scores of hideous reptiles.

The clock struck five.

THE BLIND BEGGAR WHO RODE

"He seemed a beggar such as lags
Looking for crusts and ale."

—G.K. Chesterton

The cold gray dawn was stealing over the river as we stood in the deserted bar of the Temple of Dreams. Gordon was questioning the two men who had remained on guard outside the building while their unfortunate companions went in to explore the tunnel.

"As soon as we heard the whistle, sir, Leary and Murken rushed the bar and broke into the opium room, while we waited here at the bar door according to orders. Right away several ragged dopers came tumbling out and we grabbed them. But no one else came out and we heard nothing from Leary and Murken; so we just waited until you came, sir."

"You saw nothing of a giant Negro, or of the Chinaman Yun Shatu?"

"No, sir. After a while the patrolmen arrived and we threw a cordon around the house, but no one was seen."

Gordon shrugged his shoulders; a few cursory questions had

satisfied him that the captives were harmless addicts and he had them released.

"You are sure no one else came out?"

"Yes, sir—no, wait a moment. A wretched old blind beggar did come out, all rags and dirt and with a ragged girl leading him. We stopped him but didn't hold him—a wretch like that couldn't be harmful."

No?" Gordon jerked out. "Which way did he go?"

"The girl led him down the street to the next block and then an automobile stopped and they got in and drove off, sir."

Gordon glared at him.

"The stupidity of the London detective has rightfully become an international jest," he said acidly. "No doubt it never occurred to you as being strange that a Limehouse beggar should ride about in his own automobile."

Then impatiently waving aside the man, who sought to speak further, he turned to me, and I saw the lines of weariness beneath his eyes.

"Mr. Costigan, if you will come to my apartment, we may be able to clear up some new things."

THE BLACK EMPIRE

*"Oh the new spears dipped in lifeblood as the woman
shrieked in vain!
Oh the days before the English! When will those days
come again?"*

—Talbot Mundy

G ordon struck a match and absently allowed it to flicker
and go out in his hand. His Turkish cigarette hung
unlighted between his fingers.

"This is the most logical conclusion to be reached," he was
saying. "The weak link in our chain was lack of men. But curse it,
one cannot round up an army at two o'clock in the morning,
even with the aid of Scotland Yard. I went on to Limehouse,
leaving orders for a number of patrolmen to follow me as quickly
as they could be got together, and to throw a cordon about the
house.

"They arrived too late to prevent the Master's servants slipping out of the side doors and windows, no doubt, as they could
easily do with only Finnegan and Hansen on guard at the front
of the building. However, they arrived in time to prevent the

Master himself from slipping out in that way—no doubt he lingered to effect his disguise and was caught in that manner. He owes his escape to his craft and boldness and to the carelessness of Finnegan and Hansen. The girl who accompanied him—"

"She was Zuleika, without doubt."

I answered listlessly, wondering anew what shackles bound her to the Egyptian sorcerer.

"You owe your life to her," Gordon rapped, lighting another match. "We were standing in the shadows in front of the warehouse, waiting for the hour to strike, and of course ignorant as to what was going on in the house, when a girl appeared at one of the barred windows and begged us for God's sake to do something, that a man was being murdered. So we broke in at once. However, she was not to be seen when we entered."

"She returned to the room, no doubt," I muttered, "and was forced to accompany the Master. God grant he knows nothing of her trickery."

"I do not know," said Gordon, dropping the charred match stem, "whether she guessed at our true identity or whether she just made the appeal in desperation.

"However, the main point is this: evidence points to the fact that, on hearing the whistle, Leary and Murken invaded Yun Shatu's from the front at the same instant my three men and I made our attack on the warehouse front. As it took us some seconds to batter down the door, it is logical to suppose that they found the secret door and entered the tunnel before we affected an entrance into the warehouse.

"The Master, knowing our plans beforehand, and being aware that an invasion would be made through the tunnel and having long ago made preparations for such an exigency—"

An involuntary shudder shook me.

"—the Master worked the lever that opened the chest—the screams you heard as you lay upon the altar were the death shrieks of Leary and Murken. Then, leaving the Chinaman behind to finish you, the Master and the rest descended into the tunnel—incredible as it seems—and threading their way unharmed among the serpents, entered Yun Shatu's house and escaped therefrom as I have said."

"That seems impossible. Why should not the snakes turn on them?"

Gordon finally ignited his cigarette and puffed a few seconds before replying.

"The reptiles might still have been giving their full and hideous attention to the dying men, or else—I have on previous occasions been confronted with indisputable proof of the Master's dominance over beasts and reptiles of even the lowest or most dangerous orders. How he and his slaves passed unhurt among those scaly fiends must remain, at present, one of the many unsolved mysteries pertaining to that strange man."

I stirred restlessly in my chair. This brought up a point for the purpose of clearing up which I had come to Gordon's neat but bizarre apartments.

"You have not yet told me," I said abruptly, "who this man is and what is his mission."

"As to who he is, I can only say that he is known as you name him—the Master. I have never seen him unmasked, nor do I know his real name nor his nationality."

"I can enlighten you to an extent there," I broke in. "I have seen him unmasked and have heard the name his slaves call him."

Gordon's eyes blazed and he leaned forward.

"His name," I continued, "is Kathulos and he claims to be an Egyptian."

"Kathulos!" Gordon repeated. "You say he claims to be an Egyptian—have you any reason for doubting his claim of that nationality?"

"He may be of Egypt," I answered slowly, "but he is different, somehow, from any human I ever saw or hope to see. Great age might account for some of his peculiarities, but there are certain lineal differences that my anthropological studies tell me have been present since birth—features which would be abnormal to any other man but which are perfectly normal in Kathulos. That sounds paradoxical, I admit, but to appreciate fully the horrid inhumanness of the man, you would have to see him yourself."

Gordon sat all attention while I swiftly sketched the appearance of the Egyptian as I remembered him—and that appearance was indelibly etched on my brain forever.

As I finished he nodded.

"As I have said, I never saw Kathulos except when disguised as a beggar, a leper or some such thing—when he was fairly swathed in rags. Still, I too have been impressed with a strange *difference* about him—something that is not present in other men."

Gordon tapped his knee with his fingers—a habit of his when deeply engrossed by a problem of some sort.

"You have asked as to the mission of this man," he began slowly. "I will tell you all I know."

"My position with the British government is a unique and peculiar one. I hold what might be called a roving commission—an office created solely for the purpose of suiting my special needs. As a secret service official during the war, I convinced the powers of a need of such office and of my ability to fill it.

"Somewhat over seventeen months ago I was sent to South Africa to investigate the unrest which has been growing among the natives of the interior ever since the World War and which has of late assumed alarming proportions. There I first got on the track of this man Kathulos. I found, in roundabout ways, that Africa was a seething cauldron of rebellion from Morocco to Cape Town. The old, old vow had been made again—the Negroes and the Mohammedans, banded together, should drive the white men into the sea.

"This pact has been made before but always, hitherto, broken. Now, however, I sensed a giant intellect and a monstrous genius behind the veil, a genius powerful enough to accomplish this union and hold it together. Working entirely on hints and vague whispered clues, I followed the trail up through Central

Africa and into Egypt. There, at last, I came upon definite evidence that such a man existed. The whispers hinted of a living dead man—a *skull-faced* man. I learned that this man was the high priest of the mysterious Scorpion society of northern Africa. He was spoken of variously as Skull-face, the Master, and the Scorpion.

"Following a trail of bribed officials and filched state secrets, I at last trailed him to Alexandria, where I had my first sight of him in a dive in the native quarter—disguised as a leper. I heard him distinctly addressed as 'Mighty Scorpion' by the natives, but he escaped me.

"All trace vanished then; the trail ran out entirely until rumors of strange happenings in London reached me, and I came back to England to investigate an apparent leak in the war office.

"As I thought, the Scorpion had preceded me. This man, whose education and craft transcend anything I ever met with, is simply the leader and instigator of a world-wide movement such as the world has never seen before. He plots, in a word, the overthrow of the white races!

"His ultimate aim is a black empire, with himself as emperor of the world! And to that end he has banded together in one monstrous conspiracy the black, the brown, and the yellow."

"I understand now what Yussef Ali meant when he said 'the days of the empire,'" I muttered.

"Exactly," Gordon rapped with suppressed excitement. "Kathulos' power is unlimited and unguessed. Like an octopus his tentacles stretch to the high places of civilization and the far corners of the world. And his main weapon is—dope! He has flooded Europe and no doubt America with opium and hashish, and in spite of all effort it has been impossible to discover the break in the barriers through which the hellish stuff is coming. With this he ensnares and enslaves men and women.

"You have told me of the aristocratic men and women you saw coming to Yun Shatu's dive. Without doubt they were dope addicts—for, as I said, the habit lurks in high places—holders of governmental positions, no doubt, coming to trade for the stuff they craved and giving in return state secrets, inside information, and promise of protection for the Master's crimes.

"Oh, he does not work haphazardly! Before ever the black flood breaks, he will be prepared; if he has his way, the governments of the white races will be honeycombs of corruption— the strongest men of the white races will be dead. The white men's secrets of war will be his. When it comes, I look for a simultaneous uprising against white supremacy, of all the colored races—races who, in the last war, learned the white men's ways of battle, and who, led by such a man as Kathulos and armed with white men's finest weapons, will be almost invincible.

"A steady stream of rifles and ammunition has been pouring into East Africa, and it was not until I discovered the source that it was stopped. I found that a staid and reliable Scotch firm was smuggling these arms among the natives, and I found more: the manager of this firm was an opium slave. That was enough. I saw Kathulos' hand in the matter. The manager was arrested and committed suicide in his cell—that is only one of the many situations with which I am called upon to deal.

"Again, the case of Major Fairlan Morley. He, like myself, held a very flexible commission and had been sent to the Transvaal to work upon the same case. He sent to London a number of secret papers for safekeeping. They arrived some weeks ago and were put in a bank vault. The letter accompanying them gave explicit instructions that they were to be delivered to no one but the major himself, when he called for them in person, or in event of his death, to myself.

"As soon as I learned that he had sailed from Africa I sent trusted men to Bordeaux, where he intended to make his first landing in Europe. They did not succeed in saving the major's life, but they certified his death, for they found his body in a deserted ship whose hulk was stranded on the beach. Efforts were made to keep the affair a secret but somehow it leaked into the papers with the result—"

"I begin to understand why I was to impersonate the unfortunate major," I interrupted.

"Exactly. A false beard furnished you, and your black hair dyed blond, you would have presented yourself at the bank, received the papers from the banker, who knew Major Morley just intimately enough to be deceived by your appearance, and the papers would have then fallen into the hands of the Master.

"I can only guess at the contents of those papers, for events have been taking place too swiftly for me to call for and obtain them. But they must deal with subjects closely connected with the activities of Kathulos. How he learned of them and of the provisions of the letter accompanying them, I have no idea, but as I said, London is honeycombed with his spies.

"In my search for clues, I often frequented Limehouse disguised as you first saw me. I went often to the Temple of Dreams and even once managed to enter the back room, for I suspected some sort of rendezvous in the rear of the building. The absence of any exit baffled me, and I had no time to search for secret doors before I was ejected by the giant black man Hassim, who had no suspicion of my true identity. I noticed that very often the leper entered or left Yun Shatu's, and finally it was borne on me that past a shadow of doubt this supposed leper was the Scorpion himself.

"That night you discovered me on the couch in the opium room, I had come there with no especial plan in mind. Seeing Kathulos leaving, I determined to rise and follow him, but you spoiled that."

He fingered his chin and laughed grimly.

"I was an amateur boxing champion in Oxford," said he, "but Tom Cribb himself could not have withstood that blow—or have dealt it."

"I regret it as I regret few things."

"No need to apologize. You saved my life immediately afterward—I was stunned, but not too much to know that that brown devil Yussef Ali was burning to cut out my heart."

"How did you come to be at Sir Haldred Frenton's estate? And how is it that you did not raid Yun Shatu's dive?"

"I did not have the place raided because I knew somehow Kathulos would be warned and our efforts would come to naught. I was at Sir Haldred's that night because I have contrived to spend at least part of each night with him since he returned from the Congo. I anticipated an attempt upon his life when I learned from his own lips that he was preparing, from the studies he made on this trip, a treatise on the secret native societies of West Africa. He hinted that the disclosures he intended to make therein might prove sensational, to say the least. Since it is to Kathulos' advantage to destroy such men as might be able to arouse the western world to its danger, I knew that Sir Haldred was a marked man. Indeed, two distinct attempts were made upon his life on his journey to the coast from the African interior. So I put two trusted men on guard and they are at their post even now.

"Roaming about the darkened house, I heard the noise of your entry, and, warning my men, I stole down to intercept you. At the time of our conversation, Sir Haldred was sitting in his unlighted study, a Scotland Yard man with drawn pistol on each side of him. Their vigilance no doubt accounts for Yussef Ali's failure to attempt what you were sent to do.

"Something in your manner convinced me in spite of yourself," he meditated. "I will admit I had some bad moments of doubt as I waited in the darkness that precedes dawn, outside the warehouse."

Gordon rose suddenly and going to a strong box which stood in a corner of the room, drew thence a thick envelope.

"Although Kathulos has checkmated me at almost every move," he said, "I have not been entirely idle. Noting the frequenters of Yun Shatu's, I have compiled a partial list of the Egyptian's right-hand men, and their records. What you have told me has enabled me to complete that list. As we know, his henchmen are scattered all over the world, and there are possibly hundreds of them here in London. However, this is a list of those I believe to be in his closest council, now with him in England. He told you himself that few even of his followers ever saw him unmasked."

We bent together over the list, which contained the following names: "Yun Shatu, Hongkong Chinese, suspected opium smuggler—keeper of Temple of Dreams—resident of Limehouse seven years. Hassim, ex-Senegalese Chief—wanted in French Congo for murder. Santiago, Negro—fled from Haiti under suspicion of voodoo worship atrocities. Yar Khan, Afridi, record unknown. Yussef Ali, Moor, slave-dealer in Morocco— suspected of being a German spy in the World War—an instigator of the Fellaheen Rebellion on the upper Nile. Ganra Singh, Lahore, India, Sikh—smuggler of arms into Afghanistan—took an active part in the Lahore and Delhi riots—suspected of murder on two occasions—a dangerous man. Stephen Costigan, American—resident in England since the war—hashish addict— man of remarkable strength. Li Kung, northern China, opium smuggler."

Lines were drawn significantly through three names—mine, Li Kung's, and Yussef Ali's. Nothing was written next to mine, but following Li Kung's name was scrawled briefly in Gordon's rambling characters: "Shot by John Gordon during the raid on Yun Shatu's." And following the name of Yussef Ali: "Killed by Stephen Costigan during the Yun Shatu raid."

I laughed mirthlessly. Black empire or not, Yussef Ali would never hold Zuleika in his arms, for he had never risen from where I felled him.

"I know not," said Gordon somberly as he folded the list and replaced it in the envelope, "what power Kathulos has that draws together black men and yellow men to serve him—that unites world-old foes. Hindu, Moslem, and pagan are among his followers. And back in the mists of the east where mysterious and gigantic forces are at work, this uniting is culminating on a monstrous scale."

He glanced at his watch.

"It is nearly ten. Make yourself at home here, Mr. Costigan, while I visit Scotland Yard and see if any clue has been found as to Kathulos' new quarters. I believe that the webs are closing on him, and with your aid I promise you we will have the gang located within a week at most."

THE MARK OF THE TULWAR

"The fed wolf curls by his drowsy mate
In a tight-trod earth; but the lean wolves wait."

—Talbot Mundy

I sat alone in John Gordon's apartments and laughed mirthlessly. In spite of the elixir's stimulus, the strain of the previous night, with its loss of sleep and its heartrending actions, was telling on me. My mind was a chaotic whirl wherein the faces of Gordon, Kathulos, and Zuleika shifted with numbing swiftness. All the mass of information Gordon had given to me seemed jumbled and incoherent.

Through this state of being, one fact stood out boldly. I must find the latest hiding-place of the Egyptian and get Zuleika out of his hands—if indeed she still lived.

A week, Gordon had said—I laughed again—a week and I would be beyond aiding anyone. I had found the proper amount of elixir to use—knew the minimum amount my system required—and knew that I could make the flask last me four days at most. Four days! Four days in which to comb the rat-holes of Limehouse and Chinatown—four days in which to ferret out, somewhere in the mazes of the East End, the lair of Kathulos.

I burned with impatience to begin, but nature rebelled, and staggering to a couch, I fell upon it and was asleep instantly.

Then someone was shaking me.

"Wake up, Mr. Costigan!"

I sat up, blinking. Gordon stood over me, his face haggard.

"There's devil's work done, Costigan! The Scorpion has struck again!"

I sprang up, still half-asleep and only partly realizing what he was saying. He helped me into my coat, thrust my hat at me, and then his firm grip on my arm was propelling me out of his door and down the stairs. The streetlights were blazing; I had slept an incredible time.

"A logical victim!" I was aware that my companion was saying. "He should have notified me the instant of his arrival!"

"I don't understand—" I began dazedly.

We were at the curb now and Gordon hailed a taxi, giving the address of a small and unassuming hotel in a staid and prim section of the city.

"The Baron Rokoff," he rapped as we whirled along at reckless speed, "a Russian free-lance, connected with the War Office. He returned from Mongolia yesterday and apparently went into hiding. Undoubtedly he had learned something vital in regard to the slow waking of the East. He had not yet communicated with us, and I had no idea that he was in England until just now."

"And you learned—"

"The baron was found in his room, his dead body mutilated in a frightful manner!"

The respectable and conventional hotel which the doomed baron had chosen for his hiding place was in a state of mild uproar, suppressed by the police. The management had attempted to keep the matter quiet, but somehow the guests had learned of the atrocity and many were leaving in haste—or preparing to, as the police were holding all for investigation.

The baron's room, which was on the top floor, was in a state to defy description. Not even in the Great War have I seen a more complete shambles. Nothing had been touched; all remained just as the chambermaid had found it a half-hour since. Tables and chairs lay shattered on the floor, and the furniture, floor, and walls were spattered with blood. The baron, a tall, muscular man in life, lay in the middle of the room, a fearful spectacle. His skull had been cleft to the brows, a deep gash under his left armpit had shorn through his ribs, and his left arm hung by a shred of flesh. The cold bearded face was set in a look of indescribable horror.

"Some heavy, curved weapon must have been used," said Gordon, "something like a saber, wielded with terrific force. See where a chance blow sank inches deep into the windowsill. And again, the thick back of this heavy chair has been split like a shingle. A saber, surely."

"A tulwar," I muttered, somberly. "Do you not recognize the handiwork of the Central Asian butcher? Yar Khan has been here."

"The Afghan! He came across the roofs, of course, and descended to the window-ledge by means of a knotted rope made fast to something on the edge of the roof. About one-thirty the maid, passing through the corridor, heard a terrific commotion in the baron's room—smashing of chairs and a sudden short shriek which died abruptly into a ghastly gurgle and then ceased—to the sound of heavy blows, curiously muffled, such as a sword might make when driven deep into human flesh. Then all noises stopped suddenly.

"She called the manager and they tried the door and, finding it locked, and receiving no answer to their shouts, opened it with the desk key. Only the corpse was there, but the window was open. This is strangely unlike Kathulos' usual procedure. It lacks subtlety. Often his victims have appeared to have died from natural causes. I scarcely understand."

"I see little difference in the outcome," I answered. "There is nothing that can be done to apprehend the murderer as it is."

"True," Gordon scowled. "We know who did it but there is no proof—not even a fingerprint. Even if we knew where the Afghan is hiding and arrested him, we could prove nothing—there would be a score of men to swear alibis for him. The baron returned only yesterday. Kathulos probably did not know of his arrival until tonight. He knew that on the morrow Rokoff would make known his presence to me and impart what he learned in northern Asia. The Egyptian knew he must strike quickly, and lacking time to prepare a safer and more elaborate form of murder, he sent the Afridi with his tulwar. There is nothing we can do, at least not until we discover the Scorpion's hiding place; what the baron had learned in Mongolia, we shall never know, but that it dealt with the plans and aspirations of Kathulos, we may be sure."

We went down the stairs again and out on the street, accompanied by one of the Scotland Yard men, Hansen. Gordon suggested that we walk back to his apartment, and I greeted the opportunity to let the cool night air blow some of the cobwebs out of my mazed brain.

As we walked along the deserted streets, Gordon suddenly cursed savagely.

"This is a veritable labyrinth we are following, leading nowhere! Here, in the very heart of civilization's metropolis, the direct enemy of that civilization commits crimes of the most outrageous nature and goes free! We are children, wandering in the night, struggling with an unseen evil—dealing with an incarnate devil, of whose true identity we know nothing and whose true ambitions we can only guess.

"Never have we managed to arrest one of the Egyptian's direct henchmen, and the few dupes and tools of his we have apprehended have died mysteriously before they could tell us anything. Again I repeat: what strange power has Kathulos that dominates these men of different creeds and races? The men in

London with him are, of course, mostly renegades, slaves of dope, but his tentacles stretch all over the east. Some dominance is his: the power that sent the Chinaman, Li Kung, back to kill you, in the face of certain death; that sent Yar Khan the Moslem over the roofs of London to do murder; that holds Zuleika the Circassian in unseen bonds of slavery.

"Of course we know," he continued after a brooding silence, "that the east has secret societies which are behind and above all considerations of creeds. There are cults in Africa and the Orient whose origin dates back to Ophir and the fall of Atlantis. This man must be a power in some or possibly all of these societies. Why, outside the Jews, I know of no oriental race which is so cordially despised by the other Eastern races, as the Egyptians! Yet here we have a man, an Egyptian by his own word, controlling the lives and destinies of orthodox Moslems, Hindus, Shintos and devil worshippers. It's unnatural.

"Have you ever—" he turned to me abruptly "—heard the ocean mentioned in connection with Kathulos?"

"Never."

"There is a widespread superstition in northern Africa, based on a very ancient legend, that the great leader of the colored races would come out of the sea! And I once heard a Berber speak of the Scorpion as 'The Son of the Ocean.'"

"That is a term of respect among that tribe, is it not?"

"Yes; still I wonder sometimes."

THE MUMMY WHO LAUGHED

"Laughing as littered skulls that lie
After lost battles turn to the sky
An everlasting laugh."

—G.K. Chesterton

"A shop open this late," Gordon remarked suddenly.

A fog had descended on London and along the quiet street we were traversing the lights glimmered with the peculiar reddish haze characteristic of such atmospheric conditions. Our footfalls echoed drearily. Even in the heart of a great city, there are always sections which seem overlooked and forgotten. Such a street was this. Not even a policeman was in sight.

The shop which had attracted Gordon's attention was just in front of us, on the same side of the street. There was no sign over the door, merely some sort of emblem, something like a dragon. Light flowed from the open doorway and the small show windows on each side. As it was neither a cafe nor the entrance to a hotel, we found ourselves idly speculating over its reason for being open. Ordinarily, I suppose, neither of us would have given the matter a thought, but our nerves were so keyed up that we found ourselves instinctively suspicious of anything out of the ordinary. Then something occurred which was distinctly out of the ordinary.

A very tall, very thin man, considerably stooped, suddenly loomed up out of the fog in front of us, and beyond the shop. I had only a glance of him—an impression of incredible gauntness, of worn, wrinkled garments, a high silk hat drawn close over the brows, a face entirely hidden by a muffler; then he turned aside and entered the shop. A cold wind whispered down the street, twisting the fog into wispy ghosts, but the coldness that came upon me transcended the wind's.

"Gordon!" I exclaimed in a fierce, low voice. "My senses are no longer reliable or else Kathulos himself has just gone into that house!"

Gordon's eyes blazed. We were now close to the shop, and lengthening his strides into a run he hurled himself into the door, the detective and I close upon his heels.

A weird assortment of merchandise met our eyes. Antique weapons covered the walls, and the floor was piled high with curious things. Maori idols shouldered Chinese josses, and suits of medieval armor bulked darkly against stacks of rare oriental rugs and Latin-make shawls. The place was an antique shop. Of the figure who had aroused our interest we saw nothing.

An old man clad bizarrely in red fez, brocaded jacket, and Turkish slippers came from the back of the shop; he was a Levantine of some sort.

"You wish something, sirs?"

"You keep open rather late," Gordon said abruptly, his eyes traveling swiftly over the shop for some secret hiding place that might conceal the object of our search.

"Yes, sir. My customers number many eccentric professors and students who keep very irregular hours. Often the night boats unload special pieces for me and very often I have customers later than this. I remain open all night, sir."

"We are merely looking around," Gordon returned, and in an

aside to Hansen: "Go to the back and stop anyone who tries to leave that way."

Hansen nodded and strolled casually to the rear of the shop. The back door was clearly visible to our view, through a vista of antique furniture and tarnished hangings strung up for exhibition. We had followed the Scorpion—if he it was—so closely that I did not believe he would have had time to traverse the full length of the shop and make his exit without our having seen him as we came in. For our eyes had been on the rear door ever since we had entered.

Gordon and I browsed around casually among the curios, handling and discussing some of them, but I have no idea as to their nature. The Levantine had seated himself cross-legged on a Moorish mat close to the center of the shop and apparently took only a polite interest in our explorations.

After a time Gordon whispered to me: "There is no advantage in keeping up this pretense. We have looked everywhere the Scorpion might be hiding, in the ordinary manner. I will make known my identity and authority and we will search the entire building openly."

Even as he spoke, a truck drew up outside the door and two burly Negroes entered. The Levantine seemed to have expected them, for he merely waved them toward the back of the shop and they responded with a grunt of understanding.

Gordon and I watched them closely as they made their way to a large mummy case which stood upright against the wall not far from the back. They lowered this to a level position and then started for the door, carrying it carefully between them.

"Halt!" Gordon stepped forward, raising his hand authoritatively.

"I represent Scotland Yard," he said swiftly, "and have sanction for anything I choose to do. Set that mummy down; nothing leaves this shop until we have thoroughly searched it."

The Negroes obeyed without a word and my friend turned to

the Levantine, who, apparently not perturbed or even interested, sat smoking a Turkish water pipe.

"Who was that tall man who entered just before we did, and where did he go?"

"No one entered before you, sir. Or, if anyone did, I was at the back of the shop and did not see him. You are certainly at liberty to search my shop, sir."

And search it we did, with the combined craft of a secret service expert and a denizen of the underworld—while Hansen stood stolidly at his post, the two Negroes standing over the carved mummy case watched us impassively, and the Levantine sitting like a sphinx on his mat, puffing a fog of smoke into the air. The whole thing had a distinct effect of unreality.

At last, baffled, we returned to the mummy case, which was certainly long enough to conceal even a man of Kathulos' height. The thing did not appear to be sealed as is the usual custom, and Gordon opened it without difficulty. A formless shape, swathed in moldering wrappings, met our eyes. Gordon parted some of the wrappings and revealed an inch or so of withered, brownish, leathery arm. He shuddered involuntarily as he touched it, as a man will do at the touch of a reptile or some inhumanly cold thing. Taking a small metal idol from a stand nearby, he rapped on the shrunken breast and the arm. Each gave out a solid thumping, like some sort of wood.

Gordon shrugged his shoulders. "Dead for two thousand years anyway and I don't suppose I should risk destroying a valuable mummy simply to prove what we know to be true."

He closed the case again.

"The mummy may have crumbled some, even from this much exposure, but perhaps it did not."

This last was addressed to the Levantine, who replied merely by a courteous gesture of his hand, and the Negroes once more lifted the case and carried it to the truck, where they loaded it on, and a moment later mummy, truck, and Negroes had vanished in the fog.

Gordon still nosed about the shop, but I stood stock-still in the center of the floor. To my chaotic and dope-ridden brain I attribute it, but the sensation had been mine, that through the wrappings of the mummy's face, great eyes had burned into mine, eyes like pools of yellow fire, that seared my soul and froze me where I stood. And as the case had been carried through the door, I knew that the lifeless thing in it, dead, God only knows how many centuries, was *laughing*, hideously and silently.

THE DEAD MAN FROM THE SEA

"The blind gods roar and rave and dream
Of all cities under the sea."

—G.K. Chesterton

Gordon puffed savagely at his Turkish cigarette, staring abstractedly and unseeingly at Hansen, who sat opposite him.

"I suppose we must chalk up another failure against ourselves. That Levantine, Kamonos, is evidently a creature of the Egyptian's and the walls and floors of his shop are probably honeycombed with secret panels and doors which would baffle a magician."

Hansen made some answer but I said nothing. Since our return to Gordon's apartment, I had been conscious of a feeling of intense languor and sluggishness which not even my condition could account for. I knew that my system was full of the elixir— but my mind seemed strangely slow and hard of comprehension in direct contrast with the average state of my mentality when stimulated by the hellish dope.

This condition was slowly leaving me, like mist floating from the surface of a lake, and I felt as if I were waking gradually from a long and unnaturally sound sleep.

Gordon was saying: "I would give a good deal to know if Kamonos is really one of Kathulos' slaves or if the Scorpion managed to make his escape through some natural exit as we entered."

"Kamonos is his servant, true enough," I found myself saying slowly, as if searching for the proper words. "As we left, I saw his gaze light upon the scorpion which is traced on my hand. His eyes narrowed, and as we were leaving he contrived to brush close against me—and to whisper in a quick low voice: 'Soho, 48.'"

Gordon came erect like a loosened steel bow.

"Indeed!" he rapped. "Why did you not tell me at the time?"

"I don't know."

My friend eyed me sharply.

"I noticed you seemed like a man intoxicated all the way from the shop," said he. "I attributed it to some aftermath of hashish. But no. Kathulos is undoubtedly a masterful disciple of Mesmer—his power over venomous reptiles shows that, and I am beginning to believe it is the real source of his power over humans.

"Somehow, the Master caught you off your guard in that shop and partly asserted his dominance over your mind. From what hidden nook he sent his thought waves to shatter your brain, I do not know, but Kathulos was somewhere in that shop, I am sure."

"He was. He was in the mummy case."

"The mummy case!" Gordon exclaimed rather impatiently. "That is impossible! The mummy quite filled it and not even such a thin being as the Master could have found room there."

I shrugged my shoulders, unable to argue the point but somehow sure of the truth of my statement.

"Kamonos," Gordon continued, "doubtless is not a member of the inner circle and does not know of your change of allegiance. Seeing the mark of the scorpion, he undoubtedly supposed you to be a spy of the Master's. The whole thing may be a plot to ensnare us, but I feel that the man was sincere—Soho 48 can be nothing less than the Scorpion's new rendezvous."

I too felt that Gordon was right, though a suspicion lurked in my mind.

"I secured the papers of Major Morley yesterday," he continued, "and while you slept, I went over them. Mostly they but corroborated what I already knew—touched on the unrest of the natives and repeated the theory that one vast genius was behind all. But there was one matter which interested me greatly, and which I think will interest you also."

From his strong box he took a manuscript written in the close, neat characters of the unfortunate major, and, in a monotonous droning voice which betrayed little of his intense excitement, he read the following nightmarish narrative:

"This matter I consider worth jotting down—as to whether it has any bearing on the case at hand, further developments will show. At Alexandria, where I spent some weeks seeking further clues as to the identity of the man known as the Scorpion, I made the acquaintance, through my friend Ahmed Shah, of the noted Egyptologist Professor Ezra Schuyler of New York. He verified the statement made by various laymen, concerning the legend of the 'ocean-man.' This myth, handed down from generation to generation, stretches back into the very mists of antiquity and is, briefly, that someday a man shall come up out of the sea and shall lead the people of Egypt to victory over all others. This legend has spread over the continent so that now all black races consider that it deals with the coming of a universal emperor. Professor Schuyler gave it as his opinion that the myth was somehow connected with the lost Atlantis, which, he maintains, was located between the African and South American continents and to whose inhabitants the ancestors of the Egyptians were tributary. The reasons for his connection are too lengthy and vague to note here, but, following the line of his theory, he told me a strange and fantastic tale. He said that a close friend of his, Von Lorfmon of Germany, a sort of free-lance scientist, now dead, was sailing off the coast of Senegal some years ago, for the purpose of investigating and classifying the rare specimens of sea life found there. He was using for his purpose a small trading-vessel, manned by a crew of Moors, Greeks, and Negroes.

"Some days out of sight of land, something floating was sighted, and this object, being grappled and brought aboard, proved to be a *mummy case of a most curious kind.* Professor Schuyler explained to me the features whereby it differed from the ordinary Egyptian style, but from his rather technical account I merely got the impression that it was a strangely shaped affair carved with characters neither cuneiform nor hieroglyphic. The case was heavily lacquered, being watertight and airtight, and Von Lorfmon had considerable difficulty in opening it. However, he managed to do so without damaging the case, and a most unusual mummy was revealed. Schuyler said that he never saw either the mummy or the case, but that from descriptions given him by the Greek skipper who was present at the opening of the case, the mummy differed as much from the ordinary man as the case differed from the conventional type.

"Examination proved that the subject had not undergone the usual procedure of mummification. All parts were intact just as in life, but the whole form was shrunk and hardened to a wood-like consistency. Cloth wrappings swathed the thing and they crumbled to dust and vanished the instant air was let in upon them.

"Von Lorfmon was impressed by the effect upon the crew. The Greeks showed no interest beyond that which would ordi-narily be shown by any man, but the Moors, and even more the Negroes, seemed to be rendered temporarily insane! As the case was hoisted on board, they all fell prostrate on the deck and raised a sort of worshipful chant, and it was necessary to use force in order to exclude them from the cabin wherein the mummy was exposed. A number of fights broke out between them and the Greek element of the crew, and the skipper and Von Lorfmon thought best to put back to the nearest port in all haste. The skipper attributed it to the natural aversion of seamen toward having a corpse on board, but Von Lorfmon seemed to sense a deeper meaning.

"They made port in Lagos, and that very night Von Lorfmon was murdered in his stateroom, and the mummy and its case vanished. All the Moor and Negro sailors deserted ship the same night. Schuyler said—and here the matter took on a most sinister and mysterious aspect—that immediately afterward this widespread unrest among the natives began to smolder and take tangible form; he connected it in some manner with the old legend.

"An aura of mystery, also, hung over Von Lorfmon's death. He had taken the mummy into his stateroom, and anticipating an attack from the fanatical crew, had carefully barred and bolted door and portholes. The skipper, a reliable man, swore that it was virtually impossible to affect an entrance from without. And what signs were present pointed to the fact that the locks had been worked from within. The scientist was killed by a dagger which formed part of his collection and which was left in his breast.

"As I have said, immediately afterward the African cauldron began to seethe. Schuyler said that in his opinion the natives considered the ancient prophecy fulfilled. The mummy was *the man from the sea.*

"Schuyler gave as his opinion that the thing was the work of Atlanteans and that the man in the mummy case was a native of lost Atlantis. How the case came to float up through the fathoms of water which cover the forgotten land, he does not venture to offer a theory. He is sure that somewhere in the ghost-ridden mazes of the African jungles the mummy has been enthroned as a god, and, inspired by the dead thing, the black warriors are gathering for a wholesale massacre. He believes, also, that some crafty Moslem is the direct moving power of the threatened rebellion."

Gordon ceased and looked up at me.

"Mummies seem to weave a weird dance through the warp of the tale," he said. "The German scientist took several pictures of the mummy with his camera, and it was after seeing these— which strangely enough were not stolen along with the thing— that Major Morley began to think himself on the brink of some monstrous discovery. His diary reflects his state of mind and becomes incoherent—his condition seems to have bordered on insanity. What did he learn to unbalance him so? Do you suppose that the mesmeric spells of Kathulos were used against him?"

"These pictures—" I began.

"They fell into Schuyler's hands and he gave one to Morley. I found it among the manuscripts."

He handed the thing to me, watching me narrowly. I stared, then rose unsteadily and poured myself a tumbler of wine.

"Not a dead idol in a voodoo hut," I said shakily, "but a monster animated by fearsome life, roaming the world for victims. Morley had seen the Master—that is why his brain crumbled. Gordon, as I hope to live again, *that face is the face of Kathulos!*"

Gordon stared wordlessly at me.

"The Master hand, Gordon," I laughed. A certain grim enjoyment penetrated the mists of my horror, at the sight of the steel-nerved Englishman struck speechless, doubtless for the first time in his life.

He moistened his lips and said in a scarcely recognizable voice, "Then, in God's name, Costigan, nothing is stable or certain, and mankind hovers at the brink of untold abysses of nameless horror. If that dead monster found by Von Lorfmon be in truth the Scorpion, brought to life in some hideous fashion, what can mortal effort do against him?"

"The mummy at Kamonos'——" I began.

"Aye, the man whose flesh, hardened by a thousand years of non-existence—that must have been Kathulos himself! He would have just had time to strip, wrap himself in the linens and step into the case before we entered. You remember that the case, leaning upright against the wall, stood partly concealed by a large Burmese idol, which obstructed our view and doubtless gave him time to accomplish his purpose. My God, Costigan, with what horror of the prehistoric world are we dealing?"

"I have heard of Hindu fakirs who could induce a condition closely resembling death," I began. "Is it not possible that Kathulos, a shrewd and crafty Oriental, could have placed himself in this state and his followers have placed the case in the ocean where it was sure to be found? And might not he have been in this shape tonight at Kamonos'?"

Gordon shook his head.

"No, I have seen these fakirs. None of them ever feigned death to the extent of becoming shriveled and hard—in a word, dried up. Morley, narrating in another place the description of the mummy case as jotted down by Von Lorfmon and passed on to Schuyler, mentions the fact that large portions of seaweed adhered to it—seaweed of a kind found only at great depths, on the bottom of the ocean. The wood, too, was of a kind which Von Lorfmon failed to recognize or to classify, in spite of the fact that he was one of the greatest living authorities on flora. And his notes again and again emphasize the enormous age of the thing. He admitted that there was no way of telling how old the mummy was, but his hints intimate that he believed it to be, not thousand of years old, but millions of years!

"No. We must face the facts. Since you are positive that the picture of the mummy is the picture of Kathulos—and there is little room for fraud—one of two things is practically certain: the Scorpion was never dead but ages ago was placed in that mummy-case and his life preserved in some manner, or else—he was dead and has been brought to life! Either of these theories, viewed in the cold light of reason, is absolutely untenable. Are we all insane?"

"Had you ever walked the road to hashish land," I said somberly, "you could believe anything to be true. Had you ever gazed into the terrible reptilian eyes of Kathulos the sorcerer, you would not doubt that he was both dead and alive."

Gordon gazed out the window, his fine face haggard in the gray light which had begun to steal through them.

"At any rate," said he, "there are two places which I intend exploring thoroughly before the sun rises again—Kamonos' antique shop and Soho 48."

THE GRIP OF THE SCORPION

"While from a proud tower in the town
Death looks gigantically down."

—Edgar Allan Poe

Hansen snored on the bed as I paced the room. Another day had passed over London, and again the streetlamps glimmered through the fog. Their lights affected me strangely. They seemed to beat, solid waves of energy, against my brain. They twisted the fog into strange sinister shapes. Footlights of the stage that is the streets of London; how many grisly scenes had they lighted? I pressed my hands hard against my throbbing temples, striving to bring my thoughts back from the chaotic labyrinth where they wandered.

Gordon I had not seen since dawn. Following the clue of "Soho 48" he had gone forth to arrange a raid upon the place and he thought it best that I should remain under cover. He anticipated an attempt upon my life, and again he feared that if I went searching among the dives I formerly frequented it would arouse suspicion.

Hansen snored on. I seated myself and began to study the

Turkish shoes which clothed my feet. Zuleika had worn Turkish slippers—how she floated through my waking dreams, gilding prosaic things with her witchery! Her face smiled at me from the fog; her eyes shone from the flickering lamps; her phantom footfalls re-echoed through the misty chambers of my skull.

They beat an endless tattoo, luring and haunting till it seemed that these echoes found echoes in the hallway outside the room where I stood, soft and stealthy. A sudden rap at the door and I started.

Hansen slept on as I crossed the room and flung the door swiftly open. A swirling wisp of fog had invaded the corridor, and through it, like a silver veil, I saw her—Zuleika stood before me with her shimmering hair and her red lips parted and her great dark eyes.

Like a speechless fool I stood, and she glanced quickly down the hallway and then stepped inside and closed the door.

"Gordon!" she whispered in a thrilling undertone. "Your friend! The Scorpion has him!"

Hansen had awakened and now sat gaping stupidly at the strange scene which met his eyes.

Zuleika did not heed him.

"And oh, Steephen!" she cried, and tears shone in her eyes, "I have tried so hard to secure some more elixir but I could not."

"Never mind that," I finally found my speech. "Tell me about Gordon."

"He went back to Kamonos' alone, and Hassim and Ganra Singh took him captive and brought him to the Master's house. Tonight assemble a great host of the people of the Scorpion for the sacrifice."

"Sacrifice!" A grisly thrill of horror coursed down my spine. Was there no limit to the ghastliness of this business?

"Quick, Zuleika, where is this house of the Master's?"

"Soho, 48. You must summon the police and send many men to surround it, but you must not go yourself—"

Hansen sprang up quivering for action, but I turned to him. My brain was clear now, or seemed to be, and racing unnaturally.

"Wait!" I turned back to Zuleika. "When is this sacrifice to take place?"

"At the rising of the moon."

"That is only a few hours before dawn. Time to save him, but if we raid the house, they'll kill him before we can reach them. And God only knows how many diabolical things guard all approaches."

"I do not know," Zuleika whimpered. "I must go now, or the Master will kill me."

Something gave way in my brain at that; something like a flood of wild and terrible exultation swept over me.

"The Master will kill no one!" I shouted, flinging my arms on high. "Before ever the east turns red for dawn, the Master dies! By all things holy and unholy I swear it!"

Hansen stared wildly at me, and Zuleika shrank back as I turned on her. To my dope-inspired brain had come a sudden burst of light, true and unerring.

I knew Kathulos was a mesmerist—that he understood fully the secret of dominating another's mind and soul. And I knew that at last I had hit upon the reason of his power over the girl. Mesmerism! As a snake fascinates and draws to him a bird, so the Master held Zuleika to him with unseen shackles. So absolute was his rule over her that it held even when she was out of his sight, working over great distances.

There was but one thing which would break that hold: the magnetic power of some other person whose control was stronger with her than Kathulos's. I laid my hands on her slim little shoulders and made her face me.

"Zuleika," I said commandingly, "here you are safe; you shall not return to Kathulos. There is no need of it. Now you are free."

But I knew I had failed before I ever started. Her eyes held a look of amazed, unreasoning fear and she twisted timidly in my grasp.

"Steephen, please let me go!" she begged. "I must—I must!"

I drew her over to the bed, and asked Hansen for his handcuffs. He handed them to me, wonderingly, and I fastened one cuff to the bedpost and the other to her slim wrist. The girl whimpered but made no resistance, her limpid eyes seeking mine in mute appeal.

It cut me to the quick to enforce my will upon her in this apparently brutal manner but I steeled myself.

"Zuleika," I said tenderly, "you are now my prisoner. The Scorpion cannot blame you for not returning to him when you are unable to do so—and before dawn you shall be free of his rule entirely."

I turned to Hansen and spoke in a tone which admitted of no argument.

"Remain here, just without the door, until I return. On no account allow any strangers to enter—that is, anyone whom you do not personally know. And I charge you, on your honor as a man, do not release this girl, no matter what she may say. If neither I nor Gordon have returned by ten o'clock tomorrow, take her to this address—that family once was friends of mine and will take care of a homeless girl. I am going to Scotland Yard."

"Steephen," Zuleika wailed, "you are going to the Master's lair! You will be killed. Send the police, do not go!"

I bent, drew her into my arms, felt her lips against mine, then tore myself away.

The fog plucked at me with ghostly fingers, cold as the hands of dead men, as I raced down the street. I had no plan, but one was forming in my mind, beginning to seethe in the stimulated cauldron that was my brain. I halted at the sight of a policeman pacing his beat, and beckoning him to me, scribbled a terse note on a piece of paper torn from a notebook and handed it to him.

"Get this to Scotland Yard; it's a matter of life and death and it has to do with the business of John Gordon."

At that name, a gloved hand came up in swift assent, but his assurance of haste died out behind me as I renewed my flight. The note stated briefly that Gordon was a prisoner at Soho 48 and advised an immediate raid in force—advised, nay, in Gordo's name, commanded it.

My reason for my actions was simple; I knew that the first noise of the raid sealed John Gordon's doom. Somehow I first must reach him and protect or free him before the police arrived.

The time seemed endless, but at last the grim gaunt outlines of the house that was Soho 48 rose up before me, a giant ghost in the fog. The hour grew late; few people dared the mists and the dampness as I came to a halt in the street before this forbidding building. No lights showed from the windows, either upstairs or down. It seemed deserted. But the lair of the scorpion often seems deserted until the silent death strikes suddenly.

Here I halted and a wild thought struck me. One way or another, the drama would be over by dawn. Tonight was the climax of my career, the ultimate top of life. Tonight I was the strongest link in the strange chain of events. Tomorrow it would not matter whether I lived or died. I drew the flask of elixir from my pocket and gazed at it. Enough for two more days if properly eked out. Two more days of life! Or—I needed stimulation as I never needed it before; the task in front of me was one no mere human could hope to accomplish. If I drank the entire remainder of the elixir, I had no idea as to the duration of its effect, but it would last the night through. And my legs were shaky; my mind had curious periods of utter vacuity; weakness of brain and body assailed me. I raised the flask and with one draft drained it.

For an instant I thought it was death. Never had I taken such an amount.

Sky and world reeled, and I felt as if I would fly into a million vibrating fragments, like the bursting of a globe of brittle steel. Like fire, like hellfire the elixir raced along my veins and I was a giant! A monster! A superman!

Turning, I strode to the menacing, shadowy doorway. I had no plan; I felt the need of none. As a drunken man walks blithely into danger, I strode to the lair of the Scorpion, magnificently aware of my superiority, imperially confident of my stimulation and sure as the unchanging stars that the way would open before me.

Oh, there never was a superman like that who knocked commandingly on the door of Soho 48 that night in the rain and the fog!

I knocked four times, the old signal that we slaves had used to be admitted into the idol room at Yun Shatu's. An aperture opened in the center of the door and slanted eyes looked warily out. They slightly widened as the owner recognized me, then narrowed wickedly.

"You fool!" I said angrily. "Don't you see the mark?"

I held my hand to the aperture.

"Don't you recognize me? Let me in, curse you."

I think the very boldness of the trick made for its success. Surely by now all the Scorpion's slaves knew of Stephen Costigan's rebellion, knew that he was marked for death. And the very fact that I came there, inviting doom, confused the doorman.

The door opened and I entered. The man who had admitted me was a tall, lank Chinaman I had known as a servant at Kathulos'. He closed the door behind me, and I saw we stood in a sort of vestibule, lighted by a dim lamp whose glow could not be seen from the street for the reason that the windows were heavily curtained. The Chinaman glowered at me undecided. I looked at him, tensed. Then suspicion flared in his eyes and his hand flew to his sleeve. But at the instant I was on him, and his lean neck broke like a rotten bough between my hands.

I eased his corpse to the thickly carpeted floor and listened. No sound broke the silence. Stepping as stealthily as a wolf, fingers spread like talons, I stole into the next room. This was furnished in oriental style, with couches and rugs and gold-worked drapery, but was empty of human life. I crossed it and went into the next one. Light flowed softly from the censers which were swung from the ceiling, and the eastern rugs dead-ened the sound of my footfalls; I seemed to be moving through a castle of enchantment.

Every moment I expected a rush of silent assassins from the doorways or from behind the curtains or screen with their writhing dragons. Utter silence reigned. Room after room I explored, and at last halted at the foot of the stairs. The inevitable censer shed an uncertain light, but most of the stairs were veiled in shadows. What horrors awaited me above?

But fear and the elixir are strangers and I mounted that stair of lurking terror as boldly as I had entered that house of terror. The upper rooms I found to be much like those below and with them they had this fact in common: they were empty of human life. I sought an attic, but there seemed no door letting into one. Returning to the first floor, I made a search for an entrance into the basement, but again my efforts were fruit-less. The amazing truth was borne in upon me: except for myself and that dead man who lay sprawled so grotesquely in the outer vestibule, there were no men in that house, dead or living.

I could not understand it. Had the house been bare of furni-ture I should have reached the natural conclusion that Kathulos had fled—but no signs of flight met my eye. This was unnatural, uncanny. I stood in the great shadowy library and pondered. No, I had made no mistake in the house. Even if the broken corpse in the vestibule were not there to furnish mute testimony, every-thing in the room pointed toward the presence of the Master. There were the artificial palms, the lacquered screens, the tapestries, even the idol, though now no incense smoke rose before it. About the walls were ranged long shelves of books, bound in strange and costly fashion—books in every language in the world, I found from a swift examination, and on every subject—outré and bizarre, most of them.

Remembering the secret passage in the Temple of Dreams, I investigated the heavy mahogany table which stood in the center of the room. But nothing resulted. A sudden blaze of fury surged up in me, primitive and unreasoning. I snatched a statuette from the table and dashed it against the shelf-covered wall. The noise of its breaking would surely bring the gang from their hiding place. But the result was much more startling than that!

The statuette struck the edge of a shelf and instantly the whole section of shelves with their load of books swung silently outward, revealing a narrow doorway! As in the other secret door, a row of steps led downward. At another time I would have shuddered at the thought of descending, with the horrors of the other tunnel fresh in my mind, but inflamed as I was by the elixir, I strode forward without an instant's hesitancy.

Since there was no one in the house, they must be somewhere in the tunnel or in whatever lair to which the tunnel led. I stepped through the doorway, leaving the door open; the police might find it that way and follow me, though somehow I felt as if mine would be a lone hand from start to grim finish.

I went down a considerable distance and then the stair debouched into a level corridor some twenty feet wide—a remarkable thing. In spite of the width, the ceiling was rather low and from it hung small, curiously shaped lamps which flung a dim light. I stalked hurriedly along the corridor like old Death seeking victims, and as I went I noted the work of the thing. The floor was of great broad flags and the walls seemed to be of huge blocks of evenly set stone. This passage was clearly no work of modern days; the slaves of Kathulos never tunneled there. Some secret way of medieval times, I thought—and after all, who knows what catacombs lie below London, whose secrets are greater and darker than those of Babylon and Rome?

On and on I went, and now I knew that I must be far below the earth. The air was dank and heavy, and cold moisture dripped from the stones of walls and ceiling. From time to time I saw smaller passages leading away in the darkness, but I determined to keep to the larger main one.

A ferocious impatience gripped me. I seemed to have been walking for hours and still only dank damp walls and bare flags and guttering lamps met my eyes. I kept a close watch for sinister-appearing chests or the like—saw no such things.

Then as I was about to burst into savage curses, another stair loomed up in the shadows in front of me.

DARK FURY

"The ringed wolf glared the circle round
Through baleful, blue-lit eye,
Not unforgetful of his debt.
Quoth he, 'I'll do some damage yet
Or ere my turn to die!'"

—Talbot Mundy

Like a lean wolf I glided up the stairs. Some twenty feet up there was a sort of landing from which other corridors diverged, much like the lower one by which I had come. The thought came to me that the earth below London must be honeycombed with such secret passages, one above the other.

Some feet above this landing the steps halted at a door, and here I hesitated, uncertain as to whether I should chance knocking or not. Even as I meditated, the door began to open. I shrank back against the wall, flattening myself out as much as possible. The door swung wide and a Moor came through. Only a glimpse I had of the room beyond, out of the corner of my eye, but my unnaturally alert senses registered the fact that the room was empty.

And on the instant, before be could turn, I smote the Moor a single deathly blow behind the angle of the jawbone, and he toppled headlong down the stairs, to lie in a crumpled heap on the landing, his limbs tossed grotesquely about.

My left hand caught the door as it started to slam shut, and in an instant I was through and standing in the room beyond. As I had thought, there was no occupant of this room. I crossed it swiftly and entered the next. These rooms were furnished in a manner before which the furnishings of the Soho house paled into insignificance. Barbaric, terrible, unholy—these words alone convey some slight idea of the ghastly sights which met my eyes. Skulls, bones and complete skeletons formed much of the decorations, if such they were. Mummies leered from their cases and mounted reptiles ranged the walls. Between these sinister relics hung African shields of hide and bamboo, crossed with assagais and war daggers. Here and there reared obscene idols, black and horrible.

And in between and scattered about among these evidences of savagery and barbarism were vases, screens, rugs, and hangings of the highest oriental workmanship; a strange and incongruous effect.

I had passed through two of these rooms without seeing a human being, when I came to stairs leading upward. Up these I went, several flights, until I came to a door in a ceiling. I wondered if I was still under the earth. Surely the first stairs had let into a house of some sort. I raised the door cautiously. Starlight met my eyes and I drew myself warily up and out. There I halted. A broad flat roof stretched away on all sides, and beyond its rim on all sides glimmered the lights of London. Just what building I was on, I had no idea, but that it was a tall one I could tell, for I seemed to be above most of the lights I saw. Then I saw that I was not alone.

Over against the shadows of the ledge that ran around the roof's edge, a great menacing form bulked in starlight. A pair of eyes glinted at me with a light not wholly sane; the starlight glanced silver from a curving length of steel. Yar Khan the Afghan killer fronted me in the silent shadows.

A fierce wild exultation surged over me. Now I could begin to pay the debt I owed Kathulos and all his hellish band! The dope fired my veins and sent waves of inhuman power and dark fury through me. A spring and I was on my feet in a silent, deathly rush.

Yar Khan was a giant, taller and bulkier than I. He held a tulwar, and from the instant I saw him I knew that he was full of the dope to the use of which he was addicted—heroin.

As I came in, he swung his heavy weapon high in the air, but ere he could strike I seized his sword wrist in an iron grip and with my free hand drove smashing blows into his midriff.

Of that hideous battle, fought in silence above the sleeping city with only the stars to see, I remember little. I remember tumbling back and forth, locked in a death embrace. I remember the stiff beard rasping my flesh as his dope-fired eyes gazed wildly into mine. I remember the taste of hot blood in my mouth, the tang of fearful exultation in my soul, the onrushing and upsurging of inhuman strength and fury.

God, what a sight for a human eye! Had anyone looked upon that grim roof where two human leopards, dope maniacs, tore each other to pieces!

I remember his arm breaking like rotten wood in my grip and the tulwar falling from his useless hand. Handicapped by a broken arm, the end was inevitable, and with one wild uproaring flood of might, I rushed him to the edge of the roof and bent him backward far out over the ledge. An instant we struggled there; then I tore loose his hold and hurled him over, and one single shriek came up as he hurtled into the darkness below.

I stood upright, arms hurled up toward the stars, a terrible statue of primordial triumph. And down my breast trickled streams of blood from the long wounds left by the Afghan's frantic nails, on neck and face.

Then I turned with the craft of the maniac. Had no one

heard the sound of that battle? My eyes were on the door through which I had come, but a noise made me turn, and for the first time I noticed a small affair like a tower jutting up from the roof. There was no window there, but there was a door, and even as I looked that door opened and a huge black form framed itself in the light that streamed from within. Hassim!

He stepped out on the roof and closed the door, his shoulders hunched and neck outthrust as he glanced this way and that. I struck him senseless to the roof with one hate-driven smash. I crouched over him, waiting some sign of returning consciousness; then away in the sky close to the horizon, I saw a faint red tint. The rising of the moon!

Where in God's name was Gordon? Even as I stood undecided, a strange noise reached me. It was curiously like the droning of many bees.

Striding in the direction from which it seemed to come, I crossed the roof and leaned over the ledge. A sight nightmarish and incredible met my eyes.

Some twenty feet below the level of the roof on which I stood, there was another roof, of the same size and clearly a part of the same building. On one side it was bounded by the wall; on the other three sides a parapet several feet high took the place of a ledge.

A great throng of people stood, sat and squatted, close-packed on the roof—and without exception they were *Negroes*! There were hundreds of them, and it was their low-voiced conversation which I had heard. But what held my gaze was that upon which their eyes were fixed.

About the center of the roof rose a sort of teocalli some ten feet high, almost exactly like those found in Mexico and on which the priests of the Aztecs sacrificed human victims. This, allowing for its infinitely smaller scale, was an exact type of those sacrificial pyramids. On the flat top of it was a curiously carved altar, and beside it stood a lank, dusky form whom even the ghastly mask he wore could not disguise to my gaze—Santiago, the Haiti voodoo fetish man. On the altar lay John Gordon, stripped to the waist and bound hand and foot, but conscious.

I reeled back from the roof edge, rent in twain by indecision. Even the stimulus of the elixir was not equal to this. Then a sound brought me about to see Hassim struggling dizzily to his knees. I reached him with two long strides and ruthlessly smashed him down again. Then I noticed a queer sort of contrivance dangling from his girdle. I bent and examined it. It was a mask similar to that worn by Santiago. Then my mind leaped swift and sudden to a wild desperate plan, which to my dope-ridden brain seemed not at all wild or desperate. I stepped softly to the tower and, opening the door, peered inward. I saw no one who might need to be silenced, but I saw a long silken robe hanging upon a peg in the wall. The luck of the dope fiend! I snatched it and closed the door again. Hassim showed no signs of consciousness but I gave him another smash on the chin to make sure and, seizing his mask, hurried to the ledge.

A low guttural chant floated up to me, jangling, barbaric, with an undertone of maniacal bloodlust. The Negroes, men and women, were swaying back and forth to the wild rhythm of their death chant. On the teocalli Santiago stood like a statue of black basalt, facing the east, dagger held high—a wild and terrible sight, naked as he was save for a wide silken girdle and that inhuman mask on his face. The moon thrust a red rim above the eastern horizon and a faint breeze stirred the great black plumes which nodded above the voodoo man's mask. The chant of the worshipers dropped to a low, sinister whisper.

I hurriedly slipped on the death mask, gathered the robe close about me and prepared for the descent. I was prepared to drop the full distance, being sure in the superb confidence of my insanity that I would land unhurt, but as I climbed over the ledge I found a steel ladder leading down. Evidently Hassim, one of the voodoo priests, intended descending this way. So down I went, and in haste, for I knew that the instant the moon's lower rim cleared the city's skyline, that motionless dagger would descend into Gordon's breast.

Gathering the robe close about me so as to conceal my white skin, I stepped down upon the roof and strode forward through rows of black worshipers who shrank aside to let me through. To the foot of the teocalli I stalked and up the stair that ran about it, until I stood beside the death altar and marked the dark red stains upon it. Gordon lay on his back, his eyes open, his face drawn and haggard, but his gaze dauntless and unflinching.

Santiago's eyes blazed at me through the slits of his mask, but I read no suspicion in his gaze until I reached forward and took the dagger from his hand. He was too much astonished to resist, and the black throng fell suddenly silent. That he saw my hand was not that of a Negro it is certain, but he was simply struck speechless with astonishment. Moving swiftly I cut Gordon's bonds and hauled him erect. Then Santiago with a shriek leaped upon me—shrieked again and, arms flung high, pitched headlong from the teocalli with his own dagger buried to the hilt in his breast.

Then the black worshipers were on us with a screech and a roar—leaping on the steps of the teocalli like black leopards in the moonlight, knives flashing, eyes gleaming whitely.

I tore mask and robe from me and answered Gordon's exclamation with a wild laugh. I had hoped that by virtue of my disguise I might get us both safely away, but now I was content to die there at his side.

He tore a great metal ornament from the altar, and as the attackers came he wielded this. A moment we held them at bay, and then they flowed over us like a black wave. This to me was Valhalla! Knives stung me and blackjacks smashed against me, but I laughed and drove my iron fists in straight, steam-hammer smashes that shattered flesh and bone. I saw Gordon's crude weapon rise and fall, and each time a man went down. Skulls shattered and blood splashed and the dark fury swept over me. Nightmare faces swirled about me and I was on my knees; up again and the faces crumpled before my blows. Through far mists I seemed to hear a hideous familiar voice raised in imperious command.

Gordon was swept away from me, but from the sounds I knew that the work of death still went on. The stars reeled through fogs of blood, but Hell's exaltation was on me and I reveled in the dark tides of fury until a darker, deeper tide swept over me and I knew no more.

ANCIENT HORROR

"Here now in his triumph where all things falter,
Stretched out on the spoils that his own hand spread,
As a God self-slain on his own strange altar,
Death lies dead."

—Algernon Swinburne

Slowly I drifted back into life—slowly, slowly. A mist held me and in the mist I saw a Skull—

I lay in a steel cage like a captive wolf, and the bars were too strong, I saw, even for my strength. The cage seemed to be set in a sort of niche in the wall and I was looking into a large room. This room was under the earth, for the floor was of stone flags and the walls and ceiling were composed of gigantic blocks of the same material. Shelves ranged the walls, covered with weird appliances, apparently of a scientific nature, and more were on the great table that stood in the center of the room. Beside this sat Kathulos.

The sorcerer was clad in a snaky yellow robe, and those hideous hands and that terrible head were more pronouncedly reptilian than ever. He turned his great yellow eyes toward me, like pools of livid fire, and his parchment-thin lips moved in what probably passed for a smile.

I staggered erect and gripped the bars, cursing.

"Gordon, curse you, where is Gordon?"

Kathulos took a test tube from the table, eyed it closely and emptied it into another.

"Ah, my friend awakes," he murmured in his voice—the voice of a living dead man.

He thrust his hands into his long sleeves and turned fully to me.

"I think in you," he said distinctly, "I have created a Frankenstein monster. I made of you a superhuman creature to serve my wishes and you broke from me. You are the bane of my might, worse than Gordon even. You have killed valuable servants and interfered with my plans. However, your evil comes to an end tonight. Your friend Gordon broke away but he is being hunted through the tunnels and cannot escape.

"You," he continued with the sincere interest of the scientist, "are a most interesting subject. Your brain must be formed differently from any other man that ever lived. I will make a close study of it and add it to my laboratory. How a man, with the apparent need of the elixir in his system, has managed to go on for two days still stimulated by the last draft is more than I can understand."

My heart leaped. With all his wisdom, little Zuleika had tricked him, and he evidently did not know that she had filched a flask of the life-giving stuff from him.

"The last draft you had from me," he went on, "was sufficient only for some eight hours. I repeat, it has me puzzled. Can you offer any suggestion?"

I snarled wordlessly. He sighed.

"As always the barbarian. Truly the proverb speaks: 'Jest with the wounded tiger and warm the adder in your bosom before you seek to lift the savage from his savagery.'"

He meditated awhile in silence. I watched him uneasily.

There was about him a vague and curious difference—his long fingers emerging from the sleeves drummed on the chair arms and some hidden exultation strummed at the back of his voice, lending it unaccustomed vibrancy.

"And you might have been a king of the new regime," he said suddenly. "Aye, the new—new and inhumanly old!"

I shuddered as his dry cackling laugh rasped out.

He bent his head as if listening. From far off seemed to come a hum of guttural voices. His lips writhed in a smile.

"My black children," he murmured. "They tear my enemy Gordon to pieces in the tunnels. They, Mr. Costigan, are my real henchmen and it was for their edification tonight that I laid John Gordon on the sacrificial stone. I would have preferred to have made some experiments with him, based on certain scientific theories, but my children must be humored. Later under my tutelage they will outgrow their childish superstitions and throw aside their foolish customs, but now they must be led gently by the hand.

"How do you like these under-the-earth corridors, Mr. Costigan?" he switched suddenly. "You thought of them—what? No doubt that the white savages of your Middle Ages built them? Faugh! These tunnels are older than your world! They were brought into being by mighty kings, too many eons ago for your mind to grasp, when an imperial city towered where this crude village of London stands. All trace of that metropolis has crumbled to dust and vanished, but these corridors were built by more than human skill—ha ha! Of all the teeming thousands who move daily above them, none knows of their existence save my servants—and not all of them. Zuleika, for instance, does not know of them, for of late I have begun to doubt her loyalty and shall doubtless soon make of her an example."

At that I hurled myself blindly against the side of the cage, a red wave of hate and fury tossing me in its grip. I seized the bars and strained until the veins stood out on my forehead and the muscles bulged and crackled in my arms and shoulders. And the bars bent before my onslaught—a little but no more, and finally the power flowed from my limbs and I sank down trembling and weakened. Kathulos watched me imperturbably.

"The bars hold," he announced with something almost like relief in his tone. "Frankly, I prefer to be on the opposite side of them. You are a human ape if there was ever one."

He laughed suddenly and wildly.

"But why do you seek to oppose me?" he shrieked unexpectedly. "Why defy me, who am Kathulos, the Sorcerer, great even in the days of the old empire? Today, invincible! A magician, a scientist, among ignorant savages! Ha ha!"

I shuddered, and sudden blinding light broke in on me. Kathulos himself was an addict, and was fired by the stuff of his choice! What hellish concoction was strong enough, terrible enough to thrill the Master and inflame him, I do not know, nor do I wish to know. Of all the uncanny knowledge that was his, I, knowing the man as I did, count this the most weird and grisly.

"You, you paltry fool!" he was ranting, his face lit supernaturally.

"Know you who I am? Kathulos of Egypt! Bah! They knew me in the old days! I reigned in the dim misty sea lands ages and ages before the sea rose and engulfed the land. I died, not as men die; the magic draft of life everlasting was ours! I drank deep and slept. Long I slept in my lacquered case! My flesh withered and grew hard; my blood dried in my veins. I became as one dead. But still within me burned the spirit of life, sleeping but anticipating the awakening. The great cities crumbled to dust. The sea drank the land. The tall shrines and the lofty spires sank beneath the green waves. All this I knew as I slept, as a man knows in dreams. Kathulos of Egypt? Faugh! *Kathulos of Atlantis!*"

I uttered a sudden involuntary cry. This was too grisly for sanity.

"Aye, the magician, the sorcerer.

"And down the long years of savagery, through which the barbaric races struggled to rise without their masters, the legend came of the day of empire, when one of the Old Race would rise up from the sea. Aye, and lead to victory the black people who were our slaves in the old days.

"These brown and yellow people, what care I for them? The blacks were the slaves of my race, and I am their god today. They will obey me. The yellow and the brown peoples are fools—I make them my tools, and the day will come when my black warriors will turn on them and slay at my word. And you, you white barbarians, whose ape-ancestors forever defied my race and me, your doom is at hand! And when I mount my universal throne, the only whites shall be white slaves!

"The day came as prophesied, when my case, breaking free from the halls where it lay—where it had lain when Atlantis was still sovereign of the world—where since her empery it had sunk into the green fathoms—when my case, I say, was smitten by the deep sea tides and moved and stirred, and thrust aside the clinging seaweed that masks temples and minarets, and came floating up past the lofty sapphire and golden spires, up through the green waters, to float upon the lazy waves of the sea.

"Then came a white fool carrying out the destiny of which he was not aware. The men on his ship, true believers, knew that the time had come. And I—the air entered my nostrils and I awoke from the long, long sleep. I stirred and moved and lived. And rising in the night, I slew the fool that had lifted me from the ocean, and my servants made obeisance to me and took me into Africa, where I abode awhile and learned new languages and new ways of a new world and became strong.

"The wisdom of your dreary world—ha ha! I who delved deeper in the mysteries of the old than any man dared go! All that men know today, I know, and the knowledge beside that which I have brought down the centuries is as a grain of sand beside a mountain! You should know something of that knowledge! By it I lifted you from one hell to plunge you into a greater! You fool, here at my hand is that which would lift you from this!

Aye, would strike from you the chains whereby I have bound you!"

He snatched up a golden vial and shook it before my gaze. I eyed it as men dying in the desert must eye the distant mirages. Kathulos fingered it meditatively. His unnatural excitement seemed to have passed suddenly, and when he spoke again it was in the passionless, measured tones of the scientist.

"That would indeed be an experiment worthwhile—to free you of the elixir habit and see if your dope-riddled body would sustain life. Nine times out of ten the victim, with the need and stimulus removed, would die—but you are such a giant of a brute—"

He sighed and set the vial down.

"The dreamer opposes the man of destiny. My time is not my own or I should choose to spend my life pent in my laboratories, carrying out my experiments. But now, as in the days of the old empire when kings sought my counsel, I must work and labor for the good of the race at large. Aye, I must toil and sow the seed of glory against the full coming of the imperial days when the seas give up all their living dead."

I shuddered. Kathulos laughed wildly again. His fingers began to drum his chair arms and his face gleamed with the unnatural light once more. The red visions had begun to seethe in his skull again.

"Under the green seas they lie, the ancient masters, in their lacquered cases, dead as men reckon death, but only sleeping. Sleeping through the long ages as hours, awaiting the day of awakening! The old masters, the wise men, who foresaw the day when the sea would gulp the land, and who made ready. Made ready that they might rise again in the barbaric days to come. As did I. Sleeping they lie, ancient kings and grim wizards, who died as men die, before Atlantis sank. Who, sleeping, sank with her but who shall arise again!

"Mine the glory! I rose first. And I sought out the site of old cities, on shores that did not sink. Vanished, long vanished. The barbarian tide swept over them thousands of years ago as the green waters swept over their elder sister of the deeps. On some, the deserts stretch bare. Over some, as here, young barbarian cities rise."

He halted suddenly. His eyes sought one of the dark openings that marked a corridor. I think his strange intuition warned him of some impending danger but I do not believe that he had any inkling of how dramatically our scene would be interrupted.

As he looked, swift footsteps sounded and a man appeared suddenly in the doorway—a man disheveled, tattered and bloody. *John Gordon!* Kathulos sprang erect with a cry, and Gordon, gasping as from superhuman exertion, brought down the revolver he held in his hand and fired point-blank. Kathulos staggered, clapping his hand to his breast, and then, groping wildly, reeled to the wall and fell against it. A doorway opened and he reeled through, but as Gordon leaped fiercely across the chamber, a blank stone surface met his gaze, which yielded not to his savage hammerings.

He whirled and ran drunkenly to the table where lay a bunch of keys the Master had dropped there.

"The vial!" I shrieked. "Take the vial!" And he thrust it into his pocket.

Back along the corridor through which he had come sounded a faint clamor, growing swiftly like a wolfpack in full cry. A few precious seconds spent with fumbling for the right key, then the cage door swung open and I sprang out. A sight for the gods we were, the two of us! Slashed, bruised and cut, our garments hanging in tatters—my wounds had ceased to bleed, but now as I moved they began again, and from the stiffness of my hands I knew that my knuckles were shattered. As for Gordon, he was fairly drenched in blood from crown to foot.

We made off down a passage in the opposite direction from the menacing noise, which I knew to be the black servants of the Master in full pursuit of us. Neither of us was in good shape for running, but we did our best. Where we were going I had no idea. My superhuman strength had deserted me, and I was going now on willpower alone. We switched off into another corridor and we had not gone twenty steps until, looking back, I saw the first of the black devils round the corner.

A desperate effort increased our lead a trifle. But they had seen us, were in full view now, and a yell of fury broke from them to be succeeded by a more sinister silence as they bent all efforts to overhauling us.

There a short distance in front of us we saw a stair loom suddenly in the gloom. If we might reach that—but we saw something else.

Against the ceiling, between us and the stairs, hung a huge thing like an iron grille, with great spikes along the bottom—a portcullis. And even as we looked, without halting in our panting strides, it began to move.

"They're lowering the portcullis!" Gordon croaked, his blood-streaked face a mask of exhaustion and will.

Now the blacks were only ten feet behind us—now the huge grate, gaining momentum, with a creak of rusty, unused mechanism, rushed downward. A final spurt, a gasping straining nightmare of effort—and Gordon, sweeping us both along in a wild burst of pure nerve-strength, hurled us under and through, and the grate crashed behind us!

A moment we lay gasping, not heeding the frenzied horde who raved and screamed on the other side of the grate. So close had that final leap been, that the great spikes in their descent had torn shreds from our clothing.

The blacks were thrusting at us with daggers through the bars, but we were out of reach and it seemed to me that I was content to lie there and die of exhaustion. But Gordon weaved unsteadily erect and hauled me with him.

"Got to get out," he croaked; "go to warn—Scotland Yard—honeycombs in heart of London—high explosives—arms —ammunition."

We blundered up the steps, and in front of us I seemed to

hear a sound of metal grating against metal. The stairs ended abruptly, on a landing that terminated in a blank wall. Gordon hammered against this and the inevitable secret doorway opened. Light streamed in, through the bars of a sort of grille. Men in the uniform of London police were sawing at these with hacksaws, and even as they greeted us, an opening was made through which we crawled.

"You're hurt, sir!" One of the men took Gordon's arm.

My companion shook him off.

"There's no time to lose! Out of here, as quick as we can go!"

I saw that we were in a basement of some sort. We hastened up the steps and out into the early dawn which was turning the east scarlet. Over the tops of smaller houses I saw in the distance a great gaunt building on the roof of which, I felt instinctively, that wild drama had been enacted the night before.

"That building was leased some months ago by a mysterious Chinaman," said Gordon, following my gaze. "Office building originally—the neighborhood deteriorated and the building stood vacant for some time. The new tenant added several stories to it but left it apparently empty. Had my eye on it for some time."

This was told in Gordon's jerky swift manner as we started hurriedly along the sidewalk. I listened mechanically, like a man in a trance. My vitality was ebbing fast and I knew that I was going to crumple at any moment.

"The people living in the vicinity had been reporting strange sights and noises. The man who owned the basement we just left heard queer sounds emanating from the wall of the basement and called the police. About that time I was racing back and forth among those cursed corridors like a hunted rat, and I heard the police banging on the wall. I found the secret door and opened it but found it barred by a grating. It was while I was telling the astounded policemen to procure a hacksaw that the pursuing Negroes, whom I had eluded for the moment, came into sight and I was forced to shut the door and run for it again.

By pure luck I found you and by pure luck managed to find the way back to the door.

"Now we must get to Scotland Yard. If we strike swiftly, we may capture the entire band of devils. Whether I killed Kathulos or not I do not know, or if he can be killed by mortal weapons. But to the best of my knowledge all of them are now in those subterranean corridors and—"

At that moment the world shook! A brain-shattering roar seemed to break the sky with its incredible detonation; houses tottered and crashed to ruins; a mighty pillar of smoke and flame burst from the earth and on its wings great masses of debris soared skyward. A black fog of smoke and dust and falling timbers enveloped the world, a prolonged thunder seemed to rumble up from the center of the earth as of walls and ceilings falling, and amid the uproar and the screaming I sank down and knew no more.

THE BREAKING OF THE CHAIN

"And like a soul belated,
In heaven and hell unmated;
By cloud and mist abated;
Come out of darkness morn."

—Algernon Swinburne

There is little need to linger on the scenes of horror of that terrible London morning. The world is familiar with and knows most of the details attendant to the great explosion which wiped out a tenth of that great city with a resultant loss of lives and property. For such a happening some reason must needs be given; the tale of the deserted building got out, and many wild stories were circulated. Finally, to still the rumors, the report was unofficially given out that this building had been the rendezvous and secret stronghold of a gang of international anarchists, who had stored its basement full of high explosives and who had supposedly ignited these accidentally. In a way there was a good deal to this tale, as you know, but the threat that had lurked there far transcended any anarchist.

All this was told to me, for when I sank unconscious,

Gordon, attributing my condition to exhaustion and a need of
the hashish to the use of which he thought I was addicted, lifted
me and with the aid of the stunned policemen got me to his
rooms before returning to the scene of the explosion. At his
rooms he found Hansen, and Zuleika handcuffed to the bed as I
had left her. He released her and left her to tend to me, for all
London was in a terrible turmoil and he was needed elsewhere.

When I came to myself at last, I looked up into her starry
eyes and lay quiet, smiling up at her. She sank down upon my
bosom, nestling my head in her arms and covering my face with
her kisses.

"Steephen!" she sobbed over and over, as her tears splashed
hot on my face.

I was scarcely strong enough to put my arms about her but I
managed it, and we lay there for a space, in silence, except for
the girl's hard, racking sobs.

"Zuleika, I love you," I murmured.

"And I love you, Steephen," she sobbed. "Oh, it is so hard to
part now—but I'm going with you, Steephen; I can't live without
you!"

"My dear child," said John Gordon, entering the room
suddenly, "Costigan's not going to die. We will let him have
enough hashish to tide him along, and when he is stronger we
will take him off the habit slowly."

"You don't understand, sahib; it is not hashish Steephen must
have. It is something which only the Master knew, and now that
he is dead or is fled, Steephen cannot get it and must die."

Gordon shot a quick, uncertain glance at me. His fine face
was drawn and haggard, his clothes sooty and torn from his work
among the debris of the explosion.

"She's right, Gordon," I said languidly. "I'm dying. Kathulos
killed the hashish craving with a concoction he called the elixir.
I've been keeping myself alive on some of the stuff that Zuleika
stole from him and gave me, but I drank it all last night."

I was aware of no craving of any kind, no physical or mental discomfort even. All my mechanism was slowing down fast; I had passed the stage where the need of the elixir would tear and rend me. I felt only a great lassitude and a desire to sleep. And I knew that the moment I closed my eyes, I would die.

"A strange dope, that elixir," I said with growing languor. "It burns and freezes and then at last the craving kills easily and without torment."

"Costigan, curse it," said Gordon desperately, "you can't go like this! That vial I took from the Egyptian's table—what is in it?"

"The Master swore it would free me of my curse and probably kill me also," I muttered. "I'd forgotten about it. Let me have it; it can no more than kill me and I'm dying now."

"Yes, quick, let me have it!" exclaimed Zuleika fiercely, springing to Gordon's side, her hands passionately outstretched. She returned with the vial which he had taken from his pocket, and knelt beside me, holding it to my lips, while she murmured to me gently and soothingly in her own language.

I drank, draining the vial, but feeling little interest in the whole matter. My outlook was purely impersonal, at such a low ebb was my life, and I cannot even remember how the stuff tasted. I only remember feeling a curious sluggish fire burn faintly along my veins, and the last thing I saw was Zuleika crouching over me, her great eyes fixed with a burning intensity on me. Her tense little hand rested inside her blouse, and remembering her vow to take her own life if I died I tried to lift a hand and disarm her, tried to tell Gordon to take away the dagger she had hidden in her garments. But speech and action failed me, and I drifted away into a curious sea of unconsciousness.

Of that period I remember nothing. No sensation fired my sleeping brain to such an extent as to bridge the gulf over which I drifted. They say I lay like a dead man for hours, scarcely breathing, while Zuleika hovered over me, never leaving my side an instant, and fighting like a tigress when anyone tried to coax her away to rest. Her chain was broken.

As I had carried the vision of her into that dim land of nothingness, so her dear eyes were the first thing which greeted my returning consciousness. I was aware of a greater weakness than I thought possible for a man to feel, as if I had been an invalid for months, but the life in me, faint though it was, was sound and normal, caused by no artificial stimulation. I smiled up at my girl and murmured weakly:

"Throw away your dagger, little Zuleika; I'm going to live."

She screamed and fell on her knees beside me, weeping and laughing at the same time. Women are strange beings, of mixed and powerful emotions, truly.

Gordon entered and grasped the hand which I could not lift from the bed.

"You're a case for an ordinary human physician now, Costigan," he said. "Even a layman like myself can tell that. For the first time since I've known you, the look in your eyes is entirely sane. You look like a man who has had a complete nervous breakdown, and needs about a year of rest and quiet. Great heavens, man, you've been through enough, outside your dope experience, to last you a lifetime."

"Tell me first," said I, "was Kathulos killed in the explosion?"

"I don't know," answered Gordon somberly. "Apparently the entire system of subterranean passages was destroyed. I know my last bullet—the last bullet that was in the revolver which I wrested from one of my attackers—found its mark in the Master's body, but whether he died from the wound, or whether a bullet can hurt him, I do not know. And whether in his death agonies he ignited the tons and tons of high explosives which were stored in the corridors, or whether the Negroes did it unintentionally, we shall never know.

"My God, Costigan, did you ever see such a honeycomb? And we know not how many miles in either direction the passages reached. Even now Scotland Yard men are combing the subways and basements of the town for secret openings. All known openings, such as the one through which we came and the one in Soho 48, were blocked by falling walls. The office building was simply blown to atoms."

"What about the men who raided Soho 48?"

"The door in the library wall had been closed. They found the Chinaman you killed, but searched the house without avail. Lucky for them, too, else they had doubtless been in the tunnels when the explosion came, and perished with the hundreds of Negroes who must have died then."

"Every Negro in London must have been there."

"I dare say. Most of them are voodoo worshipers at heart and the power the Master wielded was incredible. They died, but what of him? Was he blown to atoms by the stuff which he had secretly stored, or crushed when the stone walls crumbled and the ceilings came thundering down?"

"There is no way to search among those subterranean ruins, I suppose?"

"None whatever. When the walls caved in, the tons of earth upheld by the ceilings also came crashing down, filling the corridors with dirt and broken stone, blocking them forever. And on the surface of the earth, the houses which the vibration shook down were heaped high in utter ruins. What happened in those terrible corridors must remain forever a mystery."

My tale draws to a close. The months that followed passed uneventfully, except for the growing happiness which to me was paradise, but which would bore you were I to relate it. But one day Gordon and I again discussed the mysterious happenings that had had their being under the grim hand of the Master.

"Since that day," said Gordon, "the world has been quiet. Africa has subsided and the East seems to have returned to her ancient sleep. There can be but one answer—living or dead, Kathulos was destroyed that morning when his world crashed about him."

"Gordon," said I, "what is the answer to that greatest of all mysteries?"

My friend shrugged his shoulders.

"I have come to believe that mankind eternally hovers on the brinks of secret oceans of which it knows nothing. Races have lived and vanished before our race rose out of the slime of the primitive, and it is likely still others will live upon the earth after ours has vanished. Scientists have long upheld the theory that the Atlanteans possessed a higher civilization than our own, and on very different lines. Certainly Kathulos himself was proof that our boasted culture and knowledge were nothing beside that of whatever fearful civilization produced him.

"His dealings with you alone have puzzled all the scientific world, for none of them has been able to explain how he could remove the hashish craving, stimulate you with a drug so infinitely more powerful, and then produce another drug which entirely effaced the effects of the other."

"I have him to thank for two things," I said slowly; "the regaining of my lost manhood—and Zuleika. Kathulos, then, is dead, as far as any mortal thing can die. But what of those others —those 'ancient masters' who still sleep in the sea?"

Gordon shuddered.

"As I said, perhaps mankind loiters on the brink of unthink- able chasms of horror. But a fleet of gunboats is even now patrolling the oceans unobtrusively, with orders to destroy instantly any strange case that may be found floating—to destroy it and its contents. And if my word has any weight with the English government and the nations of the world, the seas will be so patrolled until doomsday shall let down the curtain on the races of today."

"At night I dream of them, sometimes," I muttered, "sleeping in their lacquered cases, which drip with strange seaweed, far down among the green surges—where unholy spires and strange towers rise in the dark ocean."

"We have been face to face with an ancient horror," said

Gordon somberly, "with a fear too dark and mysterious for the human brain to cope with. Fortune has been with us; she may not again favor the sons of men. It is best that we be ever on our guard. The universe was not made for humanity alone; life takes strange phases and it is the first instinct of nature for the different species to destroy each other. No doubt we seemed as horrible to the Master as he did to us. We have scarcely tapped the chest of secrets which nature has stored, and I shudder to think of what that chest may hold for the human race."

"That's true," said I, inwardly rejoicing at the vigor which was beginning to course through my wasted veins, "but men will meet obstacles as they come, as men have always risen to meet them. Now, I am beginning to know the full worth of life and love, and not all the devils from all the abysses can hold me."

Gordon smiled.

"You have it coming to you, old comrade. The best thing is to forget all that dark interlude, for in that course lies light and happiness."

THE CHILDREN OF THE NIGHT

There were, I remember, six of us in Conrad's bizarrely
fashioned study, with its queer relics from all over the
world and its long rows of books which ranged from the
Mandrake Press edition of Boccaccio to a *Missale Romanum*,
bound in clasped oak boards and printed in Venice, 1740.
Clemants and Professor Kirowan had just engaged in a somewhat testy anthropological argument: Clemants upholding the
theory of a separate, distinct Alpine race, while the professor
maintained that this so-called race was merely a deviation from
an original Aryan stock—possibly the result of an admixture
between the southern or Mediterranean races and the Nordic
people.

"And how," asked Clemants, "do you account for their brachy-
cephalicism? The Mediterraneans were as long-headed as the
Aryans: would admixture between these dolichocephalic peoples
produce a broad-headed intermediate type?"

"Special conditions might bring about a change in an originally long-headed race," snapped Kirowan. "Boas has demon-
strated, for instance, that in the case of immigrants to America,
skull formations often change in one generation. And Flinders

Petrie has shown that the Lombards changed from a long-headed to a round-headed race in a few centuries."

"But what caused these changes?"

"Much is yet unknown to science," answered Kirowan, "and we need not be dogmatic. No one knows, as yet, why people of British and Irish ancestry tend to grow unusually tall in the Darling district of Australia—Cornstalks, as they are called—or why people of such descent generally have thinner jaw-structures after a few generations in New England. The universe is full of the unexplainable."

"And therefore the uninteresting, according to Machen," laughed Taverel.

Conrad shook his head. "I must disagree. To me, the unknowable is most tantalizingly fascinating."

"Which accounts, no doubt, for all the works on witchcraft and demonology I see on your shelves," said Ketrick, with a wave of his hand toward the rows of books.

And let me speak of Ketrick. Each of the six of us was of the same breed—that is to say, a Briton or an American of British descent. By British, I include all-natural inhabitants of the British Isles. We represented various strains of English and Celtic blood, but basically, these strains are the same after all. But Ketrick: to me the man always seemed strangely alien. It was in his eyes that this difference showed externally. They were a sort of amber, almost yellow, and slightly oblique. At times, when one looked at his face from certain angles, they seemed to slant like a Chinaman's.

Others than I had noticed this feature, so unusual in a man of pure Anglo-Saxon descent. The usual myths ascribing his slanted eyes to some pre-natal influence had been mooted about, and I remember Professor Hendrik Brooler once remarked that Ketrick was undoubtedly an atavism, representing a reversion of type to some dim and distant ancestor of Mongolian blood—a sort of freak reversion, since none of his family showed such traces.

But Ketrick comes of the Welsh branch of the Cetrics of Sussex, and his lineage is set down in the *Book of Peers*. There you may read the line of his ancestry, which extends unbroken to the days of Canute. No slightest trace of Mongoloid intermixture appears in the genealogy, and how could there have been such intermixture in old Saxon England? For Ketrick is the modern form of Cedric, and though that branch fled into Wales before the invasion of the Danes, its male heirs consistently married with English families on the border marches, and it remains a pure line of the powerful Sussex Cedrics—almost pure Saxon. As for the man himself, this defect of his eyes, if it can be called a defect, is his only abnormality, except for a slight and occasional lisping of speech. He is highly intellectual and a good companion except for a slight aloofness and a rather callous indifference which may serve to mask an extremely sensitive nature.

Referring to his remark, I said with a laugh: "Conrad pursues the obscure and mystic as some men pursue romance; his shelves throng with delightful nightmares of every variety."

Our host nodded. "You'll find there a number of delectable dishes—Machen, Poe, Blackwood, Maturin—look, there's a rare feast—*Horrid Mysteries*, by the Marquis of Grosse—the real Eighteenth Century edition."

Taverel scanned the shelves. "Weird fiction seems to vie with works on witchcraft, Voodoo, and dark magic."

True; historians and chronicles are often dull; tale-weavers never—the masters, I mean. A Voodoo sacrifice can be described in such a dull manner as to take all the real fantasy out of it, and leave it merely a sordid murder. I will admit that few writers of fiction touch the true heights of horror—most of their stuff is too concrete, given too much earthly shape and dimensions. But in such tales as Poe's *Fall of the House of Usher*, Machen's *Black Seal*, and Lovecraft's *Call of Cthulhu*—the three master horror tales, to my mind—the reader is borne into dark and *outer* realms of imagination.

"But look there," he continued, "there, sandwiched between

that nightmare of Huysmans', and Walpole's *Castle of Otranto*—
Von Junzt's *Nameless Cults*. There's a book to keep you awake at
night!"

"I've read it," said Taverel, "and I'm convinced the man is
mad. His work is like the conversation of a maniac—it runs with
startling clarity for awhile, then suddenly merges into vagueness
and disconnected ramblings."

Conrad shook his head. "Have you ever thought that perhaps
it is his very sanity that causes him to write in that fashion?
What if he dares not put on paper all he knows? What if his
vague suppositions are dark and mysterious hints, keys to the
puzzle, to those who know?"

"Bosh!" This from Kirowan. "Are you intimating that any of
the nightmare cults referred to by Von Junzt survive to this day
—if they ever existed save in the hag-ridden brain of a lunatic
poet and philosopher?"

"Not he alone used hidden meanings," answered Conrad. "If
you will scan various works of certain great poets you may find
double meanings. Men have stumbled onto cosmic secrets in the
past and given a hint of them to the world in cryptic words. Do
you remember Von Junzt's hints of 'a city in the waste'? What do
you think of Flecker's lines:

"Pass not beneath! Men say there blows in stony deserts still a rose

"But with no scarlet to her leaf—and from whose heart no perfume
flows.'

"Men may stumble upon secret things, but Von Junzt dipped
deep into forbidden mysteries. He was one of the few men, for
instance, who could read the *Necronomicon* in the original Greek
translation."

Taverel shrugged his shoulders, and Professor Kirowan,
though he snorted and puffed viciously at his pipe, made no
direct reply; for he, as well as Conrad, had delved into the Latin
version of the book, and had found there things not even a cold-
blooded scientist could answer or refute.

"Well," he said presently, "suppose we admit the former existence of cults revolving about such nameless and ghastly gods and entities as Cthulhu, Yog Sothoth, Tsathoggua, Gol-goroth, and the like, I can not find it in my mind to believe that survivals of such cults lurk in the dark corners of the world today."

To our surprise Clemants answered. He was a tall, lean man, silent almost to the point of taciturnity, and his fierce struggles with poverty in his youth had lined his face beyond his years. Like many another artist, he lived a distinctly dual literary life, his swashbuckling novels furnishing him a generous income, and his editorial position on *The Cloven Hoof* affording him full artistic expression. *The Cloven Hoof* was a poetry magazine whose bizarre contents had often aroused the shocked interest of the conservative critics.

"You remember Von Junzt makes mention of a so-called Bran cult," said Clemants, stuffing his pipe-bowl with a peculiarly villainous brand of shag tobacco. "I think I heard you and Taverel discussing it once."

"As I gather from his hints," snapped Kirowan, "Von Junzt includes this particular cult among those still in existence. Absurd."

Again, Clemants shook his head. "When I was a boy working my way through a certain university, I had for roommate a lad as poor and ambitious as I. If I told you his name, it would startle you. Though he came of an old Scotch line of Galloway, he was obviously of a non-Aryan type.

"This is in strictest confidence, you understand. But my roommate talked in his sleep. I began to listen and put his disjointed mumbling together. And in his mutterings I first heard of the ancient cult hinted at by Von Junzt; of the king who rules the Dark Empire, which was a revival of an older, darker empire dating back into the Stone Age; and of the great, name-less cavern where stands the Dark Man—the image of Bran Mak Morn, carved in his likeness by a master-hand while the great king yet lived, and to which each worshipper of Bran makes a pilgrimage once in his or her lifetime. Yes, that cult lives today in the descendants of Bran's people—a silent, unknown current it flows on in the great ocean of life, waiting for the stone image of the great Bran to breathe and move with sudden life, and come from the great cavern to rebuild their lost empire."

"And who were the people of that empire?" asked Ketrick.

"Picts," answered Taverel, "doubtless the people known later as the wild Picts of Galloway were predominantly Celtic—a mixture of Gaelic, Cymric, aboriginal and possibly Teutonic elements. Whether they took their name from the older race, or lent their own name to that race, is a matter yet to be decided. But when Von Junzt speaks of Picts, he refers specifically to the small, dark, garlic-eating peoples of Mediterranean blood who brought the neolithic culture into Britain. The first settlers of that country, in fact, who gave rise to the tales of earth spirits and goblins."

"I can not agree to that last statement," said Conrad. "These legends ascribe a deformity and inhumanness of appearances to the characters. There was nothing about the Picts to excite such horror and repulsion in the Aryan peoples. I believe that the Mediterraneans were preceded by a Mongoloid type, very low in the scale of development, whence these tales—"

"Quite true," broke in Kirowan, "but I hardly think they preceded the Picts, as you call them, into Britain. We find troll and dwarf legends all over the Continent, and I am inclined to think that both the Mediterranean and Aryan people brought these tales with them from the Continent. They must have been of extremely inhuman aspect, those early Mongoloids."

"At least," said Conrad, "here is a flint mallet a miner found in the Welsh hills and gave to me, which has never been fully explained. It is obviously of no ordinary neolithic make. See how small it is, compared to most implements of that age; almost like a child's toy; yet it is surprisingly heavy, and no doubt a deadly blow could be dealt with it. I fitted the handle to it myself, and you would be surprised to know how difficult it was to carve it into a shape and balance corresponding with the head."

We looked at the thing. It was well made, polished somewhat like the other remnants of the neolithic I had seen, yet as Conrad said, it was strangely different. Its small size was oddly disquieting, for it had no appearance of a toy, otherwise. It was as sinister in suggestion as an Aztec sacrificial dagger. Conrad had fashioned the oaken handle with rare skill and, in carving it to fit the head, had managed to give it the same unnatural appearance as the mallet itself had. He had even copied the workmanship of primal times, fixing the head into the cleft of the haft with rawhide.

"My word!" Taverel made a clumsy pass at an imaginary antagonist and nearly shattered a costly Shang vase. "The balance of the thing is all off-center; I'd have to readjust all my mechanics of poise and equilibrium to handle it."

"Let me see it." Ketrick took the thing and fumbled with it, trying to strike the secret of its proper handling. At length, somewhat irritated, he swung it up and struck a heavy blow at a shield which hung on the wall nearby. I was standing near it; I saw the hellish mallet twist in his hand like a live serpent, and his arm wrenched out of line; I heard a shout of alarmed warning— then darkness came with the impact of the mallet against my head.

Slowly I drifted back to consciousness. First there was dull sensation with blindness and total lack of knowledge as to where I was or what I was; then vague realization of life and being, and a hard something pressing into my ribs. Then the mists cleared and I came to myself completely.

I lay on my back half-beneath some underbrush and my head throbbed fiercely. Also my hair was caked and clotted with blood, for the scalp had been laid open. But my eyes traveled down my body and limbs, naked but for a deerskin loincloth and sandals of the same material, and found no other wound. That which pressed so uncomfortably into my ribs was my ax, on which I had fallen.

Now an abhorrent babble reached my ears and stung me into clear consciousness. The noise was faintly like language, but not such language as men are accustomed to. It sounded much like the repeated hissing of many great snakes.

I stared. I lay in a great, gloomy forest. The glade was over-shadowed, so that even in the daytime it was very dark. Aye—that forest was dark, cold, silent, gigantic, and utterly grisly. And I looked into the glade.

I saw a shambles. Five men lay there—at least, what had been five men. Now as I marked the abhorrent mutilations my soul sickened. And about clustered the—things. Humans they were, of a sort, though I did not consider them so. They were short and stocky, with broad heads too large for their scrawny bodies. Their hair was snaky and stringy, their faces broad and square, with flat noses, hideously slanted eyes, a thin gash for a mouth, and pointed ears. They wore the skins of beasts, as did I, but these hides were but crudely dressed. They bore small bows and flint-tipped arrows, flint knives and cudgels. And they conversed in a speech as hideous as themselves, a hissing, reptilian speech that filled me with dread and loathing.

Oh, I hated them as I lay there; my brain flamed with white-hot fury. And now I remembered. We had hunted, we six youths of the Sword People, and wandered far into the grim forest which our people generally shunned. Weary of the chase, we had paused to rest; to me had been given the first watch, for in those days, no sleep was safe without a sentry. Now shame and revulsion shook my whole being. I had slept—I had betrayed my comrades. And now they lay gashed and mangled—butchered while they slept, by vermin who had never dared to stand before them on equal terms. I, Aryara, had betrayed my trust.

Aye—I remembered. I had slept and in the midst of a dream of the hunt, fire and sparks had exploded in my head, and I had plunged into a deeper darkness where there were no dreams.

And now the penalty. They who had stolen through the dense forest and smitten me senseless, had not paused to mutilate me. Thinking me dead, they had hastened swiftly to their grisly work. Now perhaps they had forgotten me for a time. I had sat somewhat apart from the others and, when struck, had fallen half-under some bushes. But soon they would remember me. I would hunt no more, dance no more in the dances of hunt and love and war, see no more the wattle huts of the Sword People.

But I had no wish to escape back to my people. Should I slink back with my tale of infamy and disgrace? Should I hear the words of scorn my tribe would fling at me, see the girls point their contemptuous fingers at the youth who slept and betrayed his comrades to the knives of vermin?

Tears stung my eyes, and slow hate heaved up in my bosom, and my brain. I would never bear the sword that marked the warrior. I would never triumph over worthy foes and die gloriously beneath the arrows of the Picts or the axes of the Wolf People or the River People. I would go down to death beneath a nauseous rabble, whom the Picts had long ago driven into forest dens like rats.

And mad rage gripped me and dried my tears, giving in their stead a berserk blaze of wrath. If such reptiles were to bring about my downfall, I would make it a fall long remembered—if such beasts had memories.

Moving cautiously, I shifted until my hand was on the haft of my ax; then I called on Il-marinen and bounded up as a tiger springs. And as a tiger springs I was among my enemies and mashed a flat skull as a man crushes the head of a snake. A sudden wild clamor of fear broke from my victims and for an instant they closed round me, hacking and stabbing. A knife gashed my chest, but I gave no heed. A red mist waved before my eyes, and my body and limbs moved in perfect accord with my fighting brain. Snarling, hacking, and smiting, I was a tiger among reptiles. In an instant they gave way and fled, leaving me bestriding half a dozen stunted bodies. But I was not satiated.

I was close on the heels of the tallest one, whose head would perhaps come to my shoulder, and who seemed to be their chief. He fled down a sort of runway, squealing like a monstrous lizard, and when I was close at his shoulder, he dived, snake-like, into the bushes. But I was too swift for him, and I dragged him forth and butchered him in a most gory fashion.

And through the bushes I saw the trail he was striving to reach—a path winding in and out among the trees, almost too narrow to allow the traversing of it by a man of normal size. I hacked off my victim's hideous head, and carrying it in my left hand, went up the serpent-path, with my red ax in my right.

Now as I strode swiftly along the path, and blood splashed beside my feet at every step from the severed jugular of my foe, I thought of those I hunted. Aye—we held them in so little esteem, we hunted by day in the forest they haunted. What they called themselves, we never knew, for none of our tribe ever learned the accursed hissing sibilances they used as speech; but we called them Children of the Night. And night-things they were indeed, for they slunk in the depths of the dark forests, and in subterraneous dwellings, venturing forth into the hills only when their conquerors slept. It was at night that they did their foul deeds—the quick flight of a flint-tipped arrow to slay cattle, or perhaps a loitering human, the snatching of a child that had wandered from the village.

But it was for more than this we gave them their name; they were, in truth, people of night and darkness and the ancient horror-ridden shadows of bygone ages. For these creatures were very old, and they represented an outworn age. They had once overrun and possessed this land, and they had been driven into hiding and obscurity by the dark, fierce little Picts with whom we contested now, and who hated and loathed them as savagely as did we.

The Picts were different from us in general appearance, being shorter of stature and dark of hair, eyes, and skin, whereas we were tall and powerful, with yellow hair and light eyes. But they were cast in the same mold, for all of that. These Children of the Night seemed not human to us, with their deformed dwarfish bodies, yellow skin, and hideous faces. Aye—they were reptiles —vermin.

And my brain was like to burst with fury when I thought that it was these vermin on whom I was to glut my ax and perish. Bah! There is no glory slaying snakes or dying from their bites. All this rage and fierce disappointment turned on the objects of my hatred, and, with the old red mist waving in front of me, I swore by all the gods I knew, to wreak such red havoc before I died as to leave a dread memory in the minds of the survivors.

My people would not honor me, in such contempt they held the Children. But those Children that I left alive would remember me and shudder. So I swore, gripping savagely my ax, which was of bronze, set in a cleft of the oaken haft and fastened securely with rawhide.

Now I heard ahead a sibilant, abhorrent murmur, and a vile stench filtered to me through the trees, human, yet less than human. A few moments more and I emerged from the deep shadows into a wide-open space. I had never before seen a village of the Children. There was a cluster of earthen domes, with low doorways sunk into the ground; squalid dwelling places, half-above and half-below the earth. And I knew from the talk of the old warriors that these dwelling places were connected by underground corridors, so the whole village was like an ant-bed, or a system of snake holes. And I wondered if other tunnels did not run off under the ground and emerge long distances from the villages.

Before the domes clustered a vast group of the creatures, hissing and jabbering at a great rate.

I had quickened my pace, and now as I burst from cover, I was running with the fleetness of my race. A wild clamor went up from the rabble as they saw the avenger, tall, bloodstained, and blazing-eyed, leap from the forest, and I cried out fiercely, flung the dripping head among them and bounded like a wounded tiger into the thick of them.

Oh, there was no escape for them now! They might have taken to their tunnels, but I would have followed, even to the guts of Hell. They knew they must slay me, and they closed around, a hundred strong, to do it.

There was no wild blaze of glory in my brain as there had been against worthy foes. But the old berserk madness of my race was in my blood, and the smell of blood and destruction in my nostrils.

I know not how many I slew. I only know that they thronged about me in a writhing, slashing mass, like serpents about a wolf, and I smote until the ax-edge turned and bent and the ax became no more than a bludgeon; and I smashed skulls, split heads, splintered bones, scattered blood and brains in one red sacrifice to Il-marinen, god of the Sword People.

Bleeding from half a hundred wounds, blinded by a slash across the eyes, I felt a flint knife sink deep into my groin, and, at the same instant, a cudgel laid my scalp open. I went to my knees but reeled up again and saw in a thick, red fog a ring of leering, slant-eyed faces. I lashed out as a dying tiger strikes, and the faces broke in red ruin.

And as I sagged, overbalanced by the fury of my stroke, a taloned hand clutched my throat and a flint blade was driven into my ribs and twisted venomously. Beneath a shower of blows I went down again, but the man with the knife was beneath me, and with my left hand I found him and broke his neck before he could writhe away.

Life was waning swiftly; through the hissing and howling of the Children I could hear the voice of Il-marinen. Yet once again I rose stubbornly, through a very whirlwind of cudgels and spears. I could no longer see my foes, even in a red mist. But I could feel their blows and knew they surged about me. I braced my feet, gripped my slippery ax-haft with both hands, and calling once more on Il-marinen, I heaved up the ax and struck one last terrific blow. And I must have died on my feet, for there was no sensation of falling; even as I knew, with a last thrill of savagery, that I slew, even as I felt the splintering of skulls beneath my ax, darkness came with oblivion.

I CAME suddenly to myself. I was half-reclining in a big armchair and Conrad was pouring water on me. My head ached and a trickle of blood had half-dried on my face. Kirowan, Taverel, and Clemants were hovering about, anxiously, while Ketrick stood just in front of me, still holding the mallet, his face schooled to a polite perturbation which his eyes did not show. And at the sight of those cursed eyes a red madness surged up in me.

"There," Conrad was saying, "I told you he'd come out of it in a moment; just a light crack. He's taken harder than that. All right now, aren't you, O'Donnel?"

At that I swept them aside, and with a single low snarl of hatred launched myself at Ketrick. Taken utterly by surprise, he had no opportunity to defend himself. My hands locked on his throat, and we crashed together on the ruins of a divan. The others cried out in amazement and horror and sprang to separate us—or rather, to tear me from my victim, for already Ketrick's slant eyes were beginning to start from their sockets.

"For God's sake, O'Donnel," exclaimed Conrad, seeking to break my grip, "what's come over you? Ketrick didn't mean to hit you—let go, you idiot!"

A fierce wrath almost overcame me at these men who were my friends, men of my own tribe, and I swore at them and their blindness, as they finally managed to tear my strangling fingers from Ketrick's throat. He sat up and choked and explored the blue marks my fingers had left, while I raged and cursed, nearly defeating the combined efforts of the four to hold me.

"You fools!" I screamed. "Let me go! Let me do my duty as a tribesman! You blind fools! I care nothing for the paltry blow he dealt me—he and his dealt stronger blows than that against me, in bygone ages. You fools, he is marked with the brand of the beast—the reptile—the vermin we exterminated centuries ago! I must crush him, stamp him out, rid the clean earth of his accursed pollution!"

So I raved and struggled and Conrad gasped to Ketrick over his shoulder: "Get out, quick! He's out of his head! His mind is unhinged! Get away from him."

Now I look out over the ancient dreaming downs and the hills and deep forests beyond and I ponder. Somehow, that blow from that ancient, accursed mallet knocked me back into another age and another life. While I was Aryara I had no cognizance of any other life. It was no dream; it was a stray bit of reality wherein I, John O'Donnel, once lived and died, and back into which I was snatched, across the voids of time and space by a chance blow. Time and times are but cogwheels, unmatched, grinding on oblivious to one another. Occasionally—oh, very rarely!—the cogs fit; the pieces of the plot snap together momentarily and give men faint glimpses beyond the veil of this everyday blindness we call reality.

I am John O'Donnel and I was Aryara, who dreamed dreams of war-glory, and hunt-glory, and feast-glory, and who died on a red heap of his victims in some lost age. But in what age and where?

The last I can answer for you. Mountains and rivers change their contours; the landscapes alter; but the downs least of all. I look out upon them now and I remember them, not only with John O'Donnel's eyes, but with the eyes of Aryara. They are but little changed. Only the great forest has shrunk and dwindled and in many, many places vanished utterly. But here on these very downs Aryara lived, and fought, and loved, and in yonder forest, he died. Kirowan was wrong. The little, fierce, dark Picts were not the first men in the Isles. There were beings before them—aye, the Children of the Night. Legends—why, the Children were not unknown to us when we came into what is now the isle of Britain. We had encountered them before, ages before. Already we had our myths of them. But we found them in Britain. Nor had the Picts totally exterminated them.

Nor had the Picts, as so many believe, preceded us by many centuries. We drove them before us as we came, in that long drift from the east. I, Aryara, knew old men who had marched on that century-long trek; who had been borne in the arms of yellow-haired women over countless miles of forest and plain, and who as youths had walked in the vanguard of the invaders.

As to the age—that I cannot say. But I, Aryara, was surely an Aryan and my people were Aryans—members of one of the thousand unknown and unrecorded drifts that scattered yellow-haired, blue-eyed tribes all over the world. The Celts were not the first to come into western Europe. I, Aryara, was of the same blood and appearance as the men who sacked Rome, but mine was a much older strain. Of the language spoke, no echo remains in the waking mind of John O'Donnel, but I knew that Aryara's tongue was to ancient Celtic what ancient Celtic is to modern Gaelic.

Il-marinen! I remember the god I called upon, the ancient, ancient god who worked in metals—in bronze then. For Il-marinen was one of the base gods of the Aryans from whom many gods grew; and he was Wieland and Vulcan in the ages of iron. But to Aryara he was Il-marinen.

And Aryara—he was one of many tribes and many drifts. Not alone did the Sword People come or dwell in Britain. The River People were before us, and the Wolf People came later. But they were Aryans like us, light-eyed, and tall, and blond. We fought them, for the reason that the various drifts of Aryans have always fought each other, just as the Achaeans fought the Dorians, just as the Celts and Germans cut each other's throats; aye, just as the Hellenes and the Persians, who were once one people and of the same drift, split in two different ways on the long trek and centuries later met and flooded Greece and Asia Minor with blood.

Now understand, all this I did not know as Aryara. I, Aryara, knew nothing of all these worldwide drifts of my race. I knew only that my people were conquerors, that a century ago my ancestors had dwelt in the great plains far to the east, plains populous with fierce, yellow-haired, light-eyed people like myself; that my ancestors had come westward in a great drift; and that in that drift, when my tribesmen met tribes of other races, they trampled and destroyed them, and when they met other yellow-haired, light-eyed people, of older or newer drifts, they fought savagely and mercilessly, according to the old, illogical custom of the Aryan people. This Aryara knew, and I, John O'Donnel, who know much more and much less than I, Aryara, knew, have combined the knowledge of these separate selves and have come to conclusions that would startle many noted scientists and historians.

Yet this fact is well known: Aryans deteriorate swiftly in sedentary and peaceful lives. Their proper existence is a nomadic one; when they settle down to an agricultural existence, they pave the way for their downfall; and when they pen themselves with city walls, they seal their doom. Why, I, Aryara, remember the tales of the old men—how the Sons of the Sword, on that long drift, found villages of white-skinned yellow-haired people who had drifted into the west centuries before and had quit the wandering life to dwell among the dark, garlic-eating people and gain their sustenance from the soil. And the old men told how soft and weak they were, and how easily they fell before the bronze blades of the Sword People.

Look—is not the whole history of the Sons of Aryan laid on those lines? Look—how swiftly has Persian followed Mede; Greek, Persian; Roman, Greek; and German, Roman. Aye, and the Norseman followed the Germanic tribes when they had grown flabby from a century or so of peace and idleness, and despoiled the spoils they had taken in the southland.

But let me speak of Ketrick. Ha—the short hairs at the back of my neck bristle at the very mention of his name. A reversion to type—but not to the type of some cleanly Chinaman or Mongol of recent times. The Danes drove his ancestors into the hills of Wales; and there, in what medieval century, and in what foul way did that cursed aboriginal taint creep into the clean Saxon blood of the Celtic line, there to lie dormant so long? The Celtic Welsh never mated with the Children any more than the Picts did. But there must have been survivals—vermin lurking in those grim hills, that had outlasted their time and age. In Aryara's day they were scarcely human. What must a thousand years of retrogression have done to the breed?

What foul shape stole into the Ketrick castle on some forgotten night, or rose out of the dusk to grip some woman of the line, straying in the hills?

The mind shrinks from such an image. But this I know: there must have been survivals of that foul, reptilian epoch when the Ketricks went into Wales. There still may be. But this changeling, this waif of darkness, this horror who bears the noble name of Ketrick, the brand of the serpent is upon him, and until he is destroyed there is no rest for me. Now that I know him for what he is, he pollutes the clean air and leaves the slime of the snake on the green earth. The sound of his lisping, hissing voice fills me with crawling horror and the sight of his slanted eyes inspires me with madness.

For I come of a royal race, and such as he is a continual insult and a threat, like a serpent underfoot. Mine is a regal race, though now it is become degraded and falls into decay by continual admixture with conquered races. The waves of alien blood have washed my hair black and my skin dark, but I still have the lordly stature and the blue eyes of a royal Aryan.

And as my ancestors—as I, Aryara, destroyed the scum that writhed beneath our heels, so shall I, John O'Donnel, exterminate the reptilian thing, the monster bred of the snaky taint that slumbered so long unguessed in clean Saxon veins, the vestigial serpent-things left to taunt the Sons of Aryan. They say the blow I received affected my mind; I know it but opened my eyes. Mine ancient enemy walks often on the moors alone, attracted, though he may not know it, by ancestral urgings. And on one of these lonely walks I shall meet him, and when I meet him, I will break his foul neck with my hands, as I, Aryara, broke the necks of foul night-things in the long, long ago.

Then they may take me and break my neck at the end of a rope if they will. I am not blind, if my friends are. And in the sight of the old Aryan god, if not in the blinded eyes of men, I will have kept faith with my tribe.

THE GODS OF BAL-SAGOTH

Red welter of war and bloodshed—a vivid weird adventure-tale of the Orkney Islands in the time when Canute the Dane ruled England

STEEL IN THE STORMS

Lightning dazzled the eyes of Turlogh O'Brien, and his foot slipped in a smear of blood as he staggered on the reeling deck. The clashing of steel rivaled the bellowing of the thunder, and screams of death cut through the roar of waves and wind. The incessant lightning flicker gleamed on the corpses sprawling redly, the gigantic horned figures that roared and smote like huge demons of the midnight storm, the great beaked prow looming above.

The play was quick and desperate; in the momentary illumination a ferocious bearded face shone before Turlogh, and his swift axe licked out, splitting it to the chin. In the brief, utter blackness that followed the flash, an unseen stroke swept Turlogh's helmet from his head, and he struck back blindly, feeling his ax sink into flesh, and hearing a man howl. Again the fires of the raging skies sprang, showing the Gael the ring of savage faces, the hedge of gleaming steel that hemmed him in.

Back against the mainmast Turlogh parried and smote; then through the madness of the fray a great voice thundered, and in a flashing instant the Gael caught a glimpse of a giant form—a strangely familiar face. Then the world crashed into fire-shot blackness.

Consciousness returned slowly. Turlogh was first aware of a swying, rocking motion of his whole body which he could not check. Then a dull throbbing in his head racked him, and he sought to raise his hand to it. Then it was he realized he was bound hand and foot—not an altogether new experience. Clearing sight showed him that he was tied to the mast of the dragon ship whose warriors had struck him down. Why they had spared him, he could not understand, because if they knew him at all, they knew him to be an outlaw—an outcast from his clan, who would pay no ransom to save him from the very pits of Hell.

The wind had fallen greatly, but a heavy sea was flowing, which tossed the long ship like a chip from gulf-like trough to foaming crest. A round silver moon, peering through broken clouds, lighted the tossing billows. The Gael, raised on the wild west coast of Ireland, knew that the serpent ship was crippled. He could tell it by the way she labored, plowing deep into the spume, heeling to the lift of the surge. Well, the tempest which had been raging on these southern waters had been enough to damage even such staunch craft as these Vikings built.

The same gale had caught the French vessel on which Turlogh had been a passenger, driving her off course and far southward. Days and nights had been a blind, howling chaos in which the ship had been hurled, flying like a wounded bird before the storm. And in the very rack of the tempest a bearded prow had loomed in the scud above the lower, broader craft, and the grappling irons had sunk in. Surely these Norsemen were wolves and the bloodlust that burned in their hearts was not human. In the terror and roar of the storm they leaped howling to the onslaught, and while the raging heavens hurled their full wrath upon them, and each shock of the frenzied waves threatened to engulf both vessels, these sea-wolves glutted their fury to the utmost—true sons of the sea, whose wildest rages found echo in their own bosoms. It had been a slaughter rather than a fight—the Celt had been the only fighting man aboard the doomed ship—and now he remembered the strange familiarity of the face he had glimpsed just before he was struck down. Who—?

"Good hail, my bold Dalcassian, it's long since we met!"

Turlogh stared at the man who stood before him, feet braced to the lifting of the deck. He was of huge stature, a good half-head taller than Turlogh, who stood well above six feet. His legs were like columns, his arms like oak and iron. His beard was of crisp gold, matching the massive armlets he wore. A shirt of scale-mail added to his warlike appearance as the horned helmet seemed to increase his height. But there was no wrath in the calm gray eyes which gazed tranquilly into the smoldering blue eyes of the Gael.

"Athelstane, the Saxon!"

"Aye—it's been a long day since you gave me this," the giant indicated a thin white scar on his temple. "We seem fated to meet on the nights of fury—we first crossed steel the night you burned Thorfel's skall. Then I fell before your ax, and you saved me from Brogar's Picts—alone of all the folk who followed Thorfel. Tonight it was I who struck you down." He touched the great two-handed sword strapped to his shoulders and Turlogh cursed.

"Nay, revile me not," said Athelstane with a pained expression, "I could have slain you in the press—I struck with the flat, but knowing you Irish have cursed hard skulls, I struck with both hands. You have been senseless for hours. Lodbrog would have slain you with the restof the merchant ship's crew, but I claimed your life. But the Vikings would only agree to spare you on condition that you be bound to the mast. They know you of old."

"Where are we?"

"Ask me not. The storm blew us far out of our course. We were sailing to harry the coasts of Spain. When chance threw us in with your vessel, of course we seized the opportunity, but there was scant spoil. Now we are racing with the sea flow, unknowing. The steer sweep is crippled, and the whole ship lamed. We may be riding the very rim of the world for aught I know. Swear to join us, and I will loose you."

"Swear to join the hosts of Hell!" snarled Turlogh. "Rather I will go down with the ship and sleep for ever under the green waters, bound to this mast. My only regret is that I can not send more sea-wolves to join the hundred-odd I have already sent to Purgatory!"

"Well, well," said Athelstane tolerantly, "A man must eat—here—I will loose your hands at least—now, set your teeth into this joint of meat."

Turlogh bent his head to the great joint and tore at it ravenously. The Saxon watched him for a moment, then turned away. A strange man, reflected Turlogh, this renegade Saxon who hunted with the wolf-pack of the north—a savage warrior in battle, but with fibers of kindliness in his makeup which set him apart from the men with whom he consorted.

The ship reeled on blindly in the night, and Athelstane, returning with a great horn of foaming ale, remarked on the fact that the clouds were gathering again, obscuring the seething face of the sea. He left the Gael's hands unbound but Turlogh was held fast to the mast by cords about legs and body. The rovers paid no heed to their prisoner; they were too much occupied in keeping their crippled ship from going down under their feet.

At last Turlogh believed he could catch at times a deep roaring above the wash of the waves. This grew in volume, and even as the duller-eared Norsemen heard it, the ship leaped like a spurred horse, straining in every timber. As by magic the clouds, lightening for dawn, rolled away on each side, showing a wild waste of tossing gray waters, and a long line of breakers dead ahead. Beyond the frothing madness of the reefs loomed land, apparently an island. The roaring increased to deafening proportions, as the longship, caught in the tide rip, raced headlong to her doom. Turlogh saw Lodbrog rushing about, his long beard flowing in the wind as he brandished his fists and bellowed futile commands. Athelstane came running across the deck.

"Little chance for any of us," he growled as he cut the Gael's bonds, "but you shall have as much as the rest—"

Turlogh sprang free. "Where is my ax?"

"There in that weapon-rack. But Thor's blood, man," marveled the big Saxon, "you won't burden yourself now—"

Turlogh had snatched the ax and confidence flowed like wine through his veins at the familiar feel of the slim, graceful shaft. His ax was as much a part of him as his right hand; if he must die he wished to die with it in his grip. He hastily slung it to his girdle. All armor had been stripped from him when he had been captured.

"There are sharks in these waters," said Athelstane, preparing to doff his scale-mail. "If we have to swim—"

The ship struck with a crash that snapped her masts and shivered her prow like glass. Her dragon beak shot high in the air and men tumbled like tenpins from her slanted deck. A moment she poised, shuddering like a living thing, then slid from the hidden reef and went down in a blinding smother of spray.

Turlogh had left the deck in a long dive that carried him clear. Now he rose in the turmoil, fought the waves for a mad moment, then caught a piece of wreckage that the breakers flung up. As he clambered across this, a shape bumped against him and went down again. Turlogh plunged his arm deep, caught a sword-belt and heaved the man up and on his makeshift rasft. For in that instant he had recognized the Saxon, Athelstane, still burdened with the armor he had not had time to remove. The man seemed dazed. He lay limp, limbs trailing.

Turlogh remembered that ride through the breakers as a chaotic nightmare. The tide tore them through, plunging their frail craft into the depths, then flinging them into the skies. There was naught to do but hold on and trust to luck. And Turlogh held on, gripping the Saxon with one hand and their raft with the other, while it seemed his fingers would crack with the strain. Again and again they were almost swamped; then by some miracle they were through, riding in water comparatively calm and Turlogh saw a lean fin cutting the surface a yard away. It swirled in, and Turlogh unslung his ax and struck. Red dyed the waters instantly and a rush of sinuous shapes made the craft rock. While the sharks tore their brother, Turlogh, paddling with his hands, urged the rude raft ashore until he could feel the bottom. He waded to the beach, half carrying the Saxon; then, iron though he was, Turlogh O'Brien sank down, exhausted and soon slept soundly.

GODS FROM THE ABYSS

Turlogh did not sleep long. When he awoke the sun was just risen above the sea-rim. The Gael rose, feeling as refreshed as if he had slept the whole night through, and looked about him. The broad white beach sloped gently from the water to a waving expanse of gigantic trees. There seemed no underbrush, but so close together were the huge boles, his sight could not pierce into the jungle. Athelstane was standing some distance away on a spit of sand that ran out into the sea. The huge Saxon leaned on his great sword and gazed out toward the reefs.

Here and there on the beach lay the stiff figures that had been washed ashore. A sudden snarl of satisfaction broke from Turlogh's lips. Here at his very feet was a gift from the gods; a dead Viking lay there, fully armed in the helmet and mail shirt he had not had time to doff when the ship foundered, and Turlogh saw they were his own. Even the round light buckler strapped to the Norseman's back was his. Turlogh did not pause to wonder how all his accoutrements had come into the possession of one man, but stripped the dead and donned the plain round helmet and shirt of black chain mail. Thus armed he went up the beach toward Athelstane, his eyes gleaming unpleasantly.

The Saxon turned as he approached. "Hail to you, Gael," he greeted, "We be all of Lodbrog's ship-people left alive. The hungry green sea drank them all. By Thor, I owe my life to you! What with the weight of my mail, and the crack my skull got on the rail, I had most certainly been food for the sharks but for you. It all seems like a dream now."

"You saved my life," snarled Turlogh, "I saved yours. Now the debt is paid, the accounts are squared, so up with your sword and let us make an end."

Athelstane stared. "You wish to fight me? Why—what—?"

"I hate your breed as I hate Satan!" roared the Gail, a tinge of madness in his blazing eyes, "Your wolves have ravaged my people for five hundred years! The smoking ruins of the South-land, the seas of spilled blood call for vengeance! The screams of a thousand ravished girls are ringing in my ears, night and day! Would that the north had but a single breast for my ax to cleave!"

"But I am no Norseman," rumbled the giant in worriment.

"The more shame to you, renegade," raved the maddened Gael, "Defend yourself lest I cut you down in cold blood!"

"This is not to my liking," protested Athelstane, lifting his mighty blade, his gray eyes serious but unafraid, "Men speak truly who say there is madness in you."

Words ceased as the men prepared to go into deadly action. The Gael approached his foe, crouching panther-like, eyes ablaze. The Saxon waited the onslaught, feet braced wide apart, sword held high in both hands. It was Turlogh's ax and shield against Athelstane's two-handed sword; in a contest one stroke might end either way. Like two great jungle beasts they played their deadly, wary game, then—

Even as Turlogh's muscles tensed for the death-leap, a fearful sound split the silence! Both men started and recoiled. From the depths of the forest behind them rose a ghastly and inhuman scream. Shrill, yet of great volume, it rose higher and higher until it ceased at the highest pitch, like the triumph of a demon, like the cry of some grisly ogre gloating over its human prey.

"Thor's blood!" gasped the Saxon, letting his sword-point fall, "What was that?"

Turlogh shook his head. Even his iron nerve was slightly shaken. "Some fiend of the forest. This is a strange land in a strange sea. Mayhap Satan himself reigns here, and it is the gate to Hell."

Athelstane looked uncertain. He was more pagan than Christian and his devils were heathen devil, but they were none the less grim for that.

"Well," said he, "let us drop our quarrel until we see what it may be. Two blades are better than one, whether for man or devil—"

A wild shriek cut him short. This time it was a human voice, blood-chilling in its horror and despair. Simultaneously came the swift patter of feet and the lumbering rush of some heavy body among the trees. The warriors wheeled toward the sound, and out of the deep shadows a half-naked woman came flying like a white leaf blown on the wind. Her loose hair streamed like a flame of gold behind her, her white limbs flashed in the morning sun, her eyes blazed with frenzied terror. And behind her—

Even Turlogh's hair stood up. The thing that pursued the fleeing girl was neither man nor beast. In form it was like a bird, but such a bird as the rest of the world had not seen for many an age. Some twelve feet high it towered, and its evil head with the wicked red eyes and cruel curved beak was as big as a horse's head. The long arched neck was thicker than a man's thigh, and the huge taloned feet could have gripped the fleeing woman as an eagle grips a sparrow.

This much Turlogh saw in one glance as he sprang between the monster and its prey, who sank down with a cry on the beach. It loomed above him like a mountain of death and the evil beak darted down, denting the shield he raised and staggering him with the impact. At the same instant he struck, but the keen ax sank harmlessly into a cushioning mass of spiky feathers. Again the beak flashed at him, and his sidelong leap saved his life by a hair's breadth. And then Athelstane ran in, and bracing his feet wide, swung his great sword with both hands and all his strength. The mighty blade sheared through one of the tree-like legs below the knee, and with an abhorrent screech, the monster sank on its side, flapping its short heavy wings wildly. Turlogh drove the back-spike of his ax between the glaring red eyes, and the gigantic bird kicked convulsively and lay still.

"Thor's blood!" Athelstane's gray eyes were blazing with battle lust, "Truly we've come to the rim of the world—"

"Watch the forest lest another come forth," snapped Turlogh, turning to the woman who had scrambled to her feet and stood panting, eyes wide with wonder. She was a splendid young animal, tall, clean-limbed, slim and shapely. Her only garment was a sheer bit of silk hung carelessly about her hips. But though the scantiness of her dress suggested the savage, her skin was snowy white, her loose hair of purest gold, and her eyes gray. Now she spoke hastily, stammeringly, in the tongue of the Norse, as if she had not so spoken in years.

"You—who are you men? Whence come you? What do you on the Isle of the Gods?"

"Thor's blood!" rumbled the Saxon; "she's of our own kind!"

"Not mine!" snapped Turlogh, unable even in that moment to forget his hate for the people of the north.

The girl looked curiously at the two. "The world must have changed greatly since I left it," said she, evidently in full control of herself once more, "else how is it that wolf and wild bull hunt together? By your black hair, you are a Gael, and you, big man, have a slur in your speech that can be naught but Saxon."

"We are outcasts," answered Turlogh, "You see these dead men lining the strand? They were the crew of the dragon ship which bore us here, storm-driven. This man, Athelstane, once of Wessex, was a swordsman on that ship, and I was a captive. I am

Turlogh Dubh, once a chief of Clan O'Brien. Who are you and what land is this?"

"This is the oldest land in the world," answered the girl, "Rome, Egypt, Cathay are as but infants beside it. I am Brunhild, daughter of Rane Thorfin's son, of the Orkneys, and until a few days ago, queen of this ancient kingdom."

Turlogh looked uncertainly at Athelstane. This sounded like sorcery.

"After what we have just seen," rumbled the giant, "I am ready to believe anything. But are you in truth Rane Thorfin's son's stolen child?"

"Aye!" cried the girl, "I am that one! I was stolen when Tostig the Mad raided the Orkneys and burned Rane's steading in the absence of its master—"

"And then Tostig vanished form the face of the earth—or sea!" interrupted Athelstane, "He was in truth a madman. I sailed with him for a ship-harrying many years ago when I was but a youth."

"And his madness cast me on this island," answered Brunhild; "for after he had harried the shores of England, the fire in his brain drove him out into unknown seas—south, and south, and ever south until even the fierce wolves he led murmured. Then a storm drove us on yonder reef, though at another part, rending the dragon ship even as yours was wrent last night. Tostig and all his strong men perished of wreckage and a whim of the gods cast me ashore, half dead. I was fifteen years old. That was ten years ago.

"I found a strange terrible people dwelling here, a brown-skinned folk who knew many dark secrets of magic. They found me lying senseless on the beach and because I was the first white human they had ever seen, their priests divined that I was a goddess given them by the sea, whom they worship. So they put me in the temple with the rest of their curious gods and did reverence to me. And their high-priest, old Gothan—cursed be his name!—taught me many strange and fearful things. Soon I learned their language and much of their priests' inner mysteries. And as I grew into full womanhood, the desire for power stirred in me; for the people of the north are made to rule the folk of the world, and it is not for the daughter of a sea king to sit meekly in a temple and accept the offerings of fruit, and flowers, and human sacrifices!"

She stopped for a moment, eyes blazing. Truly, she looked a worthy daughter of the fierce race she claimed.

"Well," she continued, "there was one who loved me—Kotar, a young chief. With him I plotted and at last I rose and flung off the yoke of old Gothan. That was a wild season of plot and counterplot, intrigue, and rebellion and red carnage! Men and women died like flies and the streets of Bal-Sagoth ran red—but in the end we triumphed, Kotar and I! The dynasty of Angar came to an end on a night of blood and fury, and I reigned supreme on the Isle of the Gods, queen and goddess!"

She had drawn herself up to her full height, her beautiful face alight with fierce pride, her bosom heaving. Turlogh was at once fascinated and repelled. He had seen rulers rise and fall, and between the lines of her brief narrative he read the bloodshed and carnage, the cruelty and the treachery—sensing the basic ruthlessness of this girl-woman.

"But if you were queen," he asked, "how is it that we find you hunted through the forests of your domain by this monster, like a runaway serving wench?"

Brunhild bit her lip and an angry flush mounted her to her cheeks. "What is it that brings down every woman, whatever her station? I trusted a man—Kotar, my lover, with whom I shared my rule. He betrayed me; after I had raised him to the highest power in the kingdom, next to my own, I found he secretly made love to another girl. I killed them both!"

Turlogh smiled coldly: "You are a true Brunhild! And then what?"

"Kotar was loved by the people. Old Gothan stirred them up. I made my greatest mistake when I let that old one live. Yet I dared not slay him. Well, Gothan rose against me, as I had risen against him, and the warriors rebelled, slaying those who stood faithful to me. Me they took captive but dared not kill; for after all, I was a goddess, they believed. So before dawn, fearing the people would change their minds again and restore me to power, Gothan had me taken to the lagoon which separates this part of the island from the other. The priests rowed me across the lagoon and left me, naked and helpless, to my fate."

"And that fate was—this?" Athelstane touched the huge carcass with his foot.

Brunhild shuddered. "Many ages ago there were many of these monsters on the isle, the legends say. They warred on the people of Bal-Sagoth and devoured them by hundreds. But at last all were extermninated on the main part of the isle and on this side of the lagoon all died but this one, who has abided here for centuries. In the old times hosts of men came against him, but he was the greatest of the devil-birds, and he slew all who fought him. So the priests made a god of him and left this part of the island to him. None comes here except those brought as sacrifices—as I was. He could not cross to the main island, because the lagoon swarms with great sharks which would rend even him to pieces.

"For a while I eluded him, stealing among the trees, but at last he spied me out—and you know the rest. I owe my life to you. Now what will you do with me?"

Athelstane looked at Turlogh and Turlogh shrugged. "What can we do, save starve in this forest?"

"I will tell you!" the girl cried in a ringing voice, her eyes blazing anew to the swift working of her keen brain. "There is an old legend among this people—that men of iron will come out of the sea, and the city of Bal-Sagoth will fall! You, with your mail and helmets, will seem as iron men to thcse folk who know nothing of armor! You have slain Groth-golka the bird-god—you have come out of the sea as did I—the people will look on you as gods. Come with me and aid me to win back my kingdom! You shall be my right-hand men, and I will heap honors upon you! Fine garments, gorgeous palaces, fairest girls shall be yours!"

Her promises slid from Turlogh's mind without leaving an imprint, but the mad splendor of the proposal intrigued him. Strongly he desired to look on this strange city of which Brunhild spoke, and the thought of two warriors and one girl pitted against a whole nation for a crown stirred the utmost depths of his knight-errant Celtic soul.

"It is well," said he. "And what of you, Athelstane?"

"My belly is empty," growled the giant. "Lead me to where there is food, and I'll hew my way to it, through a horde of priests and warriors."

"Lead us to the city!" said Turlogh to Brunhild.

"Hail!" she cried flinging her white arms high in wild exultation. "Now let Gothan and Ska, and Gelka tremble! With ye at my side I'll win back the crown they tore from me, and this time I'll not spare my enemy! I'll hurl old Gothan form the highest battlement, though the bellowing of his demons shake the very bowels of the earth! And we shall see if the god Gol-goroth shall stand against the sword that cut Groth-golka's leg from under him. Now hew the head from this carcass that the people may know you have overcome the bird-god, and follow me, for the sun mounts the sky, and I would sleep in my own palace tonight!"

The three passed into the shadows of the mighty forest. The interlocking branches, hundreds of feet above their heads, made dim and strange such sunlight as filtered through. No life was seen except for an occasional gayly hued bird or a huge ape. These beasts, Brunhild said, were survivors of another age, harmless except when attacked. Presently the growth changed somewhat, the trees thinned and became smaller and fruit of many kinds was seen among the branches. Brunhild told the warriors which to pluck and eat as they walked along. Turlogh was quite satisfied with the fruit, but Athelstane, though he ate enormously, did so with scant relish. Fruit was light sustenance to a man used to such solid stuff as formed his regular diet. Even among the gluttonous Danes the Saxon's capacity for beef and ale was admired.

"Look!" cried Brunhild sharply, halting and pointing. "The spires of Bal-Sagoth!"

Through the trees the warriors caught a glimmer, white and shimmery, and apparently far away. There was an illusory impression of towering battlements, high in the air, with fleecy clouds hovering about them. The sight woke strange dreams in the mystic deeps of the Gael's soul, and even Athelstane was silent as if he too were struck by the pagan beauty and mystery of the scene.

So they progressed through the forest, now losing sight of the defiant city as tree tops obstructed the view, now seeing it again. And at last they came out on the low shelving banks of a broad blue lagoon and the full beauty of the landscape burst upon their eyes. From the opposite shores the country sloped upward in long gentle undulations which broke like great slow waves a few miles away. These wide swells were covered with deep grass and many groves of trees, while miles away on either hand there was seen, curving away into the distance, the strip of thick forest which Brunhild said belted the white island. And among those blue dreaming hills brooded the age-old city of Bal-Sagoth, its white walls and sapphire towers clean-cut against the morning sky. The suggestion of great distance had been an illusion.

"Is this not a kingdom worth fighting for?" cried Brunhild, her voice vibrant. "Swift now—let us bind this dry wood together for a raft. We could not live an instant swimming in that shark-haunted water."

At that instant a figure leaped up from the tall grass on the other shore—a naked, brown-skinned man who stared for a moment, agape. Then as Athelstane shouted and held up the grim head of Groth-golka, the fellow gave a startled cry and raced away like an antelope.

"A slave Gothan left to see if I tried to swim the lagoon," said Brunhild with angry satisfaction. "Let him run to the city and tell them—but let us make haste and cross the lagoon before Gothan can arrive and dispute our passage."

Turlogh and Athelstane were already busy. A number of dead trees lay about, and these they stripped of their branches and bound together with long vines. In a short time they had built a raft, crude and clumsy, but capable of bearing them across the lagoon. Brunhild gave a frank sigh of relief when they stepped on the other shore.

"Let us go straight up to the city," said she. "The slave has reached it ere now, and they will be watching us from the walls. A bold course is our only one. Thor's hammer, but I'd like to see Gothan's face when the slave tells him Brunhild is returning with two strange warriors and the head of him to whom she was given as sacrifice!"

"Why did you not kill Gothan when you had the power?" asked Athelstane.

She shook her head, her eyes clouding with something akin to fear: "Easier said than done. Half the people hate Gothan, half love him, and all fear him. The most ancient men of the city say that he was old when they were babes. The people believe him to be more god than priest, and I myself have seen him do terrible and mysterious things, beyond the power of common man.

"Nay, when I was but a puppet in his hands, I came only to the outer fringe of his mysteries, yet I have looked on sights that froze my blood. I have seen strange shadows flit along black subterranean corridors in the dead of night. I have heard unhallowed sounds and have felt the presence of hideous beings. And once I heard the grisly slavering bellowings of the nameless thing Gothan has chained deep in the bowels of the hills on which rests the city of Bal-Sagoth."

Brunhild shuddered.

"There are many gods in Bal-Sagoth, but the greatest of them is Gol-goroth, the god of darkness who sits forever in the Temple of Shadows. When I overthrew the power of Gothan, I forbade men to worship Gol-goroth, and made the priests hail, as the one true diety, A-ala the daughter of the sea—myself. I had strong men take heavy hammers and smite the image of Gol-goroth, but their blows only shattered the hammers and gave strange hurts to the men who wielded them. Gol-goroth was indestructible and showed no mar. So I desisted and shut the doors of the Temple of Shadows, which were opened only when I was overthrown and Gothan, who had been skulking in the secret places of the city, came again into his own. Then Gol-goroth reigned again in his full terror, and the idols of A-ala were overthrown in the Temple of the Sea, and the priests of A-ala died howling on the red-stained altar before the black god. But now we shall see!"

"Surely you are a very Valkyrie," muttered Athelstane. "But three against a nation is great odds—especially such a people as this, who must assuredly be all witches and sorcerers."

"Bah!" cried Brunhild contemptuously. "There are many sorcerers, it is true, but though the people are strange to us, they are mere fools in their own way, as are all nations. When Gothan led me captive down the streets they spat on me. Now watch them turn on Ska, the new king Gothan has given them, when it seems my star rises again! But now we approach the city gates— be bold but wary!"

They had ascended the long swelling slopes and were not far from the walls which rose immensely upward. Surely, thought Turlogh, heathen gods built this city. The walls seemed of marble and with their fretted battlements and slim watchtowers, dwarfed the memory of such cities as Rome, Damascus, and

Byzantium. A broad, white, winding road led up from the lower levels to the plateau before the gates and as they came up this road, the three adventurers felt hundreds of hidden eyes fixed upon them with fierce intensity. The walls seemed deserted; it might have been a dead city. But the impact of those staring eyes was felt.

Now they stood before the massive gates, which to the amazed eyes of the warriors seemed to be of chased silver.

"Here is an emperor's ransom!" muttered Athelstane, eyes ablaze. "Thor's blood, if we had but a stout band of reavers and a ship to carry away the plunder!"

"Smite on the gate and then step back, lest something fall upon you," said Brunhild, and the thunder of Turlogh's ax on the portals woke the echoes in the sleeping hills.

The three then fell back a few paces, and suddenly the mighty gates swung inward, and a strange concourse of people stood revealed. The two white warriors looked on a pageant of barbaric grandeur. A throng of tall, slim, brown-skinned men stood in the gates. Their only garments were loincloths of silk, the fine work of which contrasted strangely with the near nudity of the wearers. Tall, waving plumes of many colors decked their heads, and armlets and leglets of gold and silver, crusted with gleaming gems, completed their ornamentation. Armor they wore none, but each carried a light shield on his left arm, made of hard wood, highly polished, and braced with silver. Their weapons were slim-bladed spears, light hatchets, and slender daggers, all bladed with fine steel. Evidently these warriors depended more on speed and skill than on brute force.

At the front of this band stood three men who instantly commanded attention. One was a lean, hawk-faced warrior, almost as tall as Athelstane, who wore about his neck a great golden chain from which was suspended a curious symbol in jade. One of the other men was young, evil-eyed; an impressive riot of colors in the mantle of parrot feathers which swung from his shoulders. The third man had nothing to set him apart from the rest save his own strange personality. He wore no mantle, bore no weapons. His only garment was a plain loincloth. He was very old; he alone of all the throng was bearded, and his beard was as white as the long hair which fell about his shoulders. He was very tall, and very lean, and his great dark eyes blazed as from a hidden fire. Turlogh knew without being told that this man was Gothan, priest of the Black God. The ancient exuded a very aura of age and mystery. His great eyes were like windows of some forgotten temple, behind which passed like ghosts his dark and terrible thoughts. Turlogh sensed that Gothan had delved too deep in forbidden secrets to remain altogether human. He had passed through doors that had cut him off from the dreams, desires, and emotions of ordinary mortals. Looking into those unwinking orbs Turlogh felt his skin crawl, as if he had looked into the eyes of a great serpent.

Now a glance upward showed that the walls were thronged with silent, dark-eyed folk. The stage was set; all was in readiness for the swift, red drama. Turlogh felt his pulse quicken with fierce exhilaration, and Athelstane's eyes began to glow with ferocious light.

Brunhild stepped forward boldly, head high, her splendid figure vibrant. The white warriors naturally could not understand what passed between her and the others, except as they read from gestures and expressions, but later Brunhild narrated the conversation almost word for word.

"Well, people of Bal-Sagoth," said she, spacing her words slowly, "what words have you for your goddess whom you mocked and reviled?"

"What will you have, false one?" exclaimed the tall man, Ska, the king set up by Gothan; "you who mocked at the customs of our ancestors, defied the laws of Bal-Sagoth, which are older than the world, murdered your lover, and defiled the shrine of Gol-goroth? You were doomed by law, king, and god, and placed in the grim forest beyond the lagoon—"

"And I, who am likewise a goddess and greater than any god," answered Brunhild mockingly, "am returned from the realm of horror with the head of Groth-golka!"

At a word from her, Athelstane held up the great beaked head, and a low whispering ran about the battlements, tense with a fear and bewilderment.

"Who are these men?" Ska bent a worried frown on the two warriors.

"They are iron men who have come out of the sea!" answered Brunhild in a clear voice that carried far; "the beings who have come in response to the old prophecy, to overthrow the city of Bal-Sagoth, whose people are traitors and whose priests are false!"

At these words the fearful murmur broke out afresh all up and down the line of the walls, till Gothan lifted his vulture-head, and the people fell silent and shrank before the icy state of his terrible eyes.

Ska glared bewilderedly, his ambition struggling with his superstitious fears.

Turlogh, looking closely at Gothan, believed that he read beneath the inscrutable mask of the old priest's face. For all his inhuman wisdom, Gothan had his limitations. This sudden return of one he thought well disposed of, and the appearance of the white-skinned giants accompanying her, had caught Gothan off his guard, Turlogh believed, rightly. There had been no time to properly prepare for their reception. The people had already begun to murmur in the streets against the severity of Ska's brief rule. They had always believed in Brunhild's divinity; now that she returned with two tall men of her own hue, bearing the grim trophy that marked the conquest of another of their gods, the people were wavering. Any small thing might turn the tide either way.

"People of Bal-Sagoth!" shouted Brunhild suddenly, springing back and flinging her arm high, gazing full into the faces that looked down at her. "I bid you avert your doom before it is too late! You cast me out and spat on me; you turned to darker gods than I! Yet all this will I forgive if you return and do obeisance to me! Once you reviled me—you called me bloody and cruel! True, I was a hard mistress—but has Ska been an easy master? You said I lashed the people with whips of rawhide—has Ska stroked you with parrot feathers?

"A virgin died on my altar at the full tide of each moon—but youths and maidens die at the waxing and the waning, the rising and the setting of each moon, before Gol-goroth, on whose altar a fresh human heart forever throbs! Ska is but a shadow! Your real lord is Gothan who sits above the city like a vulture! Once you were a mighty people; your galleys filled the seas. Now you are a remnant, and that is dwindling fast! Fools! You will all die on the altar of Gol-goroth before Gothan is done, and he will walk alone among the silent ruins of Bal-Sogoth!

"Look at him!" Her voice rose to a scream as she lashed herself to an inspired frenzy, and even Turlogh, to whom the words were meaningless, shivered. "Look at him where he stands there like an evil spirit out of the past! He is not even human! I tell you, he is a foul ghost, whose beard is dabbled with the blood of a million butcheries—an incarnate fiend out of the mist of the ages come to destroy the people of Bal-Sagoth!

"Choose now! Rise up against that ancient devil and his blasphemous gods, receive your rightful queen and deity again, and you shall regain some of your former greatness. Refuse, and the ancient prophecy shall be fulfilled, and the sun will set on the silent and crumbled ruins of Bal-Sagoth!"

Fired by dynamic words, a young warrior with the insignia of a chief sprang to the parapet and shouted: "Hail to A-ala! Down with the bloody gods!"

Among the multitude many took up the shout and steel clashed as a score of fights started. The crowd on the battlements and in the streets surged and eddied, while Ska glared, bewildered. Brunhild, forcing back her companions who quivered with eagerness for action of some kind, shouted: "Hold! Let no man strike a blow yet! People of Bal-Sagoth, it has been a tradition since the beginning of time that a king must fight for his crown! Let Ska cross steel with one of these warriors! If Ska wins, I will kneel before him and let him strike off my head! If Ska loses, then you shall accept me as your rightful queen and goddess!"

A great roar of approval went up from the walls as the people ceased their brawls, glad enough to shift the responsibility to their rulers.

"Will you fight, Ska?" asked Brunhild, turning to the king mockingly. "Or will you give me your head without further argument?"

"Slut!" howled Ska, driven to madness, "I will take the skulls of these fools for drinking-cups, and then I will rend you between two bent trees!"

Gothan laid a hand on his arm and whispered in his ear, but Ska had reached the point where he was deaf to all but his fury. His achieved ambition, he had found, had faded to the mere part of a puppet dancing on Gothan's string; now even the hollow bauble of his kingship was slipping from him and this wench mocked him to his face before his people. Ska went, to all practical effects, stark mad.

Brunhild turned to her two allies. "One of you must fight Ska."

"Let me be the one!" urged Turlogh, eyes dancing with eager battle lust. "He has the look of a man quick as a wildcat, and Athelstane, while a very bull for strength, is a thought slow for such work—"

"Slow!" broke in Athelstane reproachfully, "Why Turlogh, for a man my weight—"

"Enough," Brunhild interrupted. "He must choose for himself."

She spoke to Ska, who glared red-eyed for an instant, then indicated Athelstane, who grinned joyfully, cast aside the bird's head, and unslung his sword. Turlogh swore and stepped back. The king had decided that he would have a better chance against this huge buffalo of a man who looked slow, than against the black-haired warrior, whose cat-like quickness was evident.

"This Ska is without armor," rumbled the Saxon. "Let me likewise doff my mail and helmet so that we fight on equal terms—"

"No!" cried Brunhild. "Your armor is your only chance! I tell you, this false king fights like the play of summer lightning! You will be hard put to hold your own as it is. Keep on your armor, I say!"

"Well, well," grumbled Athelstane, "I will—I will. Though I say it is scarcely fair. But let him come on and make an end of it."

The huge Saxon strode ponderously toward his foe, who warily crouched and circled away. Athelstane held his great sword in both hands before him pointed upward, the hilt somewhat below the level of his chin, in position to strike a blow to right or left, or parry a sudden attack.

Ska had flung away his light shield, his fighting-sense telling him that it would be useless before the stroke of that heavy blade. In his right hand he held his slim spear as a man holds a throwing-dart; in his left a light, keen-edged hatchet. He meant to make a fast, shifty fight of it, and his tactics were good. But Ska, having never encountered armor before, made his fatal mistake in supposing it to be apparel or ornament through which his weapons would pierce.

Now he sprang in, thrusting Athelstane's face with his spear. The Saxon parried with ease and instantly cut tremendously at Ska's legs. The king bounded high, clearing the whistling blade, and in midair he hacked down at Athelstane's bent head. The light hatchet shivered to bits on the Viking's helmet and Ska sprang back out of reach with a bloodlusting howl.

And now it was Athelstane who rushed with unexpected quickness, like a charging bull, and before that terrible onslaught Ska, bewildered by the breaking of his hatchet, was caught off his guard—flat-footed. He caught a fleeting glimpse of the giant looming over him like an overwhelming wave and he sprang in, instead of out, stabbing ferociously. That mistake was his last. The thrusting spear glanced harmlessly from the Saxon's mail, and in that instant the great sword sang down in a stroke the king could not evade. The force of that stroke tossed him as a man is tossed by a plunging bull. A dozen feer away fell Ska, king of Bal-Sagoth, to lie shattered and dead in a ghastly welter of blood and entrails. The throng gaped, struck silent by the prowess of that deed.

"Hew off his head!" cried Brunhild her eyes flaming as she clenched her hands so that the nails hit into the palms. "Impale that carrion's head on your sword-point so that we may carry it through the city gates with us as token of victory!"

But Athelstane shook his head, cleansing his blade: "Nay, he was a brave man and I will not mutilate his corpse. It is no great feat I have done, for he was naked and I full-armed. Else it is in my mind, the brawl had gone differently."

Turlogh glanced at the people on the walls. They had recovered from their astonishment and now a vast roar went up: "A-ala! Hail to the true goddess!" And the warriors in the gateway dropped to their knees and bowed their foreheads in the dust before Brunhild, who stood proudly erect, bosom heaving with fierce triumph. Truly, thought Turlogh, she is more than a queen —she is a shield woman, a Valkyrie, as Athelstane said.

Now she stepped aside and, tearing the golden chain with its jade symbol from the dead neck of Ska, held it on high and shouted: "People of Bal-Sagoth, you have seen how your false king died before this golden-bearded giant who, being of iron, shows no single cut! Choose now—do you receive me of your own free will?"

"Aye, we do!" the multitude answered in a great shout. "Return to your people, oh mighty and all-powerful queen!"

Brunhild smiled sardonically. "Come," said she to the warriors; "they are lashing themselves into a very frenzy of love and loyalty, having already forgotten their treachery. The memory of the mob is short!"

Aye, thought Turlogh, as at Brunhild's side he and the Saxon passed through the mighty gates between files of prostrate chieftains; aye, the memory of the mob is very short. But a few days have passed since they were yelling as wildly for Ska the liberator —scant hours had passed since Ska sat enthroned, master of life and death, and the people bowed before his feet. Now—Turlogh glanced at the mangled corpse which lay deserted and forgotten before the silver gates. The shadow of a circling vulture fell across it. The clamor of the multitude filled Turlogh's ears and he smiled a bitter smile.

The great gates closed behind the three adventurers, and Turlogh saw a broad white street stretching away in front of him. Other lesser streets radiated from this one. The two warriors caught a jumbled and chaotic impression of great, white stone buildings shouldering each other; of sky-lifting towers and broad, stair-fronted palaces. Turlogh knew there must be an ordered system by which the city was laid out, but to him all seemed a waste of stone, and metal, and polished wood, without time or reason. His baffled eyes sought the street again.

Far up the street extended a mass of humanity, from which rose a rhythmic thunder of sound. Thousands of naked, gayly plumed men and women knelt there, bending forward to touch the marble flags with their foreheads, then swaying back with an upward flinging of their arms, all moving in perfect unison like the bending and rising of tall grass before the wind. And in time to their bowing they lifted a monotoned chant that sank and swelled in a frenzy of ecstasy. So her wayward people welcomed back the goddess A-ala.

Just within the gates Brunhild stopped and there came to her the young chief who had first raised the shout of revolt upon the walls. He knelt and kissed her bare feet, saying: "Oh great queen and goddess, thou knowest Zomar was ever faithful to thee!

Thou knowest how I fought for thee and barely escaped the altar of Gol-goroth for thy sake!"

"Thou hast indeed been faithful, Zomar," answered Brunhild in the stilted language required for such occasions, "nor shall thy fidelity go unrewarded. Henceforth thou art commander of my own bodyguard." Then in a lower voice she added: "Gather a band from your own retainers and from those who have espoused my cause all along, and bring them to the palace. I do not trust the people any more than I have to!"

Suddenly Athelstane, not understanding the conversation, broke in: "Where is the old one with the beard?"

Turlogh stared and glanced around. He had almost forgotten the wizard. He had not seen him go—yet he was gone! Brunhild laughed ruefully.

"He's stolen away to breed more trouble in the shadows. He and Gelka vanished when Ska fell. He has secret ways of coming and going and none may stay him. Forget him for the time being; heed ye well—we shall have plenty of him anon!"

Now the chiefs brought a finely carved and highly ornamented palanquin carried by two strong slaves, and Brunhild stepped into this, saying to her companions: "They are fearful of touching you, but ask if you would be carried. I think it better that you walk, one on each side of me."

"Thor's blood!" rumbled Athelstane, shouldering the huge sword he had never sheathed. "I'm no infant! I'll split the skull of the man who seeks to carry me!"

And so up the long white street went Brunhild, daughter of Rane Thorfin's son in the Orkneys, goddess of the sea, queen of age-old Bal-Sagoth. Borne by two great slaves she went, with a white giant striding on each side with bared steel, and a concourse of chiefs following, while the multitude gave way to right and left, leaving a wide lane down which she passed. Golden trumpets sounded a fanfare of triumph, drums thundered, chants of worship echoed to the ringing skies. Surely in this riot of glory, this barbaric pageant of splendor, the proud soul of the North-born girl drank deep and grew drunken with imperial pride.

Athelstane's eyes glowed with simple delight at this flame of pagan magnificence, but to the black-haired fighting-man of the West, it seemed that even in the loudest clamor of triumph, the trumpet, the drum, and the shouting faded away into the forgotten dust and silence of eternity. Kingdoms and empires pass away like mist from the sea, thought Turlogh; the people shout and triumph and even in the revelry of Belshazzar's feast, the Medes break the gates of Babylon. Even now the shadow of doom is over this city, and the slow tides of oblivion lap the feet of this unheeding race. So in a strange mood Turlogh O'Brien strode beside the palanquin, and it seemed to him that he and Athelstane walked in a dead city, through throngs of dim ghosts, cheering a ghost queen.

THE FALL OF THE GODS

Night had fallen on the ancient city of Bal-Sagoth. Turlogh, Athelstane, and Brunhild sat alone in a room of the inner palace. The queen half reclined on a silken couch, while the men sat on mahogany chairs, engaged in the viands that slave girls had served them on golden dishes. The walls of this room, as of all the palace, were of marble, with golden scrollwork. The ceiling was of lapis lazuli and the floor of silver-inlaid marble tiles. Heavy velvet hangings decorated the walls, and silken cushions, richly made divans, and mahogany chairs and tables littered the room in careless profusion.

"I would give much for a horn of ale, but this wine is not sour to the palate," said Athelstane, emptying a golden flagon with relish. "Brunhild, you have deceived us. You let us understand it would take hard fighting to win back your crown—yet I have struck but one blow, and my sword is thirsty as Turlogh's ax which has not drunk at all. We hammered on the gates, and the people fell down and worshipped with no more ado. And until a little while ago, we but stood by your throne in the great palace room, while you spoke to the throngs that came and knocked their heads on the floor before you—by Thor, never have I heard such chattering and jabbering! My ears ring till now—what were they saying? And where is that old conjurer Gothan?"

"Your steel will drink deep yet, Saxon," answered the girl grimly, resting her chin on her hands and eyeing the warriors with deep moody eyes. "Had you gambled with cities and crowns as I have done, you would know that seizing a throne may be easier than keeping it. Our sudden appearance with the bird-god's head, your killing of Ska, swept the people off their feet. As for the rest—I held audience in the palace as you saw, even if you did not understand, and the people who came in bowing droves were assuring me of their unswerving loyalty—ha! I graciously pardoned them all, but I am no fool. When they have time to think, they will begin to grumble again. Gothan is lurking in the shadows somewhere, plotting evil to us all, you may be sure. This city is honeycombed with secret corridors and subterranean passages of which only the priests know. Even I, who have traversed some of them when I was Gothan's puppet, know not where to look for the secret doors, since Gothan always led me through them blindfolded.

"Just now, I think I hold the upper hand. The people look on you with more awe than they regard me. They think your armor and helmets are part of your bodies, and that you are invulnerable. Did you not note them timidly touching your mail as we passed through the crowd, and the amazement on their faces as they felt the iron of it?"

"For a people so wise in some ways, they are very foolish in others," said Turlogh. "Who are they and whence came they?"

"They are so old," answered Brunhild, "that their most ancient legends give no hint of their origin. Ages ago they were a part of a great empire which spread out over the many isles of this sea. But some of the islands sank and vanished with their cities and people. Then the red-skinned savages assailed them and isle after isle fell before them. At last only this island was left unconquered, and the people have become weaker and forgotten many ancient arts. For lack of posts to sail to, the galleys rotted by the wharves which themselves crumbled into decay. Not in the memory of man has any son of Bal-Sagoth sailed the seas. At irregular intervals the red people descend upon the Isle of the Gods, traversing the seas in their long war canoes which bear grinning skulls on the prows. Not far away as a Viking would reckon a sea voyage, but out of sight over the sea rim lie the islands inhabited by these red men who centuries ago slaughtered the folk who dwelt there. We have always beaten them off; they cannot scale the walls, but still they come, and the fear of their raid is always hovering over the isle.

"But it is not them I fear; it is Gothan, who is at this moment either slipping like a loathly serpent through his black tunnels or else brewing abominations in one of his hidden chambers. In the caves, deep in the hills to which his tunnels lead, he works fearful and unholy magic. His subjects are beasts— serpents, spiders, and great apes; and men—red captives and wretches of his own race. Deep in his grisly caverns he makes beasts of men and half-men of beasts, mingling bestial with human in ghastly creation. No man dares guess at the horrors that have spawned in the darkness, or what shapes of terror and blasphemy have come into being during the ages Gothan has wrought his abominations; for he is not as other men, and he has discovered the secret of life everlasting. He has at least brought into foul life one creature that even he fears, the gibbering mowing, nameless Thing he keeps chained in the furthest cavern that no human foot save his has trod. He would loose it against me if he dared ...

"But it grows late and I would sleep. I will sleep in the room next to this, which has no other opening than this door. Not even a slave-girl will I keep with me, for I trust none of these people fully. You shall keep this room, and though the outer door is bolted, one had better watch while the other sleeps. Zomar and his guardsmen patrol the corridors outside, but I shall feel safer with two men of my own blood between me and the rest of the city."

She rose, and with a strangely lingering glance at Turlogh, entered her chamber and closed the door behind her.

Athelstane stretched and yawned. "Well, Turlogh," said he lazily, "men's fortunes are unstable as the sea. Last night I was the picked swordsman of a band of reavers and you a captive. This dawn we were lost outcasts springing at each other's throats. Now we are sword brothers and right-hand men to a queen. And you, I think, are destined to become a king."

"How so?"

"Why, have you not noticed the Orkney girl's eyes on you? Faith, there's more than friendship in her glances that rest on those black locks and that brown face of yours. I tell you—"

"Enough," Turlogh's voice, harsh as an old wound, stung the Saxon. "Women in power are white-fanged wolves. It was the spite of a woman that—" He stopped.

"Well, well," returned Athelstane tolerantly, "there are more good women than bad ones. I know—it was the intrigues of a woman that made you an outcast. Well, we should be good comrades. I am an outlaw, too. If I should show my face in Wessex I would soon be looking down on the countryside from a stout oak limb."

"What drove you out on the Viking path? So far have the Saxons forgotten the ocean ways that King Alfred was obliged to his Frisian rovers to build and man his fleet when he fought the Danes."

Athelstane shrugged his mighty shoulders and began whetting his dirk.

"I had a yearning for the sea even when I was a shock-headed child in Wessex. I was still a youth when I killed a young earl and fled the vengeance of his people. I found refuge in the Orkneys, and the ways of the Vikings were more to my liking than the ways of my own blood. But I came back to fight against Canute, and when England submitted to his rule, he gave me command of his house-carles. That made the Danes jealous because of the honor given a Saxon who had fought against them, and the

Saxons remembered I had left Wessex under a cloud once, and murmured that I was overly well-favored by the conquerors. Well, there was a Saxon thane and a Danish jarl who one night at feast assailed me with fiery words, and I forgot myself and slew them both.

"So England—was—again—barred—to—me—I—took—the —Viking—path—again—"

Athelstane's words trailed off. His hands slid limply from his lap and the whetstone and dirk dropped to the floor. His head fell forward on his broad chest and his eyes closed.

"Too much wine," muttered Turlogh. "But let him slumber; I'll keep watch."

Yet even as he spoke, the Gael was aware of a strange lassitude stealing over him. He lay back in the broad chair. His eyes felt heavy and sleep veiled his brain despite himself. And as he lay there, a strange nightmare vision came to him. One of the heavy hangings on the wall opposite the door swayed violently and from behind it slunk a fearful shape that crept slavering across the room. Turlogh watched it apathetically, aware that he was dreaming and at the same time wondering at the strangeness of the dream. The thing was grotesquely like a crooked gnarled man in shape, but its face was bestial. It bared yellow fangs as it lurched silently toward him, and from under penthouse brows small reddened eyes gleamed demonically. Yet there was something of the human in its countenance; it was neither ape nor man, but an unnatural creature horribly compounded of both.

Now the foul apparition halted before him, and as the gnarled fingers clutched his throat, Turlogh was suddenly and fearfully aware that this was no dream but a fiendish reality. With a burst of desperate effort he broke the unseen chains that held him and hurled himself from the chair. The grasping fingers missed his throat but, quick as he was, he could not elude the swift lunge of those hairy arms, and the next moment he was tumbling about the floor in a death grip with the monster, whose sinews felt like pliant steel.

That fearful battle was fought in silence save for the hissing of hard-drawn breath. Turlogh's left forearm was thrust under the apish chin, holding back the grisly fangs from his throat, about which the monster's fingers had locked. Athelstane still slept in his chair, head fallen forward. Turlogh tried to call to him, but those throttling hands had shut off his voice—were fast choking out his life. The room swam in a red haze before his distended eyes. His right hand, clenched into an iron mallet, battered desperately at the fearful face bent toward his; the beast-like teeth shattered under his blows and blood spattered, but still the red eyes gloated and the taloned fingers sank deeper and deeper until a ringing in Turlogh's ears knelled his soul's departure.

Even as he sank into semi-unconsciousness, his falling hand struck something his numbed fighting brain recognized as the dirk Athelstane had dropped on the floor. Blindly, with a dying gesture, Turlogh struck, and felt the fingers loosen suddenly. Feeling the return of life and power, he heaved up and over, with his assailant beneath him. Through red mists that slowly lightened, Turlogh Dubh saw the ape-man, now encrimsoned, writhing beneath him, and he drove the dirk home until the dumb horror lay still with wide staring eyes.

The Gael staggered to his feet, dizzy and panting, trembling in every limb. He drew in great gulps of air, and his giddiness slowly cleared. Blood trickled plentifully from the wounds in his throat. He noted with amazement that the Saxon still slumbered. And suddenly he began to feel again the tides of unnatural weariness and lassitude that had rendered him helpless before. Picking up his ax, he shook off the feeling with difficulty and stepped toward the curtain from behind which the ape-man had come. Like an invisible wave, a subtle power emanating from those hangings struck him, and with weighted limbs he forced his way across the room. Now he stood before the curtain and felt the power of a terrific evil will beating upon his own, menacing his very soul, threatening to enslave him, brain and body. Twice he raised his hand and twice it dropped limply to his side. Now for the third time he made a mighty effort and tore the hangings bodily from the wall. For a flashing instant he caught a glimpse of a bizarre, half-naked figure in a mantle of parrot feathers and a headgear of waving plumes. Then as he felt the full hypnotic blast of those blazing eyes, he closed his own eyes and struck blind. He felt his ax sink deep; then he opened his eyes and gazed at the silent figure which lay at his feet, cleft head in a widening crimson pool.

And now Athelstane suddenly heaved erect, eyes flaring bewilderedly, sword out. "What—?" he stammered, glaring wildly, "Turlogh, what in Thor's name happened? Thor's blood! That is a priest there, but what is this dead thing?"

"One of the devils of this foul city," answered Turlogh, wrenching his ax free. "I think Gothan has failed again. This one stood behind the hangings and bewitched us unawares. He put the spell of sleep on us—"

"Aye, I slept," the Saxon nodded dazedly. "But how came they here—?"

"There must be a secret door behind these hangings, although I can not find it—"

"Hark!" From the room where the queen slept there came a vague scuffling sound, that in its very faintness seemed fraught with grisly potentialities.

"Brunhild!" Turlogh shouted. A strangled gurgle answered him. He thrust against the door. It was locked. As he heaved up his ax to hew it open, Athelstane brushed him aside and hurled his full weight against it. The panels crashed, and through their ruins Athelstane plunged into the room. A roar burst from his lips. Over the Saxon's shoulder Turlogh saw a vision of delirium. Brunhild, queen of Bal-Sagoth, writhed helpless in midair, gripped by the black shadow of nightmare. Then as the great black shape turned cold flaming eyes on them, Turlogh saw it was a living creature. It stood, man-like, upon two tree-like legs, but its outline and face were not of a man, beast, or devil. This,

Turlogh felt, was the was the horror that even Gothan had hesitated to loose upon his foes; the arch-fiend that the demoniac priest had brought into life in his hidden caves of horror. What ghastly knowledge had been necessary, what hideous blending of human and bestial things with nameless shapes from outer voids of darkness?

Held like a babe in arms Brunhild writhed, eyes flaring with horror, and as the Thing took a misshapen hand from her white throat to defend itself, a scream of heart-shaking fright burst from her pale lips. Athelstane, first in the room, was ahead of the Gael. The black shape loomed over the giant Saxon, dwarfing and overshadowing him, but Athelstane, gripping the hilt with both hands, lunged upward. The great sword sank over half its length into the black body and came out crimson as the monster reeled back. A hellish pandemonium of sound burst forth, and the echoes of that hideous yell thundered through the palace and deafened the hearers. Turlogh was springing in, ax high, when the fiend dropped the girl and fled reeling across the room, vanishing in a dark opening that now gaped in the wall. Athelstane, death berserk, plunged after it.

Turlogh made to follow, but Brunhild, reading up, threw her white arms around him in a grip even he could hardly break. "No!" she screamed, eyes ablaze with terror. "Do not follow them into that fearful corridor! It must lead to Hell itself! The Saxon will never return! Let you not share his fate!"

"Loose me, woman!" roared Turlogh in a frenzy, striving to disengage himself without hurting her. "My comrade may be fighting for his life!"

"Wait till I summon the guard!" she cried, but Turlogh flung her from him, and as he sprang through the secret doorway, Brunhild smote on the jade gong until the palace re-echoed. A loud pounding began in the corridor, and Zomar's voice shouted: "Oh queen, are you in peril? Shall we burst the door?"

"Haven!" she screamed, as she rushed to the outer door and flung it open.

Turlogh, leaping recklessly into the corridor, raced along in the darkness for a few moments, hearing ahead of him the agonized bellowing of the wounded monster, and the deep fierce shouts of the Viking. Then the noises faded away in the distance as he came into a narrow passageway faintly lighted with torches stuck into niches. Face down on the floor lay a brown man, clad in gay feathers, his skull crushed like an eggshell.

How long Turlogh O'Brien followed the dizzy singings of the shadowy corridor he never knew. Other smaller passages led off to each side, but he kept to the main corridor. At last he passed under an arched doorway and came out into a strange, vasty room.

Sombre massive columns upheld a shadowy ceiling so high it seemed like a brooding cloud arched against a midnight sky. Turlogh saw that he was in a temple. Behind a black red-stained stone altar loomed a mighty form, sinister and abhorrent. The god Gol-goroth! Surely it must be he. But Turlogh spared only a single glance for the colossal figure that brooded there in the shadows. Before him was a strange tableau. Athelstane leaned on his great sword and gazed at the two shapes which sprawled in a red welter at his feet. Whatever foul magic had brought the Black Thing into life, it had taken but a thrust of English street to hurl it back into the limbo from whence it came. The monster lay half across its last victim—a gaunt white-bearded man whose eyes were starkly evil, even in death.

"Gothan!" ejaculated the startled Gael.

"Aye, the priest—I was close behind this troll or whatever it is, all the way along the corridor, but for all its size it fled like a deer. Once one in a feather mantle tried to halt it, and it smashed his skull and paused not an instant. At last we burst into the temple, I close upon the monster's heels with my sword raised for the death cut. But Thor's blood! When it saw the old one standing by the altar, it gave one fearful howl and tore him into pieces and died itself, all in an instant, before I could reach it and strike."

Turlogh gazed at the huge formless thing. Looking directly at it, he could form no estimate of its nature. He got only a chaotic impression of great size and inhuman evil. Now it lay like a vast shadow blotched out on the marble floor. Surely black wings beating from moonless gulfs had hovered over its birth, and the grisly souls of nameless demons had gone into its being.

And now Brunhild rushed from the dark corridor with Zomar and the guardsmen. And from outer doors and secret nooks came others silently—warriors, and priests in feathered mantles, until a great throng stood in the Temple of Darkness.

A fierce cry broke from the queen as she saw what had happened. Her eyes blazed terribly, and she was gripped by a strange madness.

"At last!" she screamed, spurning the corpse of her archfoe with her heel, "at last I am the true mistress of Bal-Sagoth! The secrets of the hidden ways are mine now, and old Gothan's beard is dabbled in his own blood!"

She flung her arms high in fearful triumph, and ran toward the grim idol, screaming exultant insults like a madwoman. And at that instant the temple rocked! The colossal image swayed outward, and then pitched suddenly forward as a tall tower falls. Turlogh shouted and leaped forward, but even as he did, with a thunder like the bursting of a world, the god Gol-goroth crashed down upon the doomed woman, who stood frozen. The mighty image splintered into a thousand great fragments, blotting from the sight of men forever Brunhild, daughter of Rane Thorfin's son, queen of Bal-Sagoth. From under the ruins there oozed a wide crimson stream.

Warriors and priests stood frozen, deafened by the crash of that fall, stunned by the weird catastrophe. An icy hand touched Turlogh's spine. Had that vast bulk been thrust over by the hand of a dead man? As it had rushed downward it had seemed to the Gael that the inhuman features had for an instant taken on the likeness of the dead Gothan!

Now, as all stood speechless, the acolyte Gelka saw and seized his opportunity.

"Gol-goroth has spoken!" he screamed. "He has crushed the false goddess! She was but a wicked mortal! And these strangers, too, are mortal! See—he bleeds!"

The priest's finger stabbed at the dried blood on Turlogh's throat and a wild roar went up from the throng. Dazed and bewildered by the swiftness and magnitude of the late events, they were like crazed wolves, ready to wipe out doubts and fear in a burst of bloodshed. Gelka bounded at Turlogh, hatchet flashing, and a knife in the hand of a satellite licked into Zomar's back. Turlogh had not understood the shout, but he realized the air was tense with danger for Athelstane and himself. He met the leaping Gelka with a stroke that sheared through the waving plumes and the skull beneath, then half a dozen lances broke on his buckler and a rush of bodies swept him back against a great pillar. Then Athelstane, slow of thought, who had stood gaping for the flashing second it had taken this to transpire, awoke in a blast of awesome fury. With a deafening roar he swung his heavy sword in a mighty arc. The whistling blade whipped off a head, sheared through a torso, and sank deep into a spinal column. The three corpses fell across each other and even in the madness of the strife, men cried out at the marvel of that single stroke.

But like a brown, blind tide of fury the maddened people of Bal-Sagoth rolled on their foes. The guardsmen of the dead queen, trapped in the press, died to a man without a chance to strike a blow. But the overthrow of the two white warriors was no such easy task. Back to back they smashed and smote; Athelstane's sword was a thunderbolt of death; Turlogh's ax was lightning. Hedged close by a sea of snarling brown faces and flashing steel, they backed their way slowly toward a doorway. The very mass of the attackers hindered the warriors of Bal-Sagoth, for they had no space to guide their strokes, while the weapons of the seafarers kept a bloody ring clear in front of them.

Heaping a ghastly row of corpses as they went, the comrades

slowly cut their way through the snarling press. The Temple of Shadows, witness of many a bloody deed, was flooded with gore spilled like a red sacrifice to her broken gods. The heavy weapons of the white fighters wrought fearful havoc among their naked, lighter-limbed foes, while their armor guarded their own lives. But their arms, legs and faces were cut and gashed by the frantically flying steel and it seemed the sheer number of their foes would overwhelm them ere they could reach the door.

Then they had reached it, and made desperate play until the brown warriors, no longer able to come upon them from all sides, drew back for a breathing space, leaving a torn red heap before the threshold. And in that instant the two sprang back into the corridor and, seizing the great brazen door, slammed it in the very faces of the warriors who leaped howling to prevent it. Athelstane, bracing his mighty legs, held it against their combined efforts until Turlogh had time to find and slip the bolt.

"Thor!" gasped the Saxon, shaking the blood in a red shower from his face. "This is close play! What now, Turlogh?"

"Down the corridor, quick!" snapped the Gael, "before they come on us from this way and trap us like rats against this door. By Satan, the whole city must be roused! Hark to that roaring!"

In truth, as they raced down the shadowed corridor, it seemed to them that all Bal-Sagoth had burst into rebellion and civil war. From all sides came the clashing of steel, the shouts of men, and the screams of women, overshadowed by a hideous howling. A lurid glow became apparent down the corridor, and then even as Turlogh, in the lead, rounded a corner and came out into an open courtyard, a vague figure leaped at him and a heavy weapon fell with unexpected force on his shield, almost felling him. But even as he staggered, he struck back, and the upper spike on his ax sank under the heart of his attacker, who fell at his feet. In the glare that illuminated all, Turlogh saw his victim differed from the brown warriors he had been fighting. This man was naked, powerfully muscled and of a copperish red rather than brown. The heavy animal-like jaw, the slanting low forehead showed none of the intelligence and refinement of the brown people, but only a brute ferocity. A heavy war club, rudely carved, lay beside him.

"By Thor!" exclaimed Athelstane, "the city burns!"

Turlogh looked up. They were standing on a sort of raised courtyard from which broad steps led down into the streets, and from the vantage point they had a plain view of the terrific end of Bal-Sagoth. Flames leaped madly higher and higher, paling the moon, and in the red glare pigmy figures ran to and fro, falling and dying like puppets dancing to the tune of the Black Gods. Through the roar of the flames and the crashing of the falling walls cut screams of death and shrieks of ghastly triumph. The city was swarming with naked, copper-skinned devils who burned, and ravished, and butchered in one red carnival of madness.

The red men of the isles! By the thousands they had descended on the Isle of the Gods in the night, and whether stealth of treachery let them through the walls, the comrades never knew, but now they ravened through the corpse-strewn streets, glutting their bloodlust in holocaust and massacre whole-sale. Not all the gashed forms that lay in the crimson running streets were brown; the people of the doomed city fought with desperate courage but, outnumbered and caught off guard, their courage was futile. The red men were blood-hungry tigers.

"What ho, Turlogh!" shouted Athelstane, beard abristle, eyes ablaze as the madness of the scene fired a like passion in his own fierce soul. "The world ends! Let us into the thick of it and glut our steel before we die! Who shall we strike for—the red or the brown?"

Steady!" snapped the Gael. "Either people would cut our throats. We must hack our way through to the gates, and the Devil take them all. We have no friends here. This way—down these stairs. Across the roofs in yonder direction I see the arch of a gate."

The comrades sprang down the stairs, gained the narrow

street below, and ran swiftly in the way Turlogh indicated. About them washed a red inundation of slaughter. A thick smoke veiled all now, and in the murk chaotic groups merged, writhed, and scattered, littering he shattered flags with gory shapes. It was like a nightmare in which demoniac figures leaped and capered, looming suddenly in the fire-shot mist, vanishing as suddenly. The flames from each side of the streets shouldered each other, singeing the hair of the warriors as they ran. Roofs fell in with an awesome thunder and walls crashing into ruin filled the air with flying death. Men struck blindly from the smoke and the seafarers cut them down and never knew whether their skins were brown or red.

Now a new note in the cataclysmic horror. Blinded by the smoke, confused by the winding streets, the red men were trapped in the snare of their own making. Fire is impartial; it can burn the lighter as well as the intended victim; and a falling wall is blind. The red men abandoned their prey and ran howling to and fro like beasts, seeking escape; many, finding this futile, turned back in a last unreasoning storm of madness as a blinded tiger turns, and made their last moments of life a crimson burst of slaughter.

Turlogh, with the unerring sense of direction that comes to men who live the life of the wolf, ran toward the point where he knew an outer gate to be; yet in the windings of the streets and the screen of smoke, doubt assailed him. From the flame-shot murk in front of him a fearful scream rang out. A naked girl reeled blindly into view and fell at Turlogh's feet, blood gushing from the mutilated breast. A howling, red-stained devil, close on her heels, jerked back her head and cut her throat a fraction of a second before Turlogh's ax ripped the head from its shoulders and spun it grinning into the street. And at the second a sudden wind shifted the writhing smoke, and the comrades saw the open gateway ahead of them, aswarm with red warriors. A fierce shout, a blasting rush, a mad instant of volcanic ferocity that littered the gateway with corpses, and they were through and racing down the slopes toward the distant forest and the beach beyond. Before them the sky was reddening for dawn; behind them rose the soul-shaking tumult of the doomed city.

Like hunted things they fled, seeking brief shelter among the many groves from time to time, to avoid groups of savages who ran toward the city. The whole island seemed to be swarming with them; the chiefs must have drawn on all the isles within hundreds of miles for a raid of such magnitude. And at last the comrades reached the strip of forest and breathed deeply as they came to the beach and found it abandoned save for a number of long, skull-decorated war canoes.

Athelstane sat down and gasped for breath. "Thor's blood! What now? What may we do but hide in these woods until those red devils hunt us out?"

"Help me launch this boat," snapped Turlogh. "We'll take our chance on the open main—"

The sun was just up, gleaming like a great goddess coin on the sea-rim. And limmed in the sun swam a tall, high-pooped craft. The comrades leaped into the nearest canoe, shoved off, and rowed like mad, shouting and waving their oars to attract the attention of the crew. Powerful muscles drove the long, slim craft along at an incredible clip, and it was not long before the ship stood about and allowed them to come alongside. Dark-faced men, clad in mail, looked over the rail.

"Spaniards," muttered Athelstane. "If they recognize me, I had better have stayed on the island!"

But he clambered up the chain without hesitation, and the two wanderers fronted the lean somber-faced man whose armor was that of a knight Asturias. He spoke to them in Spanish, and Turlogh answered him, for the Gael, like many of his race, was a natural linguist and had wandered far and spoken many tongues. In a few words the Dalcassian told their story and explained the great pillar of smoke which now rolled upward in the morning air from the isle.

"Tell him there is a king's ransom for the taking," put in Athelstane. "Tell him of the silver gates, Turlogh."

But when the Gael spoke of the vast loot in the doomed city, the commander shook his head.

"Good sir, we have no time to secure it, nor men to waste in the taking. Those red fiends you describe would hardly give up anything—though useless to them—without a fierce battle and neither my time nor my force is mine. I am Don Roderigo del Cortez of Castile, and this ship, the *Gray Friar*, is one of a fleet that sailed to harry the Moorish Corsairs. Some days agone we were separated from the rest of the fleet in a sea skirmish, and the tempest blew us far off our course. We are even now beating back to rejoin the fleet if we can find it; if not, to harry the infidel as well as we may. We serve God and the king, and we cannot halt for mere dross as you suggest. But you are welcome aboard this ship, and we have need of such fighting men as you appear to be. You will not regret it, should you wish to join us and strike a blow for Christendom against the Moslems."

In the narrow-bridged nose and deep dark eyes as in the lean ascetic face, Turlogh read the fanatic, the stainless cavalier, the knight-errant. He spoke to Athelstane: "This man is mad, but there are good blows to be struck and strange lands to see; anyway, we have no other choice."

"One place is as good as another to masterless men and wanderers," quoth the huge Saxon. "Tell him we will follow him to Hell and singe the tail of the Devil if there be any chance of loot."

EMPIRE

Turlogh and Athelstane leaned on the rail, gazing back at the swiftly receding Island of the Gods, from which rose a pillar of smoke, laden with the ghosts of a thousand centuries, and the shadows and mysteries of forgotten empire, and Athelstane cursed as only a Saxon can.

"A king's ransom—and after all that blood-letting—no loot!"

Turlogh shook his head. "We have seen an ancient kingdom fall—we have seen the last remnant of the world's oldest empire sink into flames and the abyss of oblivion, and barbarism rear its brute head above the ruins. So pass the glory, and the splendor and the imperial purple—in red flames and yellow smoke."

"But not one bit of plunder—" persisted the Viking.

Again Turlogh shook his head. "I brought away with me the rarest gem upon the island—something for which men and women have died and the gutters run with blood."

He drew from his girdle a small object—a curiously carved symbol of jade.

"The emblem of kingship!" exclaimed Athelstane.

"Aye—as Brunhild struggled with me to keep me from following you into the corridor, this thing caught in my mail and was torn from the golden chain that held it."

"He who bears it is king of Bal-Sagoth," ruminated the mighty Saxon. "As I predicted, Turlogh, you are a king!"

Turlogh laughed with bitter mirth and pointed to the great billowing column of smoke which floated in the sky away on the sea-rim.

"Aye—a kingdom of the dead—an empire of ghosts and smoke. I am Ard-Righ of a phantom city—I am King Turlogh of Bal-Sagoth, and my kingdom is fading in the morning sky. And therein it is like all other empires in the world—dreams, and ghosts, and smoke."

THE BLACK STONE

I read of it first in the strange book of Von Junzt, the German eccentric who lived so curiously and died in such grisly and mysterious fashion. It was my fortune to have access to his *Nameless Cults* in the original edition, the so-called Black Book, published in Dusseldorf in 1839, shortly before a hounding doom overtook the author. Collectors of rare literature were familiar with *Nameless Cults* mainly through the cheap and faulty translation, which was pirated in London by Bridewall in 1845, and the carefully expurgated edition put out by the Golden Goblin Press of New York, 1909. But the volume I stumbled upon was one of the unexpurgated German copies, with heavy black leather covers and rusty iron hasps. I doubt if there are more than half a dozen such volumes in the entire world today, for the quantity issued was not great, and when the manner of the author's demise was bruited about, many possessors of the book burned their volumes in panic.

Von Junzt spent his entire life (1795-1840) delving into forbidden subjects; he traveled in all part of the world, gained entrance into innumerable secret societies, and read countless little-known and esoteric books and manuscripts in the original; and in the chapters of the Black Book, which range from star-

tling clarity of exposition to murky ambiguity, there are state-
ments and hints to freeze the blood of a thinking man. Reading
what Von Junzt dared put in print arouses uneasy speculations as
to what it was that he dared not tell. What dark matters, for
instance, were contained in those closely written pages that
formed the unpublished manuscript on which he worked unceas-
ingly for months before his death, and which lay torn and scattered all over the floor of the locked and bolted chamber in
which Von Junzt was found dead with the marks of taloned
fingers on his throat? It will never be known, for the author's
closest friend, the Frenchman Alexis Ladeau, after having spent
a whole might piecing the fragments together and reading what
was written, burnt them to ashes and cut his own throat with a
razor.

But the contents of the published matter are shuddersome
enough, even if one accepts the general view that they but represent the ravings of a madman. There among many strange things
I found mention of the Black Stone, that curious, sinister monolith that broods among the mountains of Hungary, and about
which so many dark legends cluster. Van Junzt did not devote
much space to it—the bulk of his grim work concerns cults and
objects of dark worship which he maintained existed in his day,
and it would seem that the Black Stone represents some order or
being lost and forgotten centuries ago. But he spoke of it as one
of the keys—a phrase used many times by him, in various relations, and constituting one of the obscurities of his work. And
he hinted briefly at curious sights to be seen about the monolith
on Midsummer's Night. He mentioned Otto Dostman's theory
that this monolith was a remnant of the Hunnish invasion and
had been erected to commemorate a victory of Attila over the
Goths. Von Junzt contradicted this assertion without giving any
refutory facts, merely remarking that to attribute the origin of
the Black Stone to the Huns was as logical as assuming that
William the Conqueror reared Stonehenge.

The implication of enormous antiquity piqued my interest

immensely, and after some difficulty I succeeded in locating a rat-eaten and moldering copy of Dostman's *Remnants of Lost Empires* (Berlin, 1809, "Das Drachenhaus" Press). I was disappointed to find that Dostman referred to the Black Stone even more briefly than had Von Junzt, dismissing it with a few lines as an artifact comparatively modern in contrast with the Greco-Roman ruins of Asia Minor which were his pet theme. He admitted his liability to make out the defaced characters on the monolith, but pronounced them unmistakably Mongoloid. However, little as I learned from Dostman, he did mention the na me of the village adjacent to the Black Stone—Stregoicavar—an ominous name, meaning something like Witch-Town.

A close scrutiny of guidebooks and travel articles gave me no further information.

Stregiocavar, not on any map that I could find, lay in a wild, little-frequented region, out of the path of casual tourists. But I did find subject for thought in Dornly's *Magyar Folklore*. In his chapter on Dream Myths he mentions the Black Stone and tells some curious superstitions regarding it—especially the belief that if anyone sleeps in the vicinity of the monolith, that person will be haunted by monstrous nightmares forever after; and he cited tales of the peasants regarding too-curious people who ventured to visit the Stone on Midsummer Night and who died raving mad because of something they saw there.

That was all I could gleam from Dornly, but my interest was even more intensely roused as I sensed a distinctly sinister aura about the Stone. The suggestion of dark antiquity, the recurrent hint of unnatural events on Midsummer Night, touched some slumbering instinct in my being, as one senses, rather than hears, the flowing of some dark subterraneous river in the night.

And I suddenly saw a connection between this stone and a certain weird and fantastic poem written by the mad poet, Justin Geoffrey: The People of the Monolith. Iniquities led to the information that Geoffrey had indeed written that poem while traveling in Hungary, and I could not doubt that the Black Stone was the very monolith to which he referred in his strange verse. Reading his stanzas again, I felt once more the strange dim stirrings of subconscious promptings that I had noticed when first reading of the Stone.

I had been casting about for a place to spend a short vacation, and I made up my mind. I went to Stregiocavar. A train of obsolete style carried me from Temesvar to within striking distance, at least, of my objective, and a three days' ride in a jouncing coach brought me to the little village which lay in a fertile valley high up in the fir-clad mountains. The journey itself was uneventful, but during the first day we passed the old battlefield of Schomvaal where the brave Polish Hungarian knight, Count Boris Vladinoff, made his gallant and futile stand against the victorious hosts of Suleiman the Magnificent, when the Grand Turk swept over eastern Europe in 1526.

The driver of the coach pointed out to me a great heap of crumbling stones on a hill nearby under which, he said, the bones of the brave Count lay. I remembered a passage from Larson's *Turkish Wars*. "After the skirmish," (in which the Count with his small army had beaten back the Turkish advance-guard) "the Count was standing beneath the half-ruined walls of the old castle on the hill, giving orders as to the disposition of his forces, when an aide brought to him a small lacquered case which had been taken from the body of the famous Turkish scribe and historian, Selim Bahadur, who had fallen in the fight. The Count took therefrom a roll of parchment and began to read, but he had not read far before he turned very pale and, without saying a word, replaced the parchment in the case and thrust into his cloak. At that very instant a hidden Turkish battery suddenly opened fire, and the balls striking the old castle, the Hungarians were horrified to see the walls crash down in ruin, completely covering the brave Count. Without a leader the gallant little army was cut to pieces, and in the war-swept years which followed, the bones of the nobleman were never recovered. Today the natives point out a huge and moldering pile of ruins near Schomvaal beneath which, they say, still rests all that the centuries have left of Count Boris Vladinoff."

I found the village of Stregiocavar a dreamy, drowsy, little village that apparently belied its sinister cognomen—a forgotten back-eddy that Progress had passed by. The quaint houses and the quainter dress and manners of the people were those of an earlier century. They were friendly, mildly curious but not inquisitive, though visitors from the outside world were extremely rare.

"Ten years ago, another American came here and stayed a few days in the village," said the owner of the tavern where I had put up, "a young fellow and queer-acting—mumbled to himself—a poet, I think."

I knew he must mean Justin Geoffrey.

"Yes, he was a poet," I answered, "and he wrote a poem about a bit of scenery near this very village."

"Indeed?" Mine host's interest was aroused. "Then, since all great poets are strange in their speech and actions, he must have achieved great fame, for his actions and conversations were the strangest of any man I ever I knew."

"As is usual with artists," I answered, "most of his recognition has come since his death."

"He is dead, then?"

"He died screaming in a madhouse five years ago."

"Too bad, too bad," sighed mine host sympathetically. "Poor lad—he looked too long at the Black Stone."

My heart gave a leap, but I masked my keen interest and said casually, "I have heard something of this Black Stone; somewhere near this village, is it not?"

"Nearer than Christian folk wish," he responded. "Look!" He drew me to a latticed window and pointed up at the fir-clad slopes of the brooding blue mountains. "There beyond where you see the bare face of that jutting cliff stands that accursed stone. Would that it were ground to powder and the powder flung into the Danube to be carried to the deepest ocean! Once men tried to destroy the thing, but each man who laid hammer or maul against it came to an evil end. So now the people shun it."

"What is there so evil about it?" I asked curiously.

"It is a demon-haunted thing," he answered uneasily and with the suggestion of a shudder. "In my childhood I knew a young man who came up from below and laughed at our traditions—in his foolhardiness he went to the Stone one Midsummer Night and at dawn stumbled into the village again, stricken dumb and mad. Something had shattered his brain and sealed his lips, for until the day of his death, which came soon after, he spoke only to utter terrible blasphemies or to slaver gibberish.

"My own nephew when very small was lost in the mountains and slept in the woods near the Stone, and now in his manhood he is tortured by foul dreams, so that at times he makes the night hideous with his screams and wakes with cold sweat upon him.

"But let us talk of something else, Herr; it is not good to dwell upon such things."

I remarked on the evident age of the tavern, and he answered with pride, "The foundations are more than four hundred years old; the original house was the only one in the village which was not burned to the ground when Suleiman's devils swept through the mountains. Here, in the house that then stood on these same foundations, it is said, the scribe Selim Bahadur had his head-quarters while ravaging the country hereabouts."

I learned then that the present inhabitants of Stregoicavar are not descendants of the people who dwelt there before the Turkish raid of 1526. The victorious Moslems left no living human in the village or the vicinity thereabouts when they passed over. Men, women, and children they wiped out in one red holocaust of murder, leaving a vast stretch of country silent and utterly deserted. The present people of Stregoicavar are descended from hardy settlers from the lower valleys who came into the ruined village after the Turk was thrust back.

Mine host did not speak of the extermination of the original inhabitants with any great resentment, and I learned that his ancestors in the lower levels had looked on the mountaineers with even more hatred and aversion than they regarded the Turks. He was rather vague regarding the causes of this feud, but said that the original inhabitants of Stregoicavar had been in the habit of making stealthy raids on the lowlands and stealing girls and children. Moreover, he said that they were not exactly of the same blood as his own people; the sturdy, original Magyar-Slavic stock had mixed and intermarried with a degraded aboriginal race until the breeds had blended, producing an unsavory amalgamation. Who these aborigines were, he had not the slightest idea, but maintained that they were "pagans," and had dwelt in the mountains since time immemorial, before the coming of the conquering peoples.

I attached little importance to this tale; seeing in it merely a parallel to the amalgamation of Celtic tribes with Mediterranean aborigines in the Galloway hills, with the resultant mixed race which, as Picts, has such an extensive part in Scotch legendary. Time has a certain foreshortening effect on folklore, and just as tales of the squat primitives, whose individuality merged, in the telling, into Pictish tales, and was forgotten; so, I felt the supposed inhuman attributes of the first villagers of Stregoicavar could be traced to older, outworn myths with invading Huns and Mongols.

The morning after my arrival I received directions from mine host, who gave them worriedly, and set out to find the Black Stone. A few hours' tramp up the fir-covered slopes brought me to the face of the rugged, solid, stone cliff which jutted boldly from the mountainside. A narrow trail wound up it, and mounting this, I looked out over the peaceful valley of Stregoicavar, which seemed to drowse, guarded on either hand by the great blue mountains. No huts or any sign of human tenancy showed between the cliff whereon I stood and the village. I saw numbers of scattering farms in the valley but all lay on the other side of Stregoicavar, which itself seemed to shrink from the brooding slopes which masked the Black Stone.

The summit of the cliffs proved to be a sort of thickly wooded plateau. I made my way through the dense growth for a short distance and came into a wide glade; and in the center of the glade reared a gaunt figure of black stone.

It was octagonal in shape, some sixteen feet in height and about a foot and a half thick. It had once evidently been highly polished, but now the surface was thickly dinted as if savage efforts had been made to demolish it; but the hammers had done little more than to flake off small bits of stone and mutilate the characters which once had evidently marched up in a spiraling line round and round the shaft to the top. Up to ten feet from the base these characters were almost completely blotted out, so that it was very difficult to trace their direction. Higher up they were plainer, and I managed to squirm part of the way up the shaft and scan them at close range. All were more or less defaced, but I was positive that they symbolized no language now remembered on the face of the earth. I am fairly familiar with all hieroglyphics known to researchers and philologists, and I can say with certainty that those characters were like nothing of which I have ever read or heard. The nearest approach to them that I ever saw were some crude scratches on a gigantic and strangely symmetrical rock in a lost valley of Yucatan. I remember that when I pointed out these marks to the archeologist who was my companion, he maintained that they either represented natural weathering or the idle scratching of some Indian. To my theory that the rock was really the base of a long-vanished column, he merely laughed, calling my attention to the dimensions of it, which suggested, if it were built with any natural rules of architectural symmetry, a column a thousand feet high. But I was not convinced.

I will not say that the characters on the Black Stone were similar to those on that colossal rock in Yucatan; but one suggested the other. As to the substance of the monolith, again I was baffled. The stone of which it was composed was a dully gleaming black, whose surface, where it was not dinted and roughened, created a curious illusion of semitransparency.

I spent most of the morning there and came away baffled. No connection of the Stone with any other artifact in the world suggested itself to me. It was as if the monolith had been reared by alien hands, in an age distant and apart from human ken.

I returned to the village with my interest in no way abated. Now that I had seen the curious thing, my desire was still more keenly whetted to investigate the matter further and seek to learn by what strange hands and for what strange purpose the Black Stone had been reared in the long ago.

I sought out the tavern-keeper's nephew and questioned him in regard to his dreams, but he was vague, though willing to oblige. He did not mind discussing them, but was unable to describe them with any clarity. Though he dreamed the same dreams repeatedly, and though they were hideously vivid at the time, they left no distinct impressions on his waking mind. He remembered them only as chaotic nightmares through which huge whirling fires shot lurid tongues of flame and a black drum bellowed incessantly. One thing only he remembered clearly—in one dream he had seen the Black Stone, not on a mountain slope, but set like a spire on a colossal black castle.

As for the rest of the villagers, I found them not inclined to talk about the Stone, with the exception of the schoolmaster, a man of surprising education, who spent much more of his time out in the world than any of the rest.

He was much interested in what I told him of Von Junzt's remarks about the Stone, and warmly agreed with the German author in the alleged age of the monolith. He believed that a coven had once existed in the vicinity, and that possibly all of the original villagers had been members of that fertility cult which once threatened to undermine European civilization and gave rise to the tales of witchcraft. He cited the very name of the village to prove his point; it had not been originally named Stregoicavar, he said; according to the legends the builders had called it Xuthltan, which was the aboriginal name of the site on which the village had been built many centuries ago.

This fact roused again an indescribable feeling of uneasiness. The barbarous name did not suggest connection with any Scythic, Slavic, or Mongolian race to which an aboriginal people of these mountains would, under natural circumstances, have belonged.

That the Magyars and Slavs of the lower valleys believed the original inhabitants of the village to be members of the witchcraft cult was evident, the schoolmaster said, by the name they gave it, which name continued to be used even after the older settlers had been massacred by the Turks, and the village rebuilt by a cleaner and more wholesome breed.

He did not believe that the members of the cult erected the monolith, but he did believe that they used it as a center of their activities, and repeating vague legends which had been handed down since before the Turkish invasion, he advanced the theory that the degenerate villagers had used it as a sort of altar on which they offered human sacrifices, using as victims the girls and babies stolen from his own ancestors in the lower valleys.

He discounted the myths of weird events on Midsummer Night, as well as a curious legend of a strange deity which the witch-people of Xuthltan were said to have invoked with chants and wild rituals of flagellation and slaughter.

He had never visited the Stone on Midsummer Night, he said, but he would not fear to do so; whatever had existed or taken place there in the past, had been long engulfed in the mists of time and oblivion. The Black Stone had lost its meaning save as a link to a dead and dusty past.

It was while returning from a visit with this schoolmaster one night about a week after my arrival at Stregoicavar that a sudden recollection struck me—it was Midsummer Night! The very time that the legends linked with grisly implications to the Black Stone. I turned away from the tavern and strode swiftly through the village. Stregoicavar lay silent; the villagers retired early. I saw no one as I passed rapidly out of the village and up into the firs which masked the mountain's slopes with whispering darkness. A broad silver moon hung above the valley, flooding the crags and slopes in a weird light and etching the shadows blackly. No wind blew through the firs, but a mysterious, intangible rustling and whispering was abroad. Surely on such nights in past centuries, my whimsical imagination told me, naked witches astride magic broomsticks had flown across the valley, pursued by jeering, demoniac familiars.

I came to the cliffs and was somewhat disquieted to note that the illusive moonlight lent them a subtle appearance I had not noticed before—in the weird light they appeared less like natural cliffs and more like the ruins of cyclopean and Titan-reared battlements jutting from the mountain slope.

Shaking off this hallucination with difficulty, I came upon the plateau and hesitated a moment before I plunged into the brooding darkness of the woods. A sort of breathless tenseness hung over the shadows, like an unseen monster holding its breath lest it scare away its prey.

I shook off the sensation—a natural one, considering the eeriness of the place and its evil reputation—and made my way through the wood, experiencing a most unpleasant sensation that I was being followed, and halting once, sure that something clammy and unstable had brushed against my face in the darkness.

I came out into the glade and saw the tall monolith rearing its gaunt height above the sward. At the edge of the woods on the side toward the cliffs was a stone which formed a sort of natural seat. I sat down, reflecting that it was probably while there that the mad poet, Justin Geoffrey, had written his fantastic "People of the Monolith." Mine host thought that it was the Stone which had caused Geoffrey's insanity, but the seeds of madness had been sown in the poet's brain long before he ever came to Stregoicavar.

A glance at my watch showed that the hour of midnight was close at hand. I leaned back, waiting whatever ghostly demonstration might appear. A think night wind started up among the branches of the firs, with an uncanny suggestion of faint, unseen pipes whispering an eerie and evil tune. The monotony of the sound and my steady gazing at the monolith produced a sort of self-hypnosis upon me; I grew drowsy. I fought this feeling, but sleep stole on me in spite of myself; the monolith seemed to sway and dance, strangely distorted to my gaze, and then I slept.

I opened my eyes and sought to rise, but lay still, as if an icy hand gripped me helpless. Cold terror stole over me. The glade was no longer deserted. It was thronged by a silent crowd of strange people, and my distended eyes took in strange barbaric details of costume which my reason told me were archaic and forgotten even in this backward land. Surely, I thought, these are villagers who have come here to hold some fantastic conclave— but another glance told me that these people were not the folk of Stregoicavar. They were a shorter, more squat race, whose brows were lower, whose faces were broader and duller. Some had Slavic and Magyar features, but those features were degraded as from a mixture of some baser, alien strain I could not classify. Many wore the hides of wild beasts, and their whole appearance, both men and women, was one of sensual brutishness. They terrified and repelled me, but they gave me no heed. They formed in a vast half-circle in front of the monolith and began a sort of chant, flinging their arms in unison and waving their bodies rhythmically from the waist upward. All eyes were fixed on the top of the Stone which they seemed to be invoking. But the strangest of all was the dimness of their voices; not fifty yards from me hundreds of men and women were unmistakably lifting their voices in a wild chant, yet those voices came to me as a faint, indistinguishable murmur as if from across vast leagues of space—or time.

Before the monolith stood a sort of brazier from which a vile, nauseous yellow smoke billowed upward, curling curiously in a swaying spiral around the black shaft, like a vast, unstable snake.

On one side of this brazier lay two figures—a young girl, stark naked and bound hand and foot, and an infant, apparently only a few months old. On the other side of the brazier squatted a hideous old hag with a queer sort of black drum on her lap; this drum she beat with slow light blows of her open palms, but I could not hear the sound.

The rhythm of the swaying bodies grew faster, and into the space between the people and monolith sprang a naked young woman, her eyes blazing, her long black hair flying loose. Spinning dizzily on her toes, she whirled across the open space and fell prostrate before the Stone, where she lay motionless. The next instant a fantastic figure followed her—a man from whose waist hung a goatskin, and whose features were entirely hidden by a sort of mask made from a huge wolf's head, so that he looked like a monstrous, nightmare being, horribly compounded of elements both human and bestial. In his hand he held a bunch of long fir switches bound together at the larger ends, and the moonlight glinted on a chain of heavy gold looped about his neck. A smaller chain depending from it suggested a pendant of some sort, but this was missing.

The people tossed their arms violently and seemed to redouble their shouts as this grotesque creature loped across the open space with many a fantastic leap and caper. Coming to the woman who lay before the monolith, he began to lash her with the switches he bore, and she leaped up and spun into the wild mazes of the most incredible dance I have ever seen. And her tormentor danced with her, keeping the wild rhythm, matching her every whirl and bound, while incessantly raining cruel blows on her naked body. And at every blow he shouted a single word, over and over, and all the people shouted it back. I could see the working of their lips, and now the faint far-off murmur of their voices merged and blended into one distant shout, repeated over and over with slobbering ecstasy. But what the one word was, I could not make out.

In dizzy whirls spun the wild dancers, while the lookers-on, standing still in their tracks, followed the rhythm of their dance with swaying bodies and weaving arms. Madness grew in the eyes of the capering votaress and was reflected in the eyes of the watchers. Wilder and more extravagant grew the whirling frenzy of that mad dance—it became a bestial and obscene thing, while the old hag howled and battered the drum like a crazy woman, and the switches cracked out a devil's tune.

Blood trickled down the dancer's limbs but she seemed not to feel the lashing save as a stimulus for further enormities of outrageous motion; bounding into the midst of the yellow smoke which now spread out tenuous tentacles to embrace both flying figures, she seemed to merge with that foul fog and veil herself with it. Then emerging into plain view, closely followed by the beast-thing that flogged her, she shot into an indescribable, explosive burst of dynamic mad motion, and on the very crest of that mad wave, she dropped suddenly to the sward, quivering and panting as if completely overcome by her frenzied exertions. The lashing continued with unabated violence and intensity, and she began to wriggle toward the monolith on her belly. The priest—or such I will call him—followed, lashing her unprotected body with all the power of his arm as she writhed along leaving a heavy track of blood on the trampled earth. She reached the monolith and, gasping and panting, flung both arms about it and covered the cold stone with fierce hot kisses, as in frenzied and unholy adoration.

The fantastic priest bounded high in the air, flinging away the red-dabbled switches, and the worshippers, howling and foaming at the mouths, turned on each other with tooth and nail, rending one another's garments and flesh in a blind passion of bestiality. The priest swept up the infant with a long arm, and shouting again that Name, whirled the wailing babe high in the air and dashed its brains out against the monolith, leaving a ghastly stain on the black surface. Cold with horror I saw him rip the tiny body open with his bare brutish fingers and fling handfuls of blood on the shaft, then toss the red and torn shape into the brazier, extinguishing flame and smoke in a crimson rain, while the maddened brutes behind him howled over and over the Name. Then suddenly they all fell prostrate, writhing like snakes, while the priest flung wide his gory hands as in triumph. I opened my mouth to scream my horror and loathing, but only a dry rattle sounded; a huge monstrous toad-like thing squatted on top of the monolith!

I saw its bloated, repulsive, and unstable outline against the moonlight, and, set in what would have been the face of a natural creature, its huge, blinking eyes which reflected all the lust, abysmal greed, obscene cruelty, and monstrous evil that has stalked the sons of men since their ancestors moved blind and hairless in the treetops. In those grisly eyes were mirrored all the unholy things and vile secrets that sleep in the cities under the sea, and that skulk from the light of day in the blackness of primordial caverns. And so that ghastly thing that the unhallowed ritual of cruelty, and sadism, and blood had evoked from the silence of the hills, leered and blinked down on its bestial worshippers, who groveled in abhorrent abasement before it.

Now the beast-masked priest lifted the bound and weakly writhing girl in his brutish hands and held her up toward that horror on the monolith. And as that monstrosity sucked in its breath, lustfully, slobberingly, something snapped in my brain, and I fell into a merciful faint.

I opened my eyes on a still white dawn. All the events of the night rushed back on me and I sprang up, then stared about me in amazement. The monolith brooded gaunt and silent above the sward which waved green and untrampled, in the morning breeze. A few quick strides took me across the glade; here had the dancers leaped and bounded until the ground should have been trampled bare, and here had the votaress wiggled her painful way to the Stone, streaming blood on the earth. But no drop of crimson showed on the uncrushed sward. I looked, shudderingly, at the side of the monolith against which the bestial priest had brained the stolen baby—but no dark stain nor grisly clot showed there.

A dream! It had been a wild nightmare—or else—I shrugged my shoudlers. What vivid clarity for a dream!

I returned quietly to the village and entered the inn without being seen. And there I sat meditating over the strange events of the night. More and more was I prone to discard the dream-theory. That what I had seen was illusion and without material substance was evident. But I believed that I had looked on the mirrored shadow of a deed perpetrated in ghastly actuality in bygone days. But how was I to know? What proof to show that my vision had been a gathering of foul specters rather than a nightmare originating in my brain?

As if for answer a name flashed into my mind—Selim Bahadur! According to legend this man, who had been a soldier as well as a scribe, had commanded that part of Suleiman's army which had devastated Stregoicavar; it seemed logical enough; and if so, he had gone straight from the blotted-out countryside to the bloody field of Schomvaal, and his doom. I sprang up with a sudden shout—that manuscript which was taken from the Turk's body, and which Count Boris shuddered over—might it not contain some narration of what the conquering Turks found in Stregoicavar? What else could have shaken the iron nerves of the Polish adventurer? And since the bones of the Count had never been recovered, what more certain than that the lacquered case, with its mysterious contents, still lay hidden beneath the ruins that covered Boris Vladinoff? I began packing my bag with fierce haste.

Three days later found me ensconced in a little village a few miles from the old battlefield, and when the moon rose I was working with savage intensity on the great pile of crumbling stone that crowned the bill. It was backbreaking toil—looking back now I can not see how I accomplished it, though I labored without a pause from moonrise to dawn. Just as the sun was coming up I tore aside the last tangle of stones and looked on all that was mortal of Count Boris Vladinoff—only a few pitiful fragments of crumbling bone—and among them, crushed out of all original shape, lay a case whose lacquered surface had kept it from complete decay through the centuries.

I seized it with frenzied eagerness, and piling back some of the stones on the bones I hurried away; for I did not care to be discovered by the suspicious peasants in an act of apparent desecration.

Back in my tavern chamber I opened the case and found the parchment comparatively intact; and there was something else in the case—a small squat object wrapped in silk. I was wild to plumb the secrets of those yellowed pages, but weariness forbade me. Since leaving Stregoicavar I had hardly slept at all, and the terrific exertions of the previous night combined to overcome me. In spite of myself I was forced to stretch myself on my bed, nor did I awake until sundown.

I snatched a hasty supper, and then in the light of a flickering candle, I set myself to read the neat Turkish characters that covered the parchment. It was difficult work, for I am not deeply versed in the language, and the archaic style of the narrative baffled me. But as I toiled through it a word or a phrase here and there leaped at me and a dimly growing horror shook me in its grip. I bent my energies fiercely to the task, and as the tale grew clearer and took more tangible form my blood chilled in my veins, my hair stood up, and my tongue clove to my mouth. All external things partook of the grisly madness of that infernal manuscript until the night sounds of insects and creatures in the woods took the form of ghastly murmurings and stealthy treadings of ghoulish horrors, and the sighing of the night wind changed to tittering obscene gloating of evil over the souls of men.

At last when gray dawn was stealing the latticed window, I laid down the manuscript, and took up and unwrapped the thing in the bit of silk. Staring at it with haggard eyes I knew the truth of the matter was clinched, even had it been possible to doubt the veracity of that terrible manuscript.

And I replaced both obscene things in the case, nor did I rest nor sleep nor eat until that case containing them had been weighted with stones and flung into the deepest current of the Danube which, God grant, carried them back into the Hell from which they came.

It was no dream I dreamed on Midsummer Midnight in the hills above Stregoicavar. Well for Justin Geoffrey that he tarried there only in the sunlight and went his way, for had he gazed upon that ghastly conclave, his mad brain would have snapped before it did. How my own reason held, I do not know.

No—it was no dream—I gazed upon a foul rout of votaries long dead, come up from Hell to worship as of old; ghosts that bowed before a ghost. For Hell has long claimed their hideous god. Long, long he dwelt among the hills, a brain-shattering vestige of an outworn age; but no longer his obscene talons clutch for the souls of living men, and his kingdom is a dead kingdom, peopled only by the ghosts of those who served him in his lifetime and theirs.

By what foul alchemy or godless sorcery the Gates of Hell are opened on that one eerie night I do not know, but mine own eyes have seen. And I know I looked on no living thing that night, for the manuscript written in the careful hand of Selim

Bahadur narrated at length what he and his raiders found in the valley Stregoicavar; and I read, set down in detail, the blasphemous obscenities that torture wrung from the lips of screaming worshippers; and I read, too, of the lost, grim black cavern high in the hills where the horrified Turks hemmed a monstrous, bloated, wallowing toad-like being and slew it with flame and ancient steel blessed in old times by Muhammad, and with incantations that were old when Arabia was young. And even staunch old Selim's hand shook as he recorded the cataclysmic, earth-shaking death-howls of the monstrosity, which died not alone; for a half-score of his slayers perished with him, in ways that Selim would not or could not describe.

And that squat idol carved of gold and wrapped in silk was an image of himself, and Selim tore it from the golden chain that looped the neck of the slain high priest of the mask.

Well that the Turks swept out that foul valley with torch and cleanly steel! Such sights as those brooding mountains have looked on belong to the darkness and abysses of lost eons. No—it is not fear of the toad-thing that makes me shudder in the night. He is made fast in Hell with his nauseous horde, freed only for an hour on the most weird night of the year, as I have seen. And of his worshippers, none remains.

But it is the realization that such things once crouched beast-like above the souls of men which brings cold sweat to my brow; and I fear to peer again into the leaves of Von Junzt's abomination. For now I understand his repeated phrase of keys!—aye! Keys to Outer Doors—links with an abhorrent past and—who knows?—of abhorrent spheres of the present. And I understand why the cliffs look like battlements in the moonlight, and why the tavern-keeper's nightmare-haunted nephew saw in his dream., the Black Stone like a spire on a cyclopean black castle. If men ever excavate among those mountains, they may find incredible things below those masking slopes. For the cave wherein the Turks trapped the—thing—was not truly a cavern, and I shudder to contemplate the gigantic gulf of eons which must stretch between this age and the time when the earth shook herself and reared up, like a wave, those blue mountains that, rising, enveloped unthinkable things. May no man ever seek to uproot the ghastly spire men called the Black Stone!

A Key! Aye, it is a Key, symbol of a forgotten horror. That horror has faded into the limbo from which it crawled, loathsomely, in the black dawn of the earth. But what of the other fiendish possibilities hinted at by Von Junzt—what of the monstrous hand which strangled out his life? Since reading what Selim Bahadur wrote, I can no longer doubt anything in the Black Book. Man was not always master of the earth—and is he now?

And the thought recurs to me—if such a monstrous entity as the Master of the Monolith somehow survived its own unspeakably distant epoch so long—what nameless shapes may even now lurk in the dark places of the world?

PEOPLE OF THE DARK

I came to Dagon's Cave to kill Richard Brent. I went down the dusky avenues made by the towering trees, and my mood well-matched the primitive grimness of the scene.

The approach to Dagon's Cave is always dark, for the mighty branches and thick leaves shut out the sun, and now the somberness of my own soul made the shadows seem more ominous and gloomy than was natural.

Not far away I heard the slow wash of the waves against the tall cliffs, but the sea itself was out of sight, masked by the dense oak forest. The darkness and the stark gloom of my surroundings gripped my shadowed soul as I passed beneath the ancient branches—as I came out into a narrow glade and saw the mouth of the ancient cavern before me. I paused, scanning the cavern's exterior and the dim reaches of the silent oaks.

The man I hated had not come before me! I was in time to carry out my grim intent. For a moment my resolution faltered, then like a wave there surged over me the fragrance of Eleanor Bland, a vision of wavy, golden hair and deep, gray eyes, changing and mystic as the sea. I clenched my hands until the knuckles showed white, and instinctively touched the wicked snub-nosed revolver whose weight sagged my coat pocket.

But for Richard Brent, I felt certain I had already won this woman, desire for whom made my waking hours a torment and my sleep a torture. Whom did she love? She would not say; I did not believe she knew. Let one of us go away, I thought, and she would turn to the other. And I was going to simplify matters for her—and for myself. By chance I had overheard my blond English rival remark that he intended coming to lonely Dagon's Cave on an idle exploring outing—alone.

I am not by nature criminal. I was born and raised in a hard country and have lived most of my life on the raw edges of the world, where a man took what he wanted, if he could, and mercy was a virtue little known. But it was a torment that racked me day and night that sent me out to take the life of Richard Brent. I have lived hard, and violently, perhaps. When love overtook me, it also was fierce and violent. Perhaps I was not wholly sane, what with my love for Eleanor Bland and my hatred for Richard Brent. Under any other circumstances, I would have been glad to call him friend—a fine, rangy, upstanding young fellow, clear-eyed and strong. But he stood in the way of my desire and he must die.

I stepped into the dimness of the cavern and halted. I had never before visited Dagon's Cave, yet a vague sense of misplaced familiarity troubled me as I gazed on the high arching roof, the even stone walls, and the dusty floor. I shrugged my shoulders, unable to place the elusive feeling; doubtless it was evoked by a similarity to caverns in the mountain country of the American Southwest where I was born and spent my childhood.

And yet I knew that I had never seen a cave like this one, whose regular aspect gave rise to myths that it was not a natural cavern, but had been hewn from the solid rock ages ago by the tiny hands of the mysterious Little People, the prehistoric beings of British legend. The whole countryside thereabouts was a haunt for ancient folklore.

The country folk were predominantly Celtic; here the Saxon invaders had never prevailed, and the legends reached back, in that long-settled countryside, further than anywhere else in England—back beyond the coming of the Saxons, aye, and incredibly beyond that distant age, beyond the coming of the Romans, to those unbelievably ancient days when the native Britons warred with black-haired Irish pirates.

The Little People, of course, had their part in the lore. Legend said that this cavern was one of their last strongholds against the conquering Celts, and hinted at lost tunnels, long fallen in or blocked up, connecting the cave with a network of subterranean corridors which honeycombed the hills. With these chance meditations vying idly in my mind with grimmer speculations, I passed through the outer chamber of the cavern and entered a narrow tunnel, which, I knew by former descriptions, connected with a larger room.

It was dark in the tunnel, but not too dark for me to make out the vague, half-defaced outlines of mysterious etchings on the stone walls. I ventured to switch on my electric torch and examine them more closely. Even in their dimness I was repelled by their abnormal and revolting character. Surely no men cast in human mold as we know it, scratched those grotesque obscenities.

The Little People—I wondered if those anthropologists were correct in their theory of a squat Mongoloid aboriginal race, so low in the scale of evolution as to be scarcely human, yet possessing a distinct, though repulsive, culture of their own. They had vanished before the invading races, theory said, forming the base of all Aryan legends of trolls, elves, dwarfs, and witches. Living in caves from the start, these aborigines had retreated farther and farther into the caverns of the hills, before the conquerors, vanishing at last entirely, though folk-lore fancy pictures their descendants still dwelling in the lost chasms far beneath the hills, loathsome survivors of an outworn age.

I snapped off the torch and passed through the tunnel, to come out into a sort of doorway which seemed entirely too symmetrical to have been the work of nature. I was looking into a vast dim cavern, at a somewhat lower level than the outer chamber, and again I shuddered with a strange, alien sense of familiarity. A short flight of steps led down from the tunnel to the floor of the cavern—tiny steps, too small for normal human feet, carved into the solid stone. Their edges were greatly worn away, as if by ages of use. I started the descent—my foot slipped suddenly. I instinctively knew what was coming—It was all in part with that strange feeling of familiarity—but I could not catch myself. I fell headlong down the steps and struck the stone floor with a crash that blotted out my senses ...

Slowly consciousness returned to me, with a throbbing of my head and a sensation of bewilderment. I lifted a hand to my head and found it caked with blood. I had received a blow, or had taken a fall, but so completely had my wits been knocked out of me that my mind was an absolute blank. Where I was, who I was, I did not know. I looked about, blinking in the dim light, and saw that I was in a wide, dusty cavern. I stood at the foot of a short flight of steps which led upward into some kind of tunnel. I ran my hand dazedly through my square-cut black mane, and my eyes wandered over my massive naked limbs and powerful torso. I was clad, I noticed absently, in a sort of loin-cloth, from the girdle of which swung an empty scabbard, and leathern sandals were on my feet.

Then I saw an object lying at my feet, and stooped and took it up. It was a heavy iron sword, whose broad blade was darkly stained. My fingers fitted instinctively about its hilt with the familiarity of long usage. Then suddenly I remembered and laughed to think that a fall on his head should render me, Conan of the reavers, so completely daft. Aye, it all came back to me now. It had been a raid on the Britons, on whose coasts we continually swooped with torch and sword, from the island called Eireann. That day we of the black-haired Gael had swept suddenly down on a coastal village in our long, low ships and in the hurricane of battle which followed, the Britons had at last given up the stubborn contest and retreated, warriors, women, and bairns, into the deep shadows of the oak forests, whither we seldom dared follow.

But I had followed, for there was a girl of my foes whom I desired with a burning passion, a lithe, slim young creature with wavy golden hair and deep gray eyes, changing and mystic as the sea. Her name was Tamera—well I knew it, for there was trade between the races as well as war, and I had been in the villages of the Britons as a peaceful visitor, in times of rare truce.

I saw her white, half-clad body flickering among the trees as she ran with the swiftness of a doe, and I followed, panting with fierce eagerness. Under the dark shadows of the gnarled oaks she fled, with me in close pursuit, while far away behind us died out the shouts of slaughter and the clashing of swords. Then we ran in silence, save for her quick, labored panting, and I was so close behind her as we emerged into a narrow glade before a somber-mouthed cavern, that I caught her flying golden tresses with one mighty hand. She sank down with a despairing wail, and even so, a shout echoed her cry, and I wheeled quickly to face a rangy young Briton who sprang from among the trees, the light of desperation in his eyes.

"Vertorix!" the girl wailed, her voice breaking in a sob, and fiercer rage welled up in me, for I knew the lad was her lover.

"Run for the forest, Tamera!" he shouted, and leaped at me as a panther leaps, his bronze ax whirling like a flashing wheel about his head. And then sounded the clangor of strife and the hard-drawn panting of combat.

The Briton was as tall as I, but he was lithe where I was

massive. The advantage of sheer muscular power was mine, and soon he was on the defensive, striving desperately to parry my heavy strokes with his ax. Hammering on his guard like a smith on an anvil, I pressed him relentlessly, driving him irresistibly before me. His chest heaved, his breath came in labored gasps, his blood dripped from scalp, chest, and thigh where my whistling blade had cut the skin, and all but gone home. As I redoubled my strokes, and he bent and swayed beneath them like a sapling in a storm, I heard the girl cry: "Vertorix! Vertorix! The cave! Into the cave!"

I saw his face pale with a fear greater than that induced by my hacking sword.

"Not there!" he gasped. "Better a clean death! In Il-marenin's name, girl, run into the forest and save yourself!"

"I will not leave you!" she cried. "The cave! It is our one chance!"

I saw her flash past us like a flying wisp of white and vanish in the cavern, and with a despairing cry, the youth launched a wild desperate stroke that nigh cleft my skull. As I staggered beneath the blow I had barely parried, he sprang away, leaped into the cavern after the girl, and vanished in the gloom.

With a maddened yell that invoked all my grim Gaelic gods, I sprang recklessly after them, not reckoning if the Briton lurked beside the entrance to brain me as I rushed in. But a quick glance showed the chamber empty and a wisp of white disappearing through a dark doorway in the back wall.

I raced across the cavern and came to a sudden halt as an ax licked out of the gloom of the entrance and whistled perilously close to my black-maned head. I gave back suddenly. Now the advantage was with Vertorix, who stood in the narrow mouth of the corridor where I could hardly come at him without exposing myself to the devastating stroke of his ax.

I was near frothing with fury, and the sight of a slim, white form among the deep shadows behind the warrior drove me into a frenzy. I attacked savagely but warily, thrusting venomously at my foe, and drawing back from his strokes. I wished to draw him out into a wide lunge, avoid it, and run him through before he could recover his balance. In the open I could have beaten him down by sheer power and heavy blows, but here I could only use the point and that at a disadvantage; I always preferred the edge. But I was stubborn; if I could not come at him with a finishing stroke, neither could he or the girl escape me while I kept him hemmed in the tunnel.

It must have been the realization of this fact that prompted the girl's action, for she said something to Vertorix about looking for a way leading out, and though he cried out fiercely, forbidding her to venture away into the darkness, she turned and ran swiftly down the tunnel to vanish in the dimness. My wrath rose appallingly, and I nearly got my head split in my eagerness to bring down my foe before she found a means for their escape.

Then the cavern echoed with a terrible scream, and Vertorix cried out like a man death-stricken, his face ashy in the gloom. He whirled, as if he had forgotten me and my sword, and raced down the tunnel like a madman, shrieking Tamera's name. From far away, as if from the bowels of the earth, I seemed to hear her answering cry, mingled with a strange sibilant clamor that electrified me with nameless but instinctive horror. Then silence fell, broken only by Vertorix's frenzied cries, receding farther and farther into the earth.

Recovering myself, I sprang into the tunnel and raced after the Briton as recklessly as he had run after the girl. And to give me my due, red-handed reaver though I was, cutting down my rival from behind was less in my mind than discovering what dread thing had Tamera in its clutches.

As I ran along, I noted absently that the sides of the tunnel were scrawled with monstrous pictures, and realized suddenly and creepily that this must be the dread Cavern of the Children of the Night, tales of which had crossed the narrow sea to resound horrifically in the ears of the Gaels. Terror of me must have ridden Tamera hard to have driven her into the cavern shunned by her people, where it was said, lurked the survivors of that grisly race which inhabited the land before the coming of the Picts and Britons, and which had fled before them into the unknown caverns of the hills.

Ahead of me the tunnel opened into a wide chamber, and I saw the white form of Vertorix glimmer momentarily in the semidarkness and vanish in what appeared to be the entrance of a corridor opposite the mouth of the tunnel I had just traversed. Instantly there sounded a short, fierce shout and the crash of a hard-driven blow, mixed with the hysterical screams of a girl and a medley of serpentlike hissing that made my hair bristle. And at that instant I shot out of the tunnel, running at full speed, and realized too late the floor of the cavern lay several feet below the level of the tunnel. My flying feet missed the tiny steps, and I crashed terrifically on the solid stone floor.

Now as I stood in the semidarkness, rubbing my aching head, all this came back to me, and I stared fearsomely across the vast chamber at that black cryptic corridor into which Tamera and her lover had disappeared, and over which silence lay like a pall. Gripping my sword, I warily crossed the great, still cavern and peered into the corridor. Only a denser darkness met my eyes. I entered, striving to pierce the gloom, and as my foot slipped on a wide, wet smear on the stone floor, the raw, acrid scent of fresh-spilled blood met my nostrils. Someone or something had died there, either the young Briton or his unknown attacker.

I stood there uncertainly, all the supernatural fears that are the heritage of the Gael rising in my primitive soul. I could turn and stride out of these accursed mazes, into the clear sunlight and down to the clean blue sea where my comrades, no doubt, impatiently awaited me after the routing of the Britons. Why should I risk my life among these grisly rat dens? I was eaten with curiosity to know what manner of beings haunted the cavern, and who were called the Children of the Night by the Britons, but in it was my love for the yellow-haired girl which drove me down that dark tunnel—and love her I did, in my way, and would have been kind to her, had I carried her away to my island haunt.

I walked softly along the corridor, blade ready. What sort of creatures the Children of the Night were, I had no idea, but the tales of the Britons had lent them a distinctly inhuman nature.

The darkness closed around me as I advanced, until I was moving in utter blackness. My groping left hand encountered a strangely carven doorway, and at that instant something hissed like a viper beside me and slashed fiercely at my thigh. I struck back savagely and felt my blind stroke crunch home, and something fell at my feet and died. What thing I had slain in the dark I could not know, but it must have been at least partly human because the shallow gash in my thigh had been made with a blade of some sort, and not by fangs or talons. And I sweated with horror, for the gods know, the hissing voice of the Thing had resembled no human tongue I had ever heard.

And now in the darkness ahead of me I heard the sound repeated, mingled with horrible slitherings, as if numbers of reptilian creatures were approaching. I stepped quickly into the entrance my groping hand had discovered and came near repeating my headlong fall, for instead of letting into another level corridor, the entrance gave onto a flight of dwarfish steps on which I floundered wildly.

Recovering my balance, I went on cautiously, groping along the sides of the shaft for support. I seemed to be descending into the very bowels of the earth, but I dared not turn back. Suddenly, far below me, I glimpsed a faint eerie light. I went on, perforce, and came to a spot where the shaft opened into another great vaulted chamber; and I shrank back, aghast.

In the center of the chamber stood a grim, black altar; it had been rubbed all over with a sort of phosphorous, so that it glowed dully, lending a semi-illumination to the shadowy cavern.

Towering behind it, on a pedestal of human skulls, lay a cryptic black object, carven with mysterious hieroglyphics. The Black Stone! The ancient, ancient Stone before which, the Britons said, the Children of the Night bowed in gruesome worship, and whose origin was lost in the black mists of a hideously distant past. Once, legend said, it had stood in that grim circle of monoliths called Stonehenge, before its votaries had been driven like chaff before the bows of the Picts.

But I gave it but a passing, shuddering glance. Two figures lay, bound with rawhide thongs, on the glowing black altar. One was Tamera; the other was Vertorix, bloodstained and disheveled. His bronze ax, crusted with clotted blood, lay near the altar. And before the glowing stone squatted Horror.

Though I had never seen one of those ghoulish aborigines, I knew this thing for what it was, and shuddered. It was a man of a sort, but so low in the stage of life that its distorted humanness was more horrible than its bestiality.

Erect, it could not have been five feet in height. Its body was scrawny and deformed, its head disproportionately large. Lank, snaky hair fell over a square inhuman face with flabby, writhing lips that bared yellow fangs, flat, spreading nostrils and great yellow slant eyes. I knew the creature must be able to see in the dark as well as a cat. Centuries of skulking in dim caverns had lent the race terrible and inhuman attributes. But the most repellent feature was its skin: scaly, yellow, and mottled, like the hide of a serpent. A loincloth made of a real snake's skin girt its lean loins, and its taloned hands gripped a short stone-tipped spear and a sinister-looking mallet of polished flint.

So intently was it gloating over its captives, it evidently had not heard my stealthy descent. As I hesitated in the shadows of the shaft, far above me I heard a soft sinister rustling that chilled the blood in my veins. The Children were creeping down the shaft behind me, and I was trapped. I saw other entrances opening on the chamber, and I acted, realizing that an alliance with Vertorix was our only hope. Enemies though we were, we were men, cast in the same mold, trapped in the lair of these indescribable monstrosities.

As I stepped from the shaft, the horror beside the altar jerked up his head and glared full at me. And as he sprang up, I leaped and he crumpled, blood spurting, as my heavy sword split his reptilian heart. But even as he died, he gave tongue in an abhorrent shriek which was echoed far up the shaft. In desperate haste I cut Vertorix's bonds and dragged him to his feet. And I turned to Tamera, who in that dire extremity did not shrink from me, but looked up at me with pleading, terror-dilated eyes. Vertorix wasted no time in words, realizing chance had made allies of us. He snatched up his ax as I freed the girl.

"We can't go up the shaft," he explained swiftly; "we'll have the whole pack upon us quickly. They caught Tamera as she sought for an exit, and overpowered me by sheer numbers when I followed. They dragged us hither and all but that carrion scattered—bearing word of the sacrifice through all their burrows, I doubt not. Il-marenin alone knows how many of my people, stolen in the night, have died on that altar. We must take our chance in one of these tunnels—all lead to Hell! Follow me!"

Seizing Tamera's hand, he ran fleetly into the nearest tunnel and I followed. A glance back into the chamber before a turn in the corridor blotted it from view showed a revolting horde streaming out of the shaft. The tunnel slanted steeply upward, and suddenly ahead of us we saw a bar of gray light. But the next instant our cries of hope changed to curses of bitter disappointment. There was daylight, aye, drifting in through a cleft in the vaulted roof, but far, far above our reach. Behind us the pack gave tongue exultingly. And I halted.

"Save yourselves if you can," I growled. "Here I make my stand. They can see in the dark and I cannot. Here at least I can see them. Go!"

But Vertorix halted also. "Little use to be hunted like rats to our doom. There is no escape. Let us meet our fate like men."

Tamera cried out, wringing her hands, but she clung to her lover.

"Stand behind me with the girl," I grunted. "When I fall, dash out her brains with your ax lest they take her alive again. Then sell your own life as high as you may, for there is none to avenge us."

His keen eyes met mine squarely.

"We worship different gods, reaver," he said, "but all gods love brave men. Mayhap we shall meet again, beyond the Dark."

"Hail and farewell, Briton!" I growled, and our right hands gripped like steel.

"Hail and farewell, Gael!"

And I wheeled as a hideous horde swept up the tunnel and burst into the dim light, a flying nightmare of streaming snaky hair, foam-flecked lips, and glaring eyes. Thundering my war cry, I sprang to meet them, and my heavy sword sang, and a head spun grinning from its shoulder on an arching fountain of blood. They came upon me like a wave, and the fighting madness of my race was upon me. I fought as a maddened beast fights, and at every stroke I clove through flesh and bone, and blood spattered in a crimson rain.

Then as they surged in and I went down beneath the sheer weight of their numbers, a fierce yell cut the din, and Vertorix's ax sang above me, splattering blood and brains like water. The press slackened, and I staggered up, trampling the writhing bodies beneath my feet.

"A stair behind us!" the Briton was screaming. "Half-hidden in an angle of the wall! It must lead to daylight! Up it, in the name of Il-marenin!"

So we fell back, fighting our way inch by inch. The vermin fought like blood-hungry devils, clambering over the bodies of the slain to screech and hack. Both of us were streaming blood at every step when we reached the mouth of the shaft, into which Tamera had preceded us.

Screaming like very fiends, the Children surged in to drag us down. The shaft was not as light as had been the corridor, and it grew darker as we climbed, but our foes could only come at us from in front. By the gods, we slaughtered them till the stair was littered with mangled corpses, and the Children frothed like mad wolves! Then suddenly they abandoned the fray and raced back down the steps.

"What portends this?" gasped Vertorix, shaking the bloody sweat from his eyes.

"Up the shaft, quick!" I panted. "They mean to mount some other stair and come at us from above!"

So we raced up those accursed steps, slipping and stumbling, and as we fled past a black tunnel that opened into the shaft, far down it we heard a frightful howling. An instant later we emerged from the shaft into a winding corridor, dimly illumined by a vague gray light filtering in from above, and somewhere in the bowels of the earth I seemed to hear the thunder of rushing water. We started down the corridor and as we did so, a heavy weight smashed on my shoulders, knocking me headlong, and a mallet crashed again and again on my head, sending dull red flashes of agony across my brain. With a volcanic wrench I dragged my attacker off and under me, and tore out his throat with my naked fingers. And his fangs met in my arm in his death-bite.

Reeling up, I saw that Tamera and Vertorix had passed out of sight. I had been somewhat behind them, and they had run on, knowing nothing of the fiend which had leaped on my shoulders. Doubtless they thought I was still close on their heels. A dozen steps I took, then halted. The corridor branched, and I knew not which way my companions had taken. At blind venture I turned into the left-hand branch and staggered on in the semi-darkness. I was weak from fatigue and loss of blood, dizzy and sick from the blows I had received. Only the thought of Tamera kept me doggedly on my feet. Now distinctly I heard the sound of an unseen torrent.

That I was not far underground was evident by the dim light

which filtered in from somewhere above, and I momentarily expected to come upon another stair. But when I did, I halted in black despair; instead of up, it led down. Somewhere far behind me I heard faintly the howls of the pack, and I went down, plunging into utter darkness. At last I struck a level and went along blindly. I had given up all hope of escape, and only hoped to find Tamera—if she and her lover had not found a way of escape—and die with her. The thunder of rushing water was above my head now, and the tunnel was slimy and dank. Drops of moisture fell on my head and I knew I was passing under the river.

Then I blundered again upon steps cut in the stone, and these led upward. I scrambled up as fast as my stiffening wounds would allow—and I had taken punishment enough to have killed an ordinary man. Up I went and up, and suddenly daylight burst on me through a cleft in the solid rock. I stepped into the blaze of the sun. I was standing on a ledge high above the rushing waters of a river which raced at awesome speed between towering cliffs. The ledge on which I stood was close to the top of the cliff; safety was within arm's length. But I hesitated and such was my love for the golden-haired girl that I was ready to retrace my steps through those black tunnels on the mad hope of finding her. Then I started.

Across the river I saw another cleft in the cliff-wall which fronted me, with a ledge similar to that on which I stood, but longer. In olden times, I doubt not, some sort of primitive bridge connected the two ledges—possibly before the tunnel was dug beneath the riverbed. Now as I watched, two figures emerged upon that other ledge—one gashed, dust-stained, limping, gripping a bloodstained ax; the other slim, white and girlish.

Vertorix and Tamera! They had taken the other branch of the corridor at the fork and had evidently followed the windows of the tunnel to emerge as I had done, except that I had taken the left turn and passed clear under the river. And now I saw that they were in a trap. On that side the cliffs rose half a hundred feet higher than on my side of the river, and so sheer a spider could scarce have scaled them. There were only two ways of escape from the ledge: back through the fiend-haunted tunnels, or straight down to the river which raved far beneath.

I saw Vertorix look up the sheer cliffs and then down, and shake his head in despair. Tamara put her arms about his neck, and though I could not hear their voices for the rush of the river, I saw them smile, and then they went together to the edge of the ledge. And out of the cleft swarmed a loathsome mob, as foul reptiles writhe up out of the darkness, and they stood blinking in the sunlight like the night-things they were. I gripped my sword-hilt in the agony of my helplessness until the blood trickled from under my fingernails. Why had not the pack followed me instead of my companions?

The Children hesitated an instant as the two Britons faced them, then with a laugh Vertorix hurled his ax far out into the rushing river, and turning, caught Tamera in a last embrace. Together they sprang far out, and still locked in each other's arms, hurtled downward, struck the madly foaming water that seemed to leap up to meet them, and vanished. And the wild river swept on like a blind, insensate monster, thundering along the echoing cliffs.

A moment I stood frozen, then like a man in a dream I turned, caught the edge of the cliff above me and wearily drew myself up and over, and stood on my feet above the cliffs, hearing like a dim dream the roar of the river far beneath.

I reeled up, dazedly clutching my throbbing head, on which dried blood was clotted. I glared wildly about me. I had clambered the cliffs—no, by the thunder of Crom, I was still in the cavern! I reached for my sword—

The mists faded and I stared about dizzily, orienting myself with space and time. I stood at the foot of the steps down which I had fallen. I, who had been Conan the reaver, was John O'Brien. Was all that grotesque interlude a dream? Could a mere dream appear so vivid? Even in dreams, we often know we are dreaming, but Conan the reaver had no cognizance of any other existence. More, he remembered his own past life as a living man remembers, though in the waking mind of John O'Brien, that memory faded into dust and mist. But the adventures of Conan in the Cavern of the Children stood clear-etched in the mind of John O'Brien.

I glanced across the dim chamber toward the entrance of the tunnel into which Vertorix had followed the girl. But I looked in vain, seeing only the bare blank wall of the cavern. I crossed the chamber, switched on my electric torch—miraculously unbroken in my fall—and felt along the wall.

Ha! I started, as from an electric shock! Exactly where the entrance should have been, my fingers detected a difference in material, a section which was rougher than the rest of the wall. I was convinced that it was of comparatively modern workmanship; the tunnel had been walled up.

I thrust against it, exerting all my strength, and it seemed to me that the section was about to give. I drew back, and taking a deep breath, launched my full weight against it, backed by all the power of my giant muscles. The brittle, decaying wall gave way with a shattering crash and I catapulted through in a shower of stones and falling masonry.

I scrambled up, a sharp cry escaping me. I stood in a tunnel, and I could not mistake the feeling of similarity this time. Here Vertorix had first fallen foul of the Children, as they dragged Tamera away, and here where I now stood the floor had been awash with blood.

I walked down the corridor like a man in a trance. Soon I should come to the doorway on the left—aye, there it was, the strangely carven portal, at the mouth of which I had slain the unseen being which reared up in the dark beside me. I shivered momentarily. Could it be possible that remnants of that foul race still lurked hideously in these remote caverns?

I turned into the doorway and my light shone down a long, slanting shaft, with tiny steps cut into the solid stone. Down these had Conan the reaver gone groping and down them went I, John O'Brien, with memories of that other life filling my brain with vague phantasms. No light glimmered ahead of me, but I came into the great dim chamber I had known of yore, and I shuddered as I saw the grim black altar etched in the gleam of my torch. Now no bound figures writhed there, no crouching horror gloated before it. Nor did the pyramid of skulls support the Black Stone before which unknown races had bowed before Egypt was born out of time's dawn. Only a littered heap of dust lay strewn where the skulls had upheld the hellish thing. No, that had been no dream: I was John O'Brien, but I had been Conan of the reavers in that other life, and that grim interlude a brief episode of reality which I had relived.

I entered the tunnel down which we had fled, shining a beam of light ahead, and saw the bar of gray light drifting down from above—just as in that other, lost age. Here the Briton and I, Conan, had turned at bay. I turned my eyes from the ancient cleft high up in the vaulted roof, and looked for the stair. There it was, half-concealed by an angle in the wall.

I mounted, remembering how hurriedly Vertorix and I had gone up so many ages before, with the horde hissing and frothing at our heels. I found myself tense with dread as I approached the dark, gaping entrance through which the pack had sought to cut us off. I had snapped off the light when I came into the dim-lit corridor below, and now I glanced into the well of blackness which opened on the stair. And with a cry I started back, nearly losing my footing on the worn steps. Sweating in the semidarkness I switched on the light and directed its beam into the cryptic opening, revolver in hand.

I saw only the bare rounded sides of a small shaftlike tunnel, and I laughed nervously. My imagination was running riot; I could have sworn that hideous yellow eyes glared terribly at me from the darkness, and that a crawling something had scuttered away down the tunnel. I was foolish to let these imaginings upset me. The Children had long vanished from these caverns; a name-

less and abhorrent race closer to the serpent than the man, they
had centuries ago faded back into the oblivion from which they
had crawled in the black dawn ages of the Earth.

I came out of the shaft into the winding corridor, which, as I
remembered of old, was lighter. Here from the shadows a lurking
thing had leaped on my back while my companions ran on,
unknowing. What a brute of a man Conan had been, to keep
going after receiving such savage wounds! Aye, in that age all
men were iron.

I came to the place where the tunnel forked and as before I
took the left-hand branch and came to the shaft that led down.
Down this I went, listening for the roar of the river, but not
hearing it. Again the darkness shut in about the shaft, so I was
forced to have recourse to my electric torch again, lest I lose my
footing and plunge to my death. Oh, I, John O'Brien, am not
nearly so sure-footed as was I, Conan the reaver; no, nor as tigerishly powerful and quick, either.

I soon struck the dank lower level and felt again the dampness that denoted my position under the riverbed, but still I
could not hear the rush of the water. And indeed I knew that
whatever mighty river had rushed roaring to the sea in those
ancient times, there was no such body of water among the hills
today. I halted, flashing my light about. I was in a vast tunnel,
not very high of roof, but broad. Other smaller tunnels branched
off from it, and I wondered at the network which apparently
honeycombed the hills.

I cannot describe the grim, gloomy effect of those dark, low-
roofed corridors far below the earth. Over all hung an overpowering sense of unspeakable antiquity. Why had the little people
carved out these mysterious crypts, and in which black age?
Were these caverns their last refuge from the onrushing tides of
humanity, or their castles since time immemorial? I shook my

head in bewilderment; the bestiality of the Children I had seen, yet some how they had been able to carve these tunnels and chambers that might balk modern engineers. Even supposing they had but completed a task begun by nature, still it was a stupendous work for a race of dwarfish aborigines.

Then I realized with a start that I was spending more time in these gloomy tunnels than I cared for and began to hunt for the steps by which Conan had ascended. I found them and, following them up, breathed again deeply in relief as the sudden glow of daylight filled the shaft. I came out upon the ledge, now worn away until it was little more than a bump on the face of the cliff. And I saw the great river, which had roared like a prisoned monster between the sheer walls of its narrow canyon, had dwindled away with the passing eons until it was no more than a tiny stream, far beneath me, trickling soundlessly among the stones on its way to the sea.

Aye, the surface of the earth changes; the rivers swell or shrink, the mountains heave and topple, the lakes dry up, the continents alter; but under the earth the work of lost, mysterious hands slumbers untouched by the sweep of Time. Their work, aye, but what of the hands that reared that work? Did they, too, lurk beneath the bosoms of the hills?

How long I stood there, lost in dim speculations, I do not know, but suddenly, glancing across at the other ledge, crumbling and weathered, I shrank back into the entrance behind me. Two figures came out upon the ledge and I gasped to see that they were Richard Brent and Eleanor Bland. Now I remembered why I had come to the cavern, and my hand instinctively sought the revolver in my pocket. They did not see me. But I could see them, and hear them plainly, too, since no roaring river now thundered between the ledges.

"By gad, Eleanor," Brent was saying, "I'm glad you decided to come with me. Who would have guessed there was anything to those old tales about hidden tunnels leading from the cavern? I wonder how that section of wall came to collapse? I thought I heard a crash just as we entered the outer cave. Do you suppose some beggar was in the cavern ahead of us, and broke it in?"

"I don't know," she answered. "I remember—oh, I don't know. It almost seems as if I'd been here before, or dreamed I had. I seem to faintly remember, like a far-off nightmare, running, running, running endlessly through these dark corridors with hideous creatures on my heels ..."

"Was I there?" jokingly asked Brent.

"Yes, and John, too," she answered. "But you were not Richard Brent, and John was not John O'Brien. No, and I was not Eleanor Bland, either. Oh, it's so dim and far-off I can't describe it at all. It's hazy and misty and terrible."

"I understand, a little," he said unexpectedly. "Ever since we came to the place where the wall had fallen and revealed the old tunnel, I've had a sense of familiarity with the place. There was horror and danger and battle—and love, too."

He stepped nearer the edge to look down in the gorge, and Eleanor cried out sharply and suddenly, seizing him in a convulsive grasp.

"Don't, Richard, don't! Hold me, oh, hold me tight!"

He caught her in his arms. "Why, Eleanor, dear, what's the matter?"

"Nothing," she faltered, but she clung closer to him and I saw she was trembling. "Just a strange feeling—rushing dizziness and fright, just as if I were falling from a great height. Don't go near the edge, Dick; it scares me."

"I won't, dear," he answered, drawing her closer to him, and continuing hesitantly: "Eleanor, there's something I've wanted to ask you for a long time—well, I haven't the knack of putting things in an elegant way. I love you, Eleanor; always have. You know that. But if you don't love me, I'll take myself off and won't annoy you anymore. Only please tell me one way or another, for I can't stand it any longer. Is it I or the American?"

"You, Dick," she answered, hiding her face on his shoulder. "It's always been you, though I didn't know it. I think a great deal of John O'Brien. I didn't know which of you I really loved. But today as we came through those terrible tunnels and climbed those fearful stairs, and just now, when I thought for some strange reason we were falling from the ledge, I realized it was you I loved—that I always loved you, through more lives than this one. Always!"

Their lips met and I saw her golden head cradled on his shoulder. My lips were dry, my heart cold, yet my soul was at peace. They belonged to each other. Eons ago they lived and loved, and because of that love they suffered and died. And I, Conan, had driven them to that doom.

I saw them turn toward the cleft, their arms about each other, then I heard Tamera—I mean Eleanor—shriek. I saw them both recoil. And out of the cleft a horror came writhing, a loathsome, brain-shattering thing that blinked in the clean sunlight. Aye, I knew it of old—vestige of a forgotten age, it came writhing its horrid shape up out of the darkness of the Earth and the lost past to claim its own.

What three thousand years of retrogression can do to a race hideous in the beginning, I saw, and shuddered. And instinctively I knew that in all the world it was the only one of its kind, a monster that had lived on, God alone knows how many centuries, wallowing in the slime of its dank subterranean lairs. Before the Children had vanished, the race must have lost all human semblance, living as they did the life of the reptile. This thing was more like a giant serpent than anything else, but it had aborted legs and snaky arms with hooked talons. It crawled on its belly, writhing back mottled lips to bare needle-like fangs, which I felt must drip with venom. It hissed as it reared up its ghastly head on a horribly long neck, while its yellow slanted eyes glittered with all the horror that is spawned in the black lairs under the earth.

I knew those eyes had blazed at me from the dark tunnel opening on the stair. For some reason the creature had fled from me, possibly because it feared my light, and it stood to reason that it was the only one remaining in the caverns, else I had been set upon in the darkness. But for it, the tunnels could be traversed in safety.

Now the reptilian thing writhed toward the humans trapped on the ledge. Brent had thrust Eleanor behind him and stood, face ashy, to guard her as best he could. And I gave thanks silently that I, John O'Brien, could pay the debt I, Conan the reaver, owed these lovers since long ago.

The monster reared up and Brent, with cold courage, sprang to meet it with his naked hands. Taking quick aim, I fired once. The shot echoed like the crack of doom between the towering cliffs, and the Horror, with a hideously human scream, staggered wildly, swayed and pitched headlong, knotting and writhing like a wounded python, to tumble from the sloping ledge and fall plummetlike to the rocks far below.

WORMS OF THE EARTH

CHAPTER ONE

S trike in the nails, soldiers, and let our guest see the reality of our good Roman justice!"

The speaker wrapped his purple cloak closer about his powerful frame and settled back into his official chair, much as he might have settled back in his seat at the Circus Maximus to enjoy the clash of gladiatorial swords. Realization of power colored his every move. Whetted pride was necessary to Roman satisfaction, and Titus Sulla was justly proud; for he was military governor of Eboracum and answerable only to the emperor of Rome. He was a strongly built man of medium height, with the hawk-like features of the pure-bred Roman. Now a mocking smile curved his full lips, increasing the arrogance of his haughty aspect. Distinctly military in appearance, he wore the golden-scaled corselet and chased breastplate of his rank, with the short stabbing sword at his belt, and he held on his knee the silvered helmet with its plumed crest. Behind him stood a clump of impassive soldiers with shield and spear—blond titans from the Rhineland.

Before him was taking place the scene which apparently gave him so much real gratification—a scene common enough wherever stretched the far-flung boundaries of Rome. A rude cross lay flat upon the barren earth and on it was bound a man—half-naked, wild of aspect with his corded limbs, glaring eyes, and shock of tangled hair. His executioners were Roman soldiers, and with heavy hammers they prepared to pin the victim's hands and feet to the wood with iron spikes.

Only a small group of men watched this ghastly scene, in the dread place of execution beyond the city walls: the governor and his watchful guards; a few young Roman officers; the man to whom Sulla had referred as "guest" and who stood like a bronze image, unspeaking. Beside the gleaming splendor of the Roman, the quiet garb of this man seemed drab, almost somber.

He was dark, but he did not resemble the Latins around him. There was about him none of the warm, almost Oriental sensuality of the Mediterranean which colored their features. The blond barbarians behind Sulla's chair were less unlike the man in facial outline than were the Romans. Not his were the full curving red lips, nor the rich waving locks suggestive of the Greek. Nor was his dark complexion the rich olive of the south; rather it was the bleak darkness of the north. The whole aspect of the man vaguely suggested the shadowed mists, the gloom, the cold, and the icy winds of the naked northern lands. Even his black eyes were savagely cold, like black fires burning through fathoms of ice.

His height was only medium, but there was something about him which transcended mere physical bulk—a certain fierce, innate vitality, comparable only to that of a wolf or a panther. In every line of his supple, compact body, as well as in his coarse straight hair and thin lips, this was evident—in the hawk-like set of the head on the corded neck, in the broad square shoulders, in the deep chest, the lean loins, the narrow feet. Built with the savage economy of a panther, he was an image of dynamic potentialities, pent in with iron self-control.

At his feet crouched one like him in complexion—but there the resemblance ended. This other was a stunted giant, with gnarly limbs, thick body, a low sloping brow, and an expression of dull ferocity, now clearly mixed with fear. If the man on the cross resembled, in a tribal way, the man Titus Sulla called guest, he far more resembled the stunted crouching giant.

"Well, Partha Mac Othna," said the governor with studied effrontery, "when you return to your tribe, you will have a tale to tell of the justice of Rome, who rules the south."

"I will have a tale," answered the other in a voice which betrayed no emotion, just as his dark face, schooled to immobility, showed no evidence of the maelstrom in his soul.

"Justice to all under the rule of Rome," said Sulla. "*Pax Romana!* Reward for virtue, punishment for wrong!" He laughed inwardly at his own black hypocrisy, then continued: "You see, emissary of Pictland, how swiftly Rome punishes the transgressor."

"I see," answered the Pict in a voice which strongly-curbed anger made deep with menace, "that the subject of a foreign king is dealt with as though he were a Roman slave."

"He has been tried and condemned in an unbiased court," retorted Sulla.

"Aye! And the accuser was a Roman, the witnesses Roman, the judge Roman! He committed murder? In a moment of fury he struck down a Roman merchant who cheated, tricked and robbed him, and to injury added insult—aye, and a blow! Is his king but a dog, that Rome crucifies his subjects at will, condemned by Roman courts? Is his king too weak or foolish to do justice, were he informed and formal charges brought against the offender?"

"Well," said Sulla cynically, "you may inform Bran Mak Morn yourself. Rome, my friend, makes no account of her actions to barbarian kings. When savages come among us, let them act with discretion or suffer the consequences."

The Pict shut his iron jaws with a snap that told Sulla further badgering would elicit no reply. The Roman made a gesture to the executioners. One of them seized a spike and placing it against the thick wrist of the victim, smote heavily. The iron point sank deep through the flesh, crunching against the bones. The lips of the man on the cross writhed, though no moan escaped him. As a trapped wolf fights against his cage, the bound victim instinctively wrenched and struggled. The veins swelled in his temples, sweat beaded his low forehead, the muscles in arms and legs writhed and knotted. The hammers fell in inexorable strokes, driving the cruel points deeper and deeper, through wrists and ankles; blood flowed in a black river over the hands that held the spikes, staining the wood of the cross, and the splintering of bones was distinctly heard. Yet the sufferer made no outcry, though his blackened lips writhed back until the gums were visible, and his shaggy head jerked involuntarily from side to side.

The man called Partha Mac Othna stood like an iron image, eyes burning from an inscrutable face, his whole body hard as iron from the tension of his control. At his feet crouched his misshapen servant, hiding his face from the grim sight, his arms locked about his master's knees. Those arms gripped like steel and under his breath the fellow mumbled ceaselessly as if in invocation.

The last stroke fell; the cords were cut from arm and leg, so that the man would hang supported by the nails alone. He had ceased his struggling that only twisted the spikes in his agonizing wounds. His bright black eyes, unglazed, had not left the face of the man called Partha Mac Othna; in them lingered a desperate shadow of hope. Now the soldiers lifted the cross and set the end of it in the hole prepared, stamped the dirt about it to hold it erect.

The Pict hung in midair, suspended by the nails in his flesh, but still no sound escaped his lips. His eyes still hung on the somber face of the emissary, but the shadow of hope was fading.

"He'll live for days!" said Sulla cheerfully. "These Picts are harder than cats to kill! I'll keep a guard of ten soldiers watching night and day to see that no one takes him down before he dies.

Ho, there, Valerius, in honor of our esteemed neighbor, King Bran Mak Morn, give him a cup of wine!"

With a laugh the young officer came forward, holding a brimming wine cup, and rising on his toes, lifted it to the parched lips of the sufferer. In the black eyes flared a red wave of unquenchable hatred; writhing his head aside to avoid even touching the cup, he spat full into the young Roman's eyes. With a curse Valerius dashed the cup to the ground, and before any could halt him, wrenched out his sword and sheathed it in the man's body.

Sulla rose with an imperious exclamation of anger; the man called Partha Mac Othna had started violently, but he bit his lip and said nothing. Valerius seemed somewhat surprized at him as he sullenly cleansed his sword. The act had been instinctive, following the insult to Roman pride, the one thing unbearable.

"Give up your sword, young sir!" exclaimed Sulla. "Centurion Publius, place him under arrest. A few days in a cell with stale bread and water will teach you to curb your patrician pride in matters dealing with the will of the empire. What, you young fool, do you not realize that you could not have made the dog a more kindly gift? Who would not rather desire a quick death on the sword than the slow agony on the cross? Take him away. And you, centurion, see that guards remain at the cross so that the body is not cut down until the ravens pick bare the bones. Partha Mac Othna, I go to a banquet at the house of Demetrius —will you not accompany me?"

The emissary shook his head, his eyes fixed on the limp form which sagged on the black-stained cross. He made no reply. Sulla smiled sardonically, then rose and strode away, followed by his secretary who bore the gilded chair ceremoniously, and by the stolid soldiers, with whom walked Valerius, head sunken.

The man called Partha Mac Othna flung a wide fold of his cloak about his shoulder, halted a moment to gaze at the grim cross with its burden, darkly etched against the crimson sky, where the clouds of night were gathering. Then he stalked away, followed by his silent servant.

CHAPTER TWO

In an inner chamber of Eboracum, the man called Partha Mac Othna paced tigerishly to and fro. His sandaled feet made no sound on the marble tiles.

"Grom!" he turned to the gnarled servant. "Well I know why you held my knees so tightly—why you muttered aid of the Moon-Woman—you feared I would lose my self-control and make a mad attempt to succor that poor wretch. By the gods, I believe that was what the dog Roman wished; his iron-cased watchdogs watched me narrowly, I know, and his baiting was harder to bear than ordinarily.

"Gods black and white, dark and light!" He shook his clenched fists above his head in the black gust of his passion. "That I should stand by and see a man of mine butchered on a Roman cross—without justice and with no more trial than that farce! Black gods of R'lyeh, even you would I invoke to the ruin and destruction of those butchers! I swear by the Nameless Ones, men shall die howling for that deed, and Rome shall cry out as a woman in the dark who treads upon an adder!"

"He knew you, master," said Grom.

The other dropped his head and covered his eyes with a gesture of savage pain.

"His eyes will haunt me when I lie dying. Aye, he knew me, and almost until the last, I read in his eyes the hope that I might aid him. Gods and devils, is Rome to butcher my people beneath my very eyes? Then I am not king but dog!"

"Not so loud, in the name of all the gods!" exclaimed Grom in affright. "Did these Romans suspect you were Bran Mak Morn, they would nail you on a cross beside that other."

"They will know it ere long," grimly answered the king. "Too long I have lingered here in the guise of an emissary, spying upon mine enemies. They have thought to play with me, these Romans, masking their contempt and scorn only under polished satire. Rome is courteous to barbarian ambassadors, they give us fine houses to live in, offer us slaves, pander to our lusts with women, and gold, and wine, and games, but all the while they laugh at us; their very courtesy is an insult, and sometimes—as today—their contempt discards all veneer. Bah! I've seen through their baitings—have remained imperturbably serene and swallowed their studied insults. But this—by the fiends of Hell, this is beyond human endurance! My people look to me; if I fail them—if I fail even one—even the lowest of my people, who will aid them? To whom shall they turn? By the gods, I'll answer the gibes of these Roman dogs with black shaft and trenchant steel!"

"And the chief with the plumes?" Grom meant the governor and his gutturals thrummed with the bloodlust. "He dies?" He flicked out a length of steel.

Bran scowled. "Easier said than done. He dies—but how may I reach him? By day his German guards keep at his back; by night they stand at door and window. He has many enemies, Romans as well as barbarians. Many a Briton would gladly slit his throat."

Grom seized Bran's garment, stammering as fierce eagerness broke the bonds of his inarticulate nature.

"Let me go, master! My life is worth nothing. I will cut him down in the midst of his warriors!"

Bran smiled fiercely and clapped his hand on the stunted giant's shoulder with a force that would have felled a lesser man.

"Nay, old war-dog, I have too much need of thee! You shall not throw your life away uselessly. Sulla would read the intent in your eyes, besides, and the javelins of his Teutons would be through you ere you could reach him. Not by the dagger in the dark will we strike this Roman, not by the venom in the cup, nor the shaft from the ambush."

The king turned and paced the floor a moment, his head bent in thought. Slowly his eyes grew murky with a thought so fearful he did not speak it aloud to the waiting warrior.

"I have become somewhat familiar with the maze of Roman politics during my stay in this accursed waste of mud and marble," said he. "During a war on the Wall, Titus Sulla, as governor of this province, is supposed to hasten thither with his centuries. But this Sulla does not do; he is no coward, but the bravest avoid certain things—to each man, however bold, his own particular fear. So he sends in his place Caius Camillus, who in times of peace patrols the fens of the west, lest the Britons break over the border. And Sulla takes his place in the Tower of Trajan. Ha!"

He whirled and gripped Grom with steely fingers.

"Grom, take the red stallion and ride north! Let no grass grow under the stallion's hoofs! Ride to Cormac na Connacht and tell him to sweep the frontier with sword and torch! Let his wild Gaels feast their fill of slaughter. After a time, I will be with him. But for a time, I have affairs in the west."

Grom's black eyes gleamed and he made a passionate gesture with his crooked hand—an instinctive move of savagery.

Bran drew a heavy bronze seal from beneath his tunic.

"This is my safe-conduct as an emissary to Roman courts," he said grimly. "It will open all gates between this house and Baaldor. If any official questions you too closely—here!"

Lifting the lid of an iron-bound chest, Bran took out a small, heavy leather bag which he gave into the hands of the warrior.

"When all keys fail at a gate," said he, "try a golden key. Go now!"

There were no ceremonious farewells between the barbarian king and his barbarian vassal. Grom flung up his arm in a gesture of salute; then turning, he hurried out.

Bran stepped to a barred window and gazed out into the moonlit streets.

"Wait until the moon sets," he muttered grimly. "Then I'll take the road to—Hell! But before I go, I have a debt to pay."

The stealthy clink of a hoof on the flags reached him.

"With the safe-conduct and gold, not even Rome can hold a Pictish reaver," muttered the king. "Now I'll sleep until the moon sets."

With a snarl at the marble frieze-work and fluted columns as symbols of Rome, he flung himself down on a couch, from which he had long since impatiently torn the cushions and silk stuffs, as too soft for his hard body. Hate and the black passion of vengeance seethed in him, yet he went instantly to sleep. The first lesson he had learned in his bitter hard life was to snatch sleep any time he could, like a wolf that snatches sleep on the hunting trail. Generally, his slumber was as light and dreamless as a panther's, but tonight it was otherwise.

He sank into fleecy gray fathoms of slumber and in a time-less, misty realm of shadows he met the tall, lean, white-bearded figure of old Gonar, the priest of the Moon, high counselor to the king. And Bran stood aghast, for Gonar's face was white as driven snow, and he shook as with ague. Well might Bran stand appalled, for in all the years of his life he had never before seen Gonar the Wise show any sign of fear.

"What now, old one?" asked the king. "Goes all well in Baal-dor?"

"All is well in Baal-dor where my body lies sleeping," answered old Gonar. "Across the void I have come to battle with you for your soul. King, are you mad, this thought you have thought in your brain?"

"Gonar," answered Bran somberly, "this day I stood still and watched a man of mine die on the cross of Rome. What his name or his rank, I do not know. I do not care. He might have been a faithful unknown warrior of mine, he might have been an outlaw. I only know that he was mine; the first scents he knew were the scents of the heather; the first light he saw was the sunrise on the Pictish hills. He belonged to me, not to Rome. If punishment was just, then none but me should have dealt it. If he were to be tried, none but me should have been his judge. The same blood flowed in our veins; the same fire maddened our brains; in infancy we listened to the same old tales, and in youth we sang the same old songs. He was bound to my heartstrings, as every man, and every woman, and every child of Pictland is bound. It was mine to protect him; now it is mine to avenge him."

"But in the name of the gods, Bran," expostulated the wizard, "take your vengeance in another way! Return to the heather—mass your warriors—join with Cormac and his Gaels, and spread a sea of blood and flame the length of the great wall!"

"All that I will do," grimly answered Bran. "But *now*—now—I will have a vengeance such as no Roman ever dreamed of! Ha, what do they know of the mysteries of this ancient isle, which sheltered strange life long before Rome rose from the marshes of the Tiber?"

"Bran, there are weapons too foul to use, even against Rome!"

Bran barked short and sharp as a jackal.

"Ha! There are no weapons I would not use against Rome! My back is at the wall. By the blood of the fiends, has Rome fought me fair? Bah! I am a barbarian king with a wolfskin mantle and an iron crown, fighting with my handful of bows and broken pikes against the queen of the world. What have I? The heather hills, the wattle huts, the spears of my shock-headed tribesmen! And I fight Rome—with her armored legions, her broad fertile plains, and rich seas—her mountains, and her rivers, and her gleaming cities; her wealth, her steel, her gold, her mastery, and her wrath. By steel and fire I will fight her—and by subtlety and treachery—by the thorn in the foot, the adder in the path, the venom in the cup, the dagger in the dark; aye," his voice sank somberly, "and by the worms of the earth!"

"But it is madness!" cried Gonar. "You will perish in the attempt you plan—you will go down to Hell and you will not return! What of your people then?"

"If I can not serve them, I had better die," growled the king.

"But you can not even reach the beings you seek," cried Gonar. "For untold centuries they have dwelt apart. There is no door by which you can come to them. Long ago they severed the bonds that bound them to the world we know."

"Long ago," answered Bran somberly, "you told me that nothing in the universe was separated from the stream of Life—a saying the truth of which I have often seen evident. No race, no form of life but is close-knit somehow, by some manner, to the rest of Life and the world. Somewhere there is a thin link connecting *those* I seek to the world I know. Somewhere there is a door. And somewhere among the bleak fens of the west I will find it."

Stark horror flooded Gonar's eyes and he gave back crying, "Woe, Woe, Woe, to Pictdom! Woe to the unborn kingdom! Woe, black woe to the sons of men! Woe, woe, woe, woe!"

Bran awoke to a shadowed room and the starlight on the window bars. The moon had sunk from sight, though its glow was still faint above the housetops. Memory of his dream shook him and he swore beneath his breath.

Rising, he flung off cloak and mantle, donning a light shirt of black mesh-mail, and girding on sword and dirk. Going again to the iron-bound chest, he lifted several compact bags and emptied the clinking contents into the leathern pouch at his girdle. Then, wrapping his wide cloak about him, he silently left the house. No servants there were to spy on him—he had impatiently refused the offer of slaves which it was Rome's policy to furnish her barbarian emissaries. Gnarled Grom had attended to all Bran's simple needs.

The stables fronted on the courtyard. A moment's groping in the dark and he placed his hand over a great stallion's nose, checking the nicker of recognition. Working without a light he swiftly bridled and saddled the great brute, and went through the courtyard into a shadowy side street, leading him. The moon was setting, the border of floating shadows widening along the western wall. Silence lay on the marble palaces and mud hovels of Eboracum under the cold stars.

Bran touched the pouch at his girdle, which was heavy with minted gold that bore the stamp of Rome. He had come to Eboracum posing as an emissary of Pictdom, to act the spy. But being a barbarian, he had not been able to play his part in aloof formality and sedate dignity. He retained a crowded memory of wild feasts where wine flowed in fountains; of white-bosomed Roman women, who, sated with civilized lovers, looked with something more than favor on a virile barbarian; of gladiatorial games; and of other games where dice clicked, and spun, and tall stacks of gold changed hands. He had drunk deeply and gambled recklessly, after the manner of barbarians, and he had had a remarkable run of luck, due possibly to the indifference with which he won or lost. Gold to the Pict was so much dust, flowing through his fingers. In his land there was no need of it. But he had learned its power in the boundaries of civilization.

Almost under the shadow of the northwestern wall he saw ahead of him loom the great watchtower which was connected with and reared above the outer wall. One corner of the castle-like fortress, farthest from the wall, served as a dungeon. Bran left his horse standing in a dark alley, with the reins hanging on the ground, and stole like a prowling wolf into the shadows of the fortress.

The young officer Valerius was awakened from a light, unquiet sleep by a stealthy sound at the barred window. He sat up, cursing softly under his breath as the faint starlight which etched the window bars fell across the bare stone floor and reminded him of his disgrace. Well, in a few days, he ruminated, he'd be well out of it; Sulla would not be too harsh on a man with such high connections; then let any man or woman gibe at him! Damn that insolent Pict! But wait, he thought suddenly, remembering: what of the sound which had roused him?

"Hsssst!" it was a voice from the window.

Why so much secrecy? It could hardly be a foe—yet, why should it be a friend? Valerius rose and crossed his cell, coming close to the window. Outside all was dim in the starlight and he made out but a shadowy form close to the window.

"Who are you?" he leaned close against the bars, straining his eyes into the gloom.

His answer was a snarl of wolfish laughter, a long flicker of steel in the starlight. Valerius reeled away from the window and crashed to the floor, clutching his throat, gurgling horribly as he tried to scream. Blood gushed through his fingers, forming about his twitching body a pool that reflected the dim starlight dully and redly.

Outside Bran glided away like a shadow, without pausing to peer into the cell. In another minute the guards would round the corner on their regular routine. Even now he heard the measured tramp of their iron-clad feet. Before they came in sight he had vanished, and they clumped stolidly by the cell-window with no intimation of the corpse that lay on the floor within.

Bran rode to the small gate in the western wall, unchallenged by the sleepy watch. What fear of foreign invasion in Eboracum? —and certain well organized thieves and women-stealers made it profitable for the watchmen not to be too vigilant. But the single guardsman at the western gate—his fellows lay drunk in a nearby brothel—lifted his spear and bawled for Bran to halt and give an account of himself. Silently the Pict reined closer. Masked in the dark cloak, he seemed dim and indistinct to the Roman, who was only aware of the glitter of his cold eyes in the gloom. But Bran held up his hand against the starlight and the soldier caught the gleam of gold; in the other hand he saw a long sheen of steel. The soldier understood, and he did not hesitate between the choice of a golden bribe or a battle to the death with this unknown rider who was apparently a barbarian of some sort. With a grunt he lowered his spear and swung the gate open. Bran rode through, casting a handful of coins to the Roman. They fell about his feet in a golden shower, clinking against the flags. He bent in greedy haste to retrieve them, and Bran Mak Morn rode westward like a flying ghost in the night.

CHAPTER THREE

Into the dim fens of the west came Bran Mak Morn. A cold wind breathed across the gloomy waste and against the gray sky a few herons flapped heavily. The long reeds and marsh-grass waved in broken undulations and out across the desolation of the wastes a few still meres reflected the dull light. Here and there rose curiously regular hillocks above the general levels, and gaunt against the somber sky Bran saw a marching line of upright monoliths—menhirs, reared by what nameless hands?

A faint blue line lay to the west, the foothills that beyond the horizon grew to the wild mountains of Wales where dwelt still wild Celtic tribes, fierce blue-eyed men that knew not the yoke of Rome. A row of well-garrisoned watchtowers held them in check. Even now, far away across the moors, Bran glimpsed the unassailable keep men called the Tower of Trajan.

These barren wastes seemed the dreary accomplishment of desolation, yet human life was not utterly lacking. Bran met the silent men of the fen, reticent, dark of eye and hair, speaking a strange mixed tongue whose long-blended elements had forgotten their pristine separate sources. Bran recognized a certain kinship in these people to himself, but he looked on them with the scorn of a pure-blooded patrician for men of mixed strains.

Not that the common people of Caledonia were altogether pure-blooded; they got their stocky bodies and massive limbs from a primitive Teutonic race which had found its way into the northern tip of the isle even before the Celtic conquest of Britain was completed, and had been absorbed by the Picts. But the chiefs of Bran's folk had kept their blood from foreign taint since the beginnings of time, and he himself was a pure-bred Pict of the Old Race. But these fenmen, overrun repeatedly by British, Gaelic, and Roman conquerors, had assimilated blood of each, and in the process almost forgotten their original language and lineage.

For Bran came of a race that was very old, which had spread over western Europe in one vast Dark Empire, before the coming of the Aryans, when the ancestors of the Celts, the Hellenes, and the Germans were one primal people, before the days of tribal splitting-off and westward drift.

Only in Caledonia, Bran brooded, had his people resisted the flood of Aryan conquest. He had heard of a Pictish people called Basques, who in the crags of the Pyrenees called themselves an unconquered race; but he knew that they had paid tribute for centuries to the ancestors of the Gaels, before these Celtic conquerors abandoned their mountain realm and set sail for Ireland. Only the Picts of Caledonia had remained free, and they had been scattered into small feuding tribes—he was the first acknowledged king in five hundred years—the beginning of a new dynasty—no, a revival of an ancient dynasty under a new name. In the very teeth of Rome he dreamed his dreams of empire.

He wandered through the fens, seeking a door. Of his quest he said nothing to the dark-eyed fenmen. They told him news that drifted from mouth to mouth, a tale of war in the north, the skirl of war-pipes along the winding Wall, of gathering-fires in the heather, of flame, and smoke, and rapine, and the glutting of

Gaelic swords in the crimson sea of slaughter. The eagles of the legions were moving northward, and the ancient road resounded to the measured tramp of the ironclad feet. And Bran, in the fens of the west, laughed, well pleased.

In Eboracum, Titus Sulla gave secret word to seek out the Pictish emissary with the Gaelic name who had been under suspicion, and who had vanished the night young Valerius was found dead in his cell with his throat ripped out. Sulla felt that this sudden bursting flame of war on the Wall was connected closely with his execution of a condemned Pictish criminal, and he set his spy system to work, though he felt sure that Partha Mac Othna was by this time far beyond his reach. He prepared to march from Eboracum, but he did not accompany the considerable force of legionaries which he sent north. Sulla was a brave man, but each man has his own dread, and Sulla's was Cormac na Connacht, the black-haired prince of the Gaels, who had sworn to cut out the governor's heart and eat it raw. So Sulla rode with his ever-present bodyguard westward, where lay the Tower of Trajan with its warlike commander, Caius Camillus, who enjoyed nothing more than taking his superior's place when the red waves of war washed at the foot of the Wall. Devious politics, but the legate of Rome seldom visited this far isle, and what of his wealth and intrigues, Titus Sulla was the highest power in Britain.

And Bran, knowing all this, patiently waited his coming, in the deserted hut in which he had taken up his abode.

One gray evening he strode on foot across the moors, a stark figure, blackly etched against the dim crimson fire of the sunset. He felt the incredible antiquity of the slumbering land, as he walked like the last man on the day after the end of the world. Yet at last he saw a token of human life—a drab hut of wattle and mud, set in the reedy breast of the fen.

· · ·

A woman greeted him from the open door, and Bran's somber eyes narrowed with a dark suspicion. The woman was not old, yet the evil wisdom of ages was in her eyes; her garments were ragged and scanty, her black locks tangled and unkempt, lending her an aspect of wildness well in keeping with her grim surroundings. Her red lips laughed but there was no mirth in her laughter, only a hint of mockery, and under the lips her teeth showed sharp and pointed like fangs.

"Enter, master," said she, "if you do not fear to share the roof of the witch-woman of Dagon-moor!"

Bran entered silently and sat down on a broken bench while the woman busied herself with the scanty meal cooking over an open fire on the squalid hearth. He studied her lithe, almost serpentine motions, the ears which were almost pointed, the yellow eyes which slanted curiously.

"What do you seek in the fens, my lord?" she asked, turning toward him with a supple twist of her whole body.

"I seek a Door," he answered, chin resting on his fist. "I have a song to sing to the worms of the earth!"

She started upright, a jar falling from her hands to shatter on the hearth.

"This is an ill saying, even spoken in chance," she stammered.

"I speak not by chance but by intent," he answered.

She shook her head. "I know not what you mean."

"Well you know," he returned. "Aye, you know well! My race is very old. They reigned in Britain before the nations of the Celts and the Hellenes were born out of the womb of peoples. But my people were not first in Britain. By the mottles on your skin, by the slanting of your eyes, by the taint in your veins, I speak with full knowledge and meaning."

Awhile she stood silent, her lips smiling but her face inscrutable.

"Man, are you mad," she asked, "that in your madness you come seeking that from which strong men fled screaming in old times?"

"I seek a vengeance," he answered, "that can be accomplished only by Them I seek."

She shook her head.

"You have listened to a bird singing; you have dreamed empty dreams."

"I have heard a viper hiss," he growled, "and I do not dream. Enough of this weaving of words. I came seeking a link between two worlds; I have found it."

"I need lie to you no more, man of the north," answered the woman. "They you seek still dwell beneath the sleeping hills. They have drawn *apart*, farther and farther from the world you know."

"But they still steal forth in the night to grip women straying on the moors," said he, his gaze on her slanted eyes. She laughed wickedly.

"What would you of me?"

"That you bring me to Them."

She flung back her head with a scornful laugh. His left hand locked like iron in the breast of her scanty garment and his right closed on his hilt. She laughed in his face.

"Strike and be damned, my northern wolf! Do you think that such life as mine is so sweet that I would cling to it as a babe to the breast?"

His hand fell away.

"You are right. Threats are foolish. I will buy your aid."

"How?" the laughing voice hummed with mockery.

Bran opened his pouch and poured into his cupped palm a stream of gold.

"More wealth than the men of the fen ever dreamed of."

Again she laughed. "What is this rusty metal to me? Save it for some white-breasted Roman woman who will play the traitor for you!"

"Name me a price!" he urged. "The head of an enemy—"

"By the blood in my veins, with its heritage of ancient hate, who is mine enemy but thee?" she laughed and springing, struck catlike. But her dagger splintered on the mail beneath his cloak, and he flung her off with a loathful flick of his wrist which tossed her sprawling across her grass-strewn bunk. Lying there she laughed up at him.

"I will name you a price, then, my wolf, and it may be in days to come you will curse the armor that broke Atla's dagger!" She rose and came close to him, her disquietingly long hands fastened fiercely into his cloak. "I will tell you, Black Bran, king of Caledon! Oh, I knew you when you came into my hut with your black hair and your cold eyes! I will lead you to the doors of Hell if you wish—and the price shall be the kisses of a king!

"What of my blasted and bitter life, I, whom mortal men loathe and fear? I have not known the love of men, the clasp of a strong arm, the sting of human kisses, I, Atla, the were-woman of the moors! What have I known but the lone winds of the fens, the dreary fire of cold sunsets, the whispering of the marsh grasses?—the faces that blink up at me in the waters of the meres, the footpad of night—things in the gloom, the glimmer of red eyes, the grisly murmur of nameless beings in the night!

"I am half-human, at least! Have I not known sorrow and yearning and crying wistfulness, and the drear ache of loneliness? Give to me, king; give me your fierce kisses and your hurtful barbarian's embrace. Then in the long drear years to come I shall not utterly eat out my heart in vain envy of the white-bosomed women of men; for I shall have a memory few of them can boast —the kisses of a king! One night of love, oh king, and I will guide you to the gates of Hell!"

Bran eyed her somberly; he reached forth and gripped her arm in his iron fingers. An involuntary shudder shook him at the feel of her sleek skin. He nodded slowly and, drawing her close to him, forced his head down to meet her lifted lips.

CHAPTER FOUR

The cold gray mists of dawn wrapped King Bran like a clammy cloak. He turned to the woman whose slanted eyes gleamed in the gray gloom.

"Make good your part of the contract," he said roughly. "I sought a link between worlds, and in you I found it. I seek the one thing sacred to Them. It shall be the key opening the door that lies unseen between me and Them. Tell me how I can reach it."

"I will." The red lips smiled terribly. "Go to the mound men call Dagon's Barrow. Draw aside the stone that blocks the entrance and go under the dome of the mound. The floor of the chamber is made of seven great stones, six grouped about the seventh. Lift out the center stone—and you will see!"

"Will I find the Black Stone?" he asked.

"Dagon's Barrow is the door to the Black Stone," she answered, "if you dare follow the road."

"Will the symbol be well guarded?" He unconsciously loosened his blade in its sheath. The red lips curled mockingly.

"If you meet any on the road you will die as no mortal man has died for long centuries. The Stone is not guarded, as men guard their treasures. Why should They guard what man has never sought? Perhaps They will be near, perhaps not. It is a chance you must take, if you wish the Stone. Beware, king of Pictdom! Remember it was your folk who, so long ago, cut the thread that bound Them to human life. They were almost human then—they overspread the land and knew the sunlight. Now they have drawn apart. They know not the sunlight and they shun the light of the moon. Even the starlight they hate. Far, far apart have they drawn, who might have been men in time, but for the spears of your ancestors."

The sky was overcast with misty gray, through which the sun shone coldly yellow when Bran came to Dagon's Barrow, a round hillock overgrown with rank grass of a curious fungoid appearance. On the eastern side of the mound showed the entrance of a crudely built stone tunnel which evidently penetrated the barrow. One great stone blocked the entrance to the tomb. Bran laid hold of the sharp edges and exerted all his strength. It held fast. He drew his sword and worked the blade between the blocking stone and the sill. Using the sword as a lever, he worked carefully, and managed to loosen the great stone and wrench it out. A foul charnel house scent flowed out of the aperture, and the dim sunlight seemed less to illuminate the cavern-like opening than to be fouled by the rank darkness which clung there.

Sword in hand, ready for he knew not what, Bran groped his way into the tunnel, which was long and narrow, built up of heavy joined stones, and was too low for him to stand erect. Either his eyes became somewhat accustomed to the gloom, or the darkness was, after all, somewhat lightened by the sunlight filtering in through the entrance. At any rate he came into a round low chamber and was able to make out its general dome-like outline. Here, no doubt, in old times, had reposed the bones of him for whom the stones of the tomb had been joined and the earth heaped high above them; but now of those bones no vestige remained on the stone floor. And bending close and straining his eyes, Bran made out the strange, startlingly regular pattern of that floor: six well-cut slabs clustered about a seventh, six-sided stone.

He drove his sword-point into a crack and pried carefully. The edge of the central stone tilted slightly upward. A little work and he lifted it out and leaned it against the curving wall. Straining his eyes downward he saw only the gaping blackness of a dark well, with small, worn steps that led downward and out of sight. He did not hesitate. Though the skin between his shoulders crawled curiously, he swung himself into the abyss and felt the clinging blackness swallow him.

Groping downward, he felt his feet slip and stumble on steps too small for human feet. With one hand pressed hard against the side of the well he steadied himself, fearing a fall into unknown and unlighted depths. The steps were cut into solid rock, yet they were greatly worn away. The farther he progressed, the less like steps they became, mere bumps of worn stone. Then the direction of the shaft changed sharply. It still led down, but at a shallow slant down which he could walk, elbows braced against the hollowed sides, head bent low beneath the curved roof. The steps had ceased altogether, and the stone felt slimy to the touch, like a serpent's lair. What beings, Bran wondered, had slithered up and down this slanting shaft, for how many centuries?

The tunnel narrowed until Bran found it rather difficult to shove through. He lay on his back and pushed himself along with his hands, feet first. Still he knew he was sinking deeper and deeper into the very guts of the earth; how far below the surface he was, he dared not contemplate. Then ahead a faint witch-fire gleam tinged the abysmal blackness. He grinned savagely and without mirth. If They he sought came suddenly upon him, how could he fight in that narrow shaft? But he had put the thought of personal fear behind him when he began this hellish quest. He crawled on, thoughtless of all else but his goal.

And he came at last into a vast space where he could stand upright. He could not see the roof of the place, but he got an impression of dizzying vastness. The blackness pressed in on all sides, and behind him he could see the entrance to the shaft from which he had just emerged—a black well in the darkness. But in front of him a strange grisly radiance glowed about a grim altar built of human skulls. The source of that light he could not determine, but on the altar lay a sullen night-black object—the Black Stone!

Bran wasted no time in giving thanks that the guardians of the grim relic were nowhere near. He caught up the Stone, and gripping it under his left arm, crawled into the shaft. When a man turns his back on peril its clammy menace looms more grisly than when he advances upon it. So Bran, crawling back up the nighted shaft with his grisly prize, felt the darkness turn on him and slink behind him, grinning with dripping fangs. Clammy sweat beaded his flesh, and he hastened to the best of his ability, ears strained for some stealthy sound to betray that fell shapes were at his heels. Strong shudders shook him, despite himself, and the short hair on his neck prickled as if a cold wind blew at his back.

When he reached the first of the tiny steps he felt as if he had attained to the outer boundaries of the mortal world. Up them he went, stumbling and slipping, and with a deep gasp of relief came out into the tomb, whose spectral grayness seemed like the blaze of noon in comparison to the stygian depths he had just traversed. He replaced the central stone and strode into the light of the outer day, and never was the cold yellow light of the sun more grateful, as it dispelled the shadows of black-winged nightmares of fear and madness that seemed to have ridden him up out of the black deeps. He shoved the great blocking stone back into place, and picking up the cloak he had left at the mouth of the tomb, he wrapped it about the Black Stone and hurried away, a strong revulsion and loathing shaking his soul and lending wings to his strides.

A gray silence brooded over the land. It was desolate as the blind side of the moon, yet Bran felt the potentialities of life—

under his feet, in the brown earth—sleeping, but how soon to waken, and in what horrific fashion?

He came through the tall masking reeds to the still deep men called Dagon's Mere. No slightest ripple ruffled the cold blue water to give evidence of the grisly monster legend said dwelt beneath. Bran closely scanned the breathless landscape. He saw no hint of life, human or unhuman. He sought the instincts of his savage soul to know if any unseen eyes fixed their lethal gaze upon him, and found no response. He was alone as if he were the last man alive on earth.

Swiftly he unwrapped the Black Stone, and as it lay in his hands like a solid sullen block of darkness, he did not seek to learn the secret of its material nor scan the cryptic characters carved thereon. Weighing it in his hands and calculating the distance, he flung it far out, so that it fell almost exactly in the middle of the lake. A sullen splash and the waters closed over it. There was a moment of shimmering flashes on the bosom of the lake; then the blue surface stretched placid and unrippled again.

CHAPTER FIVE

The were-woman turned swiftly as Bran approached her
door. Her slant eyes widened.

"You! And alive! And sane!"

"I have been into Hell and I have returned," he growled.
"What is more, I have that which I sought."

"The Black Stone?" she cried. "You really dared steal it?
Where is it?"

"No matter; but last night my stallion screamed in his stall,
and I heard something crunch beneath his thundering hoofs
which was not the wall of the stable—and there was blood on his
hoofs when I came to see, and blood on the floor of the stall.
And I have heard stealthy sounds in the night, and noises
beneath my dirt floor, as if worms burrowed deep in the earth.
They know I have stolen their Stone. Have you betrayed me?"

She shook her head.

"I keep your secret; they do not need my word to know you.
The farther they have retreated from the world of men, the
greater have grown their powers in other uncanny ways. Some
dawn your hut will stand empty, and if men dare investigate they
will find nothing—except crumbling bits of earth on the dirt
floor."

Bran smiled terribly.

"I have not planned and toiled thus far to fall prey to the talons of vermin. If They strike me down in the night, They will never know what became of their idol—or whatever it be to Them. I would speak with Them."

"Dare you come with me and meet them in the night?" she asked.

"Thunder of all gods!" he snarled. "Who are you to ask me if I dare? Lead me to Them and let me bargain for a vengeance this night. The hour of retribution draws nigh. This day I saw silvered helmets and bright shields gleam across the fens—the new commander has arrived at the Tower of Trajan and Caius Camillus has marched to the Wall."

That night the king went across the dark desolation of the moors with the silent were-woman. The night was thick and still as if the land lay in ancient slumber. The stars blinked vaguely, mere points of red struggling through the unbreathing gloom. Their gleam was dimmer than the glitter in the eyes of the woman who glided beside the king. Strange thoughts shook Bran, vague, titanic, primeval. Tonight ancestral linkings with these slumbering fens stirred in his soul and troubled him with the phantasmal, eon-veiled shapes of monstrous dreams. The vast age of his race was borne upon him; where now he walked an outlaw and an alien, dark-eyed kings in whose mold he was cast had reigned in old times. The Celtic and Roman invaders were as strangers to this ancient isle beside his people. Yet his race likewise had been invaders, and there was an older race than his—a race whose beginnings lay lost and hidden back beyond the dark oblivion of antiquity.

Ahead of them loomed a low range of hills, which formed the easternmost extremity of those straying chains which far away climbed at last to the mountains of Wales. The woman led the way up what might have been a sheep-path, and halted before a wide black gaping cave.

"A door to those you seek, oh king!" her laughter rang hateful in the gloom. "Dare ye enter?"

His fingers closed in her tangled locks and he shook her viciously.

"Ask me but once more if I dare," he grated, "and your head and shoulders part company! Lead on."

Her laughter was like sweet deadly venom. They passed into the cave, and Bran struck flint and steel. The flicker of the tinder showed him a wide dusty cavern, on the roof of which hung clusters of bats. Lighting a torch, he lifted it and scanned the shadowy recesses, seeing nothing but dust and emptiness.

"Where are They?" he growled.

She beckoned him to the back of the cave and leaned against the rough wall, as if casually. But the king's keen eyes caught the motion of her hand pressing hard against a projecting ledge. He recoiled as a round black well gaped suddenly at his feet. Again her laughter slashed him like a keen silver knife. He held the torch to the opening and again saw small worn steps leading down.

"They do not need those steps," said Atla. "Once they did, before your people drove them into the darkness. But you will need them."

She thrust the torch into a niche above the well; it shed a faint red light into the darkness below. She gestured into the well, and Bran loosened his sword and stepped into the shaft. As he went down into the mystery of the darkness, the light was blotted out above him, and he thought for an instant Atla had covered the opening again. Then he realized that she was descending after him.

The descent was not a long one. Abruptly Bran felt his feet on a solid floor. Atla swung down beside him and stood in the dim circle of light that drifted down the shaft. Bran could not see the limits of the place into which he had come.

"Many caves in these hills," said Atla, her voice sounding small and strangely brittle in the vastness, "are but doors to greater caves which lie beneath, even as a man's words and deeds are but small indications of the dark caverns of murky thought lying behind and beneath."

And now Bran was aware of movement in the gloom. The darkness was filled with stealthy noises not like those made by any human foot. Abruptly sparks began to flash and float in the blackness, like flickering fireflies. Closer they came until they girdled him in a wide half-moon. And beyond the ring gleamed other sparks, a solid sea of them, fading away in the gloom until the farthest were mere tiny pinpoints of light. And Bran knew they were the slanted eyes of the beings who had come upon him in such numbers that his brain reeled at the contemplation—and at the vastness of the cavern.

Now that he faced his ancient foes, Bran knew no fear. He felt the waves of terrible menace emanating from them, the grisly hate, the inhuman threat to body, mind, and soul. More than a member of a less ancient race, he realized the horror of his position, but he did not fear, though he confronted the ultimate Horror of the dreams and legends of his race. His blood raced fiercely, but it was with the hot excitement of the hazard, not the drive of terror.

"They know you have the Stone, oh king," said Atla, and though he knew she feared, though he felt her physical efforts to control her trembling limbs, there was no quiver of fright in her voice. "You are in deadly peril; they know your breed of old—oh, they remember the days when their ancestors were men! I can not save you; both of us will die as no human has died for ten centuries. Speak to them, if you will; they can understand your speech, though you may not understand theirs. But it will avail not—you are human—and a Pict."

Bran laughed and the closing ring of fire shrank back at the savagery in his laughter. Drawing his sword with a soul-chilling rasp of steel, he set his back against what he hoped was a solid stone wall. Facing the glittering eyes with his sword gripped in his right hand and his dirk in his left, he laughed as a blood-hungry wolf snarls.

"Aye," he growled, "I am a Pict, a son of those warriors who drove your brutish ancestors before them like chaff before the storm!—who flooded the land with your blood and heaped high your skulls for a sacrifice to the Moon-Woman! You who fled of old before my race, dare ye now snarl at your master? Roll on me like a flood now, if ye dare! Before your viper fangs drink my life I will reap your multitudes like ripened barley—of your severed heads will I build a tower and of your mangled corpses will I rear up a wall! Dogs of the dark, vermin of Hell, worms of the earth, rush in and try my steel! When Death finds me in this dark cavern, your living will howl for the scores of your dead, and your Black Stone will be lost to you forever, for only I know where it is hidden and not all the tortures of all the Hells can wring the secret from my lips!"

Then followed a tense silence; Bran faced the fire-lit darkness, tensed like a wolf at bay, waiting the charge; at his side the woman cowered, her eyes ablaze. Then from the silent ring that hovered beyond the dim torchlight rose a vague abhorrent murmur. Bran, prepared as he was for anything, started. Gods, was *that* the speech of creatures which had once been called men?

Atla straightened, listening intently. From her lips came the same hideous soft sibilances, and Bran, though he had already known the grisly secret of her being, knew that never again could he touch her save with soul-shaken loathing.

She turned to him, a strange smile curving her red lips dimly in the ghostly light.

"They fear you, oh king! By the black secrets of R'lyeh, who are you that Hell itself quails before you? Not your steel, but the stark ferocity of your soul has driven unused fear into their strange minds. They will buy back the Black Stone at any price."

"Good." Bran sheathed his weapons. "They shall promise not

to molest you because of your aid of me. And," his voice hummed like the purr of a hunting tiger, "they shall deliver into my hands Titus Sulla, governor of Eboracum, now commanding the Tower of Trajan. This They can do—how, I know not. But I know that in the old days, when my people warred with these Children of the Night, babes disappeared from guarded huts and none saw the stealers come or go. Do They understand?"

Again rose the low frightful sounds and Bran, who feared not their wrath, shuddered at their voices.

"They understand," said Atla. "Bring the Black Stone to Dagon's Ring tomorrow night when the earth is veiled with the blackness that foreruns the dawn. Lay the Stone on the altar. There They will bring Titus Sulla to you. Trust Them; They have not interfered in human affairs for many centuries, but They will keep their word."

Bran nodded and turning, climbed up the stair with Atla close behind him. At the top he turned and looked down once more. As far as he could see floated a glittering ocean of slanted yellow eyes upturned. But the owners of those eyes kept carefully beyond the dim circle of torchlight and of their bodies he could see nothing. Their low hissing speech floated up to him, and he shuddered as his imagination visualized, not a throng of biped creatures, but a swarming, swaying myriad of serpents, gazing up at him with their glittering unwinking eyes.

He swung into the upper cave, and Atla thrust the blocking stone back in place. It fitted into the entrance of the well with uncanny precision; Bran was unable to discern any crack in the apparently solid floor of the cavern. Atla made a motion to extinguish the torch, but the king stayed her.

"Keep it so until we are out of the cave," he grunted. "We might tread on an adder in the dark."

Atla's sweetly hateful laughter rose maddeningly in the flickering gloom.

CHAPTER SIX

I t was not long before sunset when Bran came again to the reed-grown marge of Dagon's Mere. Casting cloak and sword-belt on the ground, he stripped himself of his short leathern breeches. Then, gripping his naked dirk in his teeth, he went into the water with the smooth ease of a diving seal. Swimming strongly, he gained the center of the small lake, and turning, drove himself downward.

The mere was deeper than he had thought. It seemed he would never reach the bottom, and when he did, his groping hands failed to find what he sought. A roaring in his ears warned him, and he swam to the surface.

Gulping deep of the refreshing air, he dived again, and again his quest was fruitless. A third time he sought the depth, and this time his groping hands met a familiar object in the silt of the bottom. Grasping it, he swam up to the surface.

The Stone was not particularly bulky, but it was heavy. He swam leisurely, and suddenly was aware of a curious stir in the waters about him which was not caused by his own exertions. Thrusting his face below the surface, he tried to pierce the blue depths with his eyes and thought to see a dim gigantic shadow hovering there.

He swam faster, not frightened, but wary. His feet struck the shallows, and he waded up on the shelving shore. Looking back he saw the waters swirl and subside. He shook his head, swearing. He had discounted the ancient legend which made Dagon's Mere the lair of a nameless water-monster, but now he had a feeling as if his escape had been narrow. The timeworn myths of the ancient land were taking form and coming to life before his eyes. What primeval shape lurked below the surface of that treacherous mere, Bran could not guess, but he felt that the fenmen had good reason for shunning the spot, after all.

Bran donned his garments, mounted the black stallion, and rode across the fens in the desolate crimson of the sunset's afterglow, with the Black Stone wrapped in his cloak. He rode, not to his hut, but to the west, in the direction of the Tower of Trajan and the Ring of Dagon. As he covered the miles that lay between, the red stars winked out. Midnight passed him in the moonless night and still Bran rode on. His heart was hot for his meeting with Titus Sulla. Atla had gloated over the anticipation of watching the Roman writhe under torture, but no such thought was in the Pict's mind. The governor should have his chance with weapons—with Bran's own sword he should face the Pictish king's dirk, and live or die according to his prowess. And though Sulla was famed throughout the provinces as a swordsman, Bran felt no doubt as to the outcome.

Dagon's Ring lay some distance from the Tower—a sullen circle of tall gaunt stones planted upright, with a rough-hewn stone altar in the center. The Romans looked on these menhirs with aversion; they thought the Druids had reared them; but the Celts supposed Bran's people, the Picts, had planted them—and Bran well knew what hands reared those grim monoliths in lost ages, though for what reasons, he but dimly guessed.

The king did not ride straight to the Ring. He was consumed with curiosity as to how his grim allies intended carrying out their promise. That They could snatch Titus Sulla from the very midst of his men, he felt sure, and he believed he knew how

They would do it. He felt the gnawings of a strange misgiving, as if he had tampered with powers of unknown breadth and depth, and had loosed forces which he could not control. Each time he remembered that reptilian murmur, those slanted eyes of the night before, a cold breath passed over him. They had been abhorrent enough when his people drove Them into the caverns under the hills, ages ago; what had long centuries of retrogression made of them? In their nighted, subterranean life, had They retained any of the attributes of humanity at all?

Some instinct prompted him to ride toward the Tower. He knew he was near; but for the thick darkness he could have plainly seen its stark outline tusking the horizon. Even now he should be able to make it out dimly. An obscure, shuddersome premonition shook him and he spurred the stallion into a swift canter.

And suddenly Bran staggered in his saddle as from a physical impact, so stunning was the surprize of what met his gaze. The impregnable Tower of Trajan was no more! Bran's astounded gaze rested on a gigantic pile of ruinsof shattered stone and crumbled granite, from which jutted the jagged and splintered ends of broken beams. At one corner of the tumbled heap one tower rose out of the waste of crumpled masonry, and it leaned drunkenly as if its foundations had been half cut away.

Bran dismounted and walked forward, dazed by bewilderment. The moat was filled in places by fallen stones and broken pieces of mortared wall. He crossed over and came among the ruins. Where, he knew, only a few hours before the flags had resounded to the martial tramp of ironclad feet, and the walls had echoed to the clang of shields and the blast of the loud-throated trumpets, a horrific silence reigned.

Almost under Bran's feet, a broken shape writhed and groaned. The king bent down to the legionary who lay in a sticky red pool of his own blood. A single glance showed the Pict that the man, horribly crushed and shattered, was dying.

Lifting the bloody head, Bran placed his flask to the pulped lips and the Roman instinctively drank deep, gulping through splintered teeth. In the dim starlight Bran saw his glazed eyes roll.

"The walls fell," muttered the dying man. "They crashed down like the skies falling on the day of doom. Ah Jove, the skies rained shards of granite and hailstones of marble!"

"I have felt no earthquake shock." Bran scowled, puzzled.

"It was no earthquake," muttered the Roman. "Before last dawn it began, the faint dim scratching and clawing far below the earth. We of the guard heard it—like rats burrowing, or like worms hollowing out the earth. Titus laughed at us, but all day long we heard it. Then at midnight the Tower quivered and seemed to settle—as if the foundations were being dug away—"

A shudder shook Bran Mak Morn. The worms of the earth! Thousands of vermin digging like moles far below the castle, burrowing away the foundations. Gods, the land must be honeycombed with tunnels and caverns—these creatures were even less human than he had thought—what ghastly shapes of darkness had he invoked to his aid?

"What of Titus Sulla?" he asked, again holding the flask to the legionary's lips; in that moment the dying Roman seemed to him almost like a brother.

"Even as the Tower shuddered we heard a fearful scream from the governor's chamber," muttered the soldier. "We rushed there—as we broke down the door we heard his shrieks—they seemed to recede—*into the bowels of the earth!* We rushed in; the chamber was empty. His bloodstained sword lay on the floor; in the stone flags of the floor a black hole gaped. Then—the—towers—reeled—the—roof—broke—through—a—storm—of—crashing—walls—I—crawled—"

A strong convulsion shook the broken figure.

"Lay me down, friend," whispered the Roman. "I die."

He had ceased to breathe before Bran could comply. The Pict rose, mechanically cleansing his hands. He hastened from the spot, and as he galloped over the darkened fens, the weight of the accursed Black Stone under his cloak was as the weight of a foul nightmare on a mortal breast.

As he approached the Ring, he saw an eery glow within, so that the gaunt stones stood etched like the ribs of a skeleton in which a witch-fire burns. The stallion snorted and reared as Bran tied him to one of the menhirs. Carrying the Stone, he strode into the grisly circle and saw Atla standing beside the altar, one hand on her hip, her sinuous body swaying in a serpentine manner. The altar glowed all over with ghastly light and Bran knew someone, probably Atla, had rubbed it with phosphorus from some dank swamp or quagmire.

He strode forward and, whipping his cloak from about the Stone, flung the accursed thing on to the altar.

"I have fulfilled my part of the contract," he growled.

"And They, theirs," she retorted. "Look!—They come!"

He wheeled, his hand instinctively dropping to his sword. Outside the Ring the great stallion screamed savagely and reared against his tether. The night wind moaned through the waving grass and an abhorrent soft hissing mingled with it. Between the menhirs flowed a dark tide of shadows, unstable and chaotic. The Ring filled with glittering eyes which hovered beyond the dim illusive circle of illumination cast by the phosphorescent altar. Somewhere in the darkness a human voice tittered and gibbered idiotically. Bran stiffened, the shadows of a horror clawing at his soul.

He strained his eyes, trying to make out the shapes of those who ringed him. But he glimpsed only billowing masses of shadow which heaved, and writhed, and squirmed with almost fluid consistency.

"Let them make good their bargain!" he exclaimed angrily.

"Then see, oh king!" cried Atla in a voice of piercing mockery.

There was a stir, a seething in the writhing shadows, and from the darkness crept, like a four-legged animal, a human shape that fell down and groveled at Bran's feet and writhed and mowed, and lifting a death's-head, howled like a dying dog. In the ghastly light, Bran, soul-shaken, saw the blank glassy eyes, the bloodless features, the loose, writhing, froth-covered lips of sheer lunacy—gods, was this Titus Sulla, the proud lord of life and death in Eboracum's proud city?

Bran bared his sword.

"I had thought to give this stroke in vengeance," he said somberly. "I give it in mercy—*Vale Caesar!*"

The steel flashed in the eery light and Sulla's head rolled to the foot of the glowing altar, where it lay staring up at the shadowed sky.

"They harmed him not!" Atla's hateful laugh slashed the sick silence. "It was what he saw and came to know that broke his brain! Like all his heavy-footed race, he knew nothing of the secrets of this ancient land. This night he has been dragged through the deepest pits of Hell, where even you might have blenched!"

"Well for the Romans that they know not the secrets of this accursed land!" Bran roared, maddened, "with its monster-haunted meres, its foul witch-women, and its lost caverns and subterranean realms where spawn in the darkness shapes of Hell!"

"Are they more foul than a mortal who seeks their aid?" cried Atla with a shriek of fearful mirth. "Give them their Black Stone!"

A cataclysmic loathing shook Bran's soul with red fury.

"Aye, take your cursed Stone!" he roared, snatching it from the altar and dashing it among the shadows with such savagery that bones snapped under its impact. A hurried babel of grisly tongues rose, and the shadows heaved in turmoil. One segment of the mass detached itself for an instant, and Bran cried out in fierce revulsion, though he caught only a fleeting glimpse of the thing, had only a brief impression of a broad strangely flattened head, pendulous writhing lips that bared curved pointed fangs, and a hideously misshapen, dwarfish body that seemed—*mottled* —all set off by those unwinking reptilian eyes. Gods!—the myths had prepared him for horror in human aspect, horror induced by bestial visage and stunted deformity—but this was the horror of nightmare and the night.

"Go back to Hell and take your idol with you!" he yelled, brandishing his clenched fists to the skies, as the thick shadows receded, flowing back and away from him like the foul waters of some black flood. "Your ancestors were men, though strange and monstrous—but gods, ye have become in ghastly fact what my people called ye in scorn!

"Worms of the earth, back into your holes and burrows! Ye foul the air and leave on the clean earth the slime of the serpents ye have become! Gonar was right—there are shapes too foul to use even against Rome!"

He sprang from the Ring as a man flees the touch of a coiling snake, and tore the stallion free. At his elbow Atla was shrieking with fearful laughter, all human attributes dropped from her like a cloak in the night.

"King of Pictland!" she cried, "King of fools! Do you blench at so small a thing? Stay and let me show you real fruits of the pits! Ha! ha! ha! Run, fool, run! But you are stained with the taint —you have called them forth, and they will remember! And in their own time they will come to you again!"

He yelled a wordless curse and struck her savagely in the mouth with his open hand. She staggered, blood starting from her lips, but her fiendish laughter only rose higher.

Bran leaped into the saddle, wild for the clean heather and the cold blue hills of the north where he could plunge his sword

into clean slaughter, and his sickened soul into the red maelstrom of battle, and forget the horror which lurked below the
fens of the west. He gave the frantic stallion the rein, and rode
through the night like a hunted ghost, until the hellish laughter
of the howling were-woman died out in the darkness behind.

THE THING ON THE ROOF

They lumber through the night
With their elephantine tread;
I shudder in affright
As I cower in my bed.
They lift colossal wings
On the high gable roofs
Which tremble to the trample
Of their mastodonic hoofs.

—Justin Geoffrey, *Out of the Old Land*

Let me begin by saying that I was surprised when Tussmann called on me. We had never been close friends; the man's mercenary instincts repelled me; and since our bitter controversy of three years before, when he attempted to discredit my *Evidences of Nahua Culture in Yucatan*, which was the result of years of careful research, our relations had been anything but cordial. However, I received him and found his manner hasty and abrupt, but rather abstracted, as if his dislike for me had been thrust aside in some driving passion that had hold of him.

His errand was quickly stated. He wished my aid in obtaining a volume in the first edition of Von Junzt's *Nameless Cults*—the edition known as the Black Book, not from its color, but because of its dark contents. He might almost as well have asked me for the original Greek translation of the *Necronomicon*. Though since my return from Yucatan I had devoted practically all my time to my avocation of book collecting, I had not stumbled onto any hint that the book in the Dusseldorf edition was still in existence.

A word as to this rare work. Its extreme ambiguity in spots, coupled with its incredible subject matter, has caused it long to be regarded as the ravings of a maniac, and the author was damned with the brand of insanity. But the fact remains that much of his assertions are unanswerable, and that he spent the full forty-five years of his life prying into strange places and discovering secret and abysmal things. Not a great many volumes were printed in the first edition, and many of these were burned by their frightened owners when Von Junzt was found strangled in a mysterious manner in his barred and bolted chamber one night in 1840, six months after he had returned from a mysterious journey to Mongolia.

Five years later a London printer, one Bridewall, pirated the work, and issued a cheap translation for sensational effect, full of grotesque woodcuts, and riddled with misspellings, faulty translations, and the usual errors of a cheap and unscholarly printing. This still further discredited the original work, and publishers and public forgot about the book until 1909 when the Golden Goblin Press of New York brought out an edition.

Their production was so carefully expurgated that fully a fourth of the original matter was cut out; the book was handsomely bound and decorated with the exquisite and weirdly imaginative illustrations of Diego Vasquez. The edition was intended for popular consumption, but the artistic instinct of the publishers defeated that end, since the cost of issuing the book was so great that they were forced to cite it at a prohibitive price.

I was explaining all this to Tussmann when he interrupted brusquely to say that he was not utterly ignorant in such matters. One of the Golden Goblin books ornamented his library, he said, and it was in it that he found a certain line which aroused his interest. If I could procure him a copy of the original 1839 edition, he would make it worth my while; knowing, he added, that it would be useless to offer me money, he would instead, in return for my trouble on his behalf, make a full retraction of his former accusations in regard to my Yucatan researches, and offer a complete apology in *The Scientific News*.

I will admit that I was astounded at this, and realized that if the matter meant so much to Tussmann that he was willing to make such concessions, it must indeed be of the utmost importance. I answered that I considered that I had sufficiently refuted his charges in the eyes of the world and had no desire to put him in a humiliating position, but that I would make the utmost efforts to procure him what he wanted.

He thanked me abruptly and took his leave, saying rather vaguely that he hoped to find a complete exposition of something in the Black Book which had evidently been slighted in the later edition.

I set to work, writing letters to friends, colleagues, and book dealers all over the world, and soon discovered that I had assumed a task of no small magnitude. Three months elapsed before my efforts were crowned with success, but at last, through the aid of Professor James Clement of Richmond, Virginia, I was able to obtain what I wished.

I notified Tussmann and he came to London by the next train. His eyes burned avidly as he gazed at the thick, dusty volume with its heavy leather covers and rusty iron hasps, and his fingers quivered with eagerness as he thumbed the time-yellowed pages.

And when he cried out fiercely and smashed his clenched fist down on the table, I knew that he had found what he hunted.

"Listen!" he commanded, and he read to me a passage that

spoke of an old, old temple in a Honduras jungle where a strange god was worshipped by an ancient tribe which became extinct before the coming of the Spaniards. And Tussmann read aloud of the mummy that had been, in life, the last high priest of that vanished people, and which now lay in a chamber hewn in the solid rock of the cliff against which the temple was built. About that mummy's withered neck was a copper chain, and on that chain a great red jewel carved in the form of a toad. This jewel was a key, Von Junzt went on to say, to the treasure of the temple which lay hidden in a subterranean crypt far below the temple's altar.

Tussmann's eyes blazed.

"I have seen that temple! I have stood before the altar. I have seen the sealed-up entrance of the chamber in which, the natives say, lies the mummy of the priest. It is a very curious temple, no more like the ruins of the prehistoric Indians than it is like the buildings of the modern Latin-Americans. The Indians in the vicinity disclaim any former connection with the place; they say that the people who built that temple were a different race from themselves, and were there when their own ancestors came into the country. I believe it to be a remnant of some long-vanished civilization which began to decay thousands of years before the Spaniards came.

"I would have liked to have broken into the sealed-up chamber, but I had neither the time nor the tools for the task. I was hurrying to the coast, having been wounded by an accidental gunshot in the foot, and I stumbled onto the place purely by chance.

"I have been planning to have another look at it, but circumstances have prevented—now I intend to let nothing stand in my way! By chance I came upon a passage in the Golden Goblin edition of this book, describing the temple. But that was all; the mummy was only briefly mentioned. Interested, I obtained one of Bridewall's translations, but ran up against a blank wall of baffling blunders. By some irritating mischance the translator had even mistaken the location of the Temple of the Toad, as Von Junzt calls it, and has it in Guatemala instead of Honduras. The general description is faulty, the jewel is mentioned and the fact that it is a 'key.' But a key to what, Bridewall's book does not state. I now felt that I was on the track of a real discovery, unless Von Junzt was, as many maintain, a madman. But that the man was actually in Honduras at one time is well attested, and no one could so vividly describe the temple—as he does in the Black Book—unless he had seen it himself. How he learned of the jewel is more than I can say. The Indians who told me of the mummy said nothing of any jewel. I can only believe that Von Junzt found his way into the sealed crypt somehow—the man had uncanny ways of learning hidden things.

"To the best of my knowledge only one other white man has seen the Temple of the Toad besides Von Junzt and myself—the Spanish traveler Juan Gonzales, who made a partial exploration of that country in 1793. He mentioned, briefly, a curious fane that differed from most Indian ruins, and spoke skeptically of a legend current among the natives that there was 'something unusual' hidden under the temple. I feel certain that he was referring to the Temple of the Toad.

"Tomorrow I sail for Central America. Keep the book; I have no more use for it. This time I am going fully prepared, and I intend to find what is hidden in that temple, if I have to demolish it. It can be nothing less than a great store of gold! The Spaniards missed it, somehow; when they arrived in Central America, the Temple of the Toad was deserted; they were searching for living Indians from whom torture could wring gold; not for mummies of lost peoples. But I mean to have that treasure."

So saying, Tussmann took his departure. I sat down and opened the book at the place where he had left off reading, and I sat until midnight, wrapt in Von Junzt's curious, wild, and at times utterly vague expoundings. And I found pertaining to the Temple of the Toad certain things which disquieted me so much that the next morning I attempted to get in touch with Tussmann, only to find that he had already sailed.

Several months passed and then I received a letter from Tussmann, asking me to come and spend a few days with him at his estate in Sussex; he also requested me to bring the Black Book with me.

I arrived at Tussmann's rather isolated estate just after nightfall. He lived in almost feudal state, his great ivy-grown house and broad lawns surrounded by high stone walls. As I went up the hedge-bordered way from the gate to the house, I noted that the place had not been well kept in its master's absence. Weeds grew rank among the trees, almost choking out the grass. Among some unkempt bushes over against the outer wall, I heard what appeared to be a horse or an ox blundering and lumbering about. I distinctly heard the clink of its hoof on a stone.

A servant who eyed me suspiciously admitted me, and I found Tussmann pacing to and fro in his study like a caged lion. His giant frame was leaner, harder than when I had last seen him; his face was bronzed by a tropic sun. There were more and harsher lines in his strong face and his eyes burned more intensely than ever. A smoldering, baffled anger seemed to underlie his manner.

"Well, Tussmann," I greeted him, "what success? Did you find the gold?"

"I found not an ounce of gold," he growled. "The whole thing was a hoax—well, not all of it. I broke into the sealed chamber and found the mummy—"

"And the jewel?" I exclaimed.

He drew something from his pocket and handed it to me.

I gazed curiously at the thing I held. It was a great jewel, clear and transparent as crystal, but of a sinister crimson, carved, as Von Junzt had declared, in the shape of a toad. I shuddered involuntarily; the image was peculiarly repulsive. I turned my attention to the heavy and curiously wrought copper chain which supported it.

"What are these characters carved on the chain?" I asked curiously.

"I can not say," Tussmann replied. "I had thought perhaps you might know. I find a faint resemblance between them and certain partly defaced hieroglyphics on a monolith known as the Black Stone in the mountains of Hungary. I have been unable to decipher them."

"Tell me of your trip," I urged, and over our whiskey-and-sodas he began, as if with a strange reluctance.

"I found the temple again with no great difficulty, though it lies in a lonely and little-frequented region. The temple is built against a sheer stone cliff in a deserted valley unknown to maps and explorers. I would not endeavor to make an estimate of its antiquity, but it is built of a sort of unusually hard basalt, such as I have never seen anywhere else, and its extreme weathering suggests incredible age.

"Most of the columns which form its facade are in ruins, thrusting up shattered stumps from worn bases, like the scattered and broken teeth of some grinning hag. The outer walls are crumbling, but the inner walls and the columns which support such of the roof as remains intact, seem good for another thousand years, as well as the walls of the inner chamber.

"The main chamber is a large circular affair with a floor composed of great squares of stone. In the center stands the altar, merely a huge, round, curiously carved block of the same material. Directly behind the altar, in the solid stone cliff which forms the rear wall of the chamber, is the sealed and hewn-out chamber wherein lay the mummy of the temple's last priest.

"I broke into the crypt with not too much difficulty and found the mummy exactly as is stated in the Black Book. Though it was in a remarkable state of preservation, I was unable to classify it. The withered features and general contour of the skull suggested certain degraded and mongrel peoples of Lower Egypt, and I feel certain that the priest was a member of a race more akin to the Caucasian than the Indian. Beyond this, I can not make any positive statement.

"But the jewel was there, the chain looped about the dried-up neck."

From this point Tussmann's narrative became so vague that I had some difficulty in following him and wondered if the tropic sun had affected his mind. He had opened a hidden door in the altar somehow with the jewel—just how, he did not plainly say, and it struck me that he did not clearly understand himself the action of the jewel-key. But the opening of the secret door had had a bad effect on the hardy rogues in his employ. They had refused point-blank to follow him through that gaping black opening which had appeared so mysteriously when the gem was touched to the altar.

Tussmann entered alone with his pistol and electric torch, finding a narrow stone stair that wound down into the bowels of the earth, apparently. He followed this and presently came into a broad corridor, in the blackness of which his tiny beam of light was almost engulfed. As he told this he spoke with strange annoyance of a toad which hopped ahead of him, just beyond the circle of light, all the time he was below ground.

Making his way along dank tunnels and stairways that were wells of solid blackness, he at last came to a heavy door fantastically carved, which he felt must be the crypt wherein was secreted the gold of the ancient worshippers. He pressed the toad-jewel against it at several places and finally the door gaped wide.

"And the treasure?" I broke in eagerly.

He laughed in savage self-mockery.

"There was no gold there, no precious gems—nothing—" he hesitated "—nothing that I could bring away."

Again, his tale lapsed into vagueness. I gathered that he had left the temple rather hurriedly without searching any further for the supposed treasure. He had intended bringing the mummy away with him, he said, to present to some museum, but when he came up out of the pits, it could not be found and he believed that his men, in superstitious aversion to having such a companion on their road to the coast, had thrown it into some well or cavern.

"And so," he concluded, "I am in England again no richer than when I left."

"You have the jewel," I reminded him. "Surely it is valuable."

He eyed it without favor, but with a sort of fierce avidness almost obsessional.

"Would you say that it is a ruby?" he asked.

I shook my head. "I am unable to classify it."

"And I. But let me see the book."

He slowly turned the heavy pages, his lips moving as he read. Sometimes he shook his head as if puzzled, and I noticed him dwell long over a certain line.

"This man dipped so deeply into forbidden things," said he, "I can not wonder that his fate was so strange and mysterious. He must have had some foreboding of his end—here he warns men not to disturb sleeping things."

Tussmann seemed lost in thought for some moments.

"Aye, sleeping things," he muttered, "that seem dead, but only lie waiting for some blind fool to awake them—I should have read further in the Black Book—and I should have shut the door when I left the crypt—but I have the key and I'll keep it in spite of Hell."

He roused himself from his reveries and was about to speak when he stopped short. From somewhere upstairs had come a peculiar sound.

"What was that?" he glared at me. I shook my head and he ran to the door and shouted for a servant. The man entered a few moments later and he was rather pale.

"You were upstairs?" growled Tussmann.

"Yes, sir."

"Did you hear anything?" asked Tussmann harshly and in a manner almost threatening and accusing.

"I did, sir," the man answered with a puzzled look on his face.

"What did you hear?" The question was fairly snarled.

"Well, sir," the man laughed apologetically, "you'll say I'm a bit off, I fear, but to tell you the truth, sir, it sounded like a horse stamping around on the roof!"

A blaze of absolute madness leaped into Tussmann's eyes.

"You fool!" he screamed. "Get out of here!" The man shrank back in amazement and Tussmann snatched up the gleaming toad-carved jewel.

"I've been a fool!" he raved. "I didn't read far enough—and I should have shut the door—but by heaven, the key is mine and I'll keep it in spite of man or devil."

And with these strange words he turned and fled upstairs. A moment later his door slammed heavily and a servant, knocking timidly, brought forth only a blasphemous order to retire and a luridly worded threat to shoot anyone who tried to obtain entrance into the room.

Had it not been so late I would have left the house, for I was certain that Tussmann was stark mad. As it was, I retired to the room a frightened servant showed me, but I did not go to bed. I opened the pages of the Black Book at the place where Tussmann had been reading.

This much was evident, unless the man was utterly insane: he had stumbled upon something unexpected in the Temple of the Toad. Something unnatural about the opening of the altar door had frightened his men, and in the subterranean crypt Tussmann had found *something* that he had not thought to find. And I believed that he had been followed from Central America, and that the reason for his persecution was the jewel he called the Key.

Seeking some clue in Von Junzt's volume, I read again of the Temple of the Toad, of the strange pre-Indian people who worshipped there, and of the huge, tittering, tentacled, hoofed monstrosity that they worshipped.

Tussmann had said that he had not read far enough when he had first seen the book. Puzzling over this cryptic phrase I came upon the line he had pored over—marked by his thumb nail. It seemed to me to be another of Von Junzt's many ambiguities, for it merely stated that a temple's god was the temple's treasure. Then the dark implication of the hint struck me, and cold sweat beaded my forehead.

The Key to the Treasure! And the temple's treasure was the temple's god! And sleeping things might awaken on the opening of their prison door! I sprang up, unnerved by the intolerable suggestion, and at that moment something crashed in the still-ness, and the death-scream of a human being burst upon my ears.

In an instant I was out of the room, and as I dashed up the stairs I heard sounds that have made me doubt my sanity ever since. At Tussmann's door I halted, essaying with shaking hand to turn the knob. The door was locked, and as I hesitated I heard from within a hideous high-pitched tittering and then the disgusting squashy sound as if a great, jelly-like bulk was being forced through the window. The sound ceased and I could have sworn I heard a faint swish of gigantic wings. Then silence.

Gathering my shattered nerves, I broke down the door. A foul and overpowering stench billowed out like a yellow mist. Gasping in nausea, I entered. The room was in ruins, but nothing was missing except that crimson, toad-carved jewel Tussmann called the Key, and that was never found. A foul, unspeakable slime smeared the windowsill, and in the center of the room lay Tussmann, his head crushed and flattened; and on the red ruin of skull and face, the plain print of an enormous hoof.

THE HAUNTER OF THE RING

As I entered John Kirowan's study I was too much engrossed in my own thoughts to notice, at first, the haggard appearance of his visitor, a big, handsome young fellow well known to me.

"Hello, Kirowan," I greeted. "Hello, Gordon. Haven't seen you for quite a while. How's Evelyn?" And before he could answer, still on the crest of the enthusiasm which had brought me there, I exclaimed: "Look here, you fellows, I've got something that will make you stare! I got it from that robber Ahmed Mektub, and I paid high for it, but it's worth it. Look!" From under my coat I drew the jewel-hilted Afghan dagger which had fascinated me as a collector of rare weapons.

Kirowan, familiar with my passion, showed only polite interest, but the effect on Gordon was shocking.

With a strangled cry he sprang up and backward, knocking the chair clattering to the floor. Fists clenched and countenance livid he faced me, crying: "Keep back! Get away from me, or—"

I was frozen in my tracks.

"What in the—" I began bewilderedly, when Gordon, with another amazing change of attitude, dropped into a chair and sank his head in his hands. I saw his heavy shoulders quiver. I

stared helplessly from him to Kirowan, who seemed equally
dumbfounded.

"Is he drunk?" I asked.

Kirowan shook his head and, filling a brandy glass, offered it
to the man. Gordon looked up with haggard eyes, seized the
drink, and gulped it down like a man half famished. Then he
straightened up and looked at us shamefacedly.

"I'm sorry I went off my handle, O'Donnel" he said. "It was
the unexpected shock of you drawing that knife."

"Well," I retorted, with some disgust, "I suppose you thought
I was going to stab you with it!"

"Yes, I did!" Then, at the utterly blank expression on my
face, he added: "Oh, I didn't actually *think* that; at least, I didn't
reach that conclusion by any process of reasoning. It was just the
blind primitive instinct of a hunted man, against whom anyone's
hand may be turned."

His strange words and the despairing way he said them sent a
queer shiver of nameless apprehension down my spine.

"What are you talking about?" I demanded uneasily.
"Hunted? For what? You never committed a crime in your life."

"Not in this life, perhaps," he muttered.

"What do you mean?"

"What if retribution for a black crime committed in a
previous life were hounding me?" he muttered.

"That's nonsense," I snorted.

"Oh, is it?" he exclaimed, stung. "Did you ever hear of my
great-grandfather, Sir Richard Gordon of Argyle?"

"Sure; but what's that got to do with—"

"You've seen his portrait: doesn't it resemble me?"

"Well, yes," I admitted, "except that your expression is frank
and wholesome whereas his is crafty and cruel."

"He murdered his wife," answered Gordon. "Suppose the
theory of reincarnation were true? Why shouldn't a man suffer in
one life for a crime committed in another?"

"You mean you think you are the reincarnation of your great-grandfather? Of all the fantastic—well, since he killed his wife, I suppose you'll be expecting Evelyn to murder you!" This last was delivered in searing sarcasm, as I thought of the sweet, gentle girl Gordon had married. His answer stunned me.

"My wife," he said slowly, "has tried to kill me three times in the past week."

There was no reply to that. I glanced helplessly at John Kirowan. He sat in his customary position, chin resting on his strong, slim hands; his white face was immobile, but his dark eyes gleamed with interest. In the silence I heard a clock ticking like a death-watch.

"Tell us the full story, Gordon," suggested Kirowan, and his calm, even voice was like a knife that cut a strangling, relieving the unreal tension.

"You know we've been married less than a year," Gordon began, plunging into the tale as though he were bursting for utterance; his words stumbled and tripped over one another. "All couples have spats, of course, but we've never had any real quarrels. Evelyn is the best natured girl in the world.

"The first thing out of the ordinary occurred about a week ago. We had driven up in the mountains, left the car, and were wandering around picking wildflowers. At last we came to a steep slope, some thirty feet in height, and Evelyn called my attention to the flowers which grew thickly at the foot. I was looking over the edge and wondering if I could climb down without tearing my clothes to ribbons, when I felt a violent shove from behind that toppled me over.

"If it had been a sheer cliff, I'd have broken my neck. As it was, I went tumbling down, rolling and sliding, and brought up at the bottom scratched and bruised, with my garments in rags. I looked up and saw Evelyn staring down, apparently frightened half out of her wits.

"'Oh Jim!' she cried. 'Are you hurt? How came you to fall?'

"It was on the tip of my tongue to tell her that there was such a thing as carrying a joke too far, but these words checked me. I decided that she must have stumbled against me unintentionally, and actually didn't know it was she who precipitated me down the slope."

"So I laughed it off, and went home. She made a great fuss over me, insisted on swabbing my scratches with iodine, and lectured me for my carelessness! I hadn't the heart to tell her it was her fault.

"But four days later, the next thing happened. I was walking along our driveway, when I saw her coming up it in the automobile. I stepped out on the grass to let her by, as there isn't any curb along the driveway. She was smiling as she approached me, and slowed down the car, as if to speak to me. Then, just before she reached me, a most horrible change came over her expression. Without warning the car leaped at me like a living thing as she drove her foot down on the accelerator. Only a frantic leap backward saved me from being ground under the wheels. The car shot across the lawn and crashed into a tree. I ran to it and found Evelyn dazed and hysterical, but unhurt. She babbled of losing control of the machine.

"I carried her into the house and sent for Doctor Donnelly. He found nothing seriously wrong with her, and attributed her dazed condition to fright and shock. Within half an hour she regained her normal senses, but she's refused to touch the wheel since. Strange to say, she seemed less frightened on her own account than on mine. She seemed vaguely to know that she'd nearly run me down, and grew hysterical again when she spoke of it. Yet she seemed to take it for granted that I knew the machine had got out of her control. But I distinctly saw her wrench the wheel around, and I know she deliberately tried to hit me—why, God alone knows."

"Still I refused to let my mind follow the channel it was getting into. Evelyn had never given any evidence of any psychological weakness or 'nerves'; she's always been a level-headed girl, wholesome and natural. But I began to think she was subject to crazy impulses. Most of us have felt the impulse to leap from tall buildings. And sometimes a person feels a blind, childish, and utterly reasonless urge to harm someone. We pick up a pistol, and the thought suddenly enters our mind how easy it would be to send our friend, who sits smiling and unaware, into eternity with a touch of the trigger. Of course we don't do it, but the impulse is there. So I thought perhaps some lack of mental discipline made Evelyn susceptible to these unguided impulses, and unable to control them."

"Nonsense," I broke in. "I've known her since she was a baby. If she has any such trait, she's developed it since she married you."

It was an unfortunate remark. Gordon caught it up with a despairing gleam in his eyes. "That's just it—since she married me! It's a curse—a black, ghastly curse, crawling like a serpent out of the past! I tell you, I was Richard Gordon and she—she was Lady Elizabeth, his murdered wife!" His voice sank to a blood-freezing whisper.

I shuddered; it is an awful thing to look upon the ruin of a keen, clean brain, and such I was certain that I surveyed in James Gordon. Why or how, or by what grisly chance it had come about I could not say, but I was certain the man was mad.

"You spoke of three attempts." It was John Kirowan's voice again, calm and stable amid the gathering webs of horror and unreality.

"Look here!" Gordon lifted, his arm, drew back the sleeve and displayed a bandage, the cryptic significance of which was intolerable.

"I came into the bathroom this morning looking for my razor," he said. "I found Evelyn just on the point of using my best shaving implement for some feminine purpose—to cut out a pattern, or something. Like many women she can't seem to realize the difference between a razor and a butcher-knife or a pair of shears.

"I was a bit irritated, and I said: 'Evelyn, how many times

have I told you not to use my razors for such things? Bring it here; I'll give you my pocket-knife.'

"'I'm sorry, Jim,' she said. 'I didn't know it would hurt the razor. Here it is.'

"She was advancing, holding the open razor toward me. I reached for it—then something warned me. It was the same look in her eyes, just as I had seen it the day she nearly ran over me. That was all that saved my life, for I instinctively threw up my hand just as she slashed at my throat with all her power. The blade gashed my arm, as you see, before I caught her wrist. For an instant she fought me like a wild thing; her slender body was taut as steel beneath my hands. Then she went limp and the look in her eyes was replaced by a strange dazed expression. The razor slipped out of her fingers.

"I let go of her and she stood swaying as if about to faint. I went to the lavatory—my wound was bleeding in a beastly fashion—and the next thing I heard her cry out, and she was hovering over me.

"'Jim!' she cried. 'How did you cut yourself so terribly?'"

Gordon shook his head and sighed heavily. "I guess I was a bit out of my head. My self-control snapped.

"'Don't keep up this pretense, Evelyn,' I said. 'God knows what's got into you, but you know as well as I that you've tried to kill me three times in the past week.'

"She recoiled as if I'd struck her, catching at her breast and staring at me as if at a ghost. She didn't say a word—and just what I said I don't remember. But when I finished, I left her standing there white and still as a marble statue. I got my arm bandaged at a drug store, and then came over here, not knowing what else to do.

"Kirowan—O'Donnel—it's damnable! Either my wife is subject to fits of insanity—" He choked on the word. "No, I can't believe it. Ordinarily her eyes are too clear and level—too utterly sane. But every time she has an opportunity to harm me, she seems to become a temporary maniac."

He beat his fists together in his impotence and agony.

"But it isn't insanity! I used to work in a psychopathic ward, and I've seen every form of mental unbalance. My wife is *not* insane!"

"Then what—" I began, but he turned haggard eyes on me.

"Only one alternative remains," he answered. "It is the old curse—from the days when I walked the earth with a heart as black as hell's darkest pits and did evil in the sight of man and of God. *She* knows, in fleeting snatches of memory. People have *seen* before—have glimpsed forbidden things in momentary liftings of the veil, which bars life from life. She was Elizabeth Douglas, the ill-fated bride of Richard Gordon, whom he murdered in jealous frenzy, and the vengeance is hers. I shall die by her hands, as it was meant to be. And she—" he bowed his head in his hands.

"Just a moment." It was Kirowan again. "You have mentioned a strange look in your wife's eyes. What sort of a look? Was it of maniacal frenzy?"

Gordon shook his head. "It was an utter blankness. All the life and intelligence simply vanished, leaving her eyes dark wells of emptiness."

Kirowan nodded and asked a seemingly irrelevant question. "Have you any enemies?"

"Not that I know of."

"You forget Joseph Roelocke," I said. "I can't imagine that elegant sophisticate going to the trouble of doing you actual harm, but I have an idea that if he could discomfort you without any physical effort on his part, he'd do it with a right good will."

Kirowan turned on me an eye that had suddenly become piercing.

"And who is this Joseph Roelocke?"

"A young exquisite who came into Evelyn's life and nearly rushed her off her feet for a while. But in the end, she came back to her first love—Gordon here. Roelocke took it pretty hard. For all his suaveness there's a streak of violence and passion in the man that might have cropped out but for his infernal indolence and blase indifference."

"Oh, there's nothing to be said against Roelocke," interrupted Gordon impatiently. "He must know that Evelyn never really loved him. He merely fascinated her temporarily with his romantic Latin air."

"Not exactly Latin, Jim," I protested. "Roelocke does look foreign, but it isn't Latin. It's almost Oriental."

"Well, what has Roelocke to do with this matter?" Gordon snarled with the irascibility of frayed nerves. "He's been as friendly as a man could be since Evelyn and I were married. In fact, only a week ago he sent her a ring which he said was a peace-offering and a belated wedding gift; said that after all, her jilting him was a greater misfortune for her than it was for him— the conceited jackass!"

"A ring?" Kirowan had suddenly come to life; it was as if something hard and steely had been sounded in him. "What sort of a ring?"

"Oh, a fantastic thing—copper, made like a scaly snake coiled three times, with its tail in its mouth and yellow jewels for eyes. I gather he picked it up somewhere in Hungary."

"He has traveled a great deal in Hungary?"

Gordon looked surprised at this questioning but answered: "Why, apparently the man's traveled everywhere. I put him down as the pampered son of a millionaire. He never did any work, so far as I know."

"He's a great student," I put in. "I've been up to his apartment several times, and I never saw such a collection of books—"

Gordon leaped to his feet with an oath, "Are we all crazy?" he cried. "I came up here hoping to get some help—and you fellows fall to talking of Joseph Roelocke. I'll go to Doctor Donnelly—"

"Wait!" Kirowan stretched out a detaining hand. "If you don't mind, we'll go over to your house. I'd like to talk to your wife."

Gordon dumbly acquiesced. Harried and haunted by grisly

forebodings, he knew not which way to turn, and welcomed anything that promised aid.

We drove over in his car, and scarcely a word was spoken on the way. Gordon was sunk in moody ruminations, and Kirowan had withdrawn himself into some strange aloof domain of thought beyond my ken. He sat like a statue, his dark, vital eyes staring into space, not blankly, but as one who looks with understanding into some far realm.

Though I counted the man as my best friend, I knew but little of his past. He had come into my life as abruptly and unannounced as Joseph Roelocke had come into the life of Evelyn Ash. I had met him at the Wanderers Club, which is composed of the drift of the world, travelers, eccentrics, and all manner of men whose paths lie outside the beaten tracks of life. I had been attracted to him, and intrigued by his strange powers and deep knowledge. I vaguely knew that he was the black sheep younger son of a titled Irish family, and that he had walked many strange ways. Gordon's mention of Hungary struck a chord in my memory; one phase of his life Kirowan had once let drop fragmentarily. I only knew that he had once suffered a bitter grief and a savage wrong, and that it had been in Hungary. But the nature of the episode I did not know.

At Gordon's house Evelyn met us calmly, showing inner agitation only by the over-restraint of her manner. I saw the beseeching look she stole at her husband. She was a slender, soft-spoken girl, whose dark eyes were always vibrant and alight with emotion. That child try to murder her adored husband? The idea was monstrous. Again, I was convinced that James Gordon himself was deranged.

Following Kirowan's lead, we made a pretense of small talk, as if we had casually dropped in, but I felt that Evelyn was not deceived. Our conversation rang false and hollow, and presently

Kirowan said: "Mrs. Gordon, that is a remarkable ring you are wearing. Do you mind if I look at it?"

"I'll have to give you my hand," she laughed. "I've been trying to get it off today, and it won't come off."

She held out her slim white hand for Kirowan's inspection, and his face was immobile as he looked at the metal snake that coiled about her slim finger. He did not touch it. I myself was aware of an unaccountable repulsion. There was something almost obscene about that dull copperish reptile wound about the girl's white finger.

"It's evil-looking, isn't it?" She involuntarily shivered. "At first I liked it, but now I can hardly bear to look at it. If I can get it off, I intend to return it to Joseph—Mr. Roelocke."

Kirowan was about to make some reply, when the doorbell rang. Gordon jumped as if shot, and Evelyn rose quickly.

"I'll answer it, Jim—I know who it is."

She returned an instant later with two more mutual friends, those inseparable cronies, Doctor Donnelly, whose burly body, jovial manner, and booming voice were combined with as keen a brain as any in the profession, and Bill Bain, elderly, lean, wiry, acidly witty. Both were old friends of the Ash family. Doctor Donnelly had ushered Evelyn into the world, and Bain was always Uncle Bill to her.

"Howdy, Jim! Howdy, Mr. Kirowan!" roared Donnelly. "Hey, O'Donnel, have you got any firearms with you? Last time your nearly blew my head off showing me an old flintlock pistol that wasn't supposed to be loaded!"

"Doctor Donnelly!"

We all turned. Evelyn was standing beside a wide table, holding it as if for support. Her face was white. Our badinage ceased instantly. A sudden tension was in the air.

"Doctor Donnelly," she repeated, holding her voice steady by an effort, "I sent for you and Uncle Bill—for the same reason for which I know Jim has brought Mr. Kirowan and Michael. There is a matter Jim and I can no longer deal with alone. There is something between us—something black and ghastly and terrible."

"What are you talking about, girl?" All the levity was gone from Donnelly's great voice.

"My husband—" She choked, then went blindly on: "My husband has accused me of trying to murder him."

The silence that fell was broken by Bain's sudden and energetic rise. His eyes blazed and his fists quivered.

"You young pup!" he shouted at Gordon. "I'll knock the living daylights—"

"Sit down, Bill!" Donnelly's huge hand crushed his smaller companion back into his chair. "No use goin' off half cocked. Go ahead, honey."

"We need help. We can not carry this thing alone." A shadow crossed her comely face. "This morning Jim's arm was badly cut. He said I did it. I don't know. I was handing him the razor. Then I must have fainted. At least, everything faded away. When I came to myself he was washing his arm in the lavatory—and—and he accused me of trying to kill him."

"Why, the young fool!" barked the belligerent Bain. "Hasn't he sense enough to know that if you did cut him, it was an accident?"

"Shut up, won't you?" snorted Donnelly. "Honey, did you say you fainted? That isn't like you."

"I've been having fainting spells," she answered. "The first time was when we were in the mountains and Jim fell down a cliff. We were standing on the edge—then everything went black, and when my sight cleared, he was rolling down the slope." She shuddered at the recollection.

"Then when I lost control of the car and it crashed into the tree. You remember—Jim called you over."

Doctor Donnelly nodded his head ponderously.

"I don't remember you ever having fainting spells before."

"But Jim says I pushed him over the cliff!" she cried hysterically. "He says I tried to run him down in the car! He says I purposely slashed him with the razor!"

Doctor Donnelly turned perplexedly toward the wretched Gordon.

"How about it, son?"

"God help me," Gordon burst out in agony; "it's true!"

"Why, you lying hound!" It was Bain who gave tongue, leaping again to his feet. "If you want a divorce, why don't you get it in a decent way, instead of resorting to these despicable tactics—"

"Damn you!" roared Gordon, lunging up, and losing control of himself completely. "If you say that I'll tear your jugular out!"

Evelyn screamed; Donnelly grabbed Bain ponderously and banged him back into his chair with no overly gentle touch, and Kirowan laid a hand lightly on Gordon's shoulder. The man seemed to crumple into himself. He sank back into his chair and held out his hands gropingly toward his wife.

"Evelyn," he said, his voice thick with laboring emotion, "you know I love you. I feel like a dog. But God help me, it's true. If we go on this way, I'll be a dead man, and you—"

"Don't say it!" she screamed. "I know you wouldn't lie to me, Jim. If you say I tried to kill you, I know I did. But I swear, Jim, I didn't do it consciously. Oh, I must be going mad! That's why my dreams have been so wild and terrifying lately—"

"Of what have you dreamed, Mrs. Gordon?" asked Kirowan gently.

She pressed her hands to her temples and stared dully at him, as if only half comprehending.

"A black thing," she muttered. "A horrible faceless black thing that mows and mumbles and paws over me with apish hands. I dream of it every night. And in the daytime I try to kill the only man I ever loved. I'm going mad! Maybe I'm already crazy and don't know it."

"Calm yourself, honey."

To Doctor Donnelly, with all his science, it was only another case of feminine hysteria. His matter-of-fact voice seemed to soothe her, and she sighed and drew a weary hand through her damp locks.

"We'll talk this all over, and everything's goin' to be okay," he said, drawing a thick cigar from his vest pocket. "Gimme a match, honey."

She began mechanically to feel about the table, and just as mechanically Gordon said: "There are matches in the drawer, Evelyn."

She opened the drawer and began groping in it, when suddenly, as if struck by recollection and intuition, Gordon sprang up, white-faced, and shouted: "No, no! Don't open that drawer—don't—"

Even as he voiced that urgent cry, she stiffened, as if at the feel of something in the drawer. Her change of expression held us all frozen, even Kirowan. The vital intelligence vanished from her eyes like a blown-out flame, and into them came the look Gordon had described as blank. The term was descriptive. Her beautiful eyes were dark wells of emptiness, as if the soul had been withdrawn from behind them.

Her hand came out of the drawer holding a pistol, and she fired point-blank. Gordon reeled with a groan and went down, blood starting from his head. For a flashing instant she looked down stupidly at the smoking gun in her hand, like one suddenly waking from a nightmare. Then her wild scream of agony smote our ears.

"Oh God, I've killed him! Jim! *Jim!*"

She reached him before any of us, throwing herself on her knees and cradling his bloody head in her arms, while she sobbed in an unbearable passion of horror and anguish. The emptiness was gone from her eyes; they were alive and dilated with grief and terror.

I was making toward my prostrate friend with Donnelly and Bain, but Kirowan caught my arm. His face was no longer immobile; his eyes glittered with a controlled savagery.

"Leave him to them!" he snarled. "We are hunters, not heal-ers! Lead me to the house of Joseph Roelocke!"

I did not question him. We drove there in Gordon's car. I had the wheel, and something about the grim face of my companion caused me to hurl the machine recklessly through the traffic. I had the sensation of being part of a tragic drama which was hurtling with headlong speed toward a terrible climax.

I wrenched the car to a grinding halt at the curb before the building where Roelocke lived in a bizarre apartment high above the city. The very elevator that shot us skyward seemed imbued with something of Kirowan's driving urge for haste. I pointed out Roelocke's door, and he cast it open without knocking and shouldered his way in. I was close at his heels.

Roelocke, in a dressing-gown of Chinese silk worked with dragons, was lounging on a divan, puffing quickly at a cigarette. He sat up, overturning a wineglass which stood with a half-filled bottle at his elbow.

Before Kirowan could speak, I burst out with our news. "James Gordon has been shot!"

He sprang to his feet. "Shot? When? When did she kill him?"

"*She?*" I glared in bewilderment. "How did you know—"

With a steely hand Kirowan thrust me aside, and as the men faced each other, I saw recognition flare up in Roelocke's face. They made a strong contrast: Kirowan, tall, pale with some white-hot passion; Roelocke, slim, darkly handsome, with the saracenic arch of his slim brows above his black eyes. I realized that whatever else occurred, it lay between those two men. They were not strangers; I could sense like a tangible thing the hate that lay between them.

"John Kirowan!" softly whispered Roelocke.

"You remember me, Yosef Vrolok!" Only an iron control kept Kirowan's voice steady. The other merely stared at him without speaking.

"Years ago," said Kirowan more deliberately, "when we delved in the dark mysteries together in Budapest, I saw whither you were drifting. I drew back; I would not descend to the foul depths of forbidden occultism and diabolism to which you sank. And because I would not, you despised me, and you robbed me of the only woman I ever loved; you turned her against me by means of your vile arts, and then you degraded and debauched her, sank her into your own foul slime. I had killed you with my hands then, Yosef Vrolok—vampire by nature as well as by name that you are—but your arts protected you from physical vengeance. But you have trapped yourself at last!"

Kirowan's voice rose in fierce exultation. All his cultured restraint had been swept away from him, leaving a primitive, elemental man, raging and gloating over a hated foe.

"You sought the destruction of James Gordon and his wife, because she unwittingly escaped your snare; you—"

Roelocke shrugged his shoulders and laughed. "You are mad. I have not seen the Gordons for weeks. Why blame me for their family troubles?"

Kirowan snarled. "Liar as always. What did you say just now when O'Donnel told you Gordon had been shot? 'When did she kill him?' You were expecting to hear that the girl had killed her husband. Your psychic powers had told you that a climax was close at hand. You were nervously awaiting news of the success of your devilish scheme.

"But I did not need a slip of your tongue to recognize your handiwork. I knew as soon as I saw the ring on Evelyn Gordon's finger; the ring she could not remove; the ancient and accursed ring of Thoth-amon, handed down by foul cults of sorcerers since the days of forgotten Stygia. I knew that ring was yours, and I knew by what ghastly rites you came to possess it. And I knew its power. Once she put it on her finger, in her innocence and ignorance, she was in your power. By your black magic you summoned the black elemental spirit, *the haunter of the ring*, out of the gulfs of Night and the ages. Here in your accursed chamber you performed unspeakable rituals to drive Evelyn Gordon's soul from her body, and to cause that body to be possessed by that godless sprite from *outside* the human universe.

"She was too clean and wholesome, her love for her husband too strong, for the fiend to gain complete and permanent possession of her body; only for brief instants could it drive her own spirit into the void and animate her form. But that was enough for your purpose. But you have brought ruin upon yourself by your vengeance!"

Kirowan's voice rose to a feline screech.

"What was the price demanded by the fiend you drew from the Pits? Ha, you blench! Yosef Vrolok is not the only man to have learned forbidden secrets! After I left Hungary, a broken man, I took up again the study of the black arts, to trap you, you cringing serpent! I explored the ruins of Zimbabwe, the lost mountains of inner Mongolia, and the forgotten jungle islands of the southern seas. I learned what sickened my soul so that I forswore occultism forever—but I learned of the black spirit that deals death by the hand of a beloved one, and is controlled by a master of magic.

"But, Yosef Vrolok, you are not an adept! You have not the power to control the fiend you have invoked. And you have sold your soul!"

The Hungarian tore at his collar as if it were a strangling noose. His face had changed, as if a mask had dropped away; he looked much older.

"You lie!" he panted. "I did not promise him *my* soul—"

"I do not lie!" Kirowan's shriek was shocking in its wild exultation. "I know the price a man must pay for calling forth the nameless shape that roams the gulfs of Darkness. Look! There in the corner behind you! A nameless, sightless thing is laughing—is mocking you! It has fulfilled its bargain, and it has come for you, Yosef Vrolok!"

"No!" shrieked Vrolok, tearing his limp collar away from his sweating throat. His composure had crumpled, and his demoralization was sickening to see. "I tell you it was not my soul—I promised it a soul, but not *my* soul—he must take the soul of the girl, or of James Gordon."

"Fool!" roared Kirowan. "Do you think *he* could take the souls of innocence? That he would not know they were beyond his reach? The girl and the youth he could kill; their souls were not his to take or yours to give. But *your* black soul is not beyond his reach, and he will have his wage. *Look!* He is materializing behind you! He is growing out of thin air!"

Was it the hypnosis inspired by Kirowan's burning words that caused me to shudder and grow cold, to feel an icy chill that was not of earth pervade the room? Was it a trick of light and shadow that seemed to produce the effect of a black anthropomorphic shadow on the wall behind the Hungarian? *No*, by heaven! It grew, it swelled—Vrolok had not turned. He stared at Kirowan with eyes starting from his head, hair standing stiffly on his scalp, sweat dripping from his livid face.

Kirowan's cry started shudders down my spine.

"Look behind you, fool! *I see him!* He has come! He is here! His grisly mouth gapes in awful laughter! His misshapen paws reach for you!"

And then at last Vrolok wheeled, with an awful shriek, throwing his arms above his head in a gesture of wild despair. And for one brain-shattering instant he was *blotted out* by a great black shadow—Kirowan grasped my arm and we fled from that accursed chamber, blind with horror.

The same paper which bore a brief item telling of James Gordon having suffered a slight scalp-wound by the accidental discharge of a pistol in his home, headlined the sudden death of Joseph Roelocke, wealthy and eccentric clubman, in his sumptuous apartments—apparently from heart-failure.

I read it at breakfast, while I drank cup after cup of black coffee, from a hand that was not too steady, even after the lapse of a night. Across the table from me Kirowan likewise seemed to lack appetite. He brooded, as if he roamed again through bygone years.

"Gordon's fantastic theory of reincarnation was wild enough," I said at last. "But the actual facts were still more incredible. Tell me, Kirowan, was that last scene the result of hypnosis? Was it the power of your words that made me seem to see a black horror grow out of the air and rip Yosef Vrolok's soul from his living body?"

He shook his head. "No human hypnotism would strike that blackhearted devil dead on the floor. No; there are beings outside the ken of common humanity, foul shapes of transcosmic evil. Such a one it was with which Vrolok dealt."

"But how could it claim his soul?" I persisted. "If indeed such an awful bargain had been struck, it had not fulfilled its part, for James Gordon was not dead, but merely knocked senseless."

"Vrolok did not know it," answered Kirowan. "He thought that Gordon was dead, and I convinced him that he himself had been trapped, and was doomed. In his demoralization he fell easy prey to the thing he called forth. *It*, of course, was always watching for a moment of weakness on his part. The powers of Darkness never deal fairly with human beings; he who traffics with them is always cheated in the end."

"It's a mad nightmare," I muttered. "But it seems to me, then, that you as much as anything else brought about Vrolok's death."

"It is gratifying to think so," Kirowan answered. "Evelyn Gordon is safe now; and it is a small repayment for what he did to another girl, years ago, and in a far country."

THE CHALLENGE FROM BEYOND

In 1935, the editor of Fantasy Magazine *asked five prominent science fiction writers and five prominent fantasy writers to write two "round-robin" stories, both called* The Challenge from Beyond. *The authors of the fantasy version were C.L. Moore, A. Merritt, H.P. Lovecraft, Robert E. Howard, and Frank Belknap Long. The science fiction version was written by Stanley G. Weinbaum, Donald Wandrei, Edward E. (E.E. "Doc") Smith, Harl Vincent, and Murray Leinster. In the following text, the name of the author of each section of the story is given in brackets.*

[C.L. MOORE]

George Campbell opened sleep-fogged eyes upon darkness and lay gazing out of the tent flap upon the pale August night for some minutes before he roused enough even to wonder what had wakened him. There was in the keen, clear air of these Canadian woods a soporific as potent as any drug. Campbell lay quiet for a moment, sinking slowly back into the delicious borderlands of sleep, conscious of an exquisite weariness, an unaccustomed sense of muscles well used, and relaxed now into perfect ease. These were vacation's most delightful moments, after all—rest, after toil, in the clear, sweet forest night.

Luxuriously, as his mind sank backward into oblivion, he assured himself once more that three long months of freedom lay before him—freedom from cities and monotony, freedom from pedagogy and the University and students with no rudiments of interest in the geology he earned his daily bread by dinning into their obdurate ears. Freedom from—

Abruptly the delightful somnolence crashed about him. Somewhere outside the sound of tin shrieking across tin slashed into his peace. George Campbell sat up jerkily and reached for his flashlight. Then he laughed and put it down again, straining his eyes through the midnight gloom outside, where among the

tumbling cans of his supplies a dark anonymous little night beast
was prowling. He stretched out a long arm and groped about
among the rocks at the tent door for a missile. His fingers closed
on a large stone, and he drew back his hand to throw.

But he never threw it. It was such a queer thing he had come
upon in the dark. Square, crystal smooth, obviously artificial,
with dull rounded corners. The strangeness of its rock surfaces
to his fingers was so remarkable that he reached again for his
flashlight and turned its rays upon the thing he held.

All sleepiness left him as he saw what it was, he had picked
up in his idle groping. It was clear as rock crystal, this queer,
smooth cube. Quartz, unquestionably, but not in its usual hexag-
onal crystallized form. Somehow—he could not guess the
method—it had been wrought into a perfect cube, about four
inches in measurement over each worn face. For it was incredibly worn. The hard, hard crystal was rounded now until its
corners were almost gone and the thing was beginning to assume
the outlines of a sphere. Ages and ages of wearing, years almost
beyond counting, must have passed over this strange clear thing.

But the most curious thing of all was that shape he could
make out dimly in the heart of the crystal. For imbedded in its
center lay a little disc of a pale and nameless substance with
characters incised deep upon its quartz-enclosed surface. Wedge-
shaped characters, faintly reminiscent of cuneiform writing.

George Campbell wrinkled his brows and bent closer above
the little enigma in his hands, puzzling helplessly. How could
such a thing as this have imbedded in pure rock crystal?
Remotely a memory floated through his mind of ancient legends
that called quartz crystals ice which had frozen too hard to melt
again. Ice—and wedge-shaped cuneiforms—yes, didn't that sort
of writing originate among the Sumerians who came down from
the north in history's remotest beginnings to settle in the primitive Mesopotamian valley? Then hard sense regained control and
he laughed. Quartz, of course, was formed in the earliest of
Earth's geological periods, when there was nothing anywhere but

heat and heaving rock. Ice had not come for tens of millions of years after this thing must have been formed.

And yet—that writing. Man-made, surely, although its characters were unfamiliar save in their faint hinting at cuneiform shapes. Or could there, in a Paleozoic world, have been things with a written language who might have graven these cryptic wedges upon the quartz-enveloped disc he held? Or—might a thing like this have fallen meteor-like out of space into the unformed rock of a still molten world? Could it—

Then he caught himself up sharply and felt his ears going hot at the luridness of his own imagination. The silence and the solitude and the queer thing in his hands were conspiring to play tricks with his common sense. He shrugged and laid the crystal down at the edge of his pallet, switching off the light. Perhaps morning and a clear head would bring him an answer to the questions that seemed so insoluble now.

But sleep did not come easily. For one thing, it seemed to him, as he flashed off the light, that the little cube had shone for a moment as if with sustained light before it faded into the surrounding dark. Or perhaps he was wrong. Perhaps it had been only his dazzled eyes that seemed to see the light forsake it reluctantly, glowing in the enigmatic deeps of the thing with queer persistence.

He lay there unquietly for a long while, turning the unanswered questions over and over in his mind. There was something about this crystal cube out of the unmeasured past, perhaps from the dawn of all history, that constituted a challenge that would not let him sleep.

[A. MERRITT]

He lay there, it seemed to him, for hours. It had been the lingering light, the luminescence that seemed so reluctant to die, which held his mind. It was as though something in the heart of the cube had awakened, stirred drowsily, become suddenly alert ... and intent upon him.

Sheer fantasy, this. He stirred impatiently and flashed his light upon his watch. Close to one o'clock; three hours more before the dawn. The beam fell and was focused upon the warm crystal cube. He held it there closely, for minutes. He snapped it out, then watched.

There was no doubt about it now. As his eyes accustomed themselves to the darkness, he saw that the strange crystal was glimmering with tiny fugitive lights deep within it like threads of sapphire lightnings. They were at its center and they seemed to him to come from the pale disk with its disturbing markings. And the disc itself was becoming larger ... the markings shifting shapes ... the cube was growing ... was it illusion brought about by the tiny lightnings ...

He heard a sound. It was the very ghost of a sound, like the ghosts of harp strings being plucked with ghostly fingers. He bent closer. It came from the cube ...

There was squeaking in the underbrush, a flurry of bodies and an agonized wailing like a child in death throes and swiftly stilled. Some small tragedy of the wilderness, killer and prey. He stepped over to where it had been enacted but could see nothing. He again snapped off the flash and looked toward his tent. Upon the ground was a pale blue glimmering. It was the cube. He stooped to pick it up; then obeying some obscure warning, drew back his hand.

And again, he saw, its glow was dying. The tiny sapphire lightnings flashing fitfully, withdrawing to the disc from which they had come. There was no sound from it.

He sat, watching the luminescence glow and fade, glow and fade, but steadily becoming dimmer. It came to him that two elements were necessary to produce the phenomenon. The electric ray itself, and his own fixed attention. His mind must travel along the ray, fix itself upon the cube's heart, if its beat were to wax, until ... what?

He felt a chill of spirit, as though from contact with some alien thing. It was alien, he knew it; not of this earth. Not of earth's life. He conquered his shrinking, picked up the cube and took it into the tent. It was neither warm nor cold; except for its weight he would not have known he held it. He put it upon the table, keeping the torch turned from it; then stepped to the flap of the tent and closed it.

He went back to the table, drew up the camp chair, and turned the flash directly upon the cube, focusing it so far as he could upon its heart. He sent all his will, all his concentration, along it; focusing will and sight upon the disc as he had the light.

As though at command, the sapphire lightnings burned forth. They burst from the disc into the body of the crystal cube, then beat back, bathing the disc and the markings. Again these began to change, shifting, moving, advancing, and retreating in the blue gleaming. They were no longer cuneiform. They were things ... objects.

He heard the murmuring music, the plucked harp strings.

Louder grew the sound and louder, and now all the body of the cube vibrated to their rhythm. The crystal walls were melting, growing misty as though formed of the mist of diamonds. And the disc itself was growing ... the shapes shifting, dividing and multiplying as though some door had been opened and into it companies of phantasms were pouring; while brighter, more bright grew the pulsing light.

He felt swift panic, tried to withdraw sight and will, dropped the flash. The cube had no need now of the ray... and he could not withdraw ... could not withdraw? Why, he himself was being sucked into that disc which was now a globe within which unnameable shapes danced to a music that bathed the globe with steady radiance.

There was no tent. There was only a vast curtain of sparkling mist behind which shone the globe ... He felt himself drawn through that mist, sucked through it as if by a mighty wind, straight for the globe.

[H.P. LOVECRAFT]

As the mist-blurred light of the sapphire suns grew more and more intense, the outlines of the globe ahead wavered and dissolved to a churning chaos. Its pallor and its motion and its music all blended themselves with the engulfing mist—bleaching it to a pale steel colour and setting it undulantly in motion. And the sapphire suns, too, melted imperceptibly into the greying infinity of shapeless pulsation.

Meanwhile the sense of forward, outward motion grew intolerably, incredibly, cosmically swift. Every standard of speed known to earth seemed dwarfed, and Campbell knew that any such flight in physical reality would mean instant death to a human being. Even as it was—in this strange, hellish hypnosis or nightmare—the quasi-visual impression of meteor-like hurtling almost paralyzed his mind. Though there were no real points of reference in the grey, pulsing void, he felt that he was approaching and passing the speed of light itself. Finally, his consciousness did go under—and merciful blackness swallowed everything.

It was very suddenly, and amidst the most impenetrable darkness, that thoughts and ideas again came to George Campbell. Of how many moments—or years—or eternities—had elapsed since his flight through the grey void, he could form no estimate. He knew only that he seemed to be at rest and without pain. Indeed, the absence of all physical sensation was the salient quality of his condition. It made even the blackness seem less solidly black—suggesting as it did that he was rather a disembodied intelligence in a state beyond physical senses, than a corporeal being with senses deprived of their accustomed objects of perception. He could think sharply and quickly— almost preternaturally so—yet could form no idea whatsoever of his situation.

Half by instinct, he realised that he was not in his own tent. True, he might have awaked there from a nightmare to a world equally black; yet he knew this was not so. There was no camp cot beneath him—he had no hands to feel the blankets and canvas surface and flashlight that ought to be around him—there was no sensation of cold in the air—no flap through which he could glimpse the pale night outside ... something was wrong, dreadfully wrong.

He cast his mind backward and thought of the fluorescent cube which had hypnotised him—of that, and all which had followed. He had known that his mind was going, yet had been unable to draw back. At the last moment there had been a shocking, panic fear—a subconscious fear beyond even that caused by the sensation of daemonic flight. It had come from some vague flash or remote recollection—just what, he could not at once tell. Some cell-group in the back of his head had seemed to find a cloudily familiar quality in the cube—and that familiarity was fraught with dim terror. Now he tried to remember what the familiarity and the terror were.

Little by little it came to him. Once—long ago, in connection with his geological lifework—he had read of something like that cube. It had to do with those debatable and disquieting clay fragments called the Eltdown Shards, dug up from pre-carboniferous strata in southern England thirty years before. Their shape and markings were so queer that a few scholars hinted at artificiality, and made wild conjectures about them and their origin. They came, clearly, from a time when no human beings could exist on the globe—but their contours and figurings were damnably puzzling. That was how they got their name.

It was not, however, in the writings of any sober scientist that Campbell had seen that reference to a crystal, disc-holding globe. The source was far less reputable, and infinitely more vivid. About 1912 a deeply learned Sussex clergyman of occultist leanings—the Reverend Arthur Brooke Winters-Hall—had professed to identify the markings on the Eltdown Shards with some of the so-called "pre-human hieroglyphs" persistently cherished and esoterically handed down in certain mystical circles, and had published at his own expense what purported to be a "translation" of the primal and baffling "inscriptions"—a "translation" still quoted frequently and seriously by occult writers. In this "translation"—a surprisingly long brochure in view of the limited number of "shards" existing—had occurred the narrative, supposedly of pre-human authorship, containing the now frightening reference.

As the story went, there dwelt on a world—and eventually on countless other worlds—of outer space a mighty order of worm-like beings whose attainments and whose control of nature surpassed anything within the range of terrestrial imagination. They had mastered the art of interstellar travel early in their career, and had peopled every habitable planet in their own galaxy—killing off the races they found.

Beyond the limits of their own galaxy—which was not ours—they could not navigate in person; but in their quest for knowledge of all space and time they discovered a means of spanning certain transgalactic gulfs with their minds. They devised peculiar objects—strangely energized cubes of a curious crystal containing hypnotic talismans and enclosed in space-resisting spherical envelopes of an unknown substance—which could be forcibly expelled beyond the limits of their universe, and which would respond to the attraction of cool solid matter only.

These, of which a few would necessarily land on various inhabited worlds in outside universes, formed the ether-bridges needed for mental communication. Atmospheric friction burned away the protecting envelope, leaving the cube exposed and subject to discovery by the intelligent minds of the world where it fell. By its very nature, the cube would attract and rivet attention. This, when coupled with the action of light, was sufficient to set its special properties working.

The mind that noticed the cube would be drawn into it by the power of the disc, and would be sent on a thread of obscure energy to the place whence the disc had come—the remote world of the worm-like space explorers across stupendous galactic abysses. Received in one of the machines to which each cube was attuned, the captured mind would remain suspended without body or senses until examined by one of the dominant race. Then it would, by an obscure process of interchange, be pumped of all its contents. The investigator's mind would now occupy the strange machine while the captive mind occupied the interrogator's worm-like body. Then, in another interchange, the interrogator's mind would leap across boundless space to the captive's vacant and unconscious body on the trans-galactic world—animating the alien tenement as best it might, and exploring the alien world in the guise of one of its denizens.

When done with exploration, the adventurer would use the cube and its disc in accomplishing his return—and sometimes the captured mind would be restored safely to its own remote world. Not always, however, was the dominant race so kind. Sometimes, when a potentially important race capable of space travel was found, the worm-like folk would employ the cube to capture and annihilate minds by the thousands, and would extirpate the race for diplomatic reasons—using the exploring minds as agents of destruction.

In other cases, sections of the worm-folk would permanently occupy a trans-galactic planet—destroying the captured minds and wiping out the remaining inhabitants preparatory to settling down in unfamiliar bodies. Never, however, could the parent civilization be quite duplicated in such a case, since the new planet would not contain all the materials necessary for the worm-race's arts. The cubes, for example, could be made only on the home planet.

Only a few of the numberless cubes sent forth ever found a landing and response on an inhabited world—since there was no such thing as aiming them at goals beyond sight or knowledge. Only three, ran the story, had ever landed on peopled worlds in our own particular universe. One of these had struck a planet near the galactic rim two thousand billion years ago, while another had lodged three billion years ago on a world near the centre of the galaxy. The third—and the only one ever known to have invaded the solar system—had reached our own earth 150,000,000 years ago.

It was with this latter that Dr. Winters-Hall's "translation" chiefly dealt. When the cube struck the earth, he wrote, the ruling terrestrial species was a huge, cone-shaped race surpassing all others before or since in mentality and achievements. This race was so advanced that it had actually sent minds abroad in both space and time to explore the cosmos, hence recognised something of what had happened when the cube fell from the sky and certain individuals had suffered mental change after gazing at it.

Realising that the changed individuals represented invading minds, the race's leaders had them destroyed—even at the cost of leaving the displaced minds exiled in alien space. They had had experience with even stranger transitions. When, through a mental exploration of space and time, they formed a rough idea of what the cube was, they carefully hid the thing from light and sight, and guarded it as a menace. They did not wish to destroy a thing so rich in later experimental possibilities. Now and then some rash, unscrupulous adventurer would furtively gain access to it and sample its perilous powers despite the consequences—

but all such cases were discovered, and safely and drastically dealt with.

Of this evil meddling the only bad result was that the worm-like outside race learned from the new exiles what had happened to their explorers on earth, and conceived a violent hatred of the planet and all its life-forms. They would have depopulated it if they could, and indeed sent additional cubes into space in the wild hope of striking it by accident in unguarded places—but that accident never came to pass.

The cone-shaped terrestrial beings kept the one existing cube in a special shrine as a relique and basis for experiments, till after aeons it was lost amidst the chaos of war and the destruction of the great polar city where it was guarded. When, fifty million years ago, the beings sent their minds ahead into the infinite future to avoid a nameless peril of inner earth, the whereabouts of the sinister cube from space were unknown.

This much, according to the learned occultist, the Eltdown Shards had said. What now made the account so obscurely frightful to Campbell was the minute accuracy with which the alien cube had been described. Every detail tallied—dimensions, consistency, heiroglyphed central disc, hypnotic effects. As he thought the matter over and over amidst the darkness of his strange situation, he began to wonder whether his whole experience with the crystal cube—indeed, its very existence—were not a nightmare brought on by some freakish subconscious memory of this old bit of extravagant, charlatanic reading. If so, though, the nightmare must still be in force; since his present apparently bodiless state had nothing of normality in it.

Of the time consumed by this puzzled memory and reflection, Campbell could form no estimate. Everything about his state was so unreal that ordinary dimensions and measurements became meaningless. It seemed an eternity, but perhaps it was not really long before the sudden interruption came. What happened was as strange and inexplicable as the blackness it succeeded. There was a sensation—of the mind rather than of the body—and all at once Campbell felt his thoughts swept or sucked beyond his control in tumultuous and chaotic fashion.

Memories arose irresponsibly and irrelevantly. All that he knew—all his personal background, traditions, experiences, scholarship, dreams, ideas, and inspirations—welled up abruptly and simultaneously, with a dizzying speed and abundance which soon made him unable to keep track of any separate concept. The parade of all his mental contents became an avalanche, a cascade, a vortex. It was as horrible and vertiginous as his hypnotic flight through space when the crystal cube pulled him. Finally, it sapped his consciousness and brought on fresh oblivion.

Another measureless blank—and then a slow trickle of sensation. This time it was physical, not mental. Sapphire light, and a low rumble of distant sound. There were tactile impressions—he could realise that he was lying at full length on something, though there was a baffling strangeness about the feel of his posture. He could not reconcile the pressure of the supporting surface with his own outlines—or with the outlines of the human form at all. He tried to move his arms, but found no definite response to the attempt. Instead, there were little, ineffectual nervous twitches all over the area which seemed to mark his body.

He tried to open his eyes more widely, but found himself unable to control their mechanism. The sapphire light came in a diffused, nebulous manner, and could nowhere be voluntarily focussed into definiteness. Gradually, though, visual images began to trickle in curiously and indecisively. The limits and qualities of vision were not those which he was used to, but he could roughly correlate the sensation with what he had known as sight. As this sensation gained some degree of stability, Campbell realised that he must still be in the throes of nightmare.

He seemed to be in a room of considerable extent—of medium height, but with a large proportionate area. On every side—and he could apparently see all four sides at once—were high, narrowish slits which seemed to serve as combined doors and windows. There were singular low tables or pedestals, but no furniture of normal nature and proportions. Through the slits streamed floods of sapphire light, and beyond them could be mistily seen the sides and roofs of fantastic buildings like clustered cubes. On the walls—in the vertical panels between the slits—were strange markings of an oddly disquieting character. It was some time before Campbell understood why they disturbed him so—then he saw that they were, in repeated instances, precisely like some of the hieroglyphs on the crystal cube's disc.

The actual nightmare element, though, was something more than this. It began with the living thing which presently entered through one of the slits, advancing deliberately toward him and bearing a metal box of bizarre proportions and glassy, mirror-like surfaces. For this thing was nothing human—nothing of earth—nothing even of man's myths and dreams. It was a gigantic, pale-grey worm or centipede, as large around as a man and twice as long, with a disc-like, apparently eyeless, cilia-fringed head bearing a purple central orifice. It glided on its rear pairs of legs, with its fore part raised vertically—the legs, or at least two pairs of them, serving as arms. Along its spinal ridge was a curious purple comb, and a fan-shaped tail of some grey membrane ended its grotesque bulk. There was a ring of flexible red spikes around its neck, and from the twistings of these came clicking, twanging sounds in measured, deliberate rhythms. Here, indeed, was outré nightmare at its height—capricious fantasy at its apex. But even this vision of delirium was not what caused George Campbell to lapse a third time into unconsciousness. It took one more thing—one final, unbearable touch—to do that. As the nameless worm advanced with its glistening box, the reclining man caught in the mirror-like surface a glimpse of what should have been his own body. Yet—horribly verifying his disordered and unfamiliar sensations—it was not his own body at all that he saw reflected in the burnished metal. It was, instead, the loathsome, pale-grey bulk of one of the great centipedes.

[ROBERT E. HOWARD & FRANK BELKNAP LONG]

From that final lap of senselessness, he emerged with a full understanding of his situation. His mind was imprisoned in the body of a frightful native of an alien planet, while, somewhere on the other side of the universe, his own body was housing the monster's personality.

He fought down an unreasoning horror. Judged from a cosmic standpoint, why should his metamorphosis horrify him? Life and consciousness were the only realities in the universe. Form was unimportant. His present body was hideous only according to terrestrial standards. Fear and revulsion were drowned in the excitement of titanic adventure.

What was his former body but a cloak, eventually to be cast off at death anyway? He had no sentimental illusions about the life from which he had been exiled. What had it ever given him save toil, poverty, continual frustration, and repression? If this life before him offered no more, at least it offered no less. Intuition told him it offered more—much more.

With the honesty possible only when life is stripped to its naked fundamentals, he realized that he remembered with pleasure only the physical delights of his former life. But he had long ago exhausted all the physical possibilities contained in that earthly body. Earth held no new thrills. But in the possession of this new, alien body he felt promises of strange, exotic joys.

A lawless exultation rose in him. He was a man without a world, free of all conventions or inhibitions of Earth, or of this strange planet, free of every artificial restraint in the universe. He was a god! With grim amusement he thought of his body moving in earth's business and society, with all the while an alien monster staring out of the windows that were George Campbell's eyes on people who would flee if they knew.

Let him walk the earth slaying and destroying as he would. Earth and its races no longer had any meaning to George Campbell. There he had been one of a billion nonentities, fixed in place by a mountainous accumulation of conventions, laws and manners, doomed to live and die in his sordid niche. But in one blind bound he had soared above the commonplace. This was not death, but re-birth—the birth of a full-grown mentality, with a new-found freedom that made little of physical captivity on Yekub.

He started. Yekub! It was the name of this planet, but how had he known? Then he knew, as he knew the name of him whose body he occupied—Tothe. Memory, deep grooved in Tothe's brain, was stirring in him—shadows of the knowledge Tothe had. Carved deep in the physical tissues of the brain, they spoke dimly as implanted instincts to George Campbell; and his human consciousness seized them and translated them to show him the way not only to safety and freedom, but to the power his soul, stripped to its primitive impulses, craved. Not as a slave would he dwell on Yekub, but as a king! Just as of old barbarians had sat on the throne of lordly empires.

For the first time he turned his attention to his surroundings. He still lay on the couch-like thing in the midst of that fantastic room, and the centipede man stood before him, holding the polished metal object, and clashing its neck-spikes. Thus it spoke to him, Campbell knew, and what it said he dimly understood, through the implanted thought processes of Tothe, just as he knew the creature was Yukth, supreme lord of science.

But Campbell gave no heed, for he had made his desperate plan, a plan so alien to the ways of Yekub that it was beyond Yukth's comprehension and caught him wholly unprepared. Yukth, like Campbell, saw the sharp-pointed metal shard on a nearby table, but to Yukth it was only a scientific implement. He did not even know it could be used as a weapon. Campbell's earthly mind supplied the knowledge and the action that followed, driving Tothe's body into movements no man of Yekub had ever made before.

Campbell snatched the pointed shard and struck, ripping savagely upward. Yukth reared and toppled, his entrails spilling on the floor. In an instant Campbell was streaking for a door. His speed was amazing, exhilarating, first fulfillment of the promise of novel physical sensations.

As he ran, guided wholly by the instinctive knowledge implanted in Tothe's physical reflexes, it was as if he were borne by a separate consciousness in his legs. Tothe's body was bearing him along a route it had traversed ten thousand times when animated by Tothe's mind.

Down a winding corridor he raced, up a twisted stair, through a carved door, and the same instincts that had brought him there told him he had found what he sought. He was in a circular room with a domed roof from which shone a livid blue light. A strange structure rose in the middle of the rainbow-hued floor, tier on tier, each of a separate, vivid color. The ultimate tier was a purple cone, from the apex of which a blue smoky mist drifted upward to a sphere that poised in mid-air—a sphere that shone like translucent ivory.

This, the deep-grooved memories of Tothe told Campbell, was the god of Yekub, though why the people of Yekub feared and worshipped it had been forgotten a million years. A worm-priest stood between him and the altar which no hand of flesh had ever touched. That it could be touched was a blasphemy that had never occurred to a man of Yekub. The worm-priest stood in frozen horror until Campbell's shard ripped the life out of him.

On his centipede-legs Campbell clambered the tiered altar, heedless of its sudden quiverings, heedless of the change that was taking place in the floating sphere, heedless of the smoke that now billowed out in blue clouds. He was drunk with the feel of power. He feared the superstitions of Yekub no more than he feared those of Earth. With that globe in his hands he would be king of Yekub. The worm men would dare deny him nothing, when he held their god as hostage. He reached a hand for the ball—no longer ivory-hued, but red as blood ...

[FRANK BELKNAP LONG]

Out of the tent into the pale August night walked the body of George Campbell. It moved with a slow, wavering gait between the bodies of enormous trees, over a forest path strewed with sweet scented pine needles. The air was crisp and cold. The sky was an inverted bowl of frosted silver flecked with stardust, and far to the north the Aurora Borealis splashed streamers of fire.

The head of the walking man lolled hideously from side to side. From the corners of his lax mouth drooled thick threads of amber froth, which fluttered in the night breeze. He walked upright at first, as a man would walk, but gradually, as the tent receded, his posture altered. His torso began almost imperceptibly to slant, and his limbs to shorten.

In a far-off world of outer space, the centipede creature that was George Campbell clasped to its bosom a god whose lineaments were red as blood, and ran with insect-like quiverings across a rainbow-hued hall and out through massive portals into the bright glow of alien suns.

Weaving between the trees of earth in an attitude that suggested the awkward loping of a werebeast, the body of George Campbell was fulfilling a mindless destiny. Long, claw-tipped fingers dragged leaves from a carpet of odorous pine needles as it moved toward a wide expanse of gleaming water.

In the far-off, extra-galactic world of the worm people, George Campbell moved between cyclopean blocks of black masonry down long, fern-planted avenues holding aloft the round red god.

There was a harsh animal cry in the underbrush near the gleaming lake on earth where the mind of a worm creature dwelt in a body swayed by instinct. Human teeth sank into soft animal fur, tore at black animal flesh. A little silver fox sank its fangs in frantic retaliation into a furry human wrist, and thrashed about in terror as its blood spurted. Slowly the body of George Campbell arose, its mouth splashed with fresh blood. With upper limbs swaying oddly it moved towards the waters of the lake.

As the variform creature that was George Campbell crawled between the black blocks of stone, thousands of worm-shapes prostrated themselves in the scintillating dust before it. A godlike power seemed to emanate from its weaving body as it moved with a slow, undulant motion toward a throne of spiritual empire transcending all the sovereignties of Earth.

A trapper stumbling wearily through the dense woods of Earth near the tent where the worm-creature dwelt in the body of George Campbell came to the gleaming waters of the lake and discerned something dark floating there. He had been lost in the woods all night, and weariness enveloped him like a leaden cloak in the pale morning light.

But the shape was a challenge that he could not ignore. Moving to the edge of the water he knelt in the soft mud and reached out toward the floating bulk. Slowly he pulled it to the shore.

Far off in outer space the worm-creature holding the glowing red god ascended a throne that gleamed like the constellation Cassiopeia under an alien vault of hyper-suns. The great deity that he held aloft energized his worm tenement, burning away in the white fire of a supermundane spirituality all animal dross.

On Earth the trapper gazed with unutterable horror into the blackened and hairy face of the drowned man. It was a bestial face, repulsively anthropoid in contour, and from its twisted, distorted mouth black ichor poured.

"He who sought your body in the abysses of time will occupy an unresponsive tenement," said the red god. "No spawn of Yekub can control the body of a human.

"On all Earth, living creatures rend one another, and feast with unutterable cruelty on their kith and kin. No worm-mind can control a bestial man-body when it yearns to raven. Only man-minds instinctively conditioned through the course of ten thousand generations can keep the human instincts in thrall. Your body will destroy itself on Earth, seeking the blood of its animal kin, seeking the cool water where it can wallow at its ease. Seeking eventually destruction, for the death-instinct is more powerful in it than the instincts of life and it will destroy itself in seeking to return to the slime from which it sprang."

Thus spoke the round red god of Yekub in a far-off segment of the space-time continuum to George Campbell as the latter, with all human desire purged away, sat on a throne and ruled an empire of worms more wisely, kindly, and benevolently than any man of earth had ever ruled an empire of men.

THE FIRE OF ASSHURBANIPAL

Yar Ali squinted carefully down the blue barrel of his Lee-Enfield, called devoutly on Allah and sent a bullet through the brain of a flying rider.

"Allaho akbar!"

The big Afghan shouted in glee, waving his weapon above his head, "God is great! By Allah, *sahib*, I have sent another one of the dogs to Hell!"

His companion peered cautiously over the rim of the sandpit they had scooped with their hands. He was a lean and wiry American, Steve Clarney by name.

"Good work, old horse," said this person. "Four left. Look—they're drawing off."

The white-robed horsemen were indeed reining away, clustering together just out of accurate rifle-range, as if in council. There had been seven when they had first swooped down on the comrades, but the fire from the two rifles in the sandpit had been deadly.

"Look, *sahib*—they abandon the fray!"

Yar Ali stood up boldly and shouted taunts at the departing riders, one of whom whirled and sent a bullet that kicked up sand thirty feet in front of the pit.

"They shoot like the sons of dogs," said Yar Ali in complacent self-esteem. "By Allah, did you see that rogue plunge from his saddle as my lead went home? Up, *sahib*; let us run after them and cut them down!"

Paying no attention to this outrageous proposal—for he knew it was but one of the gestures Afghan nature continually demands—Steve rose, dusted off his breeches and gazing after the riders, now white specks far out on the desert, said musingly: "Those fellows ride as if they had some set purpose in mind— not a bit like men running from a licking."

"Aye," agreed Yar Ali promptly and seeing nothing inconsistent with his present attitude and recent bloodthirsty suggestion, "they ride after more of their kind—they are hawks who give up their prey not quickly. We had best move our position quickly, Steve *sahib*. They will come back—maybe in a few hours, maybe in a few days—it all depends on how far away lies the oasis of their tribe. But they will be back. We have guns and lives —they want both. And behold."

The Afghan levered out the empty shell and slipped a single cartridge into the breech of his rifle.

"My last bullet, *sahib*."

Steve nodded. "I've got three left."

The raiders whom their bullets had knocked from the saddle had been looted by their own comrades. No use searching the bodies which lay in the sand for ammunition. Steve lifted his canteen and shook it. Not much water remained. He knew that Yar Ali had only a little more than he, though the big Afridi, bred in a barren land, had used and needed less water than did the American; although the latter, judged from a white man's standards, was hard and tough as a wolf. As Steve unscrewed the canteen cap and drank very sparingly, he mentally reviewed the chain of events that had led them to their present position.

Wanderers, soldiers of fortune, thrown together by chance and attracted to each other by mutual admiration, he and Yar Ali had wandered from India up through Turkistan and down through Persia, an oddly assorted but highly capable pair. Driven by the restless urge of inherent wanderlust, their avowed purpose—which they swore to and sometimes believed themselves—was the accumulation of some vague and undiscovered treasure, some pot of gold at the foot of some yet unborn rainbow.

Then in ancient Shiraz they had heard of the Fire of Asshurbanipal. From the lips of an ancient Persian trader, who only half believed what he repeated to them, they heard the tale that he in turn had heard from the babbling lips of delirium, in his distant youth. He had been a member of a caravan, fifty years before, which, wandering far on the southern shore of the Persian Gulf trading for pearls, had followed the tale of a rare pearl far into the desert.

The pearl, rumored found by a diver and stolen by a shaykh of the interior, they did not find, but they did pick up a Turk who was dying of starvation, thirst, and a bullet wound in the thigh. As he died in delirium, he babbled a wild tale of a silent, dead city of black stone set in the drifting sands of the desert far to the westward, and of a flaming gem clutched in the bony fingers of a skeleton on an ancient throne.

He had not dared bring it away with him, because of an overpowering brooding horror that haunted the place, and thirst had driven him into the desert again, where Bedouins had pursued and wounded him. Yet he had escaped, riding hard until his horse fell under him. He died without telling how he had reached the mythical city in the first place, but the old trader thought he must have come from the northwest—a deserter from the Turkish army, making a desperate attempt to reach the Gulf.

The men of the caravan had made no attempt to plunge still further into the desert in search of the city; for, said the old trader, they believed it to be the ancient City of Evil spoken of in the Necronomicon of the mad Arab Alhazred—the city of the dead on which an ancient curse rested. Legends named it vaguely: the Arabs called it *Beled-el-Djinn*, the City of Devils, and the Turks, *Kara-Shehr*, the Black City. And the gem was that ancient and accursed jewel belonging to a king of long ago, whom the Grecians called Sardanapalus and the Semitic peoples Asshurbanipal.

Steve had been fascinated by the tale. Admitting to himself that it was doubtless one of the ten thousand cock-and-bull myths booted about the East, still there was a possibility that he and Yar Ali had stumbled onto a trace of that pot of rainbow gold for which they searched. And Yar Ali had heard hints before of a silent city of the sands; tales had followed the east-bound caravans over the high Persian uplands and across the sands of Turkistan, into the mountain country and beyond— vague tales; whispers of a black city of the djinn, deep in the hazes of a haunted desert.

So, following the trail of the legend, the companions had come from Shiraz to a village on the Arabian shore of the Persian Gulf, and there had heard more from an old man who had been a pearl-diver in his youth. The loquacity of age was on him, and he told tales repeated to him by wandering tribesmen who had them in turn from the wild nomads of the deep interior; and again, Steve and Yar Ali heard of the still, black city with giant beasts carved of stone, and the skeleton sultan who held the blazing gem.

And so, mentally swearing at himself for a fool, Steve had made the plunge, and Yar Ali, secure in the knowledge that all things lay on the lap of Allah, had come with him. Their scanty supply of money had been just sufficient to provide riding-camels and provisions for a bold flying invasion of the unknown. Their only chart had been the vague rumors that placed the supposed location of Kara-Shehr.

There had been days of hard travel, pushing the beasts and conserving water and food. Then, deep in the desert they invaded, they had encountered a blinding sand-wind in which they had lost the camels. After that came long miles of staggering through the sands, battered by a flaming sun, subsisting on rapidly dwindling water from their canteens, and food Yar Ali had in a pouch. No thought of finding the mythical city now. They pushed on blindly, in hope of stumbling upon a spring; they knew that behind them, no oases lay within a distance they could hope to cover on foot. It was a desperate chance, but their only one.

Then white-clad hawks had swooped down on them, out of the haze of the skyline, and from a shallow and hastily scooped trench the adventurers had exchanged shots with the wild riders who circled them at top speed. The bullets of the Bedouins had skipped through their makeshift fortifications, knocking dust into their eyes and flicking bits of cloth from their garments, but by good chance neither had been hit.

Their one bit of luck, reflected Clarney, as he cursed himself for a fool. What a mad venture it had been, anyway! To think that two men could so dare the desert and live, much less wrest from its abysmal bosom the secrets of the ages! And that crazy tale of a skeleton hand gripping a flaming jewel in a dead city— bosh! What utter rot! He must have been crazy himself to credit it, the American decided with the clarity of view that suffering and danger bring.

"Well, old horse," said Steve, lifting his rifle, "let's get going. It's a toss-up if we die of thirst or get sniped off by the desert-brothers. Anyway, we're doin' no good here."

"God gives," agreed Yar Ali cheerfully. "The sun sinks west-ward. Soon the coolness of night will be upon us. Perhaps we shall find water yet, *sahib*. Look, the terrain changes to the south."

Clarney shaded his eyes against the dying sun. Beyond a level, barren expanse of several miles width, the land did indeed become more broken; aborted hills were in evidence. The Amer-ican slung his rifle over his arm and sighed.

"Heave ahead; we're food for the buzzards anyhow."

The sun sank and the moon rose, flooding the desert with

weird silver light. Drifted sand glimmered in long ripples, as if a sea had suddenly been frozen into immobility. Steve, parched fiercely by a thirst he dared not fully quench, cursed beneath his breath. The desert was beautiful beneath the moon, with the beauty of a cold marble lorelei to lure men to destruction. *What a mad quest!* his weary brain reiterated; the Fire of Asshurbanipal retreated into the mazes of unreality with each dragging step. The desert became not merely a material wasteland, but the gray mists of the lost eons, in whose depths dreamed sunken things.

Clarney stumbled and swore; was he failing already? Yar Ali swung along with the easy, tireless stride of the mountain man, and Steve set his teeth, nerving himself to greater effort. They were entering the broken country at last, and the going became harder. Shallow gullies and narrow ravines knifed the earth with wavering patterns. Most of them were nearly filled with sand, and there was no trace of water.

"This country was once oasis country," commented Yar Ali. "Allah knows how many centuries ago the sand took it, as the sand has taken so many cities in Turkistan."

They swung on like dead men in a gray land of death. The moon grew red and sinister as she sank, and shadowy darkness settled over the desert before they had reached a point where they could see what lay beyond the broken belt. Even the big Afghan's feet began to drag, and Steve kept himself erect only by a savage effort of will. At last they toiled up a sort of ridge, on the southern side of which the land sloped downward.

"We rest," declared Steve. "There's no water in this hellish country. No use in goin' on for ever. My legs are stiff as gun-barrels. I couldn't take another step to save my neck. Here's a kind of stunted cliff, about as high as a man's shoulder, facing south. We'll sleep in the lee of it."

"And shall we not keep watch, Steve *sahib?*"

"We don't," answered Steve. "If the Arabs cut our throats while we're asleep, so much the better. We're goners anyhow."

With which optimistic observation Clarney lay down stiffly

in the deep sand. But Yar Ali stood, leaning forward, straining his eyes into the elusive darkness that turned the star-flecked horizons to murky wells of shadow.

"Something lies on the skyline to the south," he muttered uneasily. "A hill? I cannot tell, or even be sure that I see anything at all."

"You're seeing mirages already," said Steve irritably. "Lie down and sleep."

And so saying Steve slumbered.

The sun in his eyes awoke him. He sat up, yawning, and his first sensation was that of thirst. He lifted his canteen and wet his lips. One drink left. Yar Ali still slept. Steve's eyes wandered over the southern horizon and he started. He kicked the recumbent Afghan.

"Hey, wake up, Ali. I reckon you weren't seeing things after all. There's your hill—and a queer-lookin' one, too."

The Afridi woke as a wild thing wakes, instantly and completely, his hand leaping to his long knife as he glared about for enemies. His gaze followed Steve's pointing fingers and his eyes widened.

"By Allah and by Allah!" he swore. "We have come into a land of djinn! That is no hill—it is a city of stone in the midst of the sands!"

Steve bounded to his feet like a steel spring released. As he gazed with bated breath, a fierce shout escaped his lips. At his feet the slope of the ridge ran down into a wide and level expanse of sand that stretched away southward. And far away, across those sands, to his straining sight the 'hill' slowly took shape, like a mirage growing from the drifting sands.

He saw great uneven walls, massive battlements; all about crawled the sands like a living, sensate thing, drifted high about the walls, softening the rugged outlines. No wonder that at first glance the whole had appeared like a hill.

"Kara-Shehr!" Clarney exclaimed fiercely. "Beled-el-Djinn!

The city of the dead! It wasn't a pipe-dream after all! We've found it—by Heaven, we've found it! Come on! Let's go!"

Yar Ali shook his head uncertainly and muttered something about evil djinn under his breath, but he followed. The sight of the ruins had swept from Steve his thirst and hunger, and the fatigue that a few hours' sleep had not fully overcome. He trudged on swiftly, oblivious to the rising heat, his eyes gleaming with the lust of the explorer. It was not altogether greed for the fabled gem that had prompted Steve Clarney to risk his life in that grim wilderness; deep in his soul lurked the age-old heritage of man, the urge to seek out the hidden places of the world, and that urge had been stirred to the depths by the ancient tales.

Now as they crossed the level wastes that separated the broken land from the city, they saw the shattered walls take clearer form and shape, as if they grew out of the morning sky. The city seemed built of huge blocks of black stone, but how high the walls had been there was no telling, because of the sand that drifted high about their base; in many places they had fallen away, and the sand hid the fragments entirely.

The sun reached her zenith, and thirst intruded itself in spite of zeal and enthusiasm, but Steve fiercely mastered his suffering. His lips were parched and swollen, but he would not take that last drink until he had reached the ruined city. Yar Ali wet his lips from his own canteen and tried to share the remainder with his friend. Steve shook his head and plodded on.

In the ferocious heat of the desert afternoon they reached the ruin and, passing through a wide breach in the crumbling wall, gazed on the dead city. Sand choked the ancient streets and lent fantastic form to huge, fallen and half-hidden columns. So crumbled into decay and so covered with sand was the whole that the explorers could make out little of the original plan of the city; now it was but a waste of drifted sand and crumbling stone over which brooded, like an invisible cloud, an aura of unspeakable antiquity.

But directly in front of them ran a broad avenue, the outline of which not even the ravaging sands and winds of time had been able to efface. On either side of the wide way were ranged huge columns, not unusually tall, even allowing for the sand that hid their bases, but incredibly massive. On the top of each column stood a figure carved from solid stone—great, somber images, half-human, half-bestial, partaking of the brooding brutishness of the whole city. Steve cried out in amazement.

"The winged bulls of Nineveh. The bulls with men's heads! By the saints, Ali, the old tales are true! The Assyrians did build this city! The whole tale's true! They must have come here when the Babylonians destroyed Assyria—why, this scene's a dead ringer for pictures I've seen—reconstructed scenes of old Nineveh! And look!"

He pointed down the broad street to the great building which reared at the other end, a colossal, brooding edifice whose columns and walls of solid black stone blocks defied the winds and sands of time. The drifting, obliterating sea washed about its foundations, overflowing into its doorways, but it would require a thousand years to inundate the whole structure.

"An abode of devils!" muttered Yar Ali, uneasily.

"The temple of Baal!" exclaimed Steve. "Come on!—I was afraid we'd find all the palaces and temples hidden by the sand and have to dig for the gem."

"Little good it will do us," muttered Yar Ali. "Here we die."

"I reckon so." Steve unscrewed the cap of his canteen. "Let's take our last drink. Anyway, we're safe from the Arabs. They'd never dare come here, with their superstitions. We'll drink and then we'll die, I reckon, but first we'll find the jewel. When I pass out, I want to have it in my hand. Maybe a few centuries later some lucky son-of-a-gun will find our skeletons—and the gem. Here's to him, whoever he is!"

With which grim jest Clarney drained his canteen and Yar Ali followed suit. They had played their last ace; the rest lay on the lap of Allah.

They strode up the broad way, and Yar Ali, utterly fearless in the face of human foci, glanced nervously to right and left, half expecting to see a horned and fantastic face leering at him from behind a column. Steve himself felt the somber antiquity of the place, and almost found himself fearing a rush of bronze war chariots down the forgotten streets, or to hear the sudden menacing flare of bronze trumpets. The silence in dead cities was so much more intense, he reflected, than that on the open desert.

They came to the portals of the great temple. Rows of immense columns flanked the wide doorway, which was ankle-deep in sand, and from which sagged massive bronze frame-works that had once braced mighty doors whose polished wood-work had rotted away centuries ago. They passed into a mighty hall of misty twilight whose shadowy stone roof was upheld by columns like the trunks of forest trees. The whole effect of the architecture was one of awesome magnitude and sullen, breath-taking splendor, like a temple built by somber giants for the abode of dark gods.

Yar Ali walked fearfully, as if he expected to awake sleeping gods, and Steve, without the Afridi's superstitions, yet felt the gloomy majesty of the place lay somber hands on his soul.

No trace of a footprint showed in the deep dust on the floor; half a century had passed since the affrighted and devil-ridden Turk had fled these silent halls. As for the Bedouins, it was easy to see why those superstitious sons of the desert shunned this haunted city—and haunted it was, not by actual ghosts, perhaps, but by the shadows of lost splendors.

As they trod the sands of the hall, which seemed endless, Steve pondered many questions: How did these fugitives from the wrath of frenzied rebels build this city? How did they pass through the country of their foes—for Babylonia lay between Assyria and the Arabian desert. Yet there had been no other place for them to go; westward lay Syria and the sea, and north and east swarmed the "dangerous Medes," those fierce Aryans

whose aid had stiffened the arm of Babylon to smite her foe to
the dust.

Possibly, thought Steve, Kara-Shehr—whatever its name had
been in those dim days—had been built as an outpost border city
before the fall of the Assyrian empire, whither survivals of that
overthrow fled. At any rate it was possible that Kara-Shehr had
outlasted Nineveh by some centuries—a strange, hermit city, no
doubt, cut off from the rest of the world.

Surely, as Yar Ali had said, this was once fertile country,
watered by oases; and doubtless in the broken country they had
passed over the night before, there had been quarries that
furnished the stone for the building of the city.

Then what caused its downfall? Did the encroachment of the
sands and the filling up of the springs cause the people to
abandon it, or was Kara-Shehr a city of silence before the sands
crept over the walls? Did the downfall come from within or
without? Did civil war blot out the inhabitants, or were they
slaughtered by some powerful foe from the desert? Clarney
shook his head in baffled chagrin. The answers to those questions were lost in the maze of forgotten ages.

"Allaho akbar!" They had traversed the great shadowy hall and
at its further end they came upon a hideous black stone altar,
behind which loomed an ancient god, bestial and horrific. Steve
shrugged his shoulders as he recognized the monstrous aspect of
the image—aye, that was Baal, on which black altar in other ages
many a screaming, writhing, naked victim had offered up its
naked soul. The idol embodied in its utter, abysmal, and sullen
bestiality the whole soul of this demoniac city. Surely, thought
Steve, the builders of Nineveh and Kara-Shehr were cast in
another mold from the people of today. Their art and culture
were too ponderous, too grimly barren of the lighter aspects of
humanity, to be wholly human, as modern man understands
humanity. Their architecture was repellent; of high skill, yet so
massive, sullen and brutish in effect as to be almost beyond the
comprehension of moderns.

The adventurers passed through a narrow door which opened in the end of the hall close to the idol, and came into a series of wide, dim, dusty chambers connected by column-flanked corridors. Along these they strode in the gray ghostly light, and came at last to a wide stair, whose massive stone steps led upward and vanished in the gloom. Here Yar Ali halted.

"We have dared much, *sahib*," he muttered. "Is it wise to dare more?"

Steve, aquiver with eagerness, yet understood the Afghan's mind. "You mean we shouldn't go up those stairs?"

"They have an evil look. To what chambers of silence and horror may they lead? When djinn haunt deserted buildings, they lurk in the upper chambers. At any moment a demon may bite off our heads."

"We're dead men anyhow," grunted Steve. "But I tell you— you go on back through the hall and watch for the Arabs while I go upstairs."

"Watch for a wind on the horizon," responded the Afghan gloomily, shifting his rifle and loosening his long knife in its scabbard. "No Bedouin comes here. Lead on, *sahib*. Thou'rt mad after the manner of all Franks—but I would not leave thee to face the djinn alone."

So the companions mounted the massive stairs, their feet sinking deep into the accumulated dust of centuries at each step. Up and up they went, to an incredible height until the depths below merged into a vague gloom.

"We walk blind to our doom, *sahib*," muttered Yar Ali. "*Allah il allah*—and Muhammad is his Prophet! Nevertheless, I feel the presence of slumbering Evil and never again shall I hear the wind blowing up the Khyber Pass."

Steve made no reply. He did not like the breathless silence that brooded over the ancient temple, nor the grisly, gray light that filtered from some hidden source.

Now above them the gloom lightened some what, and they emerged into a vast circular chamber, grayly illuminated by light that filtered in through the high, pierced ceiling. But another radiance lent itself to the illumination. A cry burst from Steve's lips, echoed by Yar Ali.

Standing on the top step of the broad stone stair, they looked directly across the broad chamber, with its dustcovered heavy tile floor and bare black stone walls. From about the center of the chamber, massive steps led up to a stone dais, and on this dais stood a marble throne. About this throne glowed and shimmered an uncanny light, and the awestruck adventurers gasped as they saw its source. On the throne slumped a human skeleton, an almost shapeless mass of moldering bones. A fleshless hand sagged outstretched upon the broad marble throne-arm, and in its grisly clasp there pulsed and throbbed like a living thing, a great crimson stone.

The Fire of Asshurbanipal! Even after they had found the lost city Steve had not really allowed himself to believe that they would find the gem, or that it even existed in reality. Yet he could not doubt the evidence of his eyes, dazzled by that evil, incredible glow. With a fierce shout he sprang across the chamber and up the steps. Yar Ali was at his heels, but when Steve would have seized the gem, the Afghan laid a hand on his arm.

"Wait!" exclaimed the big Muhammadan. "Touch it not yet, *sahib*! A curse lies on ancient things—and surely this is a thing triply accursed! Else why has it lain here untouched in a country of thieves for so many centuries? It is not well to disturb the possessions of the dead."

"Bosh!" snorted the American. "Superstitions! The Bedouins were scared by the tales that have come down to 'em from their ancestors. Being desertdwellers they mistrust cities anyway, and no doubt this one had an evil reputation in its lifetime. And nobody except Bedouins have seen this place before, except that Turk, who was probably half demented with suffering.

"These bones may be those of the king mentioned in the legend—the dry desert air preserves such things indefinitely—

but I doubt it. May be Assyrian—most likely Arab—some beggar that got the gem and then died on that throne for some reason or other."

The Afghan scarcely heard him. He was gazing in fearful fascination at the great stone, as a hypnotized bird stares into a serpent's eye.

"Look at it, *sahib*!" he whispered. "What is it? No such gem as this was ever cut by mortal hands! Look how it throbs and pulses like the heart of a cobra!"

Steve was looking, and he was aware of a strange undefined feeling of uneasiness. Well versed in the knowledge of precious stones, he had never seen a stone like this. At first glance he had supposed it to be a monster ruby, as told in the legends. Now he was not sure, and he had a nervous feeling that Yar Ali was right, that this was no natural, normal gem: He could not classify the style in which it was cut, and such was the power of its lurid radiance that he found it difficult to gaze at it closely for any length of time. The whole setting was not one calculated to soothe restless nerves. The deep dust on the floor suggested an unwholesome antiquity; the gray light evoked a sense of unreality, and the heavy black walls towered grimly, hinting at hidden things.

"Let's take the stone, and go!" muttered Steve, an unaccustomed panicky dread rising in his bosom.

"Wait!" Yar Ali's eyes were blazing, and he gazed, not at the gem, but at the sullen stone walls. "We are flies in the lair of the spider! *Sahib*, as Allah lives, it is more than the ghosts of old fears that lurk over this city of horror! I feel the presence of peril, as I have felt it before—as I felt it in a jungle cavern where a python lurked unseen in the darkness—as I felt it in the temple of Thuggee where the hidden stranglers of Siva crouched to spring upon us—as I feel it now, tenfold!"

Steve's hair prickled. He knew that Yar Ali was a grim veteran, not to be stampeded by silly fear or senseless panic; he well remembered the incidents referred to by the Afghan, as he remembered other occasions upon which Yar Ali's telepathic instinct had warned him of danger before that danger was seen or heard.

"What is it, Yar Ali?" he whispered.

The Afghan shook his head, his eyes filled with a weird mysterious light as he listened to the dim occult promptings of his subconsciousness.

"I know not; I know it is close to us, and that it is very ancient and very evil. I think—" Suddenly he halted and wheeled, the eery light vanishing from his eyes to be replaced by a glare of wolf-like fear and suspicion.

"Hark, *sahib*!" he snapped. "Ghosts or dead men mount the stair!"

Steve stiffened as the stealthy pad of soft sandals on stone reached his ear.

"By Judas, Ali!" he rapped; "something's out there—"

The ancient walls re-echoed to a chorus of wild yells as a horde of savage figures flooded the chamber. For one dazed insane instant Steve believed wildly that they were being attacked by re-embodied warriors of a vanished age; then the spiteful crack of a bullet past his ear and the acrid smell of powder told him that their foes were material enough. Clarney cursed; in their fancied security—they had been caught like rats in a trap by the pursuing Arabs.

Even as the American threw up his rifle, Yar Ali fired point-blank from the hip with deadly effect, hurled his empty rifle into the horde and went down the steps like a hurricane, his three-foot Khyber knife shimmering in his hairy hand. Into his gusto for battle went real relief that his foes were human. A bullet ripped the turban from his head, but an Arab went down with a split skull beneath the hillman's first, shearing stroke.

A tall Bedouin clapped his gun-muzzle to the Afghan's side, but before he could pull the trigger, Clarney's bullet scattered his brains. The very number of the attackers hindered their onslaught on the big Afridi, whose tigerish quickness made shooting as dangerous to themselves as to him. The bulk of them swarmed about him, striking with scimitar and rifle-stock while others charged up the steps after Steve. At that range there was no missing; the American simply thrust his rifle muzzle into a bearded face and blasted it into a ghastly ruin. The others came on, screaming like panthers.

And now as he prepared to expend his last cartridge, Clarney saw two things in one flashing instant—a wild warrior who, with froth on his beard and a heavy scimitar uplifted, was almost upon him, and another who knelt on the floor drawing a careful bead on the plunging Yar Ali. Steve made an instant choice and fired over the shoulder of the charging swordsman, killing the rifleman—and voluntarily offering his own life for his friend's; for the scimitar was swinging at his own head. But even as the Arab swung, grunting with the force of the blow, his sandaled foot slipped on the marble steps, and the curved blade, veering erratically from its arc, clashed on Steve's rifle-barrel. In an instant the American clubbed his rifle, and as the Bedouin recovered his balance and again heaved up the scimitar, Clarney struck with all his rangy power, and stock and skull shattered together.

Then a heavy ball smacked into his shoulder, sickening him with the shock.

As he staggered dizzily, a Bedouin whipped a turban-cloth about his feet and jerked viciously. Clarney pitched headlong down the steps, to strike with stunning force. A gun-stock in a brown hand went up to dash out his brains, but an imperious command halted the blow.

"Slay him not but bind him hand and foot."

As Steve struggled dazedly against many gripping hands, it seemed to him that somewhere he had heard that imperious voice before.

The American's downfall had occurred in a matter of seconds. Even as Steve's second shot had cracked, Yar Ali had half severed a raider's arm and himself received a numbing blow from a rifle-stock on his left shoulder. His sheepskin coat, worn despite the desert heat, saved his hide from half a dozen slashing knives. A rifle was discharged so close to his face that the powder burnt him fiercely, bringing a bloodthirsty yell from the maddened Afghan. As Yar Ali swung up his dripping blade the rifleman, ashy-faced, lifted his rifle above his head in both hands to parry the downward blow, whereat the Afridi, with a yelp of ferocious exultation, shifted as a jungle cat strikes and plunged his long knife into the Arab's belly. But at that instant a rifle-stock, swung with all the hearty ill-will its wielder could evoke, crashed against the giant's head, laying open the scalp and dashing him to his knees.

With the dogged and silent ferocity of his breed, Yar Ali staggered blindly up again, slashing at foes he could scarcely see, but a storm of blows battered him down again, nor did his attackers cease beating him until he lay still. They would have finished him in short order then, but for another peremptory order from their chief; whereupon they bound the senseless knife- man and flung him down alongside Steve, who was fully conscious and aware of the savage hurt of the bullet in his shoulder.

He glared up at the tall Arab who stood looking down at him.

"Well, *sahib*," said this one—and Steve saw he was no Bedouin—"do you not remember me?"

Steve scowled; a bullet wound is no aid to concentration.

"You look familiar—by Judas!—you are! Nureddin El Mekru!"

"I am honored! The *sahib* remembers!" Nureddin salaamed mockingly. "And you remember, no doubt, the occasion on which you made me a present of—this!"

The dark eyes shadowed with bitter menace and the shaykh indicated a thin white scar on the angle of his jaw.

"I remember," snarled Clarney, whom pain and anger did not tend to make docile. "It was in Somaliland, years ago. You were in the slave-trade then. A wretch escaped from you and took refuge with me. You walked into my camp one night in your high-handed way, started a row and in the ensuing scrap you got a butcher-knife across your face. I wish I'd cut your lousy throat."

"You had your chance," answered the Arab. "Now the tables are turned."

"I thought your stamping-ground lay west," growled Clarney; "Yemen and the Somali country."

"I quit the slave-trade long ago," answered the shaykh. "It is an outworn game. I led a band of thieves in Yemen for a time; then again I was forced to change my location. I came here with a few faithful followers, and by Allah, those wild men nearly slit my throat at first. But I overcame their suspicions, and now I lead more men than have followed me in years.

"They whom you fought off yesterday were my men—scouts I had sent out ahead. My oasis lies far to the west. We have ridden for many days, for I was on my way to this very city. When my scouts rode in and told me of two wanderers, I did not alter my course, for I had business first in Beled-el-Djinn. We rode into the city from the west and saw your tracks in the sand. We followed them, and you were blind buffalo who heard not our coming."

Steve snarled. "You wouldn't have caught us so easy, only we thought no Bedouin would dare come into Kara-Shehr."

Nureddin nodded. "But I am no Bedouin. I have traveled far and seen many lands and many races, and I have read many books. I know that fear is smoke, that the dead are dead, and that djinn and ghosts and curses are mists that the wind blows away. It was because of the tales of the red stone that I came into this forsaken desert. But it has taken months to persuade my men to ride with me here.

"But—I am here! And your presence is a delightful surprise. Doubtless you have guessed why I had you taken alive; I have more elaborate entertainment planned for you and that Pathan swine. Now—I take the Fire of Asshurbanipal and we will go."

He turned toward the dais, and one of his men, a bearded one- eyed giant, exclaimed, "Hold, my lord! Ancient evil reigned here before the days of Muhammad! The djinn howl through these halls when the winds blow, and men have seen ghosts dancing on the walls beneath the moon. No man of mortals has dared this black city for a thousand years—save one, half a century ago, who fled shrieking.

"You have come here from Yemen; you do not know the ancient curse on this foul city, and this evil stone, which pulses like the red heart of Satan! We have followed you here against our judgment, because you have proven yourself a strong man, and have said you hold a charm against all evil beings. You said you but wished to look on this mysterious gem, but now we see it is your intention to take it for yourself. Do not offend the djinn!"

"Nay, Nureddin, do not offend the djinn!" chorused the other Bedouins. The shaykh's own hard-bitten ruffians, standing in a compact group somewhat apart from the Bedouins, said nothing; hardened to crimes and deeds of impiety, they were less affected by the superstitions of the desert men, to whom the dread tale of the accursed city had been repeated for centuries. Steve, even while hating Nureddin with concentrated venom, realized the magnetic power of the man, the innate leadership that had enabled him to overcome thus far the fears and traditions of ages.

"The curse is laid on infidels who invade the city," answered Nureddin, "not on the Faithful. See, in this chamber have we overcome our *kafir* foes!"

A white-bearded desert hawk shook his head.

"The curse is more ancient than Muhammad, and recks not of race or creed. Evil men reared this black city in the dawn of the Beginnings of Days. They oppressed our ancestors of the black tents, and warred among themselves; aye, the black walls of this foul city were stained with blood and echoed to the shouts of unholy revel and the whispers of dark intrigues.

"Thus came the stone to the city: there dwelt a magician at the court of Asshurbanipal, and the black wisdom of ages was not denied to him. To gain honor and power for himself, he dared the horrors of a nameless vast cavern in a dark, untraveled land, and from those fiend-haunted depths he brought that blazing gem, which is carved of the frozen flames of Hell! By reason of his fearful power in black magic, he put a spell on the demon which guarded the ancient gem, and so stole away the stone. And the demon slept in the cavern unknowing.

"So this magician—Xuthltan by name—dwelt in the court of the sultan Asshurbanipal and did magic and forecast events by scanning the lurid deeps of the stone, into which no eyes but his could look unblinded. And men called the stone the Fire of Asshurbanipal, in honor of the king.

"But evil came upon the kingdom, and men cried out that it was the curse of the djinn, and the sultan in great fear bade Xuthltan take the gem, and cast it into the cavern from which he had taken it, lest worse ill befall them.

"Yet it was not the magician's will to give up the gem wherein he read strange secrets of pre-Adamite days, and he fled to the rebel city of Kara-Shehr, where soon civil war broke out and men strove with one another to possess the gem. Then the king who ruled the city, coveting the stone, seized the magician and put him to death by torture, and in this very room he watched him die; with the gem in his hand the king sat upon the throne—even as he has sat upon the throne—even as he has sat throughout the centuries—even as now he sits!"

The Arab's finger stabbed at the moldering bones on the marble throne, and the wild desert men blenched; even Nured-din's own scoundrels recoiled, catching their breath, but the shaykh showed no sign of perturbation.

"As Xuthltan died," continued the old Bedouin, "he cursed the stone whose magic had not saved him, and he shrieked aloud the fearful words which undid the spell he had put upon the demon in the cavern, and set the monster free. And crying out on the forgotten gods, Cthulhu, and Koth, and Yog-Sothoth, and all the pre-Adamite Dwellers in the black cities under the sea and the caverns of the earth, he called upon them—to take back that which was theirs, and with his dying breath pronounced doom on the false king, and that doom was that the king should sit on his throne holding in his hand the Fire of Asshurbanipal until the thunder of judgment Day.

"Thereat the great stone cried out as a live thing cries, and the king and his soldiers saw a black cloud spinning up from the floor, and out of the cloud blew a fetid wind, and out of the wind came a grisly shape which stretched forth fearsome paws and laid them on the king, who shriveled and died at their touch. And the soldiers fled screaming, and all the people of the city ran forth wailing into the desert, where they perished or gained through the wastes to the far oasis towns. Kara-Shehr lay silent and deserted, the haunt of the lizard and the jackal. And when some of the desert-people ventured into the city, they found the king dead on his throne, clutching the blazing gem, but they dared not lay hand upon it, for they knew the demon lurked near to guard it through all the ages—as he lurks near even as we stand here."

The warriors shuddered involuntarily and glanced about, and Nureddin said, "Why did he not come forth when the Franks entered the chamber? Is he deaf, that the sound of the combat has not awakened him?"

"We have not touched the gem," answered the old Bedouin, "nor had the Franks molested it. Men have looked on it and lived; but no mortal may touch it and survive."

Nureddin started to speak, gazed at the stubborn, uneasy faces and realized the futility of argument. His attitude changed abruptly.

"I am master here," he snapped, dropping a hand to his holster. "I have not sweat and bled for this gem to be balked at the last by groundless fears! Stand back, all! Let any man cross me at the peril of his head!"

He faced them, his eyes blazing, and they fell back, cowed by the force of his ruthless personality. He strode boldly up the marble steps, and the Arabs caught their breath, recoiling toward the door; Yar Ali, conscious at last, groaned dismally. God! thought Steve, what a barbaric scene!—bound captives on the dust-heaped floor, wild warriors clustered about, gripping their weapons, the raw acrid scent of blood and burnt powder still fouling the air, corpses strewn in a horrid welter of blood, brains and entrails—and on the dais, the hawk-faced shaykh, oblivious to all except the evil crimson glow in the skeleton fingers that rested on the marble throne.

A tense silence gripped all as Nureddin stretched forth his hand slowly, as if hypnotized by the throbbing crimson light. And in Steve's subconsciousness there shuddered a dim echo, as of something vast and loathsome waking suddenly from an age-long slumber. The American's eyes moved instinctively toward the grim cyclopean walls. The jewel's glow had altered strangely; it burned a deeper, darker red, angry and menacing.

"Heart of all evil," murmured the shaykh, "how many princes died for thee in the Beginnings of Happenings? Surely, the blood of kings throbs in thee. The sultans and the princesses and the generals who wore thee, they are dust and are forgotten, but thou blazest with majesty undimmed, fire of the world—"

Nureddin seized the stone. A shuddery wail broke from the Arabs, cut through by a sharp inhuman cry. To Steve it seemed, horribly, that the great jewel had cried out like a living thing! The stone slipped from the shaykh's hand. Nureddin might have dropped it; to Steve it looked as though it leaped convulsively, as a live thing might leap. It rolled from the dais, bounding from step to step, with Nureddin springing after it, cursing as his clutching hand missed it. It struck the floor, veered sharply, and despite the deep dust, rolled like a revolving ball of fire toward the back wall. Nureddin was close upon it—it struck the wall—the shaykh's hand reached for it.

A scream of mortal fear ripped the tense silence. Without

warning the solid wall had opened. Out of the black wall that
gaped there, a tentacle shot and gripped the shaykh's body as a
python girdles its victim and jerked him headlong into the darkness. And then the wall showed blank and solid once more; only
from within sounded a hideous, high-pitched, muffled screaming
that chilled the blood of the listeners. Howling wordlessly, the
Arabs stampeded, jammed in a battling, screeching mass in the
doorway, tore through and raced madly down the wide stairs.

Steve and Yar Ali, lying helplessly, heard the frenzied clamor
of their flight fade away into the distance, and gazed in dumb
horror at the grim wall. The shrieks had faded into a more
horrific silence. Holding their breath, they heard suddenly a
sound that froze the blood in their veins—the soft sliding of
metal or stone in a groove. At the same time the hidden door
began to open, and Steve caught a glimmer in the blackness that
might have been the glitter of monstrous eyes. He closed his
own eyes; he dared not look upon whatever horror slunk from
that hideous black well. He knew that there are strains the
human brain cannot stand, and every primitive instinct in his
soul cried out to him that this thing was nightmare and lunacy.
He sensed that Yar Ali likewise closed his eyes, and the two lay
like dead men.

Clarney heard no sound, but he sensed the presence of a
horrific evil too grisly for human comprehension—of an Invader
from Outer Gulfs and far black reaches of cosmic being. A
deadly cold pervaded the chamber, and Steve felt the glare of
inhuman eyes sear through his closed lids and freeze his
consciousness. If he looked, if he opened his eyes, he knew stark
black madness would be his instant lot.

He felt a soul-shakingly foul breath against his face and knew
that the monster was bending close above him, but he lay like a
man frozen in a nightmare. He clung to one thought: neither he
nor Yar Ali had touched the jewel this horror guarded.

Then he no longer smelled the foul odor, the coldness in the
air grew appreciably less, and he heard again the secret door

slide in its groove. The fiend was returning to its hiding-place. Not all the legions of Hell could have prevented Steve's eyes, from opening a trifle. He had only a glimpse as the hidden door slid to—and that one glimpse was enough to drive all consciousness from his brain. Steve Clarney, iron-nerved adventurer, fainted for the only time in his checkered life.

How long he lay there Steve never knew, but it could not have been long, for he was roused by Yar Ali's whisper, "Lie still, *sahib*, a little shifting of my body, and I can reach thy cords with my teeth."

Steve felt the Afghan's powerful teeth at work on his bonds, and as he lay with his face jammed into the thick dust, and his wounded shoulder began to throb agonizingly—he had forgotten it until now—he began to gather the wandering threads of his consciousness, and it all came back to him. How much, he wondered dazedly, had been the nightmares of delirium, born from suffering and the thirst that caked his throat? The fight with the Arabs had been real—the bonds and the wounds showed that—but the grisly doom of the shaykh—the thing that had crept out of the black entrance in the wall—surely that had been a figment of delirium. Nureddin had fallen into a well or pit of some sort—Steve felt his hands were free, and he rose to a sitting posture, fumbling for a pocket-knife the Arabs had over-looked. He did not look up or about the chamber as he slashed, the cords that bound his ankles, and then freed Yar Ali, working awkwardly because his left arm was stiff and useless.

"Where are the Bedouins?" he asked, as the Afghan rose, lifting him to his feet.

"Allah, *sahib*," whispered Yar Ali, "are you mad? Have you forgotten? Let us go quickly before the djinn returns!"

"It was a nightmare," muttered Steve. "Look—the jewel is back on the throne—" His voice died out. Again that red glow throbbed about the ancient throne, reflecting from the moldering skull; again in the outstretched finger-bones pulsed the Fire of Asshurbanipal. But at the foot of the throne lay

another object that had not been there before—the severed
head of Nureddin el Mekru stared sightlessly up at the gray light
filtering through the stone ceiling. The bloodless lips were drawn
back from the teeth in a ghastly grin, the staring eyes mirrored
an intolerable horror. In the thick dust of the floor three spoors
showed—one of the shaykh's where he had followed the red
jewel as it rolled to the wall, and above it two other sets of
tracks, coming to the throne and returning to the wall—vast,
shapeless tracks, as of splayed feet, taloned and gigantic, neither
human nor animal.

"My God!" choked Steve. "It was true—and the Thing—the
Thing I saw—"

Steve remembered the flight from that chamber as a rushing
nightmare, in which he and his companion hurtled headlong
down an endless stair that was a gray well of fear, raced blindly
through dusty silent chambers, past the glowering idol in the
mighty hall and into the blazing light of the desert sun, where
they fell slavering, fighting for breath.

Again, Steve was roused by the Afridi's voice: "*Sahib, sahib*, in
the Name of Allah the Compassionate, our luck has turned!"

Steve looked at his companion as a man might look in a
trance: The big Afghan's garments were in tatters, and blood-
soaked. He was stained with dust and caked with blood, and his
voice was a croak. But his eyes were alight with hope and he
pointed with a trembling finger.

"In the shade of yon ruined wall!" he croaked, striving to
moisten his blackened lips. "*Allah il allah!* The horses of the men
we killed! With canteens and food-pouches at the saddle- horns!
Those dogs fled without halting for the steeds of their
comrades!"

New life surged up into Steve's bosom and he rose,
staggering.

"Out of here," he mumbled. "Out of here, quick!"

Like dying men, they stumbled to the horses, tore them loose
and climbed fumblingly into the saddles.

"We'll lead the spare mounts," croaked Steve, and Yar Ali nodded emphatic agreement.

"Belike we shall need them ere we sight the coast."

Though their tortured nerves screamed for the water that swung in canteens at the saddle-horns, they turned the mounts aside and, swaying in the saddle, rode like flying corpses down the long sandy street of Kara-Shehr, between the ruined palaces and the crumbling columns, crossed the fallen wall and swept out into the desert. Not once did either glance back toward that black pile of ancient horror, nor did either speak until the ruins faded into the hazy distance. Then and only then did they draw rein and ease their thirst.

"Allah il allah!" said Yar Ali piously. "Those dogs have beaten me until it is as though every bone in my body were broken. Dismount, I beg thee, *sahib*, and let me probe for that accursed bullet, and dress thy shoulder to the best of my meager ability."

While this was going on, Yar Ali spoke, avoiding his friend's eye, "You said, *sahib*, you said something about—about seeing? What saw ye, in Allah's name?"

A strong shudder shook the American's steely frame.

"You didn't look when—when the—the Thing put back the jewel in the skeleton's hand and left Nureddin's head on the dais?"

"By Allah, not I!" swore Yar Ali. "My eyes were as closed as if they had been welded together by the molten irons of Satan!"

Steve made no reply until the comrades had once more swung into the saddle and started on their long trek for the coast, which, with spare horses, food, water and weapons, they had a good chance to reach.

"I looked," the American said somberly. "I wish I had not; I know I'll dream about it for the rest of my life. I had only a glance; I couldn't describe it as a man describes an earthly thing. God help me, it wasn't earthly or sane either. Mankind isn't the first owner of the earth; there were Beings here before his coming—and now, survivals of hideously ancient epochs. Maybe spheres of alien dimensions press unseen on this material universe today. Sorcerers have called up sleeping devils before now and controlled them with magic. It is not unreasonable to suppose an Assyrian magician could invoke an elemental demon out of the earth to avenge him and guard something that must have come out of Hell in the first place."

"I'll try to tell you what I glimpsed; then we'll never speak of it again. It was gigantic and black and shadowy; it was a hulking monstrosity that walked upright like a man, but it was like a toad, too, and it was winged and tentacled. I saw only its back; if I'd seen the front of it—its face—I'd have undoubtedly lost my mind. The old Arab was right; God help us, it was the monster that Xuthltan called up out of the dark blind caverns of the earth to guard the Fire of Asshurbanipal!"

DIG ME NO GRAVE

The thunder of my old-fashioned doorknocker, reverberating eerily through the house, roused me from a restless and nightmare-haunted sleep. I looked out the window. In the last light of the sinking moon, the white face of my friend John Conrad looked up at me.

"May I come up, Kirowan?" His voice was shaky and strained.

"Certainly!" I sprang out of bed and pulled on a bathrobe as I heard him enter the front door and ascend the stairs.

A moment later he stood before me, and in the light which I had turned on I saw his hands tremble and noticed the unnatural pallor of his face.

"Old John Grimlan died an hour ago," he said abruptly.

"Indeed? I had not known that he was ill."

"It was a sudden, virulent attack of peculiar nature, a sort of seizure somewhat akin to epilepsy. He has been subject to such spells of late years, you know."

I nodded. I knew something of the old hermit-like man who had lived in his great dark house on the hill; indeed, I had once witnessed one of his strange seizures, and I had been appalled at the writhings, howlings, and yammerings of the wretch, who had groveled on the earth like a wounded snake, gibbering terrible curses and black blasphemies until his voice broke in a wordless screaming which spattered his lips with foam. Seeing this, I understood why people in old times looked on such victims as men possessed by demons.

"—some hereditary taint," Conrad was saying. "Old John doubtless fell heir to some ingrown weakness brought on by some loathsome disease, which was his heritage from perhaps a remote ancestor—such things occasionally happen. Or else— well, you know old John himself pried about in the mysterious parts of the earth and wandered all over the east in his younger days. It is quite possible that he was infected with some obscure malady in his wanderings. There are still many unclassified diseases in Africa and the Orient."

"But," said I, "you have not told me the reason for this sudden visit at this unearthly hour—for I notice that it is past midnight."

My friend seemed rather confused.

"Well, the fact is that John Grimlan died alone, except for my self. He refused to receive any medical aid of any sort, and in the last few moments when it was evident that he was dying, and I was prepared to go for some sort of help in spite of him, he set up such a howling and screaming that I could not refuse his passionate pleas—which were that he should not be left to die alone.

"I have seen men die," added Conrad, wiping the perspiration from his pale brow, "but the death of John Grimlan was the most fearful I have ever seen."

"He suffered a great deal?"

"He appeared to be in much physical agony, but this was mostly submerged by some monstrous mental or psychic suffering. The fear in his distended eyes and his screams transcended any conceivable earthly terror. I tell you, Kirowan, Grimlan's fright was greater and deeper than the ordinary fear of the Beyond shown by a man of ordinarily evil life."

I shifted restlessly. The dark implications of this statement sent a chill of nameless apprehension trickling down my spine.

"I know the country people always claimed that in his youth he sold his soul to the Devil, and that his sudden epileptic attacks were merely a visible sign of the Fiend's power over him; but such talk is foolish, of course, and belongs in the Dark Ages. We all know that John Grimlan's life was a peculiarly evil and vicious one, even toward his last days. With good reason he was universally detested and feared, for I never heard of his doing a single good act. You were his only friend."

"And that was a strange friendship," said Conrad. "I was attracted to him by his unusual powers, for despite his bestial nature, John Grimlan was a highly educated man, a deeply cultured man. He had dipped deep into occult studies, and I first met him in this manner; for as you know, I have always been strongly interested in these lines of research myself.

"But, in this as in all other things, Grimlan was evil and perverse. He had ignored the white side of the occult and delved into the darker, grimmer phases of it—into Devil worship, and Voodoo and Shintoism. His knowledge of these foul arts and sciences was immense and unholy. And to hear him tell of his researches and experiments was to know such horror and repulsion as a venomous reptile might inspire. For there had been no depths to which he had not sunk, and some things he only hinted at, even to me. I tell you, Kirowan, it is easy to laugh at tales of the black world of the unknown, when one is in pleasant company under the bright sunlight; but had you sat at ungodly hours in the silent, bizarre library of John Grimlan and looked on the ancient musty volumes and listened to his grisly talk as I did, your tongue would have cloven to your palate with sheer horror as mine did, and the supernatural would have seemed very real and near to you—as it seemed to me!"

"But in God's name, man!" I cried, for the tension was growing unbearable; "come to the point and tell me what you want of me."

"I want you to come with me to John Grimlan's house and help carry out his outlandish instructions in regard to his body."

I had no liking for the adventure, but I dressed hurriedly, an occasional shudder of premonition shaking me. Once fully clad, I followed Conrad out of the house and up the silent road which led to the house of John Grimlan. The road wound uphill, and all the way, looking upward and forward, I could see that great grim house perched like a bird of evil on the crest of the hill, bulking black and stark against the stars. In the west pulsed a single dull red smear where the young moon had just sunk from view behind the low black hills. The whole night seemed full of brooding evil, and the persistent swishing of a bat's wings somewhere overhead caused my taut nerves to jerk and thrum. To drown the quick pounding of my own heart, I said:

"Do you share the belief so many hold, that John Grimlan was mad?"

We strode on several paces before Conrad answered, seemingly with a strange reluctance, "But for one incident, I would say no man was ever saner. But one night in his study, he seemed suddenly to break all bonds of reason.

"He had discoursed for hours on his favorite subject—black magic—when suddenly he cried, as his face lit with a weird unholy glow: 'Why should I sit here babbling such child's prattle to you? These voodoo rituals—these Shinto sacrifices—feathered snakes—goats without horns—black leopard cults—bah! Filth and dust that the wind blows away! Dregs of the real Unknown—the deep mysteries! Mere echoes from the Abyss!

"'I could tell you things that would shatter your paltry brain! I could breathe into your ear names that would wither you like a burnt weed! What do you know of Yog-Sothoth, of Kathulos and the sunken cities? None of these names is even included in your mythologies. Not even in your dreams have you glimpsed the black cyclopean walls of Koth or shriveled before the noxious winds that blow from Yuggoth!

"'But I will not blast you lifeless with my black wisdom! I

cannot expect your infantile brain to bear what mine holds. Were you as old as I—had you seen, as I have seen, kingdoms crumble and generations pass away—had you gathered as ripe grain the dark secrets of the centuries—'

"He was raving away, his wildly lit face scarcely human in appearance, and suddenly, noting my evident bewilderment, he burst into a horrible cackling laugh.

"'Gad!' he cried in a voice and accent strange to me, 'methinks I've frighted ye, and certes, it is not to be marveled at, sith ye be but a naked savage in the arts of life, after all. Ye think I be old, eh? Why, ye gaping lout, ye'd drop dead were I to divulge the generations of men I've known—'

"But at this point such horror overcame me that I fled from him as from an adder, and his high-pitched, diabolical laughter followed me out of the shadowy house. Some days later I received a letter apologizing for his manner and ascribing it candidly—too candidly—to drugs. I did not believe it, but I renewed our relations, after some hesitation."

"It sounds like utter madness," I muttered.

"Yes," admitted Conrad, hesitantly. "But—Kirowan, have you ever seen anyone who knew John Grimlan in his youth?"

I shook my head.

"I have been at pains to inquire about him discreetly," said Conrad. "He has lived here—with the exception of mysterious absences often for months at a time—for twenty years. The older villagers remember distinctly when he first came and took over that old house on the hill, and they all say that in the intervening years he seems not to have aged perceptibly. When he came here he looked just as he does now—or did, up to the moment of his death—of the appearance of a man about fifty.

"I met old Von Boehnk in Vienna, who said he knew Grimlan when a very young man studying in Berlin, fifty years ago, and he expressed astonishment that the old man was still living; for he said at that time Grimlan seemed to be about fifty years of age."

I gave an incredulous exclamation, seeing the implication toward which the conversation was trending.

"Nonsense! Professor Von Boehnk is past eighty himself, and liable to the errors of extreme age. He confused this man with another." Yet as I spoke, my flesh crawled unpleasantly and the hairs on my neck prickled.

"Well," shrugged Conrad, "here we are at the house."

The huge pile reared up menacingly before us, and as we reached the front door a vagrant wind moaned through the nearby trees and I started foolishly as I again heard the ghostly beat of the bat's wings. Conrad turned a large key in the antique lock, and as we entered, a cold draft swept across us like a breath from the grave—moldy and cold. I shuddered.

We groped our way through a black hallway and into a study, and here Conrad lighted a candle, for no gas lights or electric lights were to be found in the house. I looked about me, dreading what the light might disclose, but the room, heavily tapestried and bizarrely furnished, was empty save for us two.

"Where—where is—It?" I asked in a husky whisper, from a throat gone dry.

"Upstairs," answered Conrad in a low voice, showing that the silence and mystery of the house had laid a spell on him also. "Upstairs, in the library where he died."

I glanced up involuntarily. Somewhere above our head, the lone master of this grim house was stretched out in his last sleep —silent, his white face set in a grinning mask of death. Panic swept over me and I fought for control. After all, it was merely the corpse of a wicked old man, who was past harming anyone— this argument rang hollowly in my brain like the words of a frightened child who is trying to reassure himself.

I turned to Conrad. He had taken a time-yellowed envelope from an inside pocket.

"This," he said, removing from the envelope several pages of closely written, time-yellowed parchment, "is, in effect, the last word of John Grimlan, though God alone knows how many years ago it was written. He gave it to me ten years ago, immediately after his return from Mongolia. It was shortly after this that he had his first seizure.

"This envelope he gave me, sealed, and he made me swear that I would hide it carefully, and that I would not open it until he was dead, when I was to read the contents and follow their directions exactly. More, he made me swear that no matter what he said or did after giving me the envelope, I would go ahead as first directed. 'For,' he said with a fearful smile, 'the flesh is weak but I am a man of my word, and though I might, in a moment of weakness, wish to retract, it is far, far too late now. You may never understand the matter, but you are to do as I have said.'"

"Well?"

"Well," again Conrad wiped his brow, "tonight as he lay writhing in his death-agonies, his wordless howls were mingled with frantic admonitions to me to bring him the envelope and destroy it before his eyes! As he yammered this, he forced himself up on his elbows and with eyes staring and hair standing straight up on his head, he screamed at me in a manner to chill the blood. And he was shrieking for me to destroy the envelope, not to open it; and once he howled in his delirium for me to hew his body into pieces and scatter the bits to the four winds of heaven!"

An uncontrollable exclamation of horror escaped my dry lips.

"At last," went on Conrad, "I gave in. Remembering his commands ten years ago, I at first stood firm, but at last, as his screeches grew unbearably desperate, I turned to go for the envelope, even though that meant leaving him alone. But as I turned, with one last fearful convulsion in which blood-flecked foam flew from his writhing lips, the life went from his twisted body in a single great wrench."

He fumbled at the parchment.

"I am going to carry out my promise. The directions herein seem fantastic and may be the whims of a disordered mind, but I gave my word. They are, briefly, that I place his corpse on the great black ebony table in his library, with seven black candles burning about him. The doors and windows are to be firmly closed and fastened. Then, in the darkness which precedes dawn, I am to read the formula, charm or spell which is contained in a smaller, sealed envelope inside the first, and which I have not yet opened."

"But is that all?" I cried. "No provisions as to the disposition of his fortune, his estate—or his corpse?"

"Nothing. In his will, which I have seen elsewhere, he leaves estate and fortune to a certain Oriental gentleman named in the document as—Malik Tous!"

"What!" I cried, shaken to my soul. "Conrad, this is madness heaped on madness! Malik Tous—good God! No mortal man was ever so named! That is the title of the foul god worshipped by the mysterious Yezidees—they of Mount Alamout the Accursed —whose eight brazen towers rise in the mysterious wastes of deep Asia. His idolatrous symbol is the brazen peacock. And the Muhammadans, who hate his demon-worshipping devotees, say he is the essence of the evil of all the universes—the Prince of Darkness—Ahriman—the old Serpent—the veritable Satan! And you say Grimlan names this mythical demon in his will?"

"It is the truth," Conrad's throat was dry. "And look—he has scribbled a strange line at the corner of this parchment: 'Dig me no grave; I shall not need one.'"

Again, a chill wandered down my spine.

"In God's name," I cried in a kind of frenzy, "let us get this incredible business over with!"

"I think a drink might help," answered Conrad, moistening his lips. "It seems to me I've seen Grimlan go into this cabinet for wine—" He bent to the door of an ornately carved mahogany cabinet, and, after some difficulty, opened it.

"No wine here," he said disappointedly, "and if ever I felt the need of stimulants—what's this?"

He drew out a roll of parchment, dusty, yellowed, and half covered with spiderwebs. Everything in that grim house seemed, to my nervously excited senses, fraught with mysterious meaning and import, and I leaned over his shoulder as he unrolled it.

"It's a record of peerage," he said, "such a chronicle of births, deaths and so forth, as the old families used to keep, in the sixteenth century and earlier."

"What's the name?" I asked.

He scowled over the dim scrawls, striving to master the faded, archaic script.

"G-r-y-m—I've got it—Grymlann, of course. It's the records of old John's family—the Grymlanns of Toad's-heath Manor, Suffolk—what an outlandish name for an estate! Look at the last entry."

Together we read, "John Grymlann, borne, March 10, 1630." And then we both cried out. Under this entry was freshly written, in a strange scrawling hand, "Died, March 10, 1930." Below this there was a seal of black wax, stamped with a strange design, something like a peacock with a spreading tail.

Conrad stared at me speechless, all the color ebbed from his face. I shook myself with the rage engendered by fear.

"It's the hoax of a madman!" I shouted. "The stage has been set with such great care that the actors have overstepped themselves. Whoever they are, they have heaped up so many incredible effects as to nullify them. It's all a very stupid, very dull drama of illusion."

And even as I spoke, icy sweat stood out on my body, and I shook as with an ague. With a wordless motion Conrad turned toward the stairs, taking up a large candle from a mahogany table.

"It was understood, I suppose," he whispered, "that I should go through with this ghastly matter alone; but I had not the moral courage, and now I'm glad I had not."

A still horror brooded over the silent house as we went up the stairs. A faint breeze stole in from somewhere and set the heavy velvet hangings rustling, and I visualized stealthy taloned fingers drawing aside the tapestries, to fix red gloating eyes upon us. Once I thought I heard the indistinct clumping of monstrous feet somewhere above us, but it must have been the heavy pounding of my own heart.

The stairs debouched into a wide dark corridor, in which our feeble candle cast a faint gleam which but illuminated our pale faces and made the shadows seem darker by comparison. We stopped at a heavy door, and I heard Conrad's breath draw in sharply, as a man's will when he braces himself physically or mentally. I involuntarily clenched my fists until the nails bit into the palms; then Conrad thrust the door open.

A sharp cry escaped his lips. The candle dropped from his nerveless fingers and went out. The library of John Grimlan was ablaze with light, though the whole house had been in darkness when we entered it.

This light came from seven black candles placed at regular intervals about the great ebony table. On this table, between the candles—I had braced myself against the sight. Now in the face of the mysterious illumination and the sight of the thing on the table, my resolution nearly gave way. John Grimlan had been unlovely in life; in death he was hideous. Yes, he was hideous even though his face was mercifully covered with the same curious silken robe which, worked in fantastic bird-like designs, covered his whole body except the crooked claw-like hands and the bare withered feet.

A strangling sound came from Conrad. "My God!" he whispered; "what is this? I laid his body out on the table and placed the candles about it, but I did not light them, nor did I place that robe over the body! And there were bedroom slippers on his feet when I left—"

He halted suddenly. We were not alone in the death-room.

At first we had not seen him, as he sat in the great armchair in a farther nook of a corner, so still that he seemed a part of the shadows cast by the heavy tapestries. As my eyes fell upon him, a violent shuddering shook me and a feeling akin to nausea racked the pit of my stomach. My first impression was of vivid, oblique, yellow eyes which gazed unwinkingly at us. Then the man rose and made a deep *salaam*, and we saw that he was an Oriental. Now when I strive to etch him clearly in my mind, I can resurrect no plain image of him. I only remember those piercing eyes and the yellow, fantastic robe he wore.

We returned his salute mechanically and he spoke in a low, refined voice, "Gentlemen, I crave your pardon! I have made so free as to light the candles—shall we not proceed with the business pertaining to our mutual friend?"

He made a slight gesture toward the silent bulk on the table. Conrad nodded, evidently unable to speak. The thought flashed through our minds at the same time, that this man had also been given a sealed envelope—but how had he come to the Grimlan house so quickly? John Grimlan had been dead scarcely two hours, and, to the best of our knowledge, no one knew of his demise but ourselves. And how had he got into the locked and bolted house?

The whole affair was grotesque and unreal in the extreme. We did not even introduce ourselves or ask the stranger his name. He took charge in a matter-of-fact way, and so under the spell of horror and illusion were we that we moved dazedly, involuntarily obeying his suggestions, given us in a low, respectful tone.

I found myself standing on the left side of the table, looking across its grisly burden at Conrad. The Oriental stood with arms folded and head bowed at the head of the table, nor did it then strike me as being strange that he should stand there, instead of Conrad who was to read what Grimlan had written. I found my gaze drawn to the figure worked on the breast of the stranger's robe, in black silk—a curious figure, somewhat resembling a peacock and somewhat resembling a bat, or a flying dragon. I noted with a start that the same design was worked on the robe covering the corpse.

The doors had been locked and the windows fastened down. Conrad, with a shaky hand, opened the inner envelope and fluttered open the parchment sheets contained therein. These sheets seemed much older than those containing the instructions to Conrad, in the larger envelope. Conrad began to read in a monotonous drone which had the effect of hypnosis on the hearer; so at times the candles grew dim in my gaze, and the room and its occupants swam strange and monstrous, veiled and distorted like a hallucination. Most of what he read was gibberish; it meant nothing; yet the sound of it and the archaic style of it filled me with an intolerable horror.

"To ye contract elsewhere recorded, I, John Grymlann, herebye sweare by ye Name of ye Nameless One to keep goode faithe. Wherefore do I now write in blood these wordes spoken to me in thys grim & silent chamber in ye dedde citie of Koth, whereto no mortal manne hath attained but mee. These same wordes now writ down by mee to be rede over my bodie at ye appointed tyme to fulfill my parte of ye bargain which I entered intoe of mine own free will & knowledge beinge of rite mynd & fiftie years of age this yeare of 1680, A.D. Here begynneth ye incantation:

"Before manne was, ye Elder ones were, & even yet their lord dwelleth amonge ye shadows to which if a manne sette his foote he maye not turn vpon his track."

The words merged into a barbaric gibberish as Conrad stumbled through an unfamiliar language—a language faintly suggesting the Phoenician, but shuddery with the touch of a hideous antiquity beyond any remembered earthly tongue. One of the candles flickered and went out. I made a move to relight it, but a motion from the silent Oriental stayed me. His eyes burned into mine, then shifted back to the still form on the table.

The manuscript had shifted back into its archaic English.

"—And ye mortal which gaineth to ye black citadels of Koth & speaks with ye Darke Lord whose face is hidden, for a price maye he gain hys heartes desire, ryches & knowledge beyond countinge & lyffe beyond mortal span even two hundred and fiftie yeares."

Again Conrad's voice trailed off into unfamiliar gutturals. Another candle went out.

"—*Let not ye mortal flynche as ye tyme draweth nigh for payement & ye fires of Hell laye hold vpon ye vytals as the sign of reckoninge. For ye Prince of Darkness taketh hys due in ye endde & he is not to bee cozened. What ye have promised, that shall ye deliver. Augantha ne shuba—*"

At the first sound of those barbaric accents, a cold hand of terror locked about my throat. My frantic eyes shot to the candles, and I was not surprised to see another flicker out. Yet there was no hint of any draft to stir the heavy black hangings. Conrad's voice wavered; he drew his hand across his throat, gagging momentarily. The eyes of the Oriental never altered.

"—*Amonge ye sonnes of men glide strange shadows for ever. Men see ye tracks of ye talones but not ye feete that make them. Over ye souls of men spread great black wingges. There is but one Black Master though men calle hym Sathanas & Beelzebub & Apolleon & Ahriman & Malik Tous—*"

Mists of horror engulfed me. I was dimly aware of Conrad's voice droning on and on, both in English and in that other fearsome tongue whose horrific import I scarcely dared try to guess. And with stark fear clutching at my heart, I saw the candles go out, one by one. And with each flicker, as the gathering gloom darkened about us, my horror mounted. I could not speak, I could not move; my distended eyes were fixed with agonized intensity on the remaining candle. The silent Oriental at the head of that ghastly table was included in my fear. He had not moved nor spoken, but under his drooping lids, his eyes burned with devilish triumph; I knew that beneath his inscrutable exterior he was gloating fiendishly—but why—why?

I knew that the moment the extinguishing of the last candle plunged the room into utter darkness, some nameless, abominable thing would take place. Conrad was approaching the end. His voice rose to the climax in gathering crescendo.

"*Approacheth now ye moment of payement. Ye ravens are flying. Ye bats winge against ye skye. There are skulls in ye starres. Ye soul & ye bodie are promised and shall bee delivered uppe. Not to ye dust agayne nor ye elements from which springe lyfe—"*

The candle flickered slightly. I tried to scream, but my mouth gaped to a soundless yammering. I tried to flee, but I stood frozen, unable even to close my eyes.

"—Ye abysse yawns & ye debt is to paye. Ye light fayles, ye shadows gather. There is no god but evil; no lite but darkness; no hope but doom—"

A hollow groan resounded through the room. It seemed to come from the robe-covered thing on the table! That robe twitched fitfully.

"Oh winges in ye black darke!"

I started violently; a faint swish sounded in the gathering shadows. The stir of the dark hangings? It sounded like the rustle of gigantic wings.

"Oh redde eyes in ye shadows! What is promised, what is writ in bloode is fulfilled! Ye lite is gulfed in blackness! Ya—Koth!"

The last candle went out suddenly and a ghastly unhuman cry that came not from my lips or from Conrad's burst unbearably forth. Horror swept over me like a black icy wave; in the blind dark I heard myself screaming terribly. Then with a swirl and a great rush of wind something swept the room, flinging the hangings aloft and dashing chairs and tables crashing to the floor. For an instant an intolerable odor burned our nostrils, a low hideous tittering mocked us in the blackness; then silence fell like a shroud.

Somehow, Conrad found a candle and lighted it. The faint glow showed us the room in fearful disarray—showed us each other's ghastly faces—and showed us the black ebony table— empty! The doors and windows were locked as they had been, but the Oriental was gone—and so was the corpse of John Grimlan.

Shrieking like damned men, we broke down the door and fled frenziedly down the well-like staircase where the darkness seemed to clutch at us with clammy black fingers. As we tumbled down into the lower hallway, a lurid glow cut the darkness and the scent of burning wood filled our nostrils.

The outer doorway held momentarily against our frantic assault, then gave way and we hurtled into the outer starlight. Behind us the flames leaped up with a crackling roar as we fled down the hill. Conrad, glancing over his shoulder, halted suddenly, wheeled and flung up his arms like a madman, and screamed: "Soul and body he sold to Malik Tous, who is Satan, two hundred and fifty years ago! This was the night of payment—and my God—look! Look! The Fiend has claimed his own!"

I looked, frozen with horror. Flames had enveloped the whole house with appalling swiftness, and now the great mass was etched against the shadowed sky, a crimson inferno. And above the holocaust hovered a gigantic black shadow like a monstrous bat, and from its dark clutch dangled a small white thing, like the body of a man, dangling limply. Then, even as we cried out in horror, it was gone and our dazed gaze met only the shuddering walls and blazing roof which crumpled into the flames with an earth-shaking roar.

ABOUT THE AUTHOR

Robert E. (Ervin) Howard was born on January 22, 1906. He was interested in writing from an early age, and witnesses report seeing his first stories written as early as 9 years old. He mailed off his first submission to a publisher at 15 years of age. His first professional sale came three years later when "Spear and Fang," a cave man story, was accepted by *Weird Tales*, the pulp magazine with which all his greatest successes would be associated.

Howard is best known as the "father of sword & sorcery," with his most famous creations—Conan, Solomon Kane, Bran Mak Morn, and Kull the Conqueror—sliding (some more easily than others) into that genre. However, in addition to the sterling success of these fantasy adventure tales, Howard's versatility allowed him to support himself as a professional writer. He would write more than 100 stories between 1924 and his death in 1936 at age 30. He published regularly and wrote in genres as varied as westerns, weird westerns, horror, modern adventure stories, boxing stories, sailing adventures, and even "spicy" romance stories.

Of special interest to this volume is Howard's relationship to H.P. Lovecraft. Lovecraft, an elder statesman of the "weird fiction" genre, was an early contributor to *Weird Tales*, where Howard first encountered his fiction. Howard wrote an admiring letter to Lovecraft after reading "The Rats in the Walls," and eventually through their extended correspondence became part of the "Lovecraft Circle," a group of pulp writers joined primarily through H.P. Lovecraft's efforts, with Lovecraft as the hub. Howard and Lovecraft corresponded for years, debating the merits of the human conditions of barbarism and civilization. Lovecraft is best known for his stories of "the Great Old Ones," especially Cthulhu. This shared corpus of story ideas and ancient, pre-human history of Earth, became a shared mythic backdrop for many writers published in *Weird Tales*. Howard's contributions to this mythos are the focus of the current volume.

ADDITIONAL COPYRIGHT INFORMATION

IF YOU LIKED ...

The Cthulhu Tales of Robert E. Howard, you might also enjoy:

Captain Nemo
by Kevin J. Anderson

City of the Saints
D.J. Butler

Grim Tales of the Brothers Kollin
by Dani Kollin & Eytan Kollin

This book was produced as part of the Publishing MA program for Western Colorado University's Graduate Program in Creative Writing.

OTHER WORDFIRE PRESS TITLES

The Best of Penny Dread Tales
Edited by Kevin J. Anderson
& Quincy J. Allen

Selected Stories: Horror and Dark Fantasy
by Kevin J. Anderson

Monsterland
by Michael Okon

Our list of other WordFire Press authors and titles is always growing. To find out more and to see our selection of titles, visit us at:
wordfirepress.com

Made in the USA
Coppell, TX
08 October 2020

39469000R10246